THE
BRATVA'S *Bounty*

ROSE CHASE

Copyright

Other Works

Volkov Bratva:
The Bratva's Bride
The Bratva's Beast
The Bratva's Belle (Coming 2025)
The Bratva's Beloved (Coming late 2025/early 2026)

East Coast Syndicate:
Cardinal
Falcon (Coming 2025)
Dove (TBD)
Crane (TBD)
Vulture (TBD)

Serial Lover:
Killer in the Sheets
Guilty of Love (Coming 2025)

Single Chances:
Down the Aisle (February 13th, 2025)
Splash of Love (TBD)
Love Shot (TBD)
Love In Disguise (TBD)
Problems and Pound Cake (TBD)

Dracaurelian Trilogy:

Forged In Flames (April 15th, 2025)
Rise In Rage (TBD)
Born In Bane (TBD)

Umbra Demon:
Under My Bed
In My Closet
My Shadow (TBD)
Home Sweet Home (TBD)
Shadow of Love (TBD)

Content Warning

This book is a <u>**DARK MAFIA ROMANCE**</u> that contains content that some may find triggering or disturbing.

Contents include, but aren't limited to: explicit language, explicit violence, sexual violence, abuse, alcohol and drug use, explicit sexual scenes, dubious consent, consensual non-consent, BDSM elements and tones, mentions of assault, primal play, edge play, anal.

THERE IS VAGUE ON-PAGE SEXUAL ASSAULT IN ONE CHAPTER, BUT IT IS NOT WRITTEN IN DETAIL! THERE IS ALSO HEAVILY IMPLIED OFF-PAGE SEXUAL ASSAULT!

If such content triggers you then please do not continue any further or be mindful of skipping areas of trigger!

Dedication

To those who want the mafia boss to kneel before them and worship them, and to those who want the mafia boss to beg and whimper for permission while you fuck them.

Lev will be your protector in the streets and your good boy in the sheets ;)

The Bratva's Bounty

Volkov Bratva Book 3

Rose Chase

Blurb

NICOLE

"Boom!"

The best sound to ever exist, besides the irritations of Lev Volkov when I best him at every turn.

Silly wolf, he's not the hunter in this forest—I am.

Lev's beady blue orbs lock onto me, taking me for some bounty to be claimed.

Too bad I've rigged the field around my life.

But that does nothing to stop my little lion from coming to me and taking a bite of my heart.

I will no longer be the prey with my big bad wolf by my side, so I will sharpen my wits and set the field against those who hunted me.

They will know my wrath and feel its quake before their world is blown to bits—literally.

Contents

Prologue: Nicole — 1

1. Lev — 6
2. Nicole — 11
3. Lev — 16
4. Nicole — 22
5. Lev — 30
6. Nicole — 39
7. Nicole — 45
8. Lev — 53
9. Lev — 60
10. Nicole — 66
11. Lev — 71
12. Nicole — 84
13. Lev — 91
14. Nicole — 96
15. Lev — 108

16. Nicole 115

17. Lev 122

18. Nicole 128

19. Lev 135

20. Lev 145

21. Nicole 154

22. Nicole 163

23. Nicole 173

24. Lev 178

25. Lev 190

26. Lev 205

27. Nicole 218

28. Lev 228

29. Nicole 238

30. Lev 246

31. Nicole 258

32. Lev 267

33. Nicole 274

34. Lev 284

35. Nicole 294

36. Nicole 298

37. Lev 305

Epilogue: Nicole 310

Epilogue: Lev 320

Glossary 326

Thank You 329

About the Author 331

Prologue: Nicole

"You stole my own company from me!?"

The real slap to the face was the fact that it wasn't something recent. My own parents stole *my* company from right under my nose! I only found out about the change in ownership today—a whole year after it happened—because the receptionist today was a new hire who didn't know the protocol for me and let it all out of the bag.

Needless to say, I was royally pissed.

Never before have I wanted to strangle my father so much until now. "We never intended it to be yours in the first place, but we needed you to start it. So what if we omitted a huge part of it, doesn't matter. You know that women don't own things. Besides, we have something else planned for you." It hurt me how unkind and cold he was towards me, and the fact my mother stared at me with the same dead eyes made the feeling of betrayal tear at my very being.

"I'll get a damn lawyer. I never signed those damn papers, and I know that for a fact. I'm taking my company back and screwing you all over." Scoffing, I threw my hand out in a slashing motion. "I'm done. I'm so done with you and our family." Disbelief burned through my veins as my mind processed everything. "Twenty-six years I gave my damn life to you, to run with as you will, played the good daughter for your petty affections." I snapped with a seething scowl. "No more, I'm done."

I should have done this long ago: cut myself from my parents. Now that I think about it, I was so stupid for letting myself become complacent with them and the cushy life they gave me.

Before I could fully leave, after turning around, the two guards at the door grabbed my arms and held me down to the ground on my knees. "Let me go! What is the meaning of this?" No, really, what the fuck was going on?

Wait, what if this was some fucked up dream? It had to be, right? There's no way any of this was real. My company couldn't have disappeared like that, going right into my lazy brother's hands so he could live a good life on my hard work and tears. My parents weren't being heartless bastards right now. No way was I being manhandled by my own bodyguards, who *I* hired on my dime.

As he spoke to my guards, my father paid no attention to my insistent demands to be released. "Make sure she doesn't get scuffed up too much, he's expecting her to be as unscathed as possible. The plane will leave in thirty minutes, so I suggest you hurry along. Bags are packed and by the door." Okay, now I was utterly confused because I had made no plans to travel anywhere or meet anyone for anything.

"Yes, sir." Just like my father, the two guards ignored my struggle and spiteful words as they dragged me out of the house and threw me into the back of an SUV.

***

"I need to pee."

Okay, saying it out loud sounded stupid.

"Too bad, hold it, or piss your pants." Okay, and that was rude.

"Fine, I'll just piss on you then, and when my parents ask why I'm in the unruly state I am, I'll tell them that you refused to give me basic accommodations. They're not going to be happy with sending me to my new husband covered in piss." I kept blabbering on and on about how they'd regret this, and how badly my parents would react, the repercussions, just anything to get them to stop this damn car so I could escape. "Ugh, now I need to throw up too.

Seriously, I thought I was a bad driver, but you swerve so much." Faking a sick groan, I dry heaved and forced myself to gag, with the added effect of leaning over to the guard next to me to further up my antics.

"God damn it, just fucking pull over, man. I ain't sitting in a car full of piss and vomit. Just let the stupid priss piss and throw up on the side of the road real quick." The guard next to me groaned with a scrunched-up face as he tried his best to lean away from me as I kept leaning more and more toward him to press the severity of everything.

Plan B hung at the back of my mind, but one glance at the tachometer quickly changed my mind because crashing a car going 90 mph sounded like a certain death. As much as I wanted not to live this life, dying was not particularly high on my list right now. I wanted to leave my current life, as in the life of Nicole Le, the obedient and prestigious daughter of business tycoons Mark and Martha Le. If I were more pliant, I'd let them twist and bend my life as they will, but no, I'm done.

Years of being the perfect daughter for them was all for naught. If they thought I'd sit back and let them dictate my life any further, then they were mistaken. I am done. All I've worked for, all I've built, everything, gone. Everything, gone to my stupid, pathetic brother who can't even wipe his own ass without whining for mommy—oh, he's twenty, by the way, not two. Them signing everything I had ever done and owned to my younger brother was the straw that broke the camel's back, along with this stupid arranged marriage to some business Mongol as a means to create ties and shit.

I refuse to be their pawn any longer. Twenty-six years, that's how much I gave them of my life. Now, it was time for me to live my own life, and that starts today.

Steeling my nerves, I mentally psyched myself up for the stupid, and potentially deadly, escape plan I hatched.

The car slowed but showed no indication of coming to a full stop, so I faked another gag and slumped myself over against the guard next to me. "Fucking hell, man! Pull the fuck over before I throw her out!" he exclaimed with a paling face of his own as he lightly shoved me.

Groaning weakly, I pressed myself against him and heaved again as the car slowed down more to around 60 MPH. Then, I sprang into action.

Throwing my elbow back, I jammed it as hard as I could into guard one's gut, winding and stunning him enough to grab his gun from his holster. Flicking the safety off, I pulled the trigger with a surprised squeal when the recoil and sound hit me.

I don't know how many shots I let off, too lost in my own shock to count. All I knew was that the man stopped moving after a few bangs. If I wasn't sick before, the thought of possibly killing someone definitely got my stomach churning properly. I barely managed to keep myself together enough to whip the gun at the guard in the passenger seat, catching him on the temple hard enough to cause bleeding.

After a few whacks to him in the swerving car, I reached one hand out, grabbed the shift handle, and started to yank it up and down like some joystick. The vehicle jerked and skidded out of control the more I fucked around with the shift stick, and the poor driver couldn't stop me soon enough with how he had to focus on regaining control of the car.

Then, as a final 'fuck you' to this whole situation, and possibly my life, I reached over and grabbed the steering wheel, jerking it around like some child playing on a toy wheel.

The car didn't swerve around for long, though, mainly because it was forced to stop by some cars crashing into it.

And this was the point where I regretted this plan because being hit multiple times jarred my body around like a pinball in a machine. Even though I managed to brace myself, my body stood nothing against physics. So, at this point, I just hoped to stay conscious enough after the fact to escape.

Thankfully, my head didn't snap off my neck after the car came to a stop right after slamming into another vehicle. Actually, I was thankful that a semi-truck didn't hit us because I sure as hell didn't pay attention to what other cars were on the road. Nor did I care because all I wanted to do was cause mayhem to cover my escape.

Turning my head over to the driver, who was still conscious, I threw up all over his lap before stumbling over to the rear passenger door and throwing it open. Well, there wasn't much throwing because the door practically flew open against my body weight, causing me to fall out of it rather ungracefully.

Landing with a pained grunt, I struggled up to my feet, staggering with every step as the world around me blurred in and out of focus and spun like a wheel.

I need to get a grip.

With only one goal in mind, I pushed myself through the forming crowd despite being dazed. As I staggered through to the nearest functioning vehicle, my head occasionally whipped back to see if any of the bodyguards—or anyone in general—was going after me.

Shit out of luck, on one of the occasions I did look back, I noticed the guard who I whacked in the head stand out from the concerned crowd as he made his way toward me with a very heavy scowl. He shouted something at me, but I couldn't make anything out over the ringing in my ears. Then, I really didn't pay him much attention after I saw him pull his piece out at me.

Thank fucking God! Sweet Jesus, I love you so much right now!

My head spun more from the wave of relief when I threw open the first car door and saw that it was idling. With a silent apology, I slipped inside, locked the doors, and floored it after throwing it into drive. Now, I didn't feel sorry one bit for hitting the bodyguard—he hit the car with his body! But I did feel guilty about the innocent bystanders, though; I really did try to avoid them, but I was basically driving drunk in my current state. Hell, I shouldn't be behind a kiddie car, but I had to get myself to safety.

Only problem now: where the fuck to go. I needed to get to Angel, but how? The hospital she worked at was a safe way to get to her, but it also put me out in the open for my parents to come by and snatch me up again. Angel might be willing to help me, but making a bad scene in public was too risky for her.

Wait, actually, the safest way to get to her would be through her new home. If I could make it onto the property, then I would be golden. That is if I even remember how to get to her new home.

Fucking hell, and I didn't have my phone on me either to call her.

Whelp, here's to hoping my gut could lead me right for once in my life.

Chapter 1

~6 months later~

"You know she is over eighteen."

I stated the obvious, not bothering to look up at the middle-aged couple sitting across the meeting table from me. Lazily, my eyes scanned the simple information sheet and spread of polaroids before me of a young Asian woman.

"Yes, that is why we are coming to you for help. The police won't do anything because legally she is an adult. I know it is a tough ask, but we heard that you are the best of the best at this. We just want our daughter back, safe and sound with us. Nicole would never run away, she's a good girl, always punctual and on a strict schedule. This is very, very, very unlike her, very out of character. Please, we just want our daughter found and brought back." The woman, Martha Le, broke down crying into her hands, and her husband was quick to rub a soothing hand on her back.

If I was an amateur, then the tears would have done me in. Too bad I could smell bullshit a mile away. Their words carried some sincerity but with an edge; their eyes held nothing but contempt and clouds. They wanted their daughter—Nicole—back, that part was the truth, but everything else from their mouths were lies.

Either way, it was none of my business, nor did I want it to be.

This assignment seemed more trouble than it was worth but fuck it. I've got some time to kill with my latest clearance, so might as well take it easy with a locate and retrieval assignment. I mean, how hard could it be to track down a sheltered girl and drag her ass back to her parents? She didn't seem like that much of a challenge from how soft she looked in her pictures. This assignment would be easy as fuck.

"Three million, half up front and the other due upon her safe return." I sat the offer on the table as I leaned back in my chair with my arms crossed. A little much for locating and retrieving a simple girl? Probably, but Volkov services ain't cheap. Besides, if they came to us for help then they knew what they were getting into. And I might as well get a good chunk of money for shaving out some of my time doing this task; I could assign it to one of the many workers at Volkov Inc., the company I co-own with my older brother, Stepan, but I was bored enough to pick this task up myself.

Also, something about this girl intrigued me a little. She seemed innocent enough from her pictures, innocent and tame, but there was this spark in her eyes that really drew me in. Well, the fact it was muted and masked kept my interest; there were plenty of women I knew who had fire in their eyes. Yet, something about her attracted me, and I couldn't fully explain it, especially since she was somewhat average in terms of looks. Five foot three inches, according to her information sheet, and from her pictures, I could see her lovely amber eyes behind a pair of metal-rimmed glasses. She seemed to be on the skinnier side of average from a quick look, subtle curves, small chest, but she had a bit of an ass that was grabbable, and those lovely long and toned legs looked so perfect in the heeled boots she wore.

"That's a bit much, but anything for our daughter. As long as she comes back to us completely unharmed, without a single scratch on her, then we will be fine with any price. Just please, find her." The empty, emotionless tone of the father's voice grated my nerves the wrong way, but I held my tongue while offering an overly friendly smile to mask my displeasure.

A job was a job; money was money. I didn't need to know all the nitty, gritty details, and usually I didn't give a single shit, but something about these two and Nicole made my stomach lurch. Something in my mind egged me to dig deeper and learn more about what the hell was going on. I shouldn't dig my nose into things more than I needed too, but... One glance at Nicole's sad smile tugged at my dead heartstrings to help her, not her parents.

Something about all of this smelled and felt extremely fishy, and I was too enamored with this woman in the picture to let it go.

"Well," I said, getting up from my seat and holding my hand out, "I'll keep you updated as I go. As you know, this isn't an instantaneous thing, it takes a while, but I assure you, I will personally work on this case and make sure it gets done in a very timely manner. Nicole will be back in your arms before you know it." Or not, depending on what shit I find later with my research.

Yes, I took the assignment. They are the clients, but if there's something malicious going on, then like hell would I turn this innocent woman over to them. If something is going on, then I'd switch sides. Terminate the contract with the Le's and help Nicole instead. Terminating a contract was never a good thing, but my family and I didn't care. Our bratva ran the whole city of Nespin, California, along with other cities in the state. We've made our standards clear to everyone. The Le's would have no one but themselves to blame if I killed the contract and swapped sides. Hell, if I did, then they should sleep with one eye open because I wouldn't do something like that lightly with little to no thought.

Contrary to what people say about me being the dumb brute with brawns and no brains, I had functioning brain cells I used. For the most part, I let people underestimate my brain power to use their ignorance and obliviousness to my advantage. Granted, compared to my other brothers, I was definitely at the bottom of the pile when it comes to smarts; I blamed it on my father dropping me on my head too much, or maybe it was from him actually beating my head too much. Either way, the smartest out of the five of us would be the youngest twin, Alexei, who—no surprise—was a smart-ass doctor. My older brother Stepan's pretty smart, too, along with Arseny, Alexei's older twin.

Nikolai, the oldest out of all of us, was up there as well; he had to be smart, though, to run our family bratva.

Either way, dumbo me still had a functioning brain which I used on occasion, this being one I'd have to pull it out for. This Nicole better be damn worth the headache. Well, my stupid gut and heart better be right about this nagging feeling, not like Nicole asked me personally. My instincts were seldomly wrong, so I'd entertain this avenue until further notice.

"Thank you, for agreeing to take this assignment, you have no idea how thankful we are. We will make sure you are compensated nicely beyond our agreed rate." Mr. Le's overt eagerness made shaking his hand hard before we sat back down to write up the contract for the assignment.

Three months. I'll be at least three million dollars richer, not that it mattered too much because that was chump change to me. I didn't take assignments for the money most of the time; it was the assignments themselves. Yeah, I liked work for the work itself because it gave me a good avenue to vent out my frustration and energy in a productive manner.

Volkov Inc. offered a plethora of services, from simple things like accounting help to loans to more gray area matters like hits, kidnappings, and shipments. I had a tendency to stick to the more high-risk assignments, but sometimes I liked to relax with simple tasks like this seek and retrieve assignment, especially if the target was easy on the eyes.

I couldn't help but let my eyes linger on a candid photo of Nicole where she laughed at something off-screen. Her small figure was accentuated nicely in an Asian dress; I think it was some Vietnamese dress because it looked like something my sister-in-law would wear to fancy events from time to time. Either way, Nicole looked divine in the black dress adorned with gold floral embroidery.

The more I studied her, the more I engraved her into my mind. Her long but slender face had the perfect set of upturned almond-shaped eyes, a soft nose bridge to a somewhat tall and small nose, and those brownish amber eyes of hers captivated me so much because of how they popped with her glasses. I couldn't help but wonder if they'd look as shiny and glimmering in real life when I'd have her face in my hands. God, those plush little lips of hers would probably feel so soft too, so nicely sized and reddish pink.

Ugh, get a grip, Lev, she's your target, and you can't form attachments with the target.

I reminded myself with an internal and audible groan as I ran my hands down my face after tossing the picture back down on my desk.

Shoving my own thoughts and feelings aside into the fire, I recollected myself enough to focus on digging around Nicole's life, or at least whatever life the internet offered. At least she was pretty active on social media until she went missing. Countless posts gave me an insight into the young woman, along with a quick search through records by not-so-legal means.

Nicole Le seemed like a simple, successful woman who had it all in life. She had a job at her family's business as the C.O.O. right under her younger brother and father, who were the C.E.O.s. She had rich little friends, from what her posts showed. She was smiley, happy, and living the life. Yet, looking deeper, she didn't seem so simple.

Her smiles in pictures that weren't candid shots were empty, almost flat, and forced for the sake of keeping her image up.

Then her eyes, those sad, empty eyes, cried out to me.

Chapter 2

LIFE WAS GOOD.

Too good.

It felt like the calm before the storm, and I didn't like that one bit.

Just like how I didn't like this stupid rat tailing me.

I had to give him props, though, because if I weren't so paranoid and overly observant, he could have gone unnoticed. Or if I had been carefree like before, he would have slipped by. Too bad I lived my life on an anxious edge.

Even though it was a no-brainer to cut myself from my family six months ago, it didn't make living my life any easier because of their persistence. I'd let my parents run my life for too long, and I was stupid to let them get away with it for as long as they did. At least I learned to open my eyes before it was too late.

Too bad them letting me go wouldn't be easy. They had so many deals lined up, expansion opportunities, a shit load of stuff, all dependent on me marrying some creepy old man to form an alliance. Yeah, no, fuck that. Especially after they fucked me over by stealing my own cybersecurity company from right under my nose. I already played the role of the good and obedient daughter growing up, even going as far as throwing out my dream of being an engineer with my parents' constant nagging and pushing for me to go into business. I lived my life for them, and obviously, that was a huge mistake. So, now it was time to take everything back and live the life I always wanted.

After I get rid of this stupid idiot tailing me.

Yes, I did have a person following me. No, I wasn't imagining things, nor was it some coincidence that he was going in the same direction as me. This handsome man has been following me for the past week, no mistake about it. If he wasn't so darn good-looking, then he could have faded into the background to me.

Go ahead, sue me for thinking my stalker is handsome. I was no idiot, nor was I blind. This man, whoever he is, though I was willing to place my bet on him being someone my parents hired, was handsome as hell. Gotta love myself a tall and buff man, especially one with striking blue eyes because, fuck me, I was such a sucker for colored eyes. Honestly, those lovely pair of sky-blue orbs were what snatched my attention and made me zone in on him. Damn man be looking like a damn model out of a magazine. Maybe that's why he looked familiar to me.

Huffing to myself, I shook my head and shook away my little infatuation with the stud. Falling for some hired body by my parents? No thanks. If he wasn't, then, well, falling for my stalker didn't sound or seem any better either.

Actually, now that I think about it, maybe he wasn't some hired muscle from my parents. He could just damn well be some fanboy stalker. It definitely wouldn't be the first time I had fans cross the line and try to get real close and personal to me. Being a young, rich, good-looking, and available woman in this day and age slapped a huge target on my back. I've had my fair share of suitors, all of whom my parents rejected or I rejected personally. I didn't want some run-of-the-mill business tycoon as a husband, nor someone boring. Most of the men who've propositioned me were either dull, rich assholes, too posh with their heads up their asses, or were complete idiots who I couldn't stand.

I wanted someone with an actual personality, a soul made of fire. I wanted someone who would bring me excitement and true love, and someone who wouldn't stunt me as a person. I might have been a little tamer while under my parents, but I was still an outspoken and independent woman who definitely wasn't afraid to speak her own mind; apparently, not many guys I've come across like this. I wanted an equal, not to be lower or higher than anyone.

Shit. Handsome stalker guy.

Need to get my mind out of the clouds if I want to keep my pretty little ass free. Fanboy or hired man, I needed to shake him. It shouldn't be too hard of a task since the streets were pretty busy right now with the lunchtime rush.

Pulling my phone out, I snuck a quick picture of the man for later. For research, of course! I needed to find out more about my little tail. I was growing bored, so if he was hired by my parents, then I could use this opportunity to fuck around with them. If he wasn't, then, well, I'd still get some entertainment from messing around with him. This would probably bite me in the ass after the fact because I was supposed to keep a low profile, being 'in hiding' and all, but if anything went too astray, then I could call Angel for help.

Just some harmless fun with the handsome man, that's all this would be. Then again, to be fair, he's the one following me and got caught.

Smirking to myself, I dipped into my last stop of the day, a small little café for my fix of caffeine. "Hey Nicki! Your usual, along with a to-go?" The owner, a nice middle-aged woman, greeted me with a smile.

"That would be great Lia. Thank you! Oh! And I'll take a little slice of tiramisu this time, too, to go." I returned her welcoming smile with a warm one of my own before sitting at the window bar.

As I waited for my order to come out, I could spot him in the background through the window's reflection. It really was a shame I couldn't pursue him; he really was a catch looks-wise. On the other hand, I couldn't shake this eerie feeling that I'd seen him somewhere before. If it weren't for the nasty, jagged-looking scar running down the left side of his face, then I would have chunked him as some random man.

Not gonna lie, it was a nasty scar, and it gave him a scary look. Shockingly, I didn't care, even though that should have been a big red flag for me to scram and hide out of his sight, not poke at him like I planned to do. Well, the shocking part was me digging it because, fuck it, I wanted a dangerous and rugged man. I was tired of trust fund boys who didn't have a manly bone in their body (the boys my parents wanted me to get with).

Yeah, rebelling in my mid-twenties probably seemed stupid and cliché, but better late than never, I say. I only wished I'd done this sooner. Thinking back on how long I let my parents manipulate me and make most of the decisions in my life peeved me greatly. More so at myself for being so stupid and blind to let my parents go as far as they did. I can't believe it only took losing everything for me to open my eyes.

Sighing softly, I picked at the hem of my jacket while I waited for my order. I still wasn't completely free yet, either. I couldn't go about my life freely yet.

My fingers twitched as I stared at my phone sitting on the countertop. Call me immature or childish or an addict, but I wanted so badly to log onto my social media accounts. Yes, I was one of those people who wasted my time away on social media, but only because that was one of the only ways for me to connect to the outside world and get any social interaction with people who understood me.

Too bad I couldn't. I would draw too much attention to myself and give my parents a way to pinpoint my location. It was already risky for me to go out and about like this on a near-daily basis, but living in a cabin outside the bustling city limits slowly drove me mad.

Well, if anything ever went wrong, Angel was always a call away. Yeah, I felt kind of bad to lean on her like that, but she owed me big time for all the shit I've done for her throughout the years. Besides, what's the point of having a mafia boss friend if you couldn't abuse their powers vicariously through them?

Angel Vu-Volkov, wife to the esteemed Nikolai Volkov, Pakhan of the Volkov Bratva. Last I checked with Angel, ever since she overthrew her step-mother, took her mantle of Dragon Head of the Qing triad, and merged it with her husband's bratva, they nearly ran all of Nespin, California. They were working on securing San Diego, San Francisco, more of Los Angeles, and possibly another city or two, last I remember my little business chat with Angel a while back.

I had friends in high places, so might as well cash in my favors. Well, that and Angel was a good friend who would do anything for me to have a happy life. Sometimes, it was hard to remember that she was a mafia wife and head herself with how kindhearted she was as a person. That's all before the fact she was a career nurse and business owner of a shelter for the abused. Unless she was in a mood and seen in action, it was easy to forget her title as the Bratva's Bride.

I probably could have had it made like that, kind of. If I'd let my parents parade my life around how they wanted, then I'd be living it cushy with my rich husband. Yeah, maybe I was a little crazy for throwing that life away, but dwelling on such a future gave me such an ick. I didn't want to be some trophy wife or a warm body for a rich bastard to come home to.

My thoughts ran away from me at the sight of Lia out of my periphery. "Penny for your thoughts?" Lia questioned with genuine curiosity and warmth.

"Oh, just thinking about life, just in a bit of a rut and trying to get myself out." It wasn't a lie; I was basically in a life crisis.

Even after this shit with my parents got figured out, I had no idea what I'd do with my life. I couldn't pick my company back up, not after my parents and brother were dragging it through the mud and dirtying it with their mafia business. Starting another business was a possibility, but also a shit ton of work. Also, I wouldn't be truly happy running another business because it wasn't really my passion. Maybe I could go back to school and get my engineering degree, but I didn't want to waste time or run around in circles.

"Oh, you're still young with a lot ahead of you. Just do whatever makes you happy, that's all I can tell you, and have fun while you're young and still can. Oh, I miss when I could frolic around freely, give the boys a run around for their money." It was a little hard to imagine nice ol' Lia as she described herself, but one look in her eyes and I could see the simmering flame.

Peering out the window, I bit my bottom lip to suppress my widening smile as I carefully eyed the man's reflection. "You know, I might just take that advice. Have fun while I still can."

Time to fuck around and find out.

Chapter 3

WHAT THE FUCK IS she doing?

Weaving around all these people, turning these stupid street corners, and going down the shadiest streets started to get on my nerves. Something wasn't right, I could feel it. It almost felt like I was following a whole different girl around. Yes, I did wonder if she somehow caught on and did some switch-a-roo on me with a friend or something, but then I remembered the fact she basically had no friends from this little act of defiance of hers.

No, this was still the same Nicole Le I'd been stalking around for the past week; those blue, teal, and dark purple streaks on the underside of her long, black hair made her easy to spot out in the crowd. Honestly, she was doing a piss poor job of keeping low with her appearance. Okay, well, never mind, I take that back; it wasn't a completely bad job. I barely recognized her because of the appearance change. From the pictures her parents showed me, she was a complete girly girl with a soft appearance. This Nicole, the one I found and currently follow, had an edgier appearance with colored streaks in her long, black hair which she kept down rather than up all the time like in the pictures.

In a way, she looked nothing like her pictures—respectfully! The female I saw in the pictures given to me and found online was of this soft, rich, sheltered girl, but this girl a few feet ahead of me—phew! I mean, if it weren't for those fiery eyes, I'd doubt they were the same girl. I wouldn't complain one bit about her change in appearance because, honestly, I dug it. Sure, the lighter colors on her looked cute, but she made black and darker shades of color look stunning on her petite figure.

I couldn't fully comment on the shape of her body because it didn't swing fully one way or another. She may not have some full, hourglass figure, nor did she have very defined curves, but she had an athletic figure. Think maybe my sister-in-law would classify her as a rectangle, politely, of course. Nothing about her body was overtly so, nor were there any areas that were fully accentuated.

Okay, average, almost plain, would be a blunt way to put her, but I didn't mind it on her. Sure, a nice pair of tits or a juicy ass was nice to dig into, but they grew mundane after a while. A model on my arms sounded perfect, but it also sounded boring. Honestly, a huge part of me craved some kind of normality in my chaotic life. A girl was probably the last place to search for that because I seem to attract the crazy ones who only want me for my wallet or reputation.

Maybe that's why Nicole interested me because she paid no attention to me. Granted, she shouldn't be. Otherwise, I'd be doing a bitch ass job of tailing her. Damn, maybe I thought too much into this. Of course, she wouldn't fucking notice me, that's the whole point of this stupid stalking. Would she notice me, though, if she were to cross me on the street? Or if I were to approach her? Or would she shrug me off? What if—

"*Blyat*!" I hissed under my breath when she literally disappeared in the blink of an eye.

Picking up my pace, I continued to mutter cusses in Russian under my breath as I went after my target's last known location. I blinked just as she turned the corner, I think. Fucking hell, she was literally here and gone in a blink of a damn eye. No, I was not being sloppy and missed her.

Huffing and growling at myself, I rounded the corner of the building to... Nothing. Well, almost nothing. The alleyway looked like any other rubbish alleyway with dumpsters and litter, but what made me stop was the distinct crinkle under my shoe, along with a neat little takeout box with a black bow on it.

Slowly, with my eyes still scanning the alleyway, I tried to see if I could spot streaks of color amongst the dull area. When there were no signs of Nicole, I deflated with a long sigh as I bent down to pick up the piece of paper and takeout box.

A little treat for some motivation.
See you tomorrow handsome ;)

It was signed with the initials N and L with a little old-school-looking bomb with a smiley face as the center dot between the N and L.

Damn it! She knew! She fucking knew! How the hell did she figure me out?!

Needless to say, I spent a good minute berating myself for being careless somehow. Although, I didn't understand how she spotted me because I stuck to my typical routine that always worked. I kept a very fair and good distance while following her, blending into the crowd by acting mundane, and literally drew no attention to myself one bit. So, how? No one, and I mean no one, has ever made me before on an assignment unless I broke protocol.

"Blyat'!" I growled, crumpling the paper up in a fist and throwing it against the brick wall with instant regret.

Great, now I was getting worked up over some stupid note.

Sighing, I bent back down to pick the paper ball back up and straightened it back out, smoothing it between my large palms. Well, she put some effort into this note, so it felt wrong to just toss it. So, I stuffed it into the pocket of my jeans and trudged off to my car.

I was calling it a day. If she made me then she most likely made herself scarce and ran back to her hiding hole. I struck out today, and I had to accept that.

But fuck was I pissed about it.

For once in my life, I was lost.

Nicole seemed to go about her daily routine without minding me one bit of attention, which threw me off because, obviously, she knew about me. Well, she actually gave me a glance—a single glance—and that was it. So, she certainly knew I was present and tailing her. Honestly, what the hell cooked up there in her damn brain? I knew she had one; she finished college with a few business degrees, so she *definitely* had a brain. Now, whether or not it functioned properly was debatable because this woman made questionable choices.

For fuck's sake, who the hell went out and had a routine that involved the outside world and public when they're supposed to be in hiding? Unless she wasn't in hiding, but then why the paranoia and skittishness? This woman made no sense, and my head pounded with annoyance whenever I tried to figure her out below the surface.

Obviously, she actively avoided her parents, and she could have very valid reasons for doing so. Either way, she didn't seem like the runaway rebel her parents painted her to be. Honestly, I felt a little bad about having to kidnap her back to her parents, but a job was a job. Well, I could withdraw from the contract and shove it back in their face, but that would reflect badly on me and the company.

We *could* take the hit, but it would be a little risky with the Le's because of their standing and reputation in the city as one of the top cybersecurity companies out there in California. They could easily spread the word about Volkov Inc. to their customers, who were also high profile, and we could lose a lot of business that way. Also, the Le's were involved in the mafia, too, from what I dug up, but it was unclear which side of the fence they fell into.

The last thing I wanted to do was make more enemies than necessary for my family's bratva. Nikolai—the Pakhan of the Volkov Bratva and my older brother—already had a lot on his plate with the recent merge with his wife's triad after she disbanded it. Going from controlling half the city to nearly all of it in one night was *a lot* to take on. Recently, we started to branch out more because of our new connections to other cities. We might have bitten off a little more than we could chew, but we managed fine currently. Still, the fewer enemies we make right now, the better.

So, unless I had a very good reason to call off this contract, I had to keep it for now. Something in my gut refused to settle on the fact, though, because I smelt something fishy about this whole thing. Sadly, until I had solid evidence to back my decision to pull out of the contract, I couldn't.

Finally, after following her around for what felt like an eternity, she finally approached me after we stewed in some gelato café shop. "I figured ice cream as a first date sounded good. What do you think, handsome?" The gall of this woman, I swear.

Offering no words in response, I only gave her a scoffing sneer before sipping at my coffee. I was speechless, but she didn't need to know that. If it wasn't obvious, I've never been approached by a target before like this, let alone a pretty one this nonchalantly.

Without a single care, she slid into the seat across from me and settled her pretty little head up on her crossed hands after propping her elbows on the tabletop. "Oh? Shy type, huh? Strange, didn't ping you as the brooding type." She was toying with me, judging from the devious little smile paired with the little glint in her eyes.

"Either way, I'm Nicole, but I like to go by Nicki as well. What about you, handsome? It'd be nice to put a name to my silent stalker for the past week or so. Gotta say, they're not usually as good-looking as you." She chattered on with a growing smile until it became overly stretched as if she was trying to make me feel uncomfortable.

Too bad her little tactic won't work.

Refusing to engage her, I kept my lips firmly planted around the rim of my coffee cup, only offering her my intense gaze as a response.

"You're an odd one... What's your game? Want access to my underwear drawer? Some pervy pics through my window? Some weird voyeur from afar? Or is there a different reason you're following me?" She commented out loud while gesturing at me with her straw and studying me with careful eyes. "You don't seem like the typical fanboy or dude looking to score some rich bitch like me. You don't look like someone my parents would hire as a bodyguard either, but you do look of high caliber."

Do I tell her? Do I lie?

Fuck, I didn't know what to do for once in my life.

How the hell is this woman getting to me without trying?

Chapter 4

Nicole

I FUCKED AROUND, AND I found out.

And nope. Nope. Big nope.

Lev Volkov.

I fucking picked on Lev fucking Volkov.

Holy shit, how am I not dead?!

If I'd known the handsome stalker was Lev Volkov, then I wouldn't have thought about engaging him!

Oh my fucking God, I asked him if he wanted access to my underwear drawer! I totally assumed he was some pervy stalker!

Well, to be fair, he could still very well be some pervy stalker. Just because he was a handsome, hot, downright sexy mafia boss didn't mean he couldn't be pervy. Although, a guy like him probably didn't need to be. He could get anyone he wanted with his status, so no point in perving. If that was his thing, then he could easily pay someone for it too, or who knows, maybe find someone at one of the kink clubs his family owned.

Wait, shit! Why am I the target of his attention, then?

I haven't done anything to piss off the Volkov Bratva or anything that would warrant their attention on me. Plus, Angel would have informed me of such a change unless she got into the bad habit of hiding shit from me, which I highly doubt. She might be loyal to her husband, but I came before him. She wouldn't have let him push her around either to keep her lips shut—she'd probably stab him in his sleep if he dared.

So, why was Lev stalking me?

My parents weren't involved with the Volkovs either, nor would they ever. Last I remembered, they were ranting about the Russians needing to go. They also weren't very happy with Lady Qing when she formed a truce with the Volkovs, even though it was to her benefit and furthering her devious plans.

I wanted to pull my hair out because of my carelessness with the situation. I should have stayed put, lay low, and suffered cabin fever, but I couldn't do it. I was going batshit crazy at the cabin.

Yes, going out into the public kind of defeats the point of me being in hiding from my parents, but so far everything was fine. Sure, they've sent some people to try and snatch me, but I shook them off just fine. Or if I couldn't then nothing a call to Angel didn't fix.

Besides, ever since Angel overthrew her stepmother and took back the Qing Triad under her control, my parents have laid completely flat to the ground. Well, they've been kicked to the curb essentially because of their actions. Them selling me off was the last straw for Angel, which made her cut them off completely. After an investigation into them and the business revealed their noncompliance with Angel's new rules, she definitely tore into them and cut them off completely from the bratva.

The fact they were floating around in the water right now was what made me grow bold enough to go out on a near-daily basis to keep my sanity intact. So, I was somewhat in hiding? Half hiding? Under protection? I couldn't go back to living a full life without drawing too much attention and exposing myself to my would-be husband and parents. My parents already pulled the sob card and guilting on public television in on social media with their 'please find out daughter, we just want her back safe and sound' bullshit. Yeah, the public ate that shit up. I'd be shoved back into my parents' arms by the whole world if I were fully discovered right now, which was the last thing I wanted and needed.

If my parents got ahold of me again, then that would be the end of my life, literally. I knew for a damn fact that the moment I returned, I'd be shipped off to China to my would-be husband, who would then be my husband. If he was someone decent, then maybe I wouldn't mind, but he was sixty and insufferable.

Listen, when I said I liked older men, that was *not* what I meant.

It was a definite 'no' for me when he laid his hands on me the *first* time meeting me because I dared talk back to him.

I hated that it took me so long to break away from my parents, but they pushed me too far by trying to marry me off to some bastard of a person for the sake of money. I'd let them use me for their gain for too long and don't even ask me why because I didn't know the answer to it myself.

As much as I enjoyed my life right now, it was a mess. I mean, I lived in semi-hiding in a cabin located in the woods and built bombs for shit and giggles along with other little nick knacks. Yeah, it was somewhat of an ideal life for me; if I weren't isolated in the woods and wouldn't get in trouble for the shit I made, then life would be perfect.

Too bad life was unfair and shitty.

But one step at a time.

Next step, Lev. Yeah, I had to figure out what to do with him first. It's been three days since I first stepped into Lev's life, and even though it's only been me bugging him with one-sided chatter, he hasn't made any indication of his plans for me. Granted, he refused to engage in a conversation with me, only ever looking at me with his beady blue eyes in response.

Just like now.

"You know, if we're gonna make this relationship work, then you're gonna have to talk back to me. I mean, communication in a relationship is key, honey." Of course, I keep digging my grave deeper than it should be. "You have to at least give me something to work on, love. I mean, I don't even know why the hell the bratva is even interested in me, let alone the Savage Volk."

By the way his head perked up with his ears, I'd say I finally caught his full attention. Lev instantly grabbed my wrist and dragged me out of the café to the alleyway, where he proceeded to cage me against the brick wall with his massive body—seriously, dude was built like a fucking bear tank. "Do you ever know when to shut your mouth? You don't just go saying shit like that out loud in public. You're lucky there wasn't a fucking cop in there." He seethed inches away from my face with a stern face.

Surprisingly, I was unphased by his harshness. "Oh, so mister pissy face can talk," I remarked with a cute smile and tilt of my head. "But I also don't see why you would care. I mean, your family basically has all the cops in the damn city paid off to turn a blind eye or go deaf around you all." I quickly tacked on with a deep smirk while tilting my chin up at Lev.

Then, silence. What a shocker. "Seriously, what the hell is your problem? Why are you following me around? I wouldn't care if you were some obsessed fanboy, but I highly doubt that to be the case. Besides, even if it were, you need to cut this shit out because I want nothing to do with the mafia. I haven't done anything to garner any of the bratva's attention, just a simple girl trying to live her simple life." A simple life making bombs and blowing shit up.

Okay, maybe I was a little hypocritical with my words because as long as I continued to help Angel, then I would be involved with the mafia life vicariously through her. I didn't want to be fully involved in the mafia, but having my connections to Angel had its perks. If it weren't for her and her standing in the mafia world, then I wouldn't be a free woman living a cushy life right now.

I didn't help her by providing her with bombs and hacking services along with my brother Bao because I owed her or felt like I did or anything. It only started with the hacking initially because it was fun to be doing something for a good cause. Angel might be the reigning mafia queen being Nikolai Volkov's wife, but she had a good head and heart that was always pointed in the right direction. Hell, she even went on to open a safe haven shelter for victims of abuse. Which, by the way, I helped run. Angel may be a smart and caring nurse, but she was bare basics when it came to technology and anything I.T. related, so I ran her operations on that front in the background with my younger brother Bao.

Nikolai's not too bad of a person either, despite his reputation as the Devil Volk of the Volkov Bratva. Sure, he was the typical rough and brutal mafia boss, but behind closed doors, damn guy is whipped for his wife. If he wasn't a good person underneath, he wouldn't have granted Angel her request for the shelter. Granted, he did owe her a favor after she saved him from a car crash—it was how they initially met. It probably could have been a cute love story if not for the fact Angel's stepmother arranged her off into a marriage with Nikolai. He chose to go through with the marriage, but still, they were only together because their hands were somewhat forced in the matter. It would have been too cute if they had naturally made the move with each other.

Oh well, it ended very well for both of them, and I was more than happy for them. Truly, I was, especially for Angel. Poor thing had been through enough in her life, so she deserved to be happy and have someone who genuinely loved her for all she was and more.

If only I could have my little happily ever after.

Bah, who was I kidding? I was too crazy of a bitch for some man to settle with.

"What? Back to the silent treatment already?" I quipped with a quirked brow when Lev's lips continued to remain pressed in a tight line.

I thought I'd get to have some fun fucking around with Lev, but after finding out he's bratva, yeah, no thanks. If he was some little grunt worker and proved to be worth the time, then maybe I would have had some fun and entertainment in my dulling life. But ain't no way would I fuck around with a bratva boss—nah, fuck that. Besides, not like Lev was giving me anything but silence in return, so at this point, he wasn't proving worth the time.

The more entangled I became into his life, the graver I'd put mine in. If I put myself back into the spotlight, then it'd make my parents' task of dragging my ass back or finding a way to use me again that much easier.

Scooting a step up, I pressed myself right up against him, and thank God for these heeled boots of mine for giving me some inches. My 5'4 ass would pale so badly against his bulky ass 6'3? 6'2? frame. Well, he's six-foot something for sure, who cares about the inches—I mean, he was already huge compared to me either way.

Standing my ground firmly against him, I lean up to him on my tippy toes until my face was as close as possible to his.

"This will be your one and only warning, little lion. Back off. Whatever your little fascination or obsession is with me ends right here, right now. If I catch a whiff of you or see you following me out of the corner of my eyes after today, well, I won't be responsible for what bodily harm comes your way."

***

Well, I did warn him, so he couldn't say he didn't see this coming.

Okay, to be fair, no one really ever sees a wood plank straight to the face, especially from someone from me.

Even after my warning yesterday, I still found him to be tailing me today. Either he doesn't take me seriously, or something else went on I was unaware about. Unfortunately, I was more prone to opt for the latter given my strange life.

Seriously, what the hell did he want with me?

I mean, I could flat-out ask him. Actually, I did and got nothing in response, literally. My check on him still ran, so I wouldn't have much information on him for a little while. Well, it should be done tonight or tomorrow night. I couldn't do too much from my remote location without giving myself away. Limited time stretches on the internet really dampened the speed of things, but I couldn't risk my parents pinpointing my location and going after me in the middle of the night or surprising me some other way. Otherwise, all my efforts of evading them would be for naught.

In the city and general public, I was safe because of bystanders and the fact Angel had men at every corner. At the cabin, though, it was just me, and I couldn't fight for shit.

Either way, I'll probably find out what I need about Lev in the next day or so. There has to be some kind of change in his life that I could pick up because I doubt he was old school; no technology whatsoever. It won't be long now.

In the meanwhile, I'd just have to try and scare him off.

Hopefully, some innocent—not really—bodily harm would ward him off long enough until I could figure out his plans.

Just like all the other days, he followed me around—despite my warning. I made a quick detour this time after exiting the café and dodged around the corner fast enough to nearly shake him. Unfortunately, I wasn't that smooth, so I had to resort to plan B, which was to smack him in the face with the closest object, which happened to be a piece of discarded wood from a broken pallet.

I didn't feel guilty about him reeling back in pain after the sickening *crack* of his face breaking filled the area. Hey, he deserved it for not heeding my warning. "Last chance, fuck off, or I won't be so nice next time." Did I want to up the ante? No, not particularly, but if push came to shove, then I would.

Granted, it didn't have to be violent in nature. I could hack his bank account and drain all of them in a blink of an eye, make up some stupid images and videos, and post them online to completely drag his reputation through shit, or I could even take it far and blow his whole life up—literally. I might not be the best fighter out there, but I had brains and nifty bomb-making skills that made me formidable.

"Fucking... Fuck!" Lev's nasally groan gripped at my heart a little as he leaned against the wall with his face in his hands, blood dripping out from between the spaces of his fingers and splattering onto the ground at his feet.

"I warned you." I tried to remain firm and strong, but the small waver in my voice came out unconsciously.

I don't know why I was a little torn up about injuring him because he wasn't the first man I had to get physical with ever since I've been on this strange run with my parents. But he's the first person I've engaged in a playful manner because, well, actually, I don't know why besides some feeling of fascination toward him. At least, I was fascinated until I found out about his real identity. Yeah, fucking with the mafia never ended well.

"You broke my nose with a piece of wood! I didn't think you'd be crazy enough to just swing right off the bat like that," Lev groaned in response, peering up at me with pain-riddled eyes filled with fury and... Fascination? Excitement? There was an edge to his eyes that I didn't expect.

"Well, that's your fault for underestimating me," I retorted, scoffing and crossing my arms with a huffing glare. "I don't want to see your stupid handsome face again, ever, so leave me alone."

With one last look, I turned on my heels and briskly walked off with my head held down in shame.

I needed to shut him out and away, for both our sakes.

Chapter 5

I FUCKED UP.

I shouldn't have called her stupid bluff. I shouldn't have screwed around and found out.

Strings of curses in Russian spilled from my scowling mouth as I held the small towel Nicole threw at me after bashing my face in with a wooden plank.

"Seriously, what happened? You look like you lost a fight with a wall," Alexei, my younger brother, inquired as he inspected my crooked nose after removing the blood-saturated cloth. "You're usually not this grumpy either, so something went wrong."

Grumbling under my breath, I glared burning holes into the wall ahead of me. "Nothing, just a bad day in the field." No one knew much about my latest assignment besides that it was a locate and retrieval of a woman.

Yeah, like hell I would admit to them now that a little tiny Asian woman got the best of me. I'll just wrap up this damn assignment and be done with it. Nicole was still as much of a mystery to me after two weeks than before.

Yet, I couldn't bring myself to retrieve her and put her back in her parents' care, if it could even be called that. Something wasn't right with this whole situation, but I still hadn't figured that out either.

Personally, I haven't had much time to dig into her parents as I'd like because most of my day went toward tailing Nicole. Well, recently, most of my day has been focused on tolerating her yapping. For someone supposedly reserved, she sure could run her damn mouth and talk the ears off of people.

Honestly, Nicole was nothing as I anticipated thus far—but whether it was in a bad way or a good way was yet to be determined. I half expected some demure girl, but lo and behold, I got a fucking grenade that blew up in my face today.

I should be pissed and in a rage. Woman or not, if someone struck me, then it made them fair game to me. Only time I never retaliated was if my assailant was literally a child or some feeble woman who'd die from a single strike from me. Yet, I found myself unable to feel anything ill toward Nicole, even though she wasn't acting in self-defense or out of petty revenge. She fucking whacked me in the face with a piece of wood because I simply annoyed her and underestimated her. Now, she could have very well done something not so drastic, but I couldn't help the feeling of amusing shock at her bold audacity.

Seriously, who the fuck thinks, 'Oh, this person isn't listening to me, so I'll just smack them with a bat' basically. No one soft and innocent would jump from zero to a hundred like that without damn good reason. And no, my disregarding her words would not constitute as a damn good reason. I would make that jump, but I'm me, so that's fine. I mean, what can I say? I'm an amped-up man with too much to vent on the world. Nicole, though, damn woman gotta be crazy.

Sure, I deserved something thrown at my face for being an asshole to her warning, but certainly not something literally to my face like that. Still, couldn't be mad at her, which is the reason why I was pissed because I should be. Crazy enough, I wanted to see what more damage she could do when pushed.

Yeah, call me a crazy and stupid asshole because I am, but I've never met a woman who was brave enough to stand her ground against me like that after knowing exactly who I am. Not counting my sister-in-law and my new best friend because they were mafia women. From what I'm aware, Nicole wasn't involved in the mafia. Also, even though she stood up against me, I could still see the slight fear in her eyes. Yet, she didn't let that fear take over.

Nicole could have run, freeze up, or tried to appeal to my greater side for mercy—that's what people tend to do after realizing they'd fucked up against me. But not Nicole, though. Damn little hell fire was ready to face the consequences of her actions despite her fear. Then, there was also something else in her eyes; she had this look as if she dared me to doubt her more. For a sweet girl, I think she had a pretty violent bone in her cute little body.

"You rarely have a bad day in the field *bratok*, so what happened?" This time, my eyes moved over to my little brother, watching as he pulled on a pair of gloves and grabbed a wad of gauze. "Also, not every day you come to my office because of a little injury like this."

I expected him to dive right in and reset my nose, but nope. He stood there with his free hand on his hips, looking at me inquisitively. "Have you ever had someone scared of you but not? Like you can clearly see the fear in their eyes, yet they have this fire to them as well?"

Cracking a small, smug smirk, Alexei chortled out a chuckle before looking over my shoulder with a fond distance to his eyes. "Yeah, a long time ago, yeah. But it sounds like you've met your match. I feel bad for the dude who ends up with you," Alexei remarked with a cheeky gleam in his eyes before he stepped up to me and grabbed at my nose.

"Excuse you? Dude? I'll have you know I like chicks a little too much. Why the hell would you assume it's a man?" I grumbled with narrowing eyes as I braced myself for what was to come.

"Because no woman is crazy enough to put up with your insane and violent ass unless she's an insane criminal," Alexei replied before snapping my nose bridge back into place with a sudden jerk.

"*Blyat!*" I cursed with a sharp inhale. "I'm starting to wonder how insane she actually is if she had the guts to whack me in the face like this," I muttered with a soft scowl of displeasure.

"Wait, a girl did this to you? Now you have to tell me, consider it payment for fixing your ugly face to make it semi-decent again." Never a good thing when your psychopathic brother is interested in your life. "But wait, you said you got hurt in the field... Wait, please don't tell me she's some cop or something. Seriously, Arseny's already gonna get himself in a hell of a bind with his little cop crush."

With a roll of my eyes, I snatch the wad of gauze from him to hold against my leaking nose. "No, she's not some cop or anything like that, just another assignment. I just underestimated her, that's all. I've got it all handled, and she probably won't be a problem for much longer. So, don't go running your mouth to Kolya or the others. I'm pulling the patient-doctor privacy privilege shit on this one." Unless my life was in immediate danger, I knew Alexei would respect my wishes because he took his career as a doctor rather seriously enough.

I'd never go for a cop or anyone in law enforcement or politics—that was just asking for shit to go down. I honestly don't know what the hell went on in my youngest brother's—Arseny—mind with this stupid little crush of his. Well, pretty sure I could easily get the answer from Alexei because the two of them shared everything with each other and understood each other in and out. Of course, that'd be a cheap shot to ask Alexei because, of course, he'd know his own identical twin inside and out—they're practically the same person. No matter, Arseny was a grown-ass adult who could make his own bad decisions if he so wished; as long as it didn't bite our family in the ass, then I saw no harm in him having some kind of fun.

With a wary look, Alexei eyed me for a good moment before plopping back down behind his desk after discarding his gloves. "Lev, you've never let an assignment get the best of you like this, nor have you ever underestimated many people. Are you going soft now?" The little shithead teased with a cocky little smirk as he leaned back in his chair with his fingers laced and elbows propped on his legs.

Gritting my teeth, I scowled deeply at Alexei with a growl and chucked the saturated gauze at him. Alexei chuckled and easily dodged it by leaning to the side. "It's about time you simmer down and stop being a terror to everyone in the city," Alexei remarked with a cheeky smirk.

"I'm not going soft, you little psychopath. I just didn't expect her to have that spunk to her after doing all my research on her. But like I said, she won't be a problem much longer. I'm done playing around with her." Screw it. I'll just corner her at the next chance and have a nice chat with her before possibly snatching her back to her parents.

"Done playing around with who?"

Fucking great.

Internally groaning, I looked over to the office door as it shut. "Nothing, Kolya," I grumbled in response to my oldest brother, the Pakhan of our bratva.

"Lev, what the fuck did you do?" Nikolai—who we all call Kolya—sighed exasperatedly before rubbing his temple.

Feigning hurt, I scoffed softly in response while averting my eyes. "Why do you always assume I did something?" Well, to be fair, my track record wasn't the best, so I didn't blame him.

"Because you're here in Alexei's office, talking to him in a civil manner," Nikolai noted with a pointed look.

"Well, what are you doing here?" I turned the tables back on him with a quick smirk as I took in his ruffled form.

"To get medical care, why else would I be in a doctor's office," Nikolai snapped back with a soft, playful glare as he went over to the couch in Alexei's office and plopped down on it with a wince.

"No, no, let me rephrase that for you. *You* are *here* in *Alexei's* office, not just any doctor's office, nor are you at your little med ward at the estate. So, something is up." Now it was my turn to be the little shithead younger brother just to give Nikolai some grief.

"Tell me who you're done playing around with, and I'll answer you properly." Nikolai bargained with a cocky smirk.

"A woman, now your turn." Okay, now I was being an annoying smartass, and I knew it.

"Don't make me break that nose again, Lev," Nikolai playfully—not really—threatened with a slight tick of his upper lip.

"Ey! Just because I'm a doctor doesn't give you idiots permission to bang each other up every chance you get." Alexei chimed in with a glare at both of us. "I like cutting people up, not fixing them."

"Yeah, yeah, yeah, ya like to hold the power of life in your hand blah blah blah," I said dismissively with a wave of my hand, earning a chuck of a pen at me by Alexei.

Yeah, the little psychopath—yes, he is a psychopath, clinically diagnosed, too—became a doctor because he enjoyed having the power of having someone's life in his hands, literally. As a surgeon, he literally controlled everyone's life the moment they were on his operating table. At least, that was the main reason for his career choice. The other was to patch together broken people because it made him feel like God. By patching people up, I mean rearranging their insides, replacing their insides, basically making them a functioning human being again.

"Kolya, don't bleed all over my couch. Get on the exam table." Alexei sneered, pointing over to where I was currently sitting.

Rolling his eyes, Nikolai grumbled something under his breath before slowly getting up and going over to me with a strained face. "Scoot," he demanded with a shove to my shoulder.

"You know, the word 'please' exists," I smugly replied with a shit-eating grin.

Nikolai's chest rose and fell with his deep breath while his jaw tightened momentarily. "Please move your fat ass over before I lay it on the ground," he said through gritted teeth.

"Say it nicely without threatening me, and I might consider," I remarked with a widening smirk while resisting the urge to flip my older brother off to push his buttons some more.

"Lev, I swear I will stick Angel on you if you don't fucking move over this instant." Well, someone's clearly having a bad day from the snappy tone.

On the other hand, he brought something up to me. "Wait a minute. Why aren't you having your nurse or a wife patch you up if you need medical attention? I mean, you're always running your mouth about how soft her hands are and how gentle and caring she is. So, why aren't you with her instead? Hm?" I had a pretty good guess as to why he was here seeking help from our brother instead of his spunky bride, but I wanted to poke at the angry wolf some more.

"Same reason why you're here," Alexei groaned with a roll of his eyes. "What did you do this time, Kolya?" His eyes drifted over to Nikolai, who shoved me aside and took my spot on the exam table before taking his jacket off to reveal a bloody undershirt.

"Wow, what did you do this time to piss Angel off that much?" I teased with a snicker. It was a joke, of course, and everyone knew that. Angel might be a little devil underneath her caring exterior, but she'd never hurt any of us intentionally, especially her own husband.

"She won't be pissed as long as she doesn't find out about this," Nikolai grumbled, removing his button-up shirt that was nearly torn in half with whatever made the nice gash across his chest.

At least Alexei beat me to the punch this time. Otherwise, my ass probably would be laid out. "Let me guess, she told you to not go do something, then you went and did that said something, and you got injured. Now, if you go to her, not only will you get an earful of 'I fucking told you so' and shit, but you'll also be in the dog house? How close am I?" Alexei gave him a knowing smirk as he sat there, leaning back smugly in his chair.

"If any of you breathe a word about this to Angel, I swear I will make your lives a living hell for the next month. Nothing leaves this office, am I clear?" Yeah, as if going boss mode would scare us. We were too used to him after growing up with him.

That's not to say I didn't respect him and his role as the head honcho because I did during the right times. Obviously, this wasn't one of those times because we were screwing around with each other and being playful. We wouldn't snitch on each other to our prospective partners. Well, in this case, we wouldn't rat Nikolai out to his terrifying mafia wife. Alexei and I didn't have any significant other to be ousted to, so we were safe.

"What happened?" I questioned with genuine interest and worry as I moved myself to a chair.

Leaning back with a wince, Nikolai let out a deep breath before responding, "Just another unhappy customer, that's all. One who was not too happy with, and I quote, 'a damn Russian taking over business that ain't his' and whatnot."

"Oooh! Now, it's my turn to take a guess. So, let me guess, this was a merge customer. Angel said to wait for her or let her take care of it, and of course, you decide not to listen, and it blew up in your face. Right?" My brain worked sometimes, usually when it came to being an asshole.

Nikolai grumbled in response and glared at us before grumbling to Alexei to patch him up before letting his lips go tightly shut. "Although, I'm curious, how the fuck do you expect to hide this from her until you're healed?" I questioned with a snicker, earning a harsh glare from Nikolai. "I mean, with how you two go at it, pregnant or not, she's still gonna jump your bones, touch you, shower with you, other wifely duties and whatnot. And, even when you are healed up, she's still gonna notice the new scar going across your chest. You're not gonna get out of this one, *bratok*."

Angel wasn't stupid and blind, so I really don't see how Nikolai would weasel his way out of this one. "Hate to admit it, but Lev is right." Alexei chuckled as he gathered his equipment to stitch our brother up.

"Better prepare yourself to get hung out to dry by your wife." I laughed heartily, wincing with regret when I felt the painful throb from the pressure in my face from the laughing.

Yes, I still found Nikolai's marriage highly amusing because he's the tough bratva boss who feared no one until this tiny little Asian nurse came along and struck fear into him. It's funny because it could have been me instead of him. When we met Angel, it was through an arranged marriage to solidify a truce between our bratva and the Qing Triad before Angel disbanded it after she overthrew her stepmother and took over. I'd initially offered myself to be the one to marry Angel after seeing her kick ass in nothing but her underwear. I mean, who wouldn't want a tough, badass woman as theirs?

Unfortunately, Nikolai had a huge crush on the hot nurse and staked his claim with his little second chance at her. I wasn't complaining about the loss, though, not when Nikolai and Angel were so happy together. Nikolai deserved to be happy after all he's been through. Hell, all of us deserve our happy pieces for our shitty lives.

I got shit, but not as much as my two older brothers, Nikolai and Stepan. Nikolai got the brunt of it, though, being the oldest and all. Our bastard father groomed him since birth basically to take over, and our sperm donor's methods were not kind.

"Enough about me." Nikolai playfully snapped before locking his eyes with me. "What happened with you?" The pinned look and stern tone of his meant I wasn't getting out of this.

"Just a girl I was assigned to locate and retrieve. Underestimated her and got a plank to the face, that's all," I replied begrudgingly with a string of grumbling curses under my breath. "But it doesn't matter. I'll have her taken care of by the end of tomorrow. So, don't mind me any attention."

Yeah, that still didn't stop the snickering from Nikolai. "Your face got broken by a girl? Was she your size, at least?"

Embarrassed, I kept my lips sealed as I pouted in my seat. "No point in talking about it anymore if she's not gonna be a problem no more, and not like anyone else is going to find out about this because none of this shit is leaving this office." I quickly chimed up pointedly with a stern glare.

"And how did she get to the point of striking you? I mean, you've blocked and avoided much worse than some wood to the face," Nikolai pressed with an amused smirk.

Crossing my arms, I slumped in my seat. "Don't want to talk about it." Because it was too damn embarrassing for me to admit it all out loud.

I got one-upped by a girl half my size.

At least she was cute and feisty.

Chapter 6

~1 week later~

I started to wonder if Lev was deaf, stupid, or both because the damn idiot continued to follow me despite how I got physical with him.

Honestly, I thought a literal smack to the face would do the trick, especially since he ended up with at least a broken nose from it—apparently not!

His persistence unnerved me if I was being honest. Because, why? What was his reason for following me? Well, not like I cared too much at this point because I wanted nothing to do with him, given his mafia standing, nor did I want to continue feeding whatever obsession he had with me.

I needed to shake him and show him I meant business.

Which was a big shame, because his Ferrari GTS was one sexy thing. Not gonna lie, thinking about doing what I plan to do breaks my heart a little. But, all is fair in love and war—and this was war.

I'd kept to my normal routine up until it was time for me to go back to my cabin, which is when I usually had to shake Lev off my tail either way, so doing this deplorable act next wouldn't be much of a deviation from my daily routine. Still, it was gonna suck big time. I felt like it would be one of those moments where it'd gonna hurt me more than it does him.

"Are you going to knock off the stalker behavior?" I asked in a raised voice, not bothering to look back to see if Lev heard me or not because I was sure he did, considering how we were down a quiet stretch of road where we were the only two people on it.

"No, but you don't have to worry about it for much longer after today because you're coming back with me and then back to your parents." Oh, fuck that! That's why he's been tailing me for the past month?! Oh, now I really wouldn't feel bad about what's about to happen.

It wouldn't have been bad if he followed me out of his own volition for some personally sick and twisted pleasure, but he was doing this for my parents? Also, my parents sent the damn bratva after me? Why the fuck didn't Angel let me know of this? Actually, now that I think about it a little, it's only been Lev I've seen and heard about, and nothing nor anyone else. But it also didn't make much sense because surely the rest of his brothers would have known about this task of his. After all, it was my parents, and they had ties to the mafia. So, technically, this could be mafia business, and obviously, his brothers should be in the know if it was mafia business.

Fucking hell.

Pissed and frustrated, just lovely.

"Fine, catch me if you can." I didn't spare him a glance as I took off toward my Kawasaki Ninja and turned the engine over the moment I got my hands on it.

With one hand, I threw my helmet on before revving the engine and turning around full circle to face Lev as he rounded to the driver's side of his Ferrari. Under my breath, I muttered a quick apology before reaching into my bag to pull out some small bombs the size and shape of ping-pong balls. Not giving him a moment to try and figure me out, I tossed the bombs at the underside of his car before pulling my phone out and triggering the bombs through my app.

Strings of loud pops, a little louder than typical gunshots, shot off, effectively blowing the engine of the car up and setting it ablaze. God that sexy car did not deserve such an end, but my survival was more important, sadly. With a sad sigh, I tucked my phone and high-tailed it out of there with a laugh when I heard Lev's angry cries of disbelief.

I did warn him, kind of. Well, I didn't explicitly tell him what would exactly happen if he kept stalking me. I would have felt a little sorry for him if it weren't for the fact he was after me on behalf of my parents. So, fuck him.

Well, no matter, he'll be yesterday's problem tomorrow. No way he'd keep pursuing me after that.

I'd thought about calling Angel to figure out exactly what the hell was going on, but I simmered down enough by the time I got back home. Lev wouldn't be a problem anymore, so no point in bitching to Angel about something that will literally be nothing. Seriously, she didn't need this on her plate, and I handled the problem.

Or so I thought.

Yeah, Lev wasn't too happy the next day, not that I blamed him. Actually, I was surprised at the lack of outward fury when he trudged up to me in the café and dragged me out to the alleyway again. His eyes, though, were a much different story. Those bright blue eyes of his stormed over to stark ice the moment he searched for me in the café. Such a lovely pair of gems that used to melt me now pierced me like daggers to the chest.

"How much?" The question quickly slipped from between my lips the moment I recovered from being slammed and caged against the wall.

"What?" The rigidity in his eyes melted to confusion as his head tilted.

"How much are they paying you? Whatever it is, I'll triple it for you to leave me the fuck alone. Just tell them you lost me or never found me, or tell them I'm dead, I don't care, just quit going after me to drag me back to them. This really will be your final warning. If you don't quit it after today, I'll do so much worse than blow up your car." Surprisingly, I didn't waver in the slightest with the fear that coursed through my body.

Sure, I may be formidable, but I paled against Lev. The only way I'd win against him was either behind a screen paired with a remote-controlled drone or him at enough of a distance for me to chuck a bomb at him. Up close, I stood no chance, not even a hair of one.

Seriously, my short ass stood at 5'4" while he stood at a whooping 6'2". No way in hell would I win in a physical fight against him unless his hands and feet were tied—actually, that kind of sounded fun. Not gonna lie, the brief thought of a powerful man like him bound by my feet. Damn it, stupid brain, this wasn't the time for such thoughts.

The damn man would literally maul me over like a bear charging over a child. Honestly, this was a funny scene in my mind before I shoved it aside to remain serious.

Anticipating a fight, I held onto the adrenaline pumping through my body. I needed to run at the first opening because, again, fighting Lev would be the worst idea ever. So, I was shocked when Lev's tense shoulders dropped with a slow exhale. I didn't relax, though, not fully, at least because what if this was some kind of trick to get me to lower my guard?

Warily, I narrowed my eyes at him. "I just want to be left alone."

"No." With how short and pointed his replies were to me, I started to wonder if he had a fully functioning brain at this point. "Did you really have to go and blow up my damn car for not listening to you? What the fuck is wrong with you, woman? You could have killed me. I was right next to the fucking thing."

"Oh, so the brute does speak English and can string on more than five words in a sentence at a time," I teased with a coo and smirk as if I was praising some child. "But you only got yourself to blame for the tragedy of your car. I don't play around, and I damn well warned you."

Okay, blowing up his car probably wasn't warranted, but it's not like I could un-blow up his car now. "And it wouldn't have killed you unless you were directly on top of the bombs. Besides, I knew a skilled man like you would be able to dodge out of the way fast enough." They were small-scale bombs meant for distractions, not real damage. The car only blew up because of the gas component in it and the fact I threw so many down there.

Giving him a once over, I could see that he was unscathed. Literally, there wasn't even a tiny scratch on him. The only thing hurt was probably his feelings.

Honestly, dude, walk it off.

"You couldn't have tried to buy me off before you blew my car up? What kind of backward ass logic is going on in that crazy-ass mind of yours? You proposition first and then act, or at the very least, go from least harm to most harmful. Fucking crazy ass woman," Lev retorted with a roll of his eyes and a scowl.

Mocking him under my breath, I rolled my eyes in return before jabbing at his—holy shit, his pecs are fucking hard and nice as fuck. I felt like an idiot for slowly flattening my hand out against his chest while openly ogling him like a tantalizing piece of candy, but god, damn, he felt sturdy as fuck. Well, if he had any objections or complaints, then he would have pulled away or said something, but he didn't. Lev surprisingly puffed his chest out a little with his deep inhale as he looked down at me.

Taking in a deep breath, I recollected myself and reluctantly pulled my hands back to my side. Clenching my hands up into tight fists, I averted my eyes from his hypnotic ones to get my words out. "None of this would have happened if you had just come clean to me in the first place as to why you were following me." As in, I would have dropped-kicked his ass twenty miles two weeks ago.

Breathing deeply, Lev ran a hand down his face before pushing off the wall and stepping back from me. "Don't get your cute little ass killed or snatched out there."

Then he left me to my own confusion without as much as a small glance at me.

Like, what the fuck, literally.

Great, what the hell was I supposed to do with this lingering adrenaline?

Something stupid is what.

"Wait!" Yeah, I took off after him before I even realized my legs had moved. "That's it?"

Lev's body paused and went rigid briefly before his shoulders relaxed, and he looked back at me with a mysteriously playful smirk.

"No. I'll see you tomorrow, Nicole."

Chapter 7

~1 week later~

Something's not right.

I couldn't find Lev, no matter how hard I looked. Well, to be fair, I wasn't looking *that* hard because he was usually within a few feet of me if he wasn't by my side. Yet, he was nowhere to be felt or seen today. Damn asshole left me on read, too, when I texted him and asked about his whereabouts! I mean, he never really replied to my messages before with any actual responses, but he sent me a period, at the very least, to show that he acknowledged the message.

Tracking his phone was pointless as well because he either left it at home or bugged it somehow; the blinking dot on my tracking app hadn't moved one bit over the last three hours. But, considering how he saw my message, I assumed he had his phone on him, so the fucker bugged his phone somehow.

The hell is he doing? What's more important than following me around like a lost puppy? How dare he leave me on read like he did. Who the hell did he think he is? The fucker better have a good explanation for this later when I track his ass down.

45

Grumbling to myself internally, I continued to sip at my drink and pick at my salad that grew blander by the second because of my souring mood. Seriously, we should be sitting for lunch together right now. Instead, I sat here by my lonesome self without my handsome hunk to ogle between my bites of food.

My handsome hunk.

God, that was weird to think about, but not thinking about him as mine made me feel empty. As annoying as Lev was, he grew on me. A day without him lingering around felt amiss, like missing a part of a daily routine; it bugged the shit out of me if he wasn't around and didn't let me know beforehand. We weren't 'together' by any means, but a heads-up was common courtesy.

Granted, I should give him some slack. He was usually on top of things and always informed me at least a day before unless it was a true emergency or something similar.

This could be one of those situations, but the fact he hadn't moved for a few hours was suspicious.

Actually, wait, I needed to not be dumb for a second.

Huffing, I pulled my laptop out of my bag to boot up one of my tracking apps to get a better idea of Lev's current location. I could dig around in my phone's app, but the internet at the café wasn't the best for the phone. Plus, I could do a lot more on my laptop, like hack the cameras at his location to get a better view of everything.

Imagine my surprise when I pulled up his full location and saw that he was currently occupying a gentleman's club. Better yet, he was inside with some scantily clad woman who had her manicured talons on his body, and he was just letting her feel him all up.

Fucking asshole! How dare he go see other women?! Seriously, this is what he ditched me for today!? To go play hooky?!

Growling softly to myself, I slammed my laptop shut with a deep scowl. I shouldn't be bothered by this; he was his own person, and we weren't an exclusive couple. But still, I couldn't help but feel hot anger burn through my veins like lava oozing down a volcano. Lev shouldn't be paying anyone but *me* any kind of attention!

Guess he needs a reminder of who he belongs to.

Okay, maybe I've officially lost some more nuts and bolts in my brain with this impulsive plan of mine.

Well, also, I might not have really been thinking much about this whole thing... Oh well, it was too late now. But also, Lev had no one but himself to blame for this. He should have known better than to look at another woman when he should be obsessing over me.

"Girl, I knew you had a crazy bitch in you, but goddamn, this is a whole new other level of insanity to you," Mark, a good artist friend of mine, commented with a chuckle as he snapped his gloves off. "There are other ways to mark a man as yours, ya know."

Playfully shrugging my shoulders, I let out a nervous laugh. "Go big or go home?" Too late for regrets now; the deed was done.

Flashing Mark a grateful smile, I gave him a quick hug before letting him finish his packing so that he could scram before Lev woke up. "I owe ya big time."

Rolling his eyes in response, Mark waved his hand at me dismissively. "Hey, ya saved my ass too many times with my systems and finances, so this was the least I could do for you." He assured me with a smile before leaving out the door with a small wave.

The gravity of my actions sank down quickly with the silence that filled the room, along with Lev's rather cute snoring. Seriously, for a huge guy like him, I expected some kind of blaring ship horn of a snore, not the tiny baby grunts. Also, he looked so adorable asleep, as if he were a harmless little fly and not a brutish bratva boss. It kinda made me feel bad for wanting to wake him, but I haven't got all day to sit around and wait for him to naturally wake.

So, with a sigh, I walked over to the buckets of iced water, I had set out in the corner of room, and hauled them over to Lev, who remained knocked out and tied down to a chair.

Bucket in hand, I stood there for a moment to blatantly check him out. Fucking, hot ass bastard.

It really shouldn't be fair for someone so handsome and sexy like him to be walking the earth, ruining every man out there for me. Whenever I looked at another cute guy, all I could picture in their spot was Lev's bearded and scarred-up face with his dashing smile and haunting blue eyes. Then that body of his, just, fuck. He was a piece of art that belonged in a museum. Every dip and curve of his hard muscles seemed like they were carved from marble. Even when he wasn't flexing, his muscles stood out naturally.

It's not fair!

Huffing, I tightened my grip on the bucket and threw the water at him. Lev instantly sputtered and gasped for air as he was startled awake. His body jerked, and he struggled against his restraints for a second before his eyes landed on me. "What the fuck?" Quickly, his eyes narrowed into a glare, and his struggle intensified. "You crazy bitch, let me go! What did you do to me?!"

"Wow, usually people say 'thank you' when others give them a gift," I remarked sarcastically with an exaggerated roll of my eyes.

Grinning at Lev, I plopped down into his lap after pulling my phone out. "Smile. It's our first picture together as a couple." I joked with a laugh before snapping a selfie with Lev, who was most definitely not pleased or smiling.

"The fuck did you put in your coffee this morning, you psycho?" Lev bit at me with a scowl.

"Nothing," I replied in a cheery voice. "Well, maybe an extra pump or two of caramel." I joked with a giggle.

"But, no matter." Smiling, I spun around to face him fully after straddling his lap. "How do you like your little gift?" Leaning onto his shoulder, I softly poked at the fresh tattoo on his chest, right over his heart.

Lev's scowling face stretched out into shock the moment his eyes landed on the reddened area on his chest. "You have five seconds to tell me this is a stupid prank, that it's fake, or else I will throttle you against the wall and give you something permanent to remember me by after I'm done with you." His face twisted with fury and a little horror the more I just sat there smiling at him.

Giggling, I reached up and poked his scrunched-up nose. "I gotta say, think this is my favorite tattoo on you." I rubbed it into his face with a full laugh. "I figured since you like you to follow me around so much, I'd give you something to remember me by." Drawing out my last word with a soft sigh, I gripped his face. "And after what happened today, you need a constant reminder of who you belong to."

Leaning in, I ran the tip of my nose along his taut neck with a low chuckle. All while my fingernails dragged themselves down his pecs and abs, leaving trails of red in their wake until I stopped at the waistband of his pants, where his happy trail continued under. "I really hate how fucking perfect you look, smell, and feel." I groaned softly against his lips as I ghosted mine over them.

If I had no pride or came across him years ago, then I'd be shamelessly throwing myself at his feet, vying for his attention by any means possible. Too bad I grew up and found my worth in this rotten world.

I bowed to no man, even if he was perfect for me.

"If you're going to kiss me, then do it already," Lev growled under his breath with half-closed eyes.

"What if I don't want to?" I teased with a smirk, running a finger along the seam of his lips.

Leaning his head in, he brushed his lips against the corner of mine. "Yes, you do," he remarked with a smug smirk of his own. "Kiss me, Nicki. Kiss me and put us both out of our misery."

Grabbing his face, I slammed our lips together in a hot and messy kiss. Our tongues clashed wildly as our heavy breaths washed over each other, along with our moans and groans. Throwing my arms around his neck and shoulders, I held him tightly and pressed my body flush against his. "Please, tell me that's your belt," I groaned against his lips, shamelessly grinding my hips down against the bulge beneath my aching core.

Lev gritted his teeth and sucked in a sharp breath through it while bucking his hips to grind back against me. "You think my belt is that big?" He strained out a dry chuckle with a hard thrust, jerking my body forward a little.

Hot arousal poured down my body at the feeling of his tongue running along my neck. "It's just your thick pants making you feel bigger, so don't start talking a game you can't win," I mustered against his ear before nipping at it.

Gasping softly with pleasure, I rolled my hips against him, letting his straining hardness press right against my throbbing clit. The only thing that stood between us fully connecting was our clothes, but that could have been an easy fix if I really wanted to be crazy and take him. All I had to do was unzip him and take my panties off from under my dress.

"Nicki, don't start something you aren't going to finish." Lev strained out a groan as his hips started to stiffen under me as if he held himself back.

Deviously, I grinned and kissed him deeply. "Oh, I'll make sure we finish alright," I whispered hotly against his lips before pressing myself down against him, humping him. "I'll give you another thing to remind you of me."

Settling my hands on his broad shoulders, I steadied and braced myself to properly dry fuck him. "I need to be in you, please," Lev begged against my lips with a needy groan.

"No," I denied him smugly, picking up my pace while smirking. "If you want to get in my pants, then you have to at least be a gentleman and take me out on a proper date, wine, and dine me and all," I teased with a giggle, pressing down hard against him when his groaning picked up.

Throwing his head back with a deep groan, he started to buck his hips more at me. "All this for a date?" Lev said in a single breath.

Chuckling against his lips, I teasingly licked the edge of it. "We can talk later." All I wanted and needed right now was an orgasm from grinding against this sexy beast of a man. "Come with me," I whispered hotly against his lips before capturing them in a tantalizing kiss. "I'm so close." And he probably was, too, judging the way his groans were dragging and picking up in pace with his breaths.

My tongue grazed down his succulent neck to his chest, where my lips kissed the edge of my new mark on Lev. "Come on, little lion, come for me." I did my best to sound and look as sultry as possible when I locked my eyes up with his. Then, to encourage him some, I raked my nails down his chest to his abs again, this time harder than before.

Lev's body went rigid under me with his strangled gasp. *"Gavno!"* His hips sloppily jerked to a stop, and his body trembled with his heavy breaths.

I wanted to enjoy the sight of Lev coming undone a little longer, but my orgasm tore my attention away as the crash of pleasure tightened my cunt and hardened nipples, causing more pleasure to pulsate throughout my body. "Fuck, Lev," I moaned softly with a happy smile.

Unable to help myself, I slipped my fingers under his waistband, just enough to swipe at the oozing mess inside his pants. Sitting up straight, I carefully pulled my fingers out and brought them to my smirking lips.

Giggling softly, I threaded my fingers into the back of his hair, gripping it and making him look at me. "If I were a little nicer today, then I might have cleaned you up properly," I teased with a chuckle before slipping my tongue out and slowly licking my cum coated fingers with a moan.

Or maybe I should spoil both of us a little because, fuck, did he taste good! The strong, musky, tangy scent permeating the air was enough to arouse me into the mood for another orgasm. Then, the salty, bitter-sweet taste of his cum nearly drove me over the edge a little for a mini-orgasm.

A whimper of disappointment gripped my chest when I kept licking and sucking my fingers for more but found them to be clean. Without thinking, I slid off his lap to the ground, kneeling before him as I hastily licked down his abs to his pants, pulling at them impatiently to lower them enough for me to lick his pelvis and pick up more of his seed.

"Blyat!" Lev shuddered above me with darkened eyes that made his icy blues storm over dangerously.

Getting a grip on myself, I quickly fixed his pants and kissed the front of it with a pout before getting up to my feet.

Straightening myself out, I shoved my burning desire for the bratva boss into the depths of my mind.

Swallowing my emotions, I turned around to face him with a saccharin smile. "Sorry, but I gotta run," I lied through my teeth.

Going over to the corner, I picked up my bag and slung it over my shoulder. Digging through it, I fished out a pocketknife and flicked it open as I approached him again. "I would say let's do this again sometime, but there won't be another time for us," I spoke through my exaggerated smile while tapping the blade of the knife against his cheek.

Giving him one last, long kiss, I looked at him for a good moment with a cheeky smile.

Backing away, I threw the knife down by his feet, embedding it into the wooden floor.

"Bye, *anh*."

Chapter 8

THERE ARE MANY THINGS I hate in this world, and being played made the top ten.

Well, either Nicole really was the wayward child who was in her rebel stage/streak, or the Le's played me; obviously, I went for the latter because the anger and fear in Nicole's eyes at the mention of her parents were too real. Nicole wasn't some retaliating runaway child. No, she ran because of something her parents did, and I intended to find out exactly what that was.

I kind of felt a little bad for not doing my full due diligence on her parents and the whole situation before pulling what I did, which was why I backed off her ass for the past few days. I still kept an eye on her, but I kept more of a distance and out of her sight after she got irritated the day after our little confrontation... And after she drugged me and fucking tattooed me while I was out!

Yeah, I still couldn't believe that happened because that was the last thing I expected from her. Well, scratch that, the last thing I expected was for her to ride me through our clothes until we both came. Actually, never mind, what shocked me the most that day was her getting more of a taste.

Fuck, how needy her lustful eyes got when she cleaned me off her fingers. Ugh! It wasn't fair for her to look so damn sexy! And it really wasn't fair how all that plagued my mind was the sight of her enjoying herself using my body every time I shut my eyes. Seriously, I had no idea how many times I've jacked off to fantasies of her the past week—it's fucking insane!

Stop. Don't get hot and bothered by your damn assignment!

Yeah, that constant reminder did nothing for me at this point besides make me gravitate toward her more. Every second without her in my sight filled me with worry. And beating up a person didn't curb the edge to my nerves.

Dumping her and canceling the assignment probably should have been the wise thing for me to do, but I couldn't.

The thought of leaving her be didn't quite settle with me. What if something bad happened to her? I wouldn't be there to help her. I tried, though, I really did, but I found myself turning corners around the city until I was within her vicinity, and she was in my sight. She knew I was there, though, not like I kept myself hidden, but I didn't make any notion of closing in on her to give her any reason to try and blow another possession of mine up.

Sighing, I placed a hand on my chest, right over the area where her touch still lingered from the other day. To be honest, I expected her to slap me that day when I saw her lift her hand, so I was shocked when I felt the burn of her soft touch on my chest.

What's wrong with me?

Seriously, getting worked up over a brief touch from Nicole like that. I needed to get over it, but I couldn't. It was a damn blow to me, but I had to cut a date short because I couldn't get it up. Yeah, I tried to hook up with someone to fuck Nicole out of my system, but that plan flopped so badly because all I could think about during my time with the woman—don't ask me who because I honestly don't fucking remember—was Nicole. Every time I touched the woman, all I could wonder about was how Nicole's body would feel. Whenever I closed my eyes, Nicole's cute yet feisty face flashed to the forefront of my mind.

Fuck I wanted to have a taste of her lips so badly. They weren't big pillow lips, but they were perfectly sized for her petite face; a little on the smaller size, but again, they fitted her divinely. Thinking about her lips made me feel like a little creep, though. From stalking her to thinking about having her. Which was stupid because she was just some average girl in terms of appearance, but fuck would she fit perfectly in my arms.

"Mr. Volkov, the Le's are here," the office assistant announced after knocking and peering her head around my office door.

Leaning back in my chair with a deep breath, I nodded at her. "Send them in." I have a lot of bones to pick with them.

Shockingly, I did not call for this meeting. So, this ought to be interesting.

"To what do I owe the pleasure of this visit?" Okay, that was a lie; no part of this would be a pleasure.

"It's about our request with Nicole..." Mark started after clearing his throat, his wary eyes struggling to remain on me.

"Funny enough, I was about to contact you in a bit regarding that." That wasn't a lie. I really did have every intention of calling them to cancel this contract. "But please, go on. I will say my bit after yours."

Company reputation be damned, not like losing the Le's would damage it much. This whole thing was ridiculous, and I just wanted it all to be done and over with. If I had no conscience, then this whole mess would've been over days ago, but forcing Nicole back to her parents after seeing the terror and hatred in her eyes would've eaten me up until I died. It sounded crazy, letting some assignment get to me like that, but nothing made sense when it came to Nicole and her situation.

Like some unreachable itch, Nicole's been etched into my life ever since I inserted myself into her life with my stalking. Don't ask me any questions because I sure as hell won't have any answers.

"I am afraid that we will have to withdraw from our contract with you. What we paid you before is yours to keep, but your services will no longer be required of us." Well, not gonna lie, that caught me a little off guard, and I couldn't help but let it show on my face a little.

"If that is what you want, then I will honor it. Shame because I had a big update regarding Nicole and was about to work out a plan of extraction and exchange with you two since I'm at that step." Okay, big lie, and I have no idea why the fuck I let the words fly out of my mouth instead of accepting their withdrawal and sending them on their way out the damn door.

I don't know why, but my gut told me to keep them on the hook with me; otherwise, shit would go haywire. I couldn't let them go because if I did, I feared I might actually lose Nicole because of whatever her parents had planned. I needed to find out what their plan was, though, which would be another pain in the ass all on its own. Hopefully, my lie will be enough to keep their interest.

"Oh? You are that close? I apologize, but if you are that close to bringing our daughter back to us, then I do not want to terminate this contract. I thought you were still in the process of... If you are that far along, then please, we do not want all your hard work to be for naught. Consider the contract still in place, please." Yeah, something was definitely up with how fast he changed his tone.

"Did you find someone else who's going to be more efficient than me? Just curious, won't be upset if you say yes." Well, at least I wouldn't be upset for the reason I gave them. I wanna know who to fuck up later for even thinking about going after Nicole.

"A family friend of ours. We initially reached out to them, but they were busy with an assignment out of the country, which they finished early. They recently came back and asked us about our request about Nicole, and since they are a trusted family friend, well, nothing against you, Mr. Volkov, but family is family, you know? I am sure if you were in the same position as me, then you would make the same decisions." I'd give him credit for his fake ass smile filled with venom that could chill anyone to the bone—not me, though because I was used to that shit.

Matching his fake smile with one of my own, I offered him a nod of understanding. "Of course, it makes sense that you would rather work with someone you are familiar with and trust wholeheartedly. I am but a stranger to you, and the only thing you have to go on is what the public and my previous clients have told of me. I was worried that you had found someone better because not to sound cocky, I am the best there is in Nespin. Well, scratch that, the best in most of California at this rate." Hopefully, one of them will take my bait and run their lips a little.

Mark was quick to shake his head and chuckle somewhat nervously. "Oh, no, no. If Mr. Petrov wasn't someone we trusted and considered family, then we would not have even considered terminating our contract with you." Gotcha, though I kind of wish I didn't because that name made my stomach sink in the mud.

Sure, there were probably many people out there with the last name Petrov, but it was too much of a coincidence in my opinion. The Le's being involved in the mafia and having connections with someone with the Petrov name—yeah, I had my suspicions and doubts. Especially given the fact that the Le's had ties to Lady Qing, something I recently discovered after digging deeper into them at Nicole's little fumble with my revelation. The former triad head had a black-market business going on with Ivan Petrov, a small and upcoming bratva boss who played our bratva. Yeah, see the coincidences? Too much to disregard, in my opinion.

Adding a charm to my smile, I gave out a soft, friendly smile. "Ah, I have heard about Ivan Petrov. He is a formidable one. I wouldn't blame you for defaulting on him if you had a good relationship with him. I have to say, he's a crafty one." Time to chum the water more and see if they swim up for another bite.

If Igor was still sniffling around the area, then I needed to know. Well, our whole family needed to know because he was a wanted man along with his father. Both of them were wanted criminals in Russia for their activities there before they fled to the United States, and of course, us Volkovs have a huge bone to pick with them, especially after they tried to force Nikolai into an alliance with them, kidnapped him, and auctioned him off. I wouldn't mind getting my hands dirty beating their faces in for their activities with human trafficking, too, considering how they weren't so hands-off with their 'product' from what the victims told us after we saved them.

Needless to say, we wanted the Petrovs gone. Besides the father and son, there were two more, one whom we have in custody in our desert holding area, their daughter who tried to rape Nikolai during his time being kidnapped. Her twin, Nikita, was in the wind though. We didn't care too much about him since he was really only guilty by association, which sucked, but we weren't going to prosecute him because his family was shitty. So, we only had two rats to hunt and slaughter.

"Oh, you have heard of him?" Hooked line and sinker. "He is amazing and a great businessman, too. Well, Mr. Petrov will be a little disappointed, but I really don't want your hard work to go to waste like that, Mr. Volkov. I am sorry for taking up your time like this today for everything to still be the same as when my wife and I walked into your office."

God, I think I might puke up acid if this man didn't stop being nice and grateful—fake nice and grateful. If he was genuine, then I wouldn't care, but he was being overly so. Plus, his voice held any weight to it—empty words. I didn't like this man, not one bit. I couldn't say much about his wife, though, because Mrs. Le always kept her mouth shut with a stiff smile every time I've seen her. She didn't seem too happy with the situation, though, with the irritation in her eyes; there was something malicious storming in her eyes, something that made me worry for Nicole.

Which was all kind of stupid because I shouldn't be worried about her to this extent. Hell, if anything, I should forget her and let her fend for herself because she sure as hell could—my damn face still aches at the thought of her taking a plank to it. I *should* terminate this damn contract and remove myself from Nicole's life and burn her existence from mine. Yet I can't. The thought of leaving her to fend for herself when I could protect her gnawed at my burning heart.

I hated the effect she had on my life ever since I looked at her picture for the first time. Yes, I was enamored with the little spunky Asian the moment her parents slid her image across my desk. Never mind, that was a lie; I fell head over heels for her the moment she whacked me in the face and broke my nose. Anyone who had such guts to strike out against me like that got props in my book, and a hot woman at that—what more could I ask for?

Nicole wasn't afraid of me. Hell, she straight up approached me, yapped off to me, and persisted even though I showed no interest in return, or at least pretended to. No one ever approached me unless it was to pick a fight or they had a death wish, and no woman ever really approached me unless they had an ulterior motive or were drunk in the club. I had a handsome face, but it was also one of those faces that only a mother could love, thanks to the nasty scar that ran from my hairline down past my lips. I mean, sure, some girls dig the look, but for the most part, it scared a lot away because I didn't look the most welcoming out of all the men in the world.

Wonder if Nicole is put off by my scar.

She didn't seem like a shallow person, and she didn't outright stare at it. But she might have ignored it to be nice; who knows? And it's not like I should care what she thought about me. At the end of the day, it was my job to make sure she stayed safe, and she just saw me as a means of entertainment in her strange life right now. She'll probably forget all about me the moment she returns to a normal life. In a year or so, she'll probably be posting a slew of pictures on Instagram showing off her shiny new rock from her newly dubbed fiancé, who will probably be some suave businessman or hotshot actor. Yeah, I probably had a shot with her if I really tried, but an innocent woman like her didn't belong in my ruthless, bloodied world, no matter how much I wanted her.

"Don't worry about it. Do be safe out there, and I will come in touch with you within a few days once I have a solid plan about Nicole." Or at least a few days until I bring my wrath onto them after I figure out exactly what they're up to.

Chapter 9

"WHY DOES HE LOOK like that?"

"Uhh... Is he high? Please don't tell me he's fucking strung out. I am way too fucking tired to be dealing with this crap at home."

"Lev!"

A harsh slap to my face snapped me completely out of my little daze and pissed me off. Instinctively, I lashed out in the direction the hit came from while cussing them out in Russian, only to have another smack come to my face from a leather bag. "What the fuck was that for?" I snapped at Alexei with a sharp glare after I settled back into the couch with my arms spread across the back.

Alexei stared at me blankly and blinked a few times before shrugging his shoulders softly in a dismissive way. "You were looking a little too happy for our liking."

Unconsciously, I reached up and lightly rubbed my healing tattoo. "Can I not be happy?" I retorted with an offended sneer, lashing my arm out and catching Alexei softly in the midsection, causing him to grunt softly.

Turning my head to the other side, I watched Nikolai groan and rub his temples while hanging his head. "What did you do? Who did you kill? What did you collapse? What's the collateral? How much is this going to cost us?" Nikolai basically went on autopilot whenever it came to me, which I didn't blame him for. After all, I was the problem brother. Nothing good ever came from me coming home smiling like a goof—except this time!

Scrunching my face up, I followed my sister-in-law as she walked over and stopped right in front of me. "Lev, look at my finger," she directed me after she held a finger up in the air and pulled out her penlight from her scrub pocket.

Rolling my eyes, I gently lowered her hand. If it were Alexei or any of our other male employees, then I would have smacked their hand away. However, I was raised with manners by my mother and brothers. I would never hit or harm a woman, intentionally, at least. If a woman attacked me, then I would defend myself with the least harm to her in return—duh. But I would never abuse a female or raise a hand against them for any reason—if that made any sense.

"His pupils seem fine," Angel stated her observation out loud as looked at me. "Not on any drugs." But the devious little smile that spread on her face had my face dropping. "But I think I know what is wrong with Lev," she said in a sing-song voice, giggling evilly at the end.

Standing straight, she stuck her tongue out at me and flipped me off real quick. "*Rasplata eto suka,*" she sassed me before looking at her husband with a cheeky grin. "He's in—mhmphf!"

I shot up from the couch and slapped my hand against her mouth before she could utter the last of her sentence. "You finish that sentence, and I will tell Kolya what you did at the club that one time," I threatened her with a glare.

Angel's eyes widened as she pried my hand away. "You wouldn't. You swore you'd never let him know," she hissed under her breath, narrowing her sharp and dangerous eyes at me.

"*Lisichka,* room. Now," Nikolai commanded in an authoritative tone, making Angel's body tense up for a split second, and then she relaxed submissively with her hung head.

Glaring at me, she muttered something at me in Vietnamese before looking at Nikolai defiantly. Her lips pursed for a second before she broke out into a smile and waddled—she was a few months pregnant with twins—off with a cheeky giggle and a middle finger at Nikolai, who let out another stressed-out groan.

Running a hand down his face, he looked at me pointedly. "When I am done dealing with my wife, I am coming after your ass next," he told me, jabbing a finger in my direction before taking off after Angel.

Well, at least I could deal with Alexei, or at the very least, I could easily shake him. "Whelp, I got shit I need to do." I half lied with a grin, turning on my heel to disappear back to my place located on the Volkov Estate.

Unfortunately, Alexei wasn't going to let me off the hook today. Before I could make a full step toward my retreat, I felt the back of my shirt get grabbed before my body got thrown down onto the couch. For being one of the less muscular among us, he had a lot of strength to him still.

"Don't fucking think so." Alexei deadpanned with a soft glare. "Talk. Now," he demanded, jabbing a finger at me. "You are way too suspicious."

No getting past the ever-so-observant doctor.

Rolling my eyes, I shoved him aside—gently-ish—to get up and leave. "I'm just happy for once. Is that so much of a crime?" Not gonna lie, I was getting a little pissy about everyone getting on me.

Scoffing, Alexei gave me a stern look with a cocked eyebrow. "For you? Yes," he replied with flat sarcasm. "Seriously, if it's a girl, just tell us, or a guy, we don't care. We just care and worry about you, that's all." His stiff posture softened ever so slightly, giving me the impression that he actually cared.

Sighing softly, I rubbed at my chest in response to the bubbling feeling, groaning internally at the longing ache for Nicole's presence. "It's complicated, but I'm figuring it out," I assured Alexei with a confident smile.

The plan was simple: figure out the problem with Nicole and her parents, protect Nicole, take care of Nicole's problem, and then lock Nicole away with me on a remote island. Okay, that last one needed a little work, but something along those lines.

The spunky woman was impossible to resist, and since she'll no longer be my assignment after I figured shit out, there would be no problem dating her.

"Who is it? Is it someone we know?" Alexei pressed with some interest to his voice while his face remained rather flat affected. "How did you two meet?"

Scoffing, I flung a hand at my younger brother. "Go back to your patients. Don't you have a full schedule lined up today?" I didn't want to open this can of worm with him, or anyone for that fact.

My life has always been an open book to my brothers, mainly because they gave me no peace until they knew every little detail of it. Yeah, in a way, it was their way of showing they cared about me, but it was annoying sometimes. I don't think there was any part of my life—besides Nicole—remained out of at least one of my brother's eyes. Nikolai practically knew everything because he's usually the person I went to for everything, mainly to bail me out of trouble. Stepan was close to my life because we shared a company together. Then, the twins, they were just nosey little shits.

I didn't mind sharing my life with my brothers, but there were some things I wanted to keep to myself until I was ready. These are things I never really got the chance to keep because of how aggressive they were with knowing every inch of my life. But it would be different this time. I won't let them know about Nicole until we were solid; no point in telling them if I couldn't secure her—I'd make a fool of myself to my brothers.

Also, if I told them about Nicole, they'd dig her whole life up and get involved, then things would get messy. I wanted to have some peace for once in my life to take things at my pace.

"You know we're going to find out sooner rather than later," Alexei commented with a roll of his eyes. "Just save yourself the trouble and just tell us. We're not going to go on a witch hunt for her or something. We just want to make sure she's a good fit for you and, well, ya know, a good person..." His voice slowly trailed out with his insinuating words.

"Hey, I stopped sticking my dick in crazy after that one chick," I retorted with a scoffing chuckle. "I'll really be fine with Ni—"

A loud slap echoed through the room with how fast and hard my hand flew against my own mouth. Warily, I narrowed my eyes at Alexei, who cracked a small smirk as he leaned onto one leg. "I'm sorry. I think you were trying to tell me something and didn't finish." His smugness made me want to swing one across his face—okay, maybe the throw pillow, not my fist.

"Fine with *not* telling you," I gritted out through my teeth before standing straight up from the couch. "I need to go do something for work," I lied, in a hurry to leave to avoid being grilled until my lips flapped loosely in the wind.

"It's only a matter of time, *bratok*," Alexei teased with an uptick in his voice.

Of course, leave it to Alexei to pick at every little hair before I could make my full escape. "And are you okay? You've been rubbing your chest a lot lately. Heartburn? Impending heart attack?" Okay, at least it was out of concern for my health, so I couldn't be irked at him.

Assuring him with a quick smile, I shook my head as I began to round the corner. "Yeah, just a little comfort habit as of late."

Shaking the thoughts out of my head, I darted away before Alexei could have another chance at questioning me.

The walk home was quick, mainly because I lived next door to Nikolai. Nikolai and his wife lived in the mansion, something my eldest brother built after we killed our father and took over the bratva. I lived in our old house about half a football field away.

Actually, it was more or less the location of our old home, not the house itself. My brothers and I burned down the original house after we painted the walls red with our bastard father's blood. We wanted nothing to remain of our bastard father's that would remind us of the suffering we all endured, along with my mother, by our sperm donor.

I used to live in the mansion with Nikolai until I decided to build a house at the location as a way to spite my father in death—and to dance on his grave. Also, I wanted to build a good life on the earth that my mother used to walk and touch. The house and everything was just a way to show my mother that something good could come from the rotten place she tried to love.

Besides, I couldn't let her garden die; she loved that area so much. It was also one of the few places I ever really got to spend time with her, away from everyone and everything. It was as much her happy place as it was mine. I mean, I couldn't even begin to count how many nights I spent hiding out in the rosebushes or up in the apple trees from my father before inevitably falling asleep in the comfort of nature.

When we got rid of the house, the garden was the one place I refused to let anything bad happen to. I continued to tend to it to this very day and use it as my escape still.

Hopefully, I can share it with Nicole.

The thought of us sitting out at the patio set or in the swing or, hell, even on a little picnic blanket on the grass, was such a divine fantasy. To spend our nights laying around to look at the stars or if that wasn't her thing then she could do whatever she wanted while I had my head in her lap, and we basked under the moonlight.

Then, hopefully, one day, I could share it with my own children. Okay, maybe child, as in *one* kid, because I doubt I could handle more than one duplicate of me running around.

Chuckling and shaking my head at myself, I ran a tired hand through my hair as I entered my garden, letting the fresh scent of lilies and roses fill my system until I felt drunk.

God, if any of my brothers knew what went on in my head right now or saw how dopey I was getting over some girl, then they'd probably wonder if I had a stroke or send me for a psych evaluation.

Yeah, I've always wanted to settle down and have a family of my own, but I never really made any serious steps toward that kind of lifestyle. Nor did I put much effort or thought into it besides knowing I wanted it further down the road.

Honestly, the need to put a leash on myself and open my heart up to someone never surfaced until I saw those pictures of Nicole and dug into her life.

I wanted my ambitions to come true, but only with Nicole.

Chapter 10

"Did you poison that?"

My wary eyes narrowed at Lev when he took a seat across from me and placed the coffee cup in front of me.

"Come on, if I were to kill you, it'd be bloody. Do I look like a loser who'd poison a hot girl's cup to watch her choke on her own spit?" He faked his offense with a scoffing chuckle before taking the cup back, sipping it, and then returning it to me. "There, not dead yet, so it's safe."

Rolling my eyes, I quickly flipped him off before picking the cup up and drinking from it. The moment the taste hit my lips, I couldn't help but look at him with wide eyes. "Caramel latte with vanilla and salted caramel whipped cream." I knew he stalked me, but he got my order down to a tee, and I never said my order out loud at this point in time because the baristas knew what I wanted with simple words. At most, all I ever said whenever they asked me what I wanted was 'caramel,' and they automatically knew my add-ins.

So, how in the fuck did this bozo know?

"I believe the words you're looking for are 'thank you'," Lev smugly replied with a smirking chuckle.

Now that was another surprise, him responding and not in a grouchy way. "Are you sick? Oh my God, are you high right now?" This did not feel too much like the Lev I'd been bugging the past few week.

Actually, now that I think about it, he hasn't been himself—or at least my version of him—ever since our confrontation that day when I tried to bribe him. What changed? What was he getting at now?

"Listen, we got off on the wrong foot," he started with a long sigh, running a hand down his face as he looked at me somewhat cautiously.

"You stalked me, pretty sure we started out in the wrong universe," I quipped back with a roll of my eyes, taking a few sips of the drink as I eyed him warily. "If you think being nice to me will make me go easily with you, then you're dead wrong. I will not hesitate to blow up your car again, this time I might even aim for you." Which would be a shame because I didn't want to make him look more rugged and handsome.

Or maybe I might mark him up a little more and keep the other girls away from him.

Shit, the hell am I thinking?

Why should I give a single damn about other women going near him? Not like he was mine or anything. Nor did I want him to be. A fat wall of muscles with little brains and creepy stalker tendencies too. Besides, he was working for my parents, so that put him in the trash for me.

Sighing heavily, Lev leaned over onto the table on his elbows and looked at me a soft frown and apologetic eyes. "I'm going to terminate the contract I have with your parents. I really am sorry for being a little pain in the ass to you for the past few weeks, and it's partially my fault for not doing my due diligence with digging further into your parents and their request."

He seemed sincere enough, or at least he could lie sweetly enough to keep me interested. "Go on," I urged, narrowing my eyes softly while pursing my lips to express my wariness with my cocked eyebrow.

"They told me you ran away and hit some weird rebellious stage in your adult life. I shouldn't have let them play me and all, but when they showed me some pictures of you, I had to take the assignment," he strained that last bit out with a long sigh as he ran a hand through his hair.

"What? Saw pretty lil' me, and you couldn't resist? Thought you might take a bite before giving me back?" I don't know why I got a little snappy with him. He probably didn't mean anything bad by his words, but I kind of took it wrong. He made it sound like I was some pretty prize to go after and claim.

Holding his hands up, he leaned back a bit in his seat while chuckling. "Oy, cool it. I didn't mean it in any bad way. I just saw how pretty and cute you were, and those sad eyes of yours, and my heartstrings were snagged," he stammered out the last part, almost embarrassingly as he averted his eyes from me.

My posture relaxed into a playful one as his words sank in. Smirking, I leaned onto the table on my elbows and rested my tilted head on clasped hands. "You think I'm pretty and cute?" The part about my having sad eyes could be touched on later; I needed something to make me feel good. So, yeah, sue me for fishing Lev a little for some compliments.

"W-well duh, have you seen yourself? Someone would have to be blind to not see how pretty you are. And if they were blind, then I'd be sorry for them because they wouldn't be able to witness such perfection." Lev paused with his mouth opened slightly, his face twisting in thought before a lightbulb moment seemed to go off. "Actually, I take that back. I'd be glad they're blind because then I don't have to worry about them looking at you or sharing your beauty with them." Arrogantly, he grinned and crossed his arms as he leaned back in his seat.

Not gonna lie, that flattered me more than I cared to admit. "Greedy one, aren't we? What makes you think I'd let you have such a joy of having me in your life? This could be our last little date for all you know." I teased with an empty smile.

I don't know why, but the thought of this possibly being our last encounter with each other punched me in the gut. I mean, this wouldn't be our last, but hypothetically speaking.

Yeah, Lev was a little annoying with his stalking, but I grew used to him sooner rather than later and appreciated the sense of safety I got from him. It was a little weird feeling safe with my stalker around, but I had a somewhat good feeling about him under my paranoia.

"What makes you think I want your crazy ass in my life?" Lev shot back with an offended scoff. "You beat me with a wooden stick and tattooed me after gassing me," he added with a tilt of his head and pointed eyes.

Rolling his eyes with another scoff of disbelief, he chuckled and shook his head softly at me. "And if you think this is a date, then you gotta raise your damn standards. Also, I feel a little offended that you would think if I were to take you on a date, then it'd be something shabby and simple like this. Seriously, who do you take me for? You'd be wined and dined at a five-star restaurant or some other bougie place or whatever you like, and of course, I'd be a fucking gentleman and kiss your damn feet the whole time."

Clicking my tongue, I chuckled playfully and tossed him a challenging look. "What if I didn't like that shit? What if I wanted to go dumpster diving? Or out into the middle of the desert?" Okay, now I wanted to be difficult for shit and giggles.

"Then I'll pack us some food for a picnic if we're going to the damn desert for some stupid ass reason, and if you wanted to get down and dirty, then I'd make sure you're dressed properly so you don't get fucking tetanus from a cut or some shit like that," Lev replied with a sarcastic sneer and roll of his eyes. "Though, I would have to question why the hell you'd want to go out into the desert like that." His eyes raised at me quizzically as he quickly raked his eyes up and down my body.

Smiling my eyes, I painted an innocent smile on my lips while my eyes remained mischievous. "Take me out to the desert, and you'll find out."

Narrowing his eyes suspiciously at me, he studied me for a moment with his lips slightly pursed. "Planning to kill me and leave me for the vultures?" he questioned with a voice full of suspicion.

I denied it instantly with a scoff and wave of my hand. "Oh god no, that would be way too boring." It was the truth, and I was so glad the café was so dead at this time, and there wasn't anyone near us because this conversation would be very worrisome to anyone in their right mind.

"Honestly, if I were to kill you..." Trailing off, I looked at him with a nervously playful smile as I debated whether or not I should finish that sentence.

Intrigued, Lev's smirk morphed into an excited and interested smile as he leaned forward. "What? Go on, don't leave me hanging, baby." His icy blue eyes sharpened with a crazed look as he eagerly awaited my answer. "How would you kill the Savage Volk of the Volkov Bratva?" It was almost as if he challenged me to do it.

"Tick, tick." My finger wagged along with the words as my own smirk deepened almost crazily before I smacked them together to make a *pop* with my lips.

"Boom."

Chapter 11

~2 weeks later~

"I still can't believe you tattooed me," I grumbled softly as I trailed right behind Nicole with my hands stuffed in the pockets of my jacket.

"Well, you needed a reminder of who you belong to," she remarked rather haughtily, tossing her head back to flash me a smirk before continuing off to wherever. "Besides, not like it's something stupid. I mean, I could have tattooed a dick on you for all you know, or some misspelled word like 'regart' or something stupid."

Stopping, she snickered softly while smirking smugly at me. "I could have tattooed a stupid phrase in Vietnamese or a crude word," she remarked arrogantly. "So, be thankful I was being thoughtful and nice."

Scoffing in disbelief, I crossed my arms and stepped up to her. "If you ever do something like that, I will tattoo something in Cyrillic across your ass," I retorted, glaring down softly at her.

"As long as it's something cute." She laughed in my face before whipping around, smacking me in the face with her colored hair.

71

Gritting my teeth, I let out a soft scowl. "We're not done." Reaching out, I grabbed her arm and spun her back around, pulling her flush against my body. "I don't know whether to kiss you or spank you," I strained with my lips hanging a hair away from hers.

Inhaling deeply, I quickly shifted my hands around her body. One arm wrapped itself around her lower back, anchoring her plush body against mine, while my other arm snaked itself around her upper body. Sliding my hand down, I gently groped her bubbly butt with an internal groan at the softness melting in my palm. Sharply inhaling, I fisted the back of her hair with my other hand. "You are so insufferable sometimes, you know that?" I groaned softly, resting my forehead against hers.

Giggling, Nicole grinned and reached up to grip my nape with her hand. "I know, but only because you love it," she shot back, ghosting her lips across mine. "You love that I am a pain in your ass because you like suffering." Her nails dug into my sensitive skin, making me wince softly. "Kiss me."

Giving in with a groan, I let my lips fall into hers, letting her softly suck my soul out of me. "Only because I wanted to," I argued with a reddening face.

No matter how desirable they were, there was no way I'd let some woman boss me around.

I was in charge, always.

Smiling sweetly, Nicole patted my cheek. "Whatever floats your boat, sweetie." She chuckled mockingly, pushing me away. "Come on, we have an appointment to keep. If you're good, then I might let you kiss me again later," she said with a hook of her finger after turning her back to me.

Grumbling softly to myself, I rubbed at the soft ache in my chest. "I'll kiss you if I want to and whenever I want to," I muttered while following behind her.

"Where the hell are we going anyways?" This was most definitely not part of her routine. Yeah, she liked to go and do whatever, but she had her typical spots and routes.

"Just keep following me like the good little lion you are, and you will see," Nicole replied smugly with a snicker while continuing her merry way.

Rolling my eyes, I stretched my strides out until I was beside Nicole, matching her pace to keep steady with her. "You're not going to take me to get another tattoo against my will, are you?" I flatly joked with a sneer, hoping to dear lord that I would make it through the rest of the day unscathed from Nicole's antics.

I still wasn't too thrilled about being tattooed against my will, nor was I excited about the wonky design of Nicole's initials with a little cartoon bomb. But, I couldn't bring myself to go get it removed because it was from Nicole. Besides, it was unique compared to all the other ink on my body, and it grew on me a little. Also, it was sweet for her to tattoo me, mark me as hers with her unique little mark.

Just thinking about it brought a goofy smile to my face, the ones where your cheeks ached from how uncontrolled the spread was. I mean, Nicole always brought a smile to my face, but the tattoo made a huge wave of warmth shiver and melt my body.

My body jolted from another stroke of heat from Nicole's fingers brushing against my palm before my hand became engulfed by hers. "Would you lighten up, little lion? It's something fun for both of us." Yeah, as if that made me feel any better. I couldn't help but feel a little wary of her innocent smile because I don't think I've ever seen anything innocent with her.

Letting her drag me to my doom, I grumbled under my breath. "I swear, I'm going to wake up in a cage or something." Or probably something equivalent. Hell, I wouldn't be surprised if I woke up with a kidney missing.

Nicole didn't entertain me with a response as she continued to lead me down the block until we came to a stop at a shady-looking building. "Frenzy Fury Fun..." Okay, that was a stupid name for any kind of business; I didn't even want to try and think about what kind of establishment Nicole would lead me into in a moment.

"Aka, the best thing next to therapy and blowing stuff up." Nicole grinned and giddily bounced on the balls of her feet for a few seconds before throwing the door open and dragging me in behind her.

"Nicki!" A middle-aged man with a graying beard greeted her with a grin.

"Room's set up as always for you. See you brought a friend this time." His observant eyes did a quick sweep over me and lingered warily for a moment. Then, the friendliness in them hardened. "You better not be giving sweet Nicki a hard time now, boy. I don't give a shit if you're bratva, you so much as split a hair on Nicki's head, and I will come after you like a hellhound on a trail." Well, so much for friendly old(ish) man over here.

The sound of my teeth creaking echoed in my skull from my jaw clenching, and every hot exhale from me heated the room to where a knife could cut through the tension. "I would mind your own business, old man, before you find yourself without it," I strained out between my gritted teeth. "I may be bratva, but that doesn't mean I don't have any manners. So, I would watch your mouth next time before you go running it because the next person might not be as tolerable as me."

Well, if Nicole wasn't here, then I would have smashed the man's face into the glass counter he stood behind and turned him into a display.

I hated it when people made assumptions about me or my family. Yes, we were bratva, and I knew having any kind of ties to anything mafia-related carried a bad notion, but still. What happened to not judging a book by its cover and shit? I mean, sure, I looked quite rough, but I wasn't *that* horrible underneath. Besides, I was only ever bad to those who deserved it... And those who pissed me off... And maybe those who looked at me the wrong way... And perhaps many others...

Point was, I wasn't a *bad* person.

If I punched, stabbed, or shot someone, they deserved it one way or another.

"Robby, relax, Lev is harmless to me." Nicole's assurance eased a lot of the tension out of the room.

I didn't begin to relax until Nicole's hand tightened around mine. Her presence invaded my very being with how she hugged my arm and leaned into me as if we were some couple. Then, like the cherry on top, she leaned up on her tippy toes and placed a kiss on my cheek with a giggle. "He knows better than to upset me," she said with an exaggerated smile at me.

Little minx, I wanted to bend her over the counter and teach her a lesson for that comment.

Forcing a smile, I slipped an arm around Nicole's waist, pulling her against me and gripping her hip a little to assert some dominance. "I know how much of a firecracker she can be." Well, that wasn't a lie; she was rather explosive and dangerous.

Robby's eyes fluttered towards Nicole, softening with concern. "If he bothers you one bit or so much as raises a finger to you, you let me know." Honestly, if Robby didn't piss me off, I would feel a little more warmth with his concern about Nicole's well-being; too bad I wanted to smash his face in still.

"Don't worry, like I said," Nicole paused to grin up at me and lock her warm eyes on me, "he's a good boy."

Instinctively, my grip around her tightened at the words. Something about them, along with the coquettish smirk and look in her eyes, sent shivers down my spine, straight to my dick. Her sweet praise flicked some switch in my mind and body, making my insides melt with pleasure. Some stupid part of me wanted to drop to her feet and roll over to get in her good graces and hear more praise from her. I wanted to let go and not worry about anything besides how to get more sweet words from Nicole.

God, what am I thinking?

Biting the inside of my cheek, I quickly shoved my thoughts away, shutting them into a dark closet that would never be opened again. None of that was me, and I refused to go down that route. I was in charge, always have, always will. Besides, if I ever did try to entertain that unknown side, it wouldn't be with an unstable, bomb-loving tech geek.

"Well, we'll be on our way, and I promise I'll keep my Lev in check." Nicole waved at Robby as she dragged us past him, taking us down a hallway and past a few doors.

Opening my mouth, I was about to ask Nicole about what the fuck was going on but never got a chance. "So, rules are simple: break everything you want in the room *besides* the walls, windows, ceiling, and floor." Stopping at the door, she turned to look at me fully with her excited grin. "Oh, and other people, of course," she added before eagerly throwing the door open.

Warily, I walked into the concrete room behind Nicole. The room was bare except for a wooden desk stacked with various objects like vases, cups, a flat-screen TV, and other little nickknacks. On the floor were stocks of objects as well, all in a random assortment. Then, the walls were sparsely lined with various wall decorations, except one wall would be nearly bare if it weren't for the objects lined against it.

Squealing and clapping happily, Nicole shut the door with her foot and pulled her phone out to put on some... "K-Pop? Really?" I mused with a flat sigh as I watched her go over to the wall lined with various bats, clubs, wrenches, and what have you. "What the hell are we even doing?"

Without looking back at me, Nicole replied while browsing the weapons. "Oh, come on, don't act like you've never been to a rage room."

The fuck?

Approaching her, I grabbed her wrist and spun her around to face me. "I do not have anger issues," I remarked with an offended scowl.

Raising an eyebrow, Nicole studied me with a quizzical look for a moment. "I never said that. What would even make you think that, little lion?" She scoffed with a dry chuckle.

Irritated at her reaction, I grabbed her shoulders and pushed her against the wall, trapping her between my arms. "Why else would you take me to a *rage* room? Obviously, you're trying to tell me something." I sneered, baring my teeth at her when my scowl deepened greatly. "I do not need to get my anger out or any of that shit, so there's no point in taking me here unless it's to tell me I got a *real* problem with my temper."

Scoffing, Nicole rolled her eyes at me. "Wow, you are so taking all of this the wrong way," she remarked with a low chuckle, almost sounding like she pitied me. "The only thing I'm trying to tell you is to loosen up. Seriously, you're always so tense and mister macho serious." She chuckled weakly, placing a hand on my chest and stroking the area of the tattoo.

Hooking her other arm around my neck, she pulled herself up close to me. "I just thought this would be a nice way for us to blow off some steam, relax, have fun. I mean, anger issues or not, I don't care as long as you don't direct any of it toward me." Her voice was soft and sincere enough to get my nerves to calm down. "I mean, yeah, you're a little hot-headed, but at least you've got your head on straight in the right direction," she teased with a giggle.

Unable to help it, I let my eyes flutter close with my soft groan when I felt the back of my head being stroked by her fingers. "Stop doing that." I dragged out with a soft sigh. "I'm trying to stay firm with you." I was fucking putty in her hands.

"Aww, but you're so much better being my good boy." She cooed with a deep chuckle. "Don't you want to be my good boy?"

I should be offended right now. She was treating me like some damn dog! But by God, did it make me melt. Something about her rubbing and scratching my head felt amazing, and her saturated voice was lovely. "Nicki... If you don't stop, I'm going to break that table because I fucked you too hard on it." I was somewhat serious.

My cock was straining against my pants right now, and fuck did it hurt. I wanted, no needed, to bury myself into her hot cunt. I wanted to make her come undone on my cock until she wouldn't be able to form a single thought, let alone talk back to me and be in charge.

"Don't threaten me with a good time before the date's even started." Nicole's sultry voice whispered into my ear with a hot sigh. "Finish breaking shit in the room with me first, then maybe I'll let you break the bed with me later." Oh, as if she wasn't being a sly vixen herself.

Giggling, Nicole patted my cheek before picking up a crowbar, giving it a few practice swings before approaching a podium with a vase on top of it. Then, pulling back, she swung at the vase, shattering the thing into two big chunks with a squeal. "Come on, Lev!" She encouraged me with a grin before swinging repeatedly at the wooden podium, chipping away at it.

Hesitantly, I picked up a metal bat and approached Nicole from the side. "Uhh, are you sure about this?" It felt weird to think about smashing things in such a calm and casual manner.

It was one thing to utilize and break objects in a fight, but in a controlled setting? Even for a destructive and violent guy like me, that didn't feel too right.

Well, maybe it felt wrong to me because of all the reprimands I got in my life for breaking shit around the house.

"Little lion, it's okay, just take a swing," Nicole assured me with a warm smile and nudge. "This whole place is meant for breaking, so swing, be a destructive little shit."

With a shaky breath, I smacked the bat against my palm a few times to get a feel of it while I looked for my target. I mean, I knew what I wanted to hit, but I was reluctant about it because it felt like the moment I shattered the TV, Nikolai would bust down the door and scold me. Or worse, Nicole would scold me because maybe it was some test that I failed.

After a few nervous flickers of my eyes at Nicole, I took some tentative steps toward the TV on the wooden desk. Then, with one last look at Nicole, I gulped and swung the bat that suddenly weighed a thousand pounds to me. My tense heart exploded with the screen of the TV the moment the bat shattered it, and I held my breath in anticipation of the raised voice that would burst my eardrums.

Yet, it never came.

The only thing that filled my ears was the sound of my heart pounding away in my chest, along with Nicole's cheery giggle.

"There you go! Keep going!" she encouraged me with a soft laugh before the sounds of glass breaking filled the room from her going at more objects.

Well, I started, so might as well finish it.

Plus, not gonna lie, it felt good to break something and *not* get in trouble for it.

Unable to hold back my excitement, I let my face break out in a crazed grin as my arms swung freely. From the TV to the desk, the bat took out everything in its path as I let loose. The little trinkets that lined the table either fell to the ground and broke, or they were broken because I brought the bat down on them.

Object after object, anything I set my eyes on became nothing but pieces. Shards of wood and glass flew in every direction with every swing of our weapons, and the sting of cuts kept the rush of excitement alive. I should be a little more mindful since I didn't put on any safety gear, but what's life without a risk?

Pausing for a second, I looked at Nicole, watching with amazement as she destroyed a small table with a gleeful grin. Her attention slowly went to me after she was done decimating the object. "What? Do I have something in my hair?" she asked with a tilt of her head.

Chuckling, I shook my head softly and waved her over, watching as she scrunched her eyebrows together and approached me warily. Grinning widely, I waited until she was within arm's length before grabbing at her, causing her to squeal.

Without a word, I wrapped an arm around her waist, locking her against me while my other hand tangled itself into the back of her hair. Instantly, my lips devoured hers, and my groan drowned out her sounds of surprise. Using her stunned state to my advantage, I forced my tongue into her mouth, claiming every inch of her as my lower hand roamed her body.

Then, carefully, I lifted her with a hand groping her plush bottom, and I placed her on top of the dusty table with a soft grunt. The hand around her waist slipped around her body to her breasts to greedily fondle them while my other hand pulled at her hair, forcing her head back. With access to her neck, I tore myself away from her delicious lips, inhaling deeply for a much-needed breath after I pulled at her bottom lip and made it swell.

A glimmer of red caught my frenzied eyes as I leaned in again, causing me to change my intended course. Tilting my head, I angled myself along her cheek, where I dragged my tongue along the small cuts and marks on my way down to her succulent neck. Shivers vibrated down my body with my groan of delight at the taste of her mixed with blood on my tastebuds. "I can't get enough of you, baby," I whispered hotly against her neck before kissing a trail down to the swell of her small breasts.

"Good," Nicole chuckled breathlessly. "Don't forget who you belong to at the end of the day."

The sharp feeling of her nails raking against my bare back after she slipped her hand under my shirt had me hissing and cussing in Russian under my breath. "Well, your crazy ass fucking tattooed me," I remarked with a roll of my eyes.

A harsh jerk of my head pulled a soft gasp from me, and I felt myself lowering until Nicole's smug face loomed over me. "That's because you need something permanent to remind you who owns you." Then, I felt my body fall to its knees with a firm shove from Nicole. "You needed me to get through to your thick skull. Otherwise, you wouldn't have gone on that stupid date with that spoiled billionaire brat who can't tell her left from her right."

I was probably in no position to be a smart-ass, but I wasn't known to be the brightest bulb in the shed. "Oh? Hennie? I thought she was rather sweet and willing to do whatever I wanted. Hot too, especially with—" My words were cut off from my head slamming into the edge of the table.

Nicole's glaring eyes grew close as she lowered herself. "Don't you ever dare say another girl's name while you are in my presence." Lifting her leg, she pressed her foot against my chest. "You are mine. You have my mark etched into your body, so you belong to me. I am the only woman you are allowed to see, speak, and think about." Her grip on the back of my hair tightened painfully, making me wince slightly. "Am I understood?"

Whatever stubbornness and arrogance I had in my body disappeared at the authoritative gleam in her darkened brown eyes. "Yes, *zhizn moya.*"

What the fuck is wrong with me?

"Good boy," Nicole praised with a proud smile, her hand releasing me to pet my head. "Now, here's what's gonna happen." Her finger trailed along my jawline, scratching at my beard. "We're going to make out some more, then we're going to finish smashing shit before heading out to dinner, alright?"

Letting out a deep sigh, I nodded in response as I relaxed into her touch. "Yes, darling." Cupping her hand, I pressed a kiss against her palm before standing up and grabbing her face to kiss her heavily.

Of course, I wasn't satisfied with just kissing her and tasting every inch of her mouth. I needed more. "Let me taste you, please," I begged against her lips with a needy groan.

Giggling deeply, she looked up at me with cheeky eyes. "Am I going to have to teach you how to pleasure a woman as well?" She teased.

Rolling my eyes, I reached out and poked her forehead. "I know how to please a woman. I might be an idiot, but I'm not *that* clueless." Besides, I had a reputation to hold up, especially back in high school.

Getting back down on my knees, I quickly worked her jeans and panties off in my eagerness. The sight of her bare cunt made my mouth water so much that I was sure I had become a drooling idiot before her. With her pants pooled around her ankles, I spread her knees apart while scooting her to the edge of the table.

Throwing her legs over my shoulders, I hooked my arms around her thighs and held her firm against me before peppering kisses along her inner thighs to her glistening cunt. The fact she was mere inches from me, paired with her intoxicating scent invading my system, drove me up the wall.

A part of me wanted to dive in and eat her out like she was my first meal in forever, but the other part wanted to enjoy this precious moment she had allowed me. Unable to decide, I let my instincts take over as I sealed my mouth around her juicy cunt and licked every inch of her from her clit down to her ass.

Fuck me.

Letting my eyes flutter close, I savored her sweet, salty, tangy taste as I lapped at her like a thirsty dog. Scratch that; I was a thirsty dog. But only because it was Nicole. I'd never be caught dead doing something like this with another woman. Only Nicole had the privilege of bossing me around because I let her. It wasn't because I liked it or anything. No, definitely not that.

She's had it rough, so the least I could do was spoil her a little by letting her have some fun. I mean, not like anyone else would know about this happening between us. Nicole didn't have anyone she talked to, and I certainly wasn't about to blabber my mouth to my brothers about this.

"Fuck. Shit. That's it, Lev. Oh, that feels amazing," Nicole moaned happily with a contagious grin as her hands fondled her breasts. "Shit, I didn't think it would be this good." Her reluctant hips slowly became smooth in rhythm the more she bucked against my face.

A witty remark had me smirking as I licked her teasingly, making her whimper and whine a little. "Lev, don't tease me, please. I'm so close," she said through her heavy breaths, reaching a hand down to grab the top of my head and shove me back against her. "Eat me out until your face is soaked with my cum," she commanded in a rather dominant voice, making me shudder.

Peering up at her, I couldn't help the zap of pleasure from shooting down my spine to my aching cock when I saw her smug smirk. Then, like an obedient mutt, I complied. My tongue pressed and lashed against her swollen clit while my mouth groaned against her to give her some stimulation from the vibrations.

I buried my face into her, moving my head from side to side as I slid the pad of my tongue against her clit while dipping the tip into her entrance. Shifting my mouth down, I pressed my nose against her throbbing clit while I worked more of my tongue in and out of her tight walls with a hungry need.

"Oh, my G—ah!" I didn't let her finish that sentence with a hard slap to her ass that had her squealing. "Fuck, do that again, that hurt so good." She wasn't begging or asking—she was telling.

The sounds of my hand meeting her plush ass cheeks joined the rest of our lewd sounds that filled the room. It only took a few spanks for her to crack under all the stimulations, filling the room with her sweet moans and screams.

I should have taken some mercy on her and pulled away when I felt her hips buck away, but the constant flow of her juices made me press on for more.

"Oh fuckfuckfuck, it's too much, but fuck. Fuck, I want you to stop, but I also don't. My—fuck!" Her body fell back flat against the desk, and her body went rigid while her mouth hung open in a silent scream.

Concern immediately flooded my body, and I would've pulled away if it wasn't for the feeling of something spraying and drenching my face. Granted, I should have eased up a little, but seeing Nicole's squirting body spasm with pleasure while her eyes rolled to the back of her head was too much of a divine sight to stop.

Biting my bottom lip, I let out a deep groaning as I vigorously rubbed her clit with my hand to keep her on that edge of mind-shattering pleasure. "Fuck, that's it, *zhizn moya*, don't stop." I only pulled my hand away to deliver a few slaps to her twitching cunt, making her moan and gush with each impact. "Come on, one more for me," I practically begged as I put my mouth and tongue back to work, pushing her until her body tensed under me one last time and her rush of juices filled my eager mouth.

"Oh, fuck..." Nicole's body shook with her sob as she came crashing down.

Quickly, I stood up and grabbed her. Holding her tightly, I stroked her hair while whispering sweet nothings to her in Russian. "Thank you." I pressed a tender kiss against her forehead.

Once she felt steady, I let go to put her back together. "God, you're going to make it impossible for me to get rid of you if that's what you can do." Nicole chuckled dryly with a lopsided smile.

"Then don't get rid of me," I quickly remarked, holding back the wince that wounded my heart.

Giggling, Nicole scratched the back of my head, making me groan internally and roll my eyes. "Well, you're certainly going to make it impossible," she teased. "I just... Things are kind of complicated with me right now, and I don't want to drag you into my mess." A tired sigh dragged out of her slumping shoulders.

"Does it have to do with your parents?" Probably a stupid question, but I had to make sure.

Nicole chuckled dryly and nodded her head before flashing me a flat smile. "But it's my mess to deal with, so don't try to butt in." Her voice hardened a little, but I could hear the exhaustion behind it.

"No." Cupping her face, I looked at her tenderly and smiled defiantly. "Your problems are mine too, *zhizn moya*."

Pressing my lips against hers, I held the passionate kiss for a while before breaking it with a deep breath. "We'll make it through everything together." Kissing her forehead, I kept my lips against her for a few seconds as I breathed in her citrusy and earthy scent of wood and fresh soil.

"I will take care of you, Nicole."

Chapter 12

~2 weeks later~

"Girl, shouldn't you be laying around in bed with your husband at your beck and call?" I chuckled as I watched Angel walk around the living room.

Rolling her eyes at me, Angel quickly flipped me off before sitting on the couch across from me. "I'm pregnant, not invalid." Exhaling heavily, she rests her hands on her growing stomach. "Besides, moving around is good for my hips and will make birth easier. But also, I'm only barely six months along, so not like I need bed rest or anything when everything is completely fine." And leave it to her to argue for her independence.

Not wanting to get into it with her, I let the subject drop with a shake of my head. "How is everything, though? Am I going to need to bury a bomb into Nikolai any time soon?" I joked, chuckling dryly with a wary look at my friend.

With a reassuring smile, Angel waved her hand at me while chuckling, "Nikolai and I are perfectly fine, like always." Looking at me for a second, she opened her mouth to say something but quickly shut it with a shake of her head. "What about you and your mystery man? What's going to happen there?"

Sighing sadly, I leaned back in my seat and sipped at my glass of water. "What has to happen..." I replied in a dying voice.

Frowning at me disapprovingly, Angel scoffed and shook her head. "You are way too stubborn, you know that?" Scoffing again, she muttered something under her breath about me being stupid. "Seriously, just let me take care of your stupid parents. They're not just a pain in the ass to you, but they are to the bratva as well. They've been stonewalling us at every chance, and I've just about had it with them." Her hands clenched at her arms, which sat loosely wrapped above her stomach.

"They're the only part left of Lady Qing's who hasn't bowed to Nikolai and me, and they're starting to push, which pisses me off," she seethed through a scowl. "I just haven't done anything drastic out of respect for you and your wishes not to harm them, but they are *really*, and I mean *really*, fucking toeing that line with me."

"Okay, okay." Holding my hands up in defeat, I shrunk back a little from the suffocating anger that rolled off Angel in torrent waves. "I get it. You want them kicked off their pedestal."

Sighing heavily, I took an interest in my nails for a good moment to gather my thoughts. "I want them to get their dues, but I don't want them dead." Or physically hurt, much, but that part was debatable. "I still haven't gotten all I need from them, either."

Well, that was more on me because I was being cautious. Hacking the system I created should have been a cakewalk, but I didn't want to risk giving my location away. I knew for a fact that my parents had people tracking my on-line footprints, so I've had to limit my presence and time spent with electronic connections to the world. If I weren't so conscious about it all, then shit would have blown to bits by now. Not gonna lie, sometimes I toyed with the idea.

I've nothing to lose, really; my old life died the day I ran away from being my parents' pawn. Relocating with a whole new identity and life would be as easy with my connection to Angel, but a part of me didn't want to uproot whatever stability I had here in Nespin. I didn't want to leave my younger brother here, nor did I want to be away from those I considered to be my family.

And I didn't want to leave Lev.

"Well, I know you're trying to lay low or whatever, but you need to do something about your parents, and soon." Angel huffed with a scowl. "They're up to something, and I don't like it."

"I haven't noticed anything suspicious in their accounts," I remarked with a quirked eyebrow and a dip in my voice.

Shaking her head, Angel looked at me with grave seriousness. "They went old school with cold, hard cash, burner phones and smashing them right after use, paper and pen, like really old school." Sighing heavily, she sits up as much as possible. "We've been keeping a close eye on them, and they've been having a lot of meetings not on any books. And whoever they're meeting knows how to give our men the slip."

That wasn't good.

Groaning, I ran a hand through my hair. "Just..." Oh man, I was going to regret it but fuck it. "Don't worry about it. They're my problem to start with, so I need to set them straight."

"Straight down six feet underground?" Angel joked darkly with a very dry chuckle.

"If there will be anything left of them to bury. Then, yeah, sure," I joked back half-seriously with my own sardonic chuckle.

"Nicki," Angel began in a chiding tone. "You're a pyromaniac bomb-loving tech geek, not a killer." She teased with a hearty laugh.

Unable to help it, I joined in with my own laugh when I found myself agreeing with everything she said about me. "Well, if they die from the blast of the bombs, then there's nothing I can do about that," I said nonchalantly, shrugging my shoulders. "I'll just leave the killing part to my *đại ca*."

Angel's posture relaxed with her piqued interest. The corners of her lips curved up and spread wide as she shot up from the couch and darted over to me, invading my bubble when she plopped down next to me. "Girl, you gotta stop teasing me like that, seriously! Tell me who this handsome hunk is already," she demanded playfully with a giggle.

Stifling a laugh, I chewed at my bottom lip to keep my thoughts inside my head. Honestly, if she knew who my man was, she would not be using those words. "You might or might not find out soon." I snickered, earning a playful slap on the arm. "It's not even like official or anything, and I just want to be completely sure before telling you guys, you know?"

Actually, I didn't know what we were. Labels might be overrated, but they were needed for clarity. We acted like a couple, but were we really? I claimed him as mine, even went as far as physically marking him, but that didn't...

Okay, what am I saying? After all of that, he is mine in every sense.

Rolling her eyes, she slapped my arm again. "Girl, you just told me the other day that he ate you out like you were a five-star meal with dessert!" Angel remarked with a playful scoff. "You can't just tell me shit like that and not show me who this wonder worker is."

"Weeeell, I guess I can show you soooomething," I dragged my words out teasingly, shoving her squealing body away when she grabbed me excitedly. "Just a little peek, that's it."

Hiding my phone from her with a giggle, I pulled up a candid picture I took of Lev the other day with our little lunch date and cropped it from his nose down. Of course, Angel wasn't too thrilled to see a nearly faceless man with the unamused glare she gave me when I showed her the picture. "Nicki, that could be like half the people from Meri's Men Magazine." She deadpanned with a teasing voice. "I mean, lovely catch, but I wanna see who he is!" she whined.

Flashing her a mischievous grin, I shook my head while pocketing my phone. "Maybe next time." Or the next, or whenever I felt like it.

Rolling her eyes, Angel crossed her arms and leaned back onto the couch. "Rude, you all knew about Nikolai right away," she retorted.

Quirking a brow at her, I scoffed in disbelief. "Girl, you got *married* to the man, and it wasn't like your stepmother kept quiet about it." Didn't help that all of us practically stalked her because we were overprotective of our precious Angel.

Angel's shoulders tightened with her straightening back. "Does this mean you're staying then? No more foot out the door?" She sounded hopeful as she looked at me with a bright smile.

Forcing out an unsure chuckle, I shrugged my shoulders. "Maybe not a foot, but definitely a toe." The thought of escaping and disappearing from all my problems was still rather tempting.

Taking in a deep breath, I tap my finger against my glass of water while looking out the window. "What have my parents been doing?" If they were doing things off the books with no electronic footprints, then I would have absolutely no idea about it all.

Dragging out a heavy sigh and groan, Angel grumbled under her breath for a minute. "The only thing we know is that they're meeting someone unknown to us. I mean, the only thing we do know about this mystery person is that they're not affiliated with the local gangs." Letting out another sigh, Angel sipped at her water. "Like I said, we haven't been able to grasp at any ends to unravel this whole situation because your parents spin some stupid tale to lead us to dead ends, and this person they're doing business with gives us the slip every time we target them."

Seeing Angel's face weighted down with stress as she talked about things made me feel a little guilty. They were my parents, therefore my problem. My pregnant friend shouldn't be burdened by something I possibly created.

Scooting over, I hugged Angel tightly and rubbed her stomach. "Don't worry about them. I'll handle it with my man." Some more excitement in Lev's life won't kill him. Besides, he wouldn't say no to me. "Send me all the information you have, and I'll take care of it all, promise."

Angel's lips pressed into a tight smile, and she hugged me back. "Thanks, and I'm sorry you're being pulled back into your family drama when that's what you're trying to run from."

Chuckling softly, I patted her back reassuringly. "Hey, my circus, my problem. It's not fair for you to be stressed out about it all, especially being pregnant."

"Ugh, I swear, all you guys are going to make me snap before this pregnancy is over," Angel grumbled with a groan. "I'm pregnant, not invalid. I am still more than capable of handling everything still."

Rolling my eyes, I playfully shoved her. "You really need to learn how to take a step back. Honestly, you are the head of the bratva with your husband. You have all the men and power at your disposal, so delegate, take a step back, and breathe."

Sometimes, I found it hard to understand Angel. Yes, I understood that she was the kind of person who had to keep themselves busy, hence why she loved being an emergency department nurse. Still, I often wondered how she didn't get tired of piling everything onto her plate.

I mean, if I was her, I'd totally abuse the power of being the head of the most powerful mafia group in California. I'd love to do nothing but sit around my work desk and tinker my life away on my ideas while everyone else handled everything to my whims. Oh, to be the boss again, that's the dream.

The couch shifted and creaked as Angel scooted over and hugged me. "Hey, what's wrong? You have that mopey look." Angel's soft concern had me smiling sadly.

"I just..." Sighing heavily, I ran a hand through my hair. "I enjoy this free life, but I kind of miss being the boss of my own company."

Laughing softly, Angel lightly shoved at me. "Oh, you just miss busting men's balls," she teased. "You miss bossing men around, having them kiss your feet, worship the ground you walk on, all that shit." Well, she wasn't wrong, but she didn't have to put it like *that*. "Which, honestly, wish I had the confidence you do." Angel pouted softly with a small huff.

My eyes rolled before I could help myself. "Bitch, have you seen yourself? You might not be as outward as me, but you're one boss-ass bitch in your own right. Besides, who cares if you're submissive. I mean, it takes a lot of guts and respect to give yourself up to someone." Sometimes, I wish I could be a little more demure like her.

"What's your plan now, then?" Angel's voice toned back down as she looked at me inquisitively.

After a moment of thought, I shrugged my shoulders. "Don't know right now, but I'll work something out with my man."

Chapter 13

~3 days later~

"Mr. Volkov, someone is here to see you."

The tired voice of my assistant instantly pulled my attention away from the mindless assignment Stepan had just dropped on my desk.

"And? If they don't have an appointment, then send—"

I didn't get a chance to finish before I broke out in a smile from Nicole barging her way into my office. "And as I told your stupid assistant, I am VIP. No appointment needed," Nicole argued, shoving the assistant out of my office and closing the door.

Instantly, I shot out of my seat, rounded my desk, and greeted Nicole with a big hug. "*Zhizn moya.*" Unable to help myself, I pressed a kiss against her temple. "Did I miss a message about you coming? Did the assistant give you a lot of trouble? I would have told them to let you through if I'd known."

Nicole didn't look too peeved, but the assistant surely did.

Flashing me a reassuring smile, Nicole shook her head. "It's fine. I've handled much worse." Her smile quickly faded with the softening of her voice. "We need to talk."

Uh oh, those words were never good, especially in such a somber tone.

Without a word, I led her over to the couch and sat down with her in my lap. "If you're going to break up with me, then you better carve the tattoo out of my chest and take it with you." Having my ex permanently inked on me was not on my bucket list.

I hoped that wasn't the reason for this serious conversation, though. We barely started this complicated relationship of ours, if this whole thing could even be considered a relationship. It was a relationship to me because, well, why else would she continue to put up with me after I quit hunting her? Also, why the fuck would she brand me with a tattoo!?

Granted, we never really labeled this situationship, but at this point, I was more than confident that we were together after everything.

Even if that weren't the case, like hell would I let her end us.

No, she claimed me as hers, and she damn well belonged to me now. *Mine.*

A surge of possessiveness tightened my arms around Nicole, trapping her against my body. "*Shakhta.*" Grabbing her jaw, I forced her head back to attack her neck with aggressive kisses.

Gasping softly, Nicole reached back to shove at my head. "Lev, stop. We really need to talk." She struggled out between her heavy breaths.

"Tell me we're not breaking up, and I will." I bargained, dragging my teeth down the column of her delicate neck.

Scoffing, Nicole slapped my thigh and shoved her hand right into my face. "Okay, for one," she grunted softly as she spun around to face me fully and straddled me. "That's not even what the talk is about, little lion." Reaching up, she lightly slapped my cheek—playfully—a few times with a cheeky smile.

Snaking her arms around my neck, she leaned in close, ghosting her lips over mine. "Secondly, if that's how you're going to act with the impending threat of separation, I might actually try to see how far you go," she whispered deviously against my lips with a chuckle. "How far are you willing to go to keep me? How desperate will your love for me become?"

Those damn four letters had my body freezing up as if my bastard father had risen from the dead before me and brutally murdered everyone dear to me before my very eyes.

Liked? Yes. Coveted? Yes. Infatuated? Yes. Love!? No, no, no, that's where the line was drawn. No.

Swallowing the lump in my throat, I averted my eyes from Nicole as I shoved her away to put some breathing space between us. "W-what did you want to talk about?" Safe to say, my mood was ruined, and a change of subject was desperately needed.

Nicole's face twisted with concern and confusion as she studied me momentarily. Her mouth opened and closed with what seemed like a pressing matter, but she dropped it with a sigh. "My parents... and my whole situation," she paused briefly to sigh heavily. "I'm going to stay, but I need some help dealing with them."

Shoving my thoughts and feelings of stupor from before away completely, I recollected myself. "What about your parents? Besides them being a pain in the ass." I was no stranger to the issues that her parents have been to the bratva.

Besides being on my ass about their assignment for me with Nicole, they've been causing our bratva some trouble with some shady business dealings that were starting to affect some of our current client base. Some of our customers were jumping ship, yet we couldn't figure out what kind of ammo the Le's had. They were also in business with someone who kept on eluding us, and that was what pissed us off the most about the whole situation with them.

"I don't really know where to start, so I'll just kind of start with when my problem with them started," Nicole said with a sigh, slouching into me until her head rested comfortably against my chest. "It was a few months ago, a little over six or so, not too sure at this point. Either way, around that time, I found out that my parents stole my company from me, cut me out completely, and transferred everything to them and my younger brother."

I sensed that wasn't the end of the story, just the beginning. And I would be right because she proceeded to unload over the next few minutes. "If having my own company pulled from right under my nose by my own parents wasn't bad enough, they proceed to try and cart me off to some old man over in China who wants a wife for himself and his bum of a son. Some old friend of my father's is what my parents claimed." Scoffing, Nicole muttered something in a different language before continuing. "A load of bullshit is what that all was. It was some business deal, and I was the bargaining chip. Like hell was I going to let some stupid misogynistic man and his equally shitty son beat me and use me."

Tension clenched my jaw as red-hot anger burned through my veins until the veil of anger threatened to cloud my vision. "Give me one good reason why I shouldn't storm your parent's gaudy mansion and tear it to the ground with my bare hands to bury them alive in their deceit." I seethed with a silent anger that kept a deep scowl permanently etched on my face.

"Because I need to rob them of everything they have and figure out what they're up to before they can die," Nicole replied flatly with some sarcasm in her voice. "I owe a friend a favor, and my parent's business dealings with this mystery person is putting a big nail in her coffin."

I've never had much reason to doubt Nicole until now. Something about the slight strain in her voice, her slight reluctance set my gut off—and my gut was never wrong. So, what was my empress hiding? And why? Who was this friend of hers who she didn't name?

Although, one thing did bug me a little. "Why do your parents want you back?" No matter how much I dug into her parents, I couldn't find a reason as to why they wanted me to locate and retrieve her.

Pursing her lips, Nicole shrugged her shoulders at me and sighed heavily. "Your guess beats mine. I mean, they took everything from me, so I literally have nothing left to give them." Tilting her head from side to side, she let out an unsure sound. "Well, I mean, I have what I do now, but it's nothing compared to what they got."

Sighing, I tucked the subject away for a later time. "Well, what's your plan now, then? Oh great, Queen Nicki." I snarked the last part out rather sarcastically with a chuckle, earning an eye roll from Nicole.

Playful lust darkened her eyes as her lips curled into a smirk. Walking her fingers up my arm, she sneaked her fingers across my shoulder and down my chest to my tie. One by one, her slender fingers coiled around my tie. Then, with a firm tug, she jerked me closer until our lips were a breath away from touching.

"It's empress to you, little lion." Her whispering words sounded like a ghost as they fanned over my face. "Only my friends call me Nicki or Queen Nicki."

My words became caught in her mouth from the sudden kiss, where she stole my breath away with each press of her soft lips. "And you're not my friend." Again, before I could argue, her frenzied mouth silenced me. "You are far beyond that."

I quickly grabbed her chuckling face, not giving her a chance to take my voice from me again. "Oh? Beyond a friend? So, a boyfriend?"

"Mhmm, more than that." She giggled, grinning at me rather deviously.

Prying my hand away, she set it on her ass as she leaned in and hugged me tightly.

Her heavy breaths made my skin prickle with excitement as her delicate lips and tongue danced along my sensitive neck. All I could do was melt under her care, letting the room grow hot and heavy with my desire for her. Then, when her lips brushed against the shell of my ear and her breathy words whispered into my ear, I nearly lost it then and there.

I wanted to throw her down onto the couch, pin her down by her neck, and fuck her full of my cum.

God, pump her full and make her round with my baby.

Fuck.

What is wrong with me?

I don't even know if she wants kids, so why the fuck am I even thinking about that?

"You. Are. *Mine.*"

Click!

Chapter 14

Nicole

I SHOULD HAVE SET up a camera.

"Did you just—take it off!" Lev was quick to shove me off to dart into his private bathroom. "I swear to God, *zhizn moya*, this better be a fucking joke."

Laughing haughtily, I propped myself up on my arms across the back of the couch, watching Lev grab and tug at the metal collar around his neck in the bathroom mirror. "We are really going to have to work on your manners, *đại ca*." I teased him with a mocking laugh. "I mean, first the cake, then the tattoo. I mean, I gave you so much yet received no gratitude." Clicking my tongue chidingly, I shook my head. "So rude."

Growling, Lev spun around and glared at me with burning eyes. "That's it."

Confused, I tilted my head at him as I raised a brow. "Wha—ah!" My squeak cut out into a sharp gasp from the shock of Lev lunging at me and pinning me down onto the couch by my neck.

His strong hand tightened around my neck. "I've about had it with your antics. If anyone needs to be taught a lesson, it's you." The pressure around my neck increased with each word until I felt the world around me buzz and blur out.

Lev's hand released, letting me suck in the sweet air. The sudden rush of oxygen back into my lungs caused my vision to white out with the burning inhale. "Oh? I beg—" My words choked out again from Lev's hand necklace.

Slamming his lips against mine, he kisses me sloppily with a groan. Weight presses against my hips, forcing my legs to open wider the more Lev pressed himself into me. "Oh, you're going to beg, alright." His heated growl shook my body with arousal, making me suck in a sharp breath at the feeling of my panties getting soaked. "You're going to be begging me to fuck you harder and harder until you can't, and I'm not going to stop pounding away at you until you're nothing but a moaning and mumbling mess under me."

Rolling his hips into me, he dug his hard-on into my sensitive core. "I'm not stopping until you ruin this couch, which won't be hard with how much I'm going to make you squirt and gush your sweet juices." Lev had to pause his teasing thrusts to get ahold of himself. "Then, the mess you're going to make after I fill you, mhmm fuck."

The taste of his lips invading my mind chased my retorting thoughts away. I couldn't fight him—he was too irresistible. "I won't stop until I've stuffed you so full of my cum that you'll have me running down your thighs every time you stand up for days." He groaned hotly against my lips.

"Fuck and stuff you until you get all plump with—" Our exciting and tender moment was interrupted by his sudden pause, which smeared the air with tension.

Before I could further ruin the mood by questioning him, he shuts me up with another heavy kiss that ignites the inferno of lust in me again. The needy ache between my legs flared back to life, making me buck my hips against his restrained cock out of instinct. "Little lion, be a good boy and fuck me already," I whispered hastily between our kisses. "I need you so bad, please."

Smirking against my lips, he teasingly nips at my bottom lip. "Not yet, empress." Briefly, he tightened his hand around my neck as he leaned down to my ear. "I want to worship your body before I ruin it."

Oh fuck.

Shuddering, I hooked my legs around his waist, pressing my lower half against him fully to rub my covered sex against him. Burning need for Lev consumed me the more I ground my hips against his covered cock. "Lev." I let out a soft, needy moan.

Letting go of my neck, he grabbed both my wrists, pinning them above my head with one of his large hands. With me secured, he reached into his back pocket, fishing out a pocketknife. "Lev, do not do what I think you're going to do." I gave him a stern, threatening glare as I tried to shrink away from the blade the closer it came to my body.

"I'll take you shopping after and buy out whatever store you like," he promised, chuckling against my lips with a chaste kiss before trailing his rough kisses along my jawline to my neck.

Lingering around my neck with kisses and nips, he fell into a pattern of moving from one side of my neck to the other, almost like he was tracing something. "What if I gave you a collar in return?" he asked with a breathy chuckle while moving back and forth across my sensitive skin.

"Do it," I remarked smugly with a grin. "Show the world who owns you. Let them see who I allow the pleasure of touching my body, marking it, and being mine."

I belonged to Lev as much as he belonged to me. Yeah, I basically owned his ass at this point, but relationships, dominant and submissive ones included, are always a two-way street. I could drag Lev around on a leash all I wanted, lead him into a lake or off a cliff for all it mattered, but if he wasn't willing or actively consenting and participating, then there was no point to it all. I wasn't the type of person who liked to take and give nothing back.

Sure, some D/s relationships operated like so, but it wasn't my flow. I wanted a submissive, yeah, but not a slave per se. Also, I desired more of a switch submissive to curb my need to be put in my place at times; it was rare for me to have those moments, but they happened—like now.

I wanted Lev to snap and take me, claim me, and possess me.

God, Lev. He was just so perfect.

Honestly, I didn't think this relationship between us would have unfolded as well as it has so far. A hunch was all I got from Lev the moment I realized his lingering presence around me. One look at him, and I knew I had to make him kneel at my feet and that he would like it. There was this soft gleam in his eyes deep down, buried under all the roughness, his wall of confidence. It was a yearning, one I've seen too often in men like him.

Usually, I felt no inclination to fill that void in people, but something about Lev's gruff and protective demeanor drew me in like a moth to a flame. He had so much to live up to, and I could see the exhaustion underneath everything. He needed a safety net, a safe space, and I wanted to be that for him—no, I *needed* to be his safety and comfort.

I wanted to embrace him so badly the day I confronted him and got sucked into his soul the moment I locked eyes with him. Such a strong face for someone so broken underneath. He needed to be adored and cared for. The burden he carried on his back didn't have to be his to suffer alone.

My Lev. My little lion. My đại ca.

Then, whatever thoughts sweetened my desire for him ripped away along with my clothes after he sliced through my clothes and tore them off my body, leaving me completely bare for his wolfish eyes to devour me. "*Ty chertovski bozhestvenna.*" Hearing his raspy voice sent a wave of heat straight to my tight nipples and throbbing core.

A sharp bite and tug against my neck had me gasping and moaning breathily as I threw my head back to give Lev more access. My aroused body shuddered in response to every kiss, suck, lick, and bite from Lev as he took his sweet time marking my neck up. Thank God I didn't have to worry about keeping up some professional image for the media and shit. Otherwise, I'd be having a hell of a time trying to cover up Lev's little crime scene on my succulent skin.

"You better not try to hide your neck." Lev's deep voice vibrated in my ear. "I want the whole world to see that my empress is taken."

Fuck me.

Biting my bottom lip, I let out a muffled moan as I arched my body up against his, whimpering a bit at the feeling of my nipples rubbing against the fabric of his shirt. I couldn't lose myself, though, not yet. Reeling myself back in, I tried my best to keep my needy grinding to a minimum to talk properly. "Bomb. Our safe-word is Bomb." I barely managed to get it out in an audible sigh of pleasure.

"I was thinking Grenade, but Bomb works too." Lev mused with a chuckle as he continued to kiss down my chest and around my breasts. "If you can't talk, then just pull my ear." His words vibrated against my sensitive breast, making me shiver.

"Alright, sounds good. The same goes for you, though. If you need a break or to slow down, tug my ear if you can't use your words." Tough guy or not, he had his limits, which I didn't know about yet.

Hot bliss melted my body when I felt Lev's eager mouth take my hard nipple in. His tongue whipped around the bud, sending shockwaves of pleasure straight down to my aching cunt. "Oh fuck... *Đại ca*, careful, I'm sensitive," I gasped out between my moans while I twisted under him.

Lev hummed softly against me before easing a bit with his sucking and nipping. He also became more cautious with his tongue, focusing on slow and caressing movements rather than hard flicks and presses. After a while, he pulled off to move to my other nipple, giving it the same tender treatment before kissing a trail down my stomach to my nether regions.

Biting his bottom lip, Lev sucked in a deep breath as he looked down between our pelvic regions. "Fuck, look at the mess you've made already, *zhizn moya*." He groaned, leaning up and jutting his hip out to show me the darkened spot at the center of his pants. "Makes me want to dry fuck you so you can squirt and gush all over my pants." Almost as if he couldn't help himself, he leaned in and rolled his hips against me a few times, making the wet spot worse.

The sudden weight winded me, and the only thing I could breathe in was Lev because his lips sealed over mine in a desperate kiss. "I'm going to let go of your wrists to strip. Do not move them." His dominating voice brought a small smile to my nodding head.

"Yes, *đại ca*." I'd let him take care of me... for now.

Feeling the weight off my wrists, I resisted the urge to reach out and help release his immaculate body from the confines of his clothes. I wanted to burn the tips of my fingers and the palms of my hands from touching his body. His perfect body was begging to be touched until every inch of him became burned into my mind.

Over the next few seconds, I couldn't tear my eyes away from Lev as he quickly stripped down to nothing. The moment his pants and boxers came off, my eyes instantly darted down to get a glimpse of what fun he had going on down there, only to have him grab my face and kiss me. "Look at me, *zhizn moya*. I want to see your face when I take you for the first time."

Pouting and whimpering, I lightly stomped my foot against the couch in protest. "Not fair," I grumbled, shuddering at the feeling of something thick and hard running along the length of my cunt. "Oh fuck..." Gripping the couch, I groaned softly while bucking my hips at him to get more of a feel.

He felt huge! My lower lips were being parted so far apart as he kept running his bulbous tip along it. Damn it, I needed to see this monstrosity to prepare myself. Just a peek!

I tried to peer around his arm to get a glimpse, but my eyes snapped back up and rolled to the back of my head with a silent scream from the sudden penetration. It all happened in the blink of an eye, and I was in no way prepared to take all of Lev's huge cock in one thrust like that. "You son of a—fuck! Holy shit, you're gonna break me in half!" Gasping and whimpering, I struggled against his hold on my wrists—don't know when he grabbed them again, probably when he shoved himself into me without warning!

Shifting my hips, I couldn't help but wince at the feeling of some bulge rubbing my insides. "W-what is that? Something feels weird." There was an odd sensation against my tightened walls that became more evident the more I moved, and I could have sworn I felt a slight pinch a few times when Lev slid in.

Lev grinned down at me and bellowed out a laugh before giving me a few hard thrusts, only stopping when his hips pressed against the back of my thighs. "Oh, did I forget to mention how endowed I am? And how I'm decked out with some lovely piercings?" I wanted to slap the smug smirk off his face as he gave me some teasing thrusts.

Laughing haughtily, Lev pulled back a bit before ramming back into me, jerking my squealing body. "From tip to base, all for her pleasure." He teased with a shit-eating grin.

Asshole.

Recollecting myself, I plastered a mocking smirk on my own face. "Making up for your *short*-comings with some hardware?" I remarked with a scoff while trying to pretend that his cock wasn't the best thing ever.

"Shortcomings? Short!?" Lev seemed rather offended, which made my arrogance skyrocket.

With a nonchalant shrug, I dragged out a sarcastic sigh. "I mean, why else would you need piercings on your dick?" Steeling my gaze, I gave him my best asshole grin. "You're compensating."

The sight of Lev's neck muscles popping from clenching his jaw made a victorious laugh bubble in my chest. It vanished as fast as it came on, though. My face scrunched up quizzically when Lev's jaw relaxed with a smirk. "I'm gonna pull out, and you're going to count each one as they go in."

His massive body loomed over mine as he leaned down to whisper deeply in my ear, "And just so you know, each one marks an inch." His teeth grazed against the lobe of my ear with a harsh bite. "So, let's see how *short* I am."

My protest became nothing but a moaning gasp at the emptying feeling of Lev's cock leaving me. "Count." His command cut through my lustful haze so clearly, and it was the only thing my muddled mind clung to.

The pleasureful pain of his girthy length arched my back as he slowly, like very slowly, slid himself in. I almost forgot to count because I was too focused on keeping myself centered, but Lev sternly reminded me with a soft slap to the face, followed by a look.

Damn asshole purposedly slowed down more when the piercing reached my entrance, making me feel the extra stretch over the metal barbell.

One. Two. Three. Four. Five. It kept going, and every time I glanced down to see the progress... Well, that was a big mistake on my part.

"Nine." A quick glance, and fuck! There had to be a few inches left to go!

"Lev, no more, please. I'm so full already." How the hell my body managed to fit in nine inches of thick dick without breaking was beyond me.

Well, maybe it wasn't nine. Maybe he was lying about every piercing being an inch. I mean, it seemed like something he'd say to tease and rouse me. Yeah, maybe—

"Fuck, ten!" Nope, that definitely felt like an inch apart from the last.

Some soft and warm presses against my forehead, followed by some Russian. "That's my girl. You're doing so amazing, *zhizn moya*. Almost there, almost done." His lips grazed down my face to my lips, where he pressed a deep and sensual kiss against it. "You are being such a good girl for me. Taking this cock like a pro," he teased with a playful chuckle before kissing me again.

Then, with one final push, I felt his hips press against me after one more soft stretch over some metal balls. "Oh God, eleven." I let out an audible sigh of relief as I relaxed fully under Lev.

Leaning down, Lev sank his teeth into me, making me hiss a bit from the sting. "That's not eleven inches of God in you, *zhizn moya*." Cocky bastard pulled back briefly to slam into me, making me gasp out a sharp moan. "That's all *me* that's stretching and stuffing this cunt of yours. *My cock*," he growled possessively against my neck.

Pushing himself up with an arm, he situated himself properly before grabbing my neck to anchor me. Then, with a wolfish grin and darkened eyes full of nothing but adoration and lust for me, he started to thrust in and out of me at a fast and hard pace.

I didn't care how much of the damn building could hear our bodies colliding or my moans. There was no controlling the sinful song from slipping past my parted lips. Every thrust rubbed his stupid piercings right against my tight walls, and it was impossible not to feel them with how big he was. If the added stimulation wasn't bad enough, the way his cock bullied every sweet spot I had, and ones I didn't know I had, added to the tormenting pleasure.

God, if he wasn't holding my wrists down, I'd be clawing and clinging to him for dear life because he was my anchor in this churning sea of lust and mind-breaking rapture. "Lev, my body... I can't... Fuck! I can't stop coming, and it—fuck!" I was so frustrated with myself.

My body was overstimulated, that much I knew and accepted, but I couldn't decide whether I wanted it all to slow down and stop or for him to keep pounding away at me with no mercy until I completely broke.

"Fuck, Lev, I don't know how much more I can take." My body wouldn't stop trembling and shaking from the constant aftershocks of my orgasms.

Gritting his teeth, he let out a feral groan before laughing smugly. "I'm almost there, *zhizn moya*, just a little more." Leaning down, he rests his forehead against mine, his lips barely touching mine with each jarring thrust. "One more, baby, come one more time for me, and milk me for all I got."

That last part was a bucket of iced water to my brain. "What? No." I instantly struggled a bit against him, quitting halfway because of an orgasm. "Lev, you can't come in me. I'm not on birth control," I quickly protested, removing a leg from him to try and get him off, only to have him grab it after releasing my neck.

Letting go of my wrists, he grabbed his discarded tie off the ground and bound my wrists together to use both his hands to press my thighs wide apart. After folding me into a damn pretzel, he adjusted his angle to thrust into me without abandon.

The sound of our bodies pounding against each other shook the room, along with Lev's hard fucking. There was no stopping him. I could hit and struggle all I wanted against him, but the frenzied look in his determined eyes told me all I needed to know.

Those five words set off a bomb in him. It was as if I flung open the cage to a rabid animal by telling him I wasn't on birth control.

After a brief string of Russian, followed by a loud groan, Lev's hips jerked out of rhythm before stilling in me to unload his cum. Of course, I was silly to think that'd be the end because not even ten seconds later, Lev went back to bucking at me wildly. "Can't fucking stop now after hearing that." Lev groaned between his heavy pants.

Hissing something under his breath in Russian, he pressed my legs more into the couch. "We're not stopping until I can't fill you anymore," he growled.

Every rough thrust from him sent a sloosh of cum rushing out of my spasming cunt. He was making such a mess of me, but I didn't care at this point. I wanted him to fuck me until our juices ran down my legs and stomach and until I'd be leaking his cum for days. I could already feel his hot seed dripping out and down my abdomen with how upright he pressed my body.

The crazed gleam in his eyes slowly faded with his second release, and by the time he groaned out his third, everything disappeared from him. His sweaty muscles shined under the lights, and they were exaggerated with every heaving breath his trembling body took.

Weakly laughing, he leaned down and kissed me sloppily. "Shit, never done that before." He struggled to get his words out between his breaths. "But fuck, that was amazing. Best fuck of my life, ever."

Replying with a weak chuckle of my own, I lightly slapped his tense pecs with my bound hands. "If you weren't the infamous Lev Volkov, I'd be inclined to believe that," I remarked with a playful scoff.

Grabbing my face, he kissed me deeply and passionately, not letting up until I pounded at his chest because I needed to breathe properly. "You really are the first I've ever desired and craved like an addict craves their next high." His expression was serious, and his voice was genuine as he looked deeply into my eyes.

"Do I have you hooked then?" I joked with a dry chuckle, worrying my bottom lip between my teeth as the fear of Lev giving me the boot slipped back into my mind.

Leaning in, Lev adored every inch of my face with kisses and sweet reassurance. "Empress, you had me enamored and chained to you the moment your parents slid your picture across my desk." The pause felt long, and I couldn't help but feel as if there was a 'but' to follow.

Kissing my temple, he quickly untied my wrists. "Stay. I'm going to grab some stuff to clean you up."

I had to press my lips into a thin line and force myself to smile at the coldness I felt from Lev. Well, to say he was cold would be a gross overstatement; it felt as if he pulled a curtain between us.

The slight movement from Lev had me wincing at the sudden pain. Then, the surge of cum flowing out of my had me shuddering at the stark feeling of heat against my chilling body.

"*Blyat*! Nicole, why didn't you stop me?" Lev's eyes darted between me and his cock.

I didn't comprehend his concern until I followed his gaze to his bloodied member. "Oh... I didn't... I mean, it's normal to bleed with your first time, isn't it?" Yeah, it hurt a little at first when I was adjusting, but sex with Lev felt amazing, even if he did get a little wild at the end.

Lev's face dropped with the rest of his shocked body. "What?" His frantic eyes searched my face and pleaded with me for something, but when all I did was give him a confused look in return, he let out a frustrated sigh while running his hand through his hair. "Nicole, why didn't you tell me you were a virgin!? I wouldn't have fucked you like some rabid animal nor push you that far if I had known. I could have really hurt you!"

Seeing his face twist with guilt as he beat himself up made me frown and feel bad about it all.

So, with a sigh, I pushed myself up to sit, wincing some more at the soreness between my legs. "Lev," I barked out, reaching over and pulling him to me by the ring of his collar. "I am fine," I assured him with a confident smile.

With a forceful pull, I forced him forward into my body to hold him. "I didn't think it was that big of a deal. I mean, people have sex all the time, and I knew my time would come eventually." I honestly didn't see why he was fussing about my decisions about my body. "I wasn't really waiting for Mister Right or anything, not to say that you aren't, because you are." Flashing him a grin, I giggled softly. "I knew you were who I wanted to give myself to the moment you came back around after I tried so hard to get rid of you."

Leaning down, I pressed a kiss to the top of his head before stroking my fingers along his scalp. "Don't beat yourself up, little lion. I didn't tell you because I really didn't place too much importance on it." Stroking his hair, I held his head firm against my chest. "You didn't hurt me, promise. I would have let you know if you did and if it had gotten to be too much, then I would have used the safe word."

Grasping his chin, I tilted his head up to face my smiling one. "You gave me one of the best moments in my life just now, so don't be upset or anything."

No one likes a sourpuss.

Craning my neck down, I kissed him deeply. "Now, clean me up, cuddle me, and let me use you as a pillow to nap." The exhaustion from our activities started to set into my bones and weigh my eyelids down.

"Yes, empress." Kissing my chest with a chuckle, Lev held me for a moment before tearing himself away.

And treat me like a fucking empress he did. He was so meticulous with making sure the water was kept warm enough while he wiped my body clean inch by inch, being extra careful at more sore areas. Then, when he was done, he slipped his shirt on me before laying down on the couch with me tucked cozily against him.

"You feel so perfect," I groaned contently against his chest, burying my face into it with a huge smile.

"My Lev." Pressing a kiss against his tattoo, I grinned up at him pridefully. "My little lion."

Chapter 15

"Sir, Mr. Volkov is busy! And you do not have permission to be back here!" The faint voice of the assistant grew louder and louder, along with sets of footsteps.

"Do you know who I am?" Hearing Mark Le's familiar voice made me groan internally. "I always have permission whenever and wherever."

Great, this is where shit is gonna go? Fuck me.

"Mr. Le!" My assistant's voice was right outside the door now, and I was still bundled on the couch with a stirring Nicole in my arms.

"What's go—"

Nicole didn't get a chance to finish waking before the door was thrown open rather rudely. "Mis—" Nicole's father paused for a few seconds of shock before flying into a rage.

If Nicole wasn't awake, she surely was now, with how she shot up from the couch and shouted back at her father. Now, I had no idea what they were arguing about because it was all in Vietnamese, but given Nicole's situation and what she told me, I could take a few good guesses.

Also, it was a good thing I'd put my shirt on her and my pants back on earlier before we conked out. Otherwise, we'd both be stark ass naked.

As the shouting match dragged on, I slowly got up from the couch, standing beside a fuming Nicole. My movement caused Mark's stark eyes to lock onto me. "What is the meaning of this? I hired you to find my daughter and safely return her to me," he seethed, taking a cautious step toward me. "And I come in to see you taking advantage of her."

My jaw ticked with an irritated click of my tongue. "Do not make me out to be some predator, Mark. I do not take kindly to such accusations." Glowering at him, I slipped an arm around Nicole's waist and pulled her close. "What Nicole and I chose to do is none of your business, and per my last communication with you, the contract between us is null and void because you broke some of the clauses." Okay, that last part was a big stretch, but her parents failed to argue and immediately went on the offensive.

I already made the overdue phone call days—no, nearly over a week ago to terminate the contract with the Le's. Needless to say, that call was not pleasant, but it took a huge weight off my shoulders. Then, when I pulled the bit about them breaking one of the terms and conditions, they instantly attacked me, saying their family business was none of mine, that I needed to remain professional and indifferent, and that I should be understanding of them because I was in the same business and lifestyle.

Honestly, after a few shots of hard liquor after that call, I hardly remembered it, let alone give a shit about it.

Clearing my throat, I gathered myself back together. "When I agreed to your contract, it was to bring Nicole back to you because you wanted to care for her again, provide her a safe home and shit." Gritting my teeth, I tightened my hold on Nicole protectively. "I did not agree to return her to you so that you could use her for your own gain." Again, lies, and I might be digging my own grave with each word, but I was in too deep now.

"What I do with my daughter is none of your business," Mark scowled deeply, his eyes darting over to Nicole briefly.

"It is fully my business what you do with Nicole because she is under Volkov Bratva protection. *My* protection." Now, *that* wasn't a lie because I made it my personal assignment when I realized Nicole's life was in jeopardy somehow.

I was determined to protect her until I ceased to exist.

Sputtering in disbelief, Mark's body did a double take before tensing up again. "What lies did she feed you to turn you against me? Do you know the consequences of such decisions? Do you think that you can just cancel on *me*?" Whatever lies I'd thrown out earlier had to have more truth to them than I anticipated, given how flustered Mark became.

Clicking my tongue in annoyance, I scowled angrily at him and took a threatening step toward him, making him flinch. "Watch your tone with me, old man," I warned him with a grave voice and glare. "You broke the terms and conditions, so I have more than every right to terminate our contract." Not like that mattered anyhow; they may have proposed the job, and I may have taken it, but I damn well had the right to change my mind and pull out. "Even if you hadn't, I still retain the rights to null the contract, per its terms and conditions."

As my brothers would tell me, 'Cover your ass.' This was why all my contracts had a clear condition stating that I held full rights to terminate the assignment no matter what. I seldom canceled assignments, though, only when they went against my rules and morals or if there was some kind of other shitty conflict.

"I gave you an assignment, and I expect you to complete it as we had agreed." Mark stood his shaky ground with a determined look. "Hand over Nicole right now, and I'll forgive and forget about all this."

Scoffing in disbelief, I waited for a second to see if Mark was being serious. When he showed no signs of changing the hard look on his face, I laughed. "Listen here, you may have come to me with the request, but I do not work for you at the end of the day. You and your family are under Volkov control. You work for us, not the other way around." Pushing Nicole behind me, I crossed my arms and stood protectively before her. "Unless you want trouble, I suggest you turn your ass around and leave. Then, you forget about Nicole and never bother her again, or else."

Baring his teeth at me, he glared at me harshly, muttering something foreign under his breath. "You Volkovs think you're all in charge now because of what happened with Lady Qing, but you're all naïve to think that was the end of it all." He switched his tongue again, shouting at me in Vietnamese.

My body jarred with a shove from Nicole. Rounding around me, Nicole seethed at her father. "You fucking try." With one hand gripping my arm, she lashed out at Mark. "You've done more than enough damage and got more than you ever need in this stupid life. Your greed will get you killed if you dare try and carry out a fraction of your stupid plans."

Nicole spat something at Mark in Vietnamese before suddenly grabbing my gun from the coffee table. "Leave and never look in my direction ever again, or I'll show you what I'm really capable of." Placing her finger over the trigger, she steadied her aim. "I'm not your daughter anymore. That girl died the day you ripped the life I had built up from me and handed it to my brother on a golden platter and tried to ship me off to a different country to be married off to some old fart and his useless son for money!"

Was it wrong for me to root for Nicole to pull the trigger on her father? I mean, I could easily disarm her and prevent the 'unnecessary' violence in the office, but Mark deserved to be shot in the face—in my humble opinion. Also, if she wasn't gonna do it, then I might take the gun from her and do it myself.

Would his untimely death cause a lot more trouble than it'd be worth? Yes, very much. But! But the satisfaction of getting rid of this arrogant bastard would be so amazing!

"You made it clear where Bao and I stand to you, mother, and the whole family. You decided to cut us out the way you did. So, whatever happens from here on out is all on you." Nicole's chilling voice sent shivers down my spine as I watched her take an angry step toward Mark, who instantly held his hands up. "You have until the count of three."

Nicole barely finished counting to one before her father spun around and ran out with his tail tucked between his legs, making me bellow an amused laugh that shook the office.

"Empress, as hot as you look all riled up with a gun, you're lucky your father didn't call you out on the fact you wouldn't shoot him." I teased her with a snicker, watching her body spin around.

Huffing, Nicole scowled and pointed the gun at me. "I would have! You don't think I'm serious!?" I couldn't help but laugh at her for her tough-guy act. "Lev! I'm being serious!" She growled, stomping her foot.

Slapping a lid on myself, I stifled my laughter. "My empress, you're not going to be shooting anyone with the safety on." I pointed out the little switch with an arrogant little smile.

Now, I probably shouldn't shove it in her face, but I was too much of a jerk to resist. So, to add the cherry on top of everything, I pulled a loaded magazine out of the pocket of my pants. "Nor will you hurt anyone with an empty gun." For extra effect, I waved the magazine in front of her face. "It was cute that you tried, though."

Pouting at me with a glare, Nicole muttered something under her breath before tossing the gun onto the coffee table with a huff. "Well, why the fuck do you have an empty gun for? Mister bratva boss," she snarked.

"I needed to reload it because I spent all the bullets on some idiot who didn't listen to me when I told him not to run," I answered with a nonchalant shrug of my shoulders.

"Did you really call off the contract with my parents?" she asked sheepishly while hiding a smile.

Smiling softly to myself, I trap her in my arms before pulling us back down to the couch. "I had no intentions of keeping to it after you reacted how you did when I told you about your parents sending me after you," I assured her with a kiss on the cheek. "I didn't feel good about it from the start, but my gut really punched me when I saw the anger and fear in your eyes that day."

If I were a heartless bastard, the outcomes would be different. Luckily for Nicole and everyone else in the world, I was raised better and actually had a functioning brain cell and heart.

Money was no issue for me; even if I needed money, I would never place it above someone else's livelihood. A person and their life are priceless—well, most are anyway. I wouldn't be able to sleep at night if I knew I sent someone to their doom when they didn't deserve it.

I did beat myself up a little with Nicole's case for jumping the gun and not listening to my gut initially. I should have done my research before agreeing. Instead, I let my stupid instant infatuation take the wheel.

Well, at least being impulsive this time resulted in something good.

Keeping my arms tightly around Nicole, I held her tenderly as she remained draped over me. "Do you need to nap some more, *zhizn moya*?" She had barely been napping for an hour before her father barged in.

Humming softly, Nicole snuggled herself into me. "No, I think I'll be fine. I need to get home soon anyway." She sighed heavily, pouting softly. "I don't like driving back to my place in the dark."

Looking down at her, I stroked her hair while replying, "Stay then. I'll take you home later." Simple enough of a fix to her problem. "Or let me take you back to my place. You'll be safer there."

Given what had transpired with her father just now, I didn't like the thought of letting her go back to wherever she lived. Her parents could very well send someone else after her, ambush her, kidnap her in the middle of the night, and many other things as a means to get her. They hired *me*, of all people, to go after her, and I wasn't the first, from what I found out recently. So, them hiring some other unsavory person to track and retrieve Nicole wouldn't surprise me. Even if I did make it known that Nicole was under my protection, I highly doubt they would be deterred.

Shaking her head, Nicole gave me a confident smile. "My place is safe, so don't worry." Giggling softly, she reaches up to ruffle my hair. "Unless that's your way of asking me to move in." She cheekily teased me with a grin.

Narrowing my eyes at her, I stared at her for a good moment before cracking a devious grin. "Or I can just take you back to my place and chain you to my bed," I joked, laughing at the way Nicole's face dropped.

Growling softly, Nicole dug her fist into my side, causing my laughter to increase from the ticklish sensation. "I'm kidding," I assured her, pushing her hand away. "My brothers would kill me if you don't do it first."

No matter how ruthless my brothers and I were, we had our boundaries. If they ever found out that I held a girl captive in my home for the sake of keeping her, then I'd be lucky if they gave a quick death with a bullet to the brain.

It wasn't abnormal for us to keep prisoners, though. We actually had a whole compound in the desert with prisoners in it currently. The only difference between them and Nicole if I were to go through with the absurd plan was the intention. Locking Nicole away was more of a selfish reason to benefit me. As opposed to the other prisoners, who were all bad people the bratva had an issue with. Everyone locked away right now had a damn good reason to be in a cage.

My brothers and I weren't in the business of bartering around with human lives or trafficking them. The only thing that happened in our mafia business regarding humans was prostitution, but even that was more along the lines of regulation and protection. A lot of our clubs had sex workers in it, but they're all there of their own accord. We merely provided a place of employment and a roof over their heads to protect them from abusive pimps and other unsavory bastards out in the streets.

Sighing softly, I looked at Nicole pleadingly as I stroked her cheek with the back of my fingers. "Empress, please, come stay with me. I really just want to keep you safe, and I don't know anything about where you live and how the area is." Every time I've tried to follow her back home, I've failed. I don't know how she does it, but she had an uncanny ability to shake me off her tail.

Propping herself up onto her forearms, she looked at me pensively, frowning a little as her eyes slowly furrowed together. "I'm sorry, but I can't." She was genuinely apologetic, and I felt a small tug at my heart with how guarded and hurt she looked. "But, I promise, I swear, if anything happens, no matter how tiny, I'll show up at your door and claim your bed," she promised with a smile.

Well, call me a bastard for what I'm about to do then.

Chapter 16

~1 week later~

Letting out an annoyed sigh, I pushed Lev's fretting hands off my bandaged arm. "I'm fine," I bit out harsher than I intended, but I hated how much he worried over me for nothing.

Gritting his teeth and scowling at me, he grabbed my arm again, holding it up for both of us to see. "If you were, your arm wouldn't be bandaged up," he retorted, waving my arm a little. "What happened to what you promised me before?"

Groaning internally, I rolled my eyes and wrenched my arm from him. "It happened while I was in the city, not when I was making my way back home," I argued, hoping it would be enough to keep me from Lev's home.

"Nicole." Lev's pointed voice made my jaw clench with extreme irritation. "We had an agreement."

Grumbling under my breath, I picked at my nails while glaring at my feet. I could argue with him, but we would get nowhere. Also, I wouldn't win because he was right. I promised him I'd live with him if anything were to happen, which, obviously, something did. Otherwise, we wouldn't be having this stupid tiff. Well, we were having this argument because I was stubborn and reluctant.

Sucking in a deep breath, I held it for a few seconds before letting my chest deflate, relishing a bit in the dizzying feeling from the tension leaving my body. "Tomorrow," I bargained with a determined gaze. "Just give me until tomorrow to gather my shit and swallow this whole thing." Just one last day of independent freedom, that's all I was asking for.

A part of me regretted making such a promise to Lev now that the moment came. It wasn't as if I didn't want to live with him; I needed more time to adjust to our dynamic. Yes, I loved the asshole, but I was used to living on my own now that I needed more time to process the idea of sharing a home with someone else.

Also, as much as I loved seeing Lev nearly every day, seeing him 24/7 would be a whole different story. The eager part of me wanted the sweet moments of cooking meals together, cuddling on the couch and in bed, showering together, waking up and going to bed together, and all the sappy shit couples did. It was the reasonable part of me that made me hesitate. Mentally and emotionally, I wasn't ready for such a commitment yet.

On the other hand, sharing a home with Lev meant spending more time with him and having an easier time keeping track of him. So, there was an upside to the whole thing, kind of.

What if he has some unsavory habit, and I won't be able to stand it? Or what if my habits rub him the wrong way?

Okay, stupid thoughts. Of course, there would be habits we'd find irksome about each other as time went on. I was grasping at straws to poke holes into this abrupt change in my life.

Clicking his tongue, Lev straightened and crossed his arms. "Fine," he reluctantly agreed through gritted teeth. "But I'm going back with you tonight to your place as a safety measure," he decided with certainty, throwing me an arrogant smile as he unfurled his arms and relaxed them in his lap.

I looked at him flatly for a few seconds before scoffing dryly, waiting for his smug expression to change to indicate that what he said was a joke. Unfortunately, that never came. Crossing my arms, I narrowed my eyes at him.

"It's one night. I'll be fine, and we're going to meet first thing in the morning," I argued with a stubborn scowl.

Maintaining the smirk, he raised a brow while slouching a bit in his seat. "Nope. I already gave you a lot of slack by granting you an extra day. So, either I go back with you today, or I throw you into the back seat of my car and take you back to my place right now." That was the ultimatum, it would seem.

Scowling, I let my attitude come out in an overly exaggerated scoff and groan. "Since when were you in charge?" I asked in a mocking voice.

Perking up, Lev leaned over onto the café table with an arrogant grin. "When it became clear to me that you have no street skills and can't keep yourself safe outside the safety of four walls," he retorted pompously, snickering a little with a tilt of his head.

Scooting in closer, he leaned fully over the table, reached a hand out, and pulled me in by my neck until our lips were a breath apart. "You may be in charge when we're at home and in bed, but the moment we cross the threshold into the streets, it's my game we're playing." His grip around my neck loosened, so the hold was more tender and less commanding. "I will still respect you as my empress, but you also need to respect my authority outside the safety of our home. I'm not doing it to be a dick to you. It's to keep you safe and alive."

Tingles of comfort and pleasure rippled from his touch as he ran his thumb across my jawline. "I only do it because I care about and for you." The rough pad of his thumb dances across my bottom lip. "Because I want to go home with you every day and fall asleep with you in my arms. I want to wake up to your face that will brighten my day more than the sun could ever. But you need to be alive and well for all of that to happen."

His other hand reached for my face, cupping it and stroking my cheek before bringing me into a breathtaking kiss that made my heart explode with bliss. "Also, you call me boss for a reason," he remarked, chuckling softly against my lips.

"Oh hush, it's fitting because you literally are a gang leader being a bratva boss and all." I defended myself with a playful scoff and roll of my eyes. "But fine, only because it eases my anxiety to not have to think about the shit I have to do out on the streets."

Yeah, I loved being in charge, but being the badass boss lady gets exhausting. I guess, deep down, I did yearn for someone to take care of me from time to time so that I could actually relax and not have to think for myself. The need has always been there, just buried under layers of who knows what.

It also never really surfaced much until recently... Specifically not until Lev screwed my brains out and pampered me like the queen I was afterward. He was so gentle and tender with how he wiped up every inch of my body clean, peppering delicate kisses on any area that was blemished. Then, he fed me after putting his shirt on me and held me until I dosed off.

No man has ever come close to spoiling me as Lev has, and maybe that was the reason why my deep-rooted need came careening to the surface. I finally found someone I truly trusted and wanted, someone I felt deeply for.

I never thought I'd feel fine with giving anyone control over my life. It was how I've always been ever since I can remember. Even when I was little, I wouldn't let my parents make many decisions for me, and when they did and gave me no choice, I was never happy with any of it and always bent the conditions my way as much as possible. Once I grew up and started my own tech company, well, I was the top dog in charge of the whole shit show.

My parents were co-owners because they were my parents and bullied their way through. Otherwise, I refused to let anyone else have any kind of authoritative role in the company that was on par with mine because I didn't trust anyone to carry out the same quality of work as I did.

Of course, none of that mattered now, not after the shit my parents pulled. The only thing I had now was my own name, what money I pulled from my accounts before my parents took those over and shut me out, and what I had scrapped together and built thus far. Well, I also still had my warehouses full of my shit, thankfully, but still. I had everything set for life, only to have it all crumble to nothing because I had been too naïve and ignorant with my parents.

Before my mind could spiral down the endless pit of resentment, Lev's long kiss pulled me away. "What's on your mind, *zhizn moya*? You got all frowny and angry," he asked in a soft voice, pulling away a few inches to give me some room to breathe.

Taking in a deep breath, I dismissed him with a small smile and a shake of my head. "Thinking about the past when I shouldn't, but I'm not anymore," I assured him with a half-convincing smile. "Also, just thinking about what you said about taking control outside of our private lives." My smile faltered a little

Lev urged my full attention with a firm stroke of my jaw and grasp of my chin. "If it really makes you that uncomfortable, or if you're not fine with it, then we don't have to," he told me with an understanding smile. "I'm fine letting you be in charge of it all... Just..." His eyes averted from me. "You'll have to be a little patient with me..." Lev shifted uncomfortably in his seat with a wary frown.

Chuckling softly, I reached out and traced the edge of the collar adorning his neck, running the tip of my finger against his neck. "I gotta say, I'm surprised you have a submissive side to you." His softening eyes hardened a bit with inner turmoil. "Nothing wrong with that, though. I think it's admirable of you to show your belly to someone."

Leaning up, I kissed his forehead. "Don't worry, I'll take it slow and easy, and I'm not some sadistic Dominant." I mean, not gonna lie, the thought of having Lev bend over for a whipping got my body a little hot and bothered. But still, I got off more on the power and control aspect of it all.

"Now, be a good boy and go get me another drink," I commanded with a hint of playfulness.

Rolling his eyes, Lev kissed my cheek before getting up and going to the counter to order.

He was so good to me, which made me feel a little bad for what I had planned. I mean, on the upside, I'd get to drive his sweet Bugatti La Voiture Noire. Lev wasn't gonna be happy with the aftermath of my little plan, but it was harmless fun... mostly.

"Nicole, if you don't stop brake-checking me, I'm going to hit you." Lev's voice grumbled through my earpiece as I continued to lead him around the road on my motorcycle.

"Sorry, I'm just a little jittery from yesterday," I lied smoothly, smirking behind my helmet as I continued to tap away at the small screen between my handles. "So, what do you want to do when we get back to my place?" I stalled with a stupid question, needing to buy myself some more time to successfully hack his car.

"*Zhizn moya*, I'm here. You've got nothing to worry about," he assured me confidently, and no doubt he had a smile to match plastered on his face. "Are we getting close to your place?"

I purposely drove at the slowest speed possible to keep on stalling. With just a few more taps, his whole system would be at my whims. "Almost ish," I lied again.

The insistent blinking on my screen ceased with one final tap, causing me to break into a huge, victorious smile. Gritting my teeth, I held back my mischievous snicker as I sent the command to slow down and stop to Lev's car.

Blurring trees slowly came into focus as my vehicle came to a stop with Lev's car. Then, the sweet sounds of Lev's irritation and confusion filled my ears. Every spat of his infused my steps with an energetic pep as I went over to the driver-side door with a mad grin behind my helmet.

It took so much effort to wipe the cocky grin off my face, but I had to act innocent to give Lev the slip. So, begrudgingly, I wiped my face clean, painting on a confused and concerned expression before removing my helmet.

I wanted to smack Lev over the head when he threw the door open, nearly hitting me. The near miss wasn't why I wanted to whack him. It was how rough he handled the precious car. "*Đại ca*, what's wrong?" I asked in an overly sweetened voice, nearly cringing at how fake I sounded; I was afraid that I gave myself away with how off I seemed.

Huffing, Lev cussed under his breath while running a very frustrated hand through his hair. "I don't know, the car just stopped, and it won't respond or anything," he grumbled with a soft scowl.

Patting his arm to urge him out of the way, I lightly shoved his reluctant body when he dug his heels in a bit. "It's probably just a technical issue or something. Let me take a look." I lightly shoved him away from the car to give myself some more distance.

Climbing into the car with a smile, I shut and locked the doors before pulling my phone out to disable the system lock. Flashing Lev a grin, I flipped him off before flooring the pedal with an unhinged laugh filled with excitement.

Busting a U-turn, I rolled the window down as I passed a stunned Lev. "Thanks for the new car, babe!" My laughter echoed with the roar of the car as I sped down the road.

Humming to myself, I happily drove to the sweet hums and vibrations of the car, along with Lev's voice through my earpiece. I didn't reply to him, though, no matter how much he commanded me to turn around and pick him up, or else I would regret it later when he got his hands on me.

"Now, now, don't threaten me with a good time, little lion. I might just let you bend me over for a good spanking before I bend you over and turn your ass just as red," I teased back, laughing arrogantly to try and rile him up some.

"*Ty, malen'kaya shalun'ya, ya sobirayus'.*" Lev's shout of frustration echoed through my ear, along with a string of Russian. "Nicole! I swear, if I have to walk home in the rain, I'm going to fuck you until you drench yourself from head to toe in your own juices from squirting so much." As if that was a punishment.

"See you at home later, *đại ca.*"

Chapter 17

"Achoo!" My aching body jerked violently with my painful sneeze.

"*Bud' zdorov.*" Stepan chuckled in response, side-eyeing me smugly. "Feeling under the weather because of a girl?"

Slumping into the couch, I bundled the blanket around myself tighter before flipping Stepan off.

"Stepan, you're the last of us to talk." Nikolai chided in an almost flat voice as he entered the living room with a tray of stuff. "Or need I remind you of how you nearly broke your ankle and ended up in a boot a few weeks ago, along with a bad cold, after you let Hanna hunt your masochistic ass through the forest at 3 AM?"

Scoffing in disbelief, Stepan sputtered a denial out, only to have Nikolai deadpan him. "That—! How the hell did you even know about that!?" Stepan huffed with a red face, his arms crossing as he shrunk a little.

"I'm your big brother. It's my job to know everything," Nikolai replied with a smug chuckle.

A sharp scoff and curt laugh caused all of us to turn our heads in the direction of Angel as she approached us to set out another tray, this one filled with snacks. "Oh, that's a load of bullshit," she retorted, throwing Nikolai a teasing look. "He saw you and Hanna come in and asked about it. I didn't say anything, but Alexei did."

Nikolai's shoulders shook with a dry chuckle. "That's not how I remember getting the information." His eyes flashed Angel a knowing look, his lips curling into a devious smirk that lasted a split second. "But, whatever floats your boat, *lisichka*."

Scoffing, Angel rolled her eyes before turning her attention to me. "There's some water and medicine. Drink it all," she bit out, pointing at the tray Nikolai had brought out.

Nervously, I eyed the different glasses with a wary frown. "That looks like a glass of sewage, and the other looks like a cocktail of hot sauces." I deadpanned, shoving the tray away with my foot. "I'm not drinking that shit. I'll just tough it out." I stubbornly decided, doubling down by curling up on myself with a determined look.

Rolling her eyes, Angel waved her hand dismissively. "Fine, suffer then," she snapped back sarcastically as she turned around and walked away.

A moment of silence filled the room as Nikolai got situated in the armchair between Stepan and me. It wasn't too awkward of silence, thank God, just really tense as the three of us looked back and forth between each other.

"So... Are you going to tell us why you showed up to Kolya's house all soaking wet and grumpy as fuck? Or are we going to have to grill it out of you?" Stepan prodded with a curious but smug smirk. "Also, why the hell are you wearing a turtleneck? Actually, where the hell did you even get that? Pretty sure the only things you own is tactical gear, t-shirts, jeans, and business shit for work."

Okay, maybe this was a bad idea.

Groaning internally, I fought the feeling of regret that made my legs ache to book it out the door to avoid the embarrassment of confessing to my brothers.

"Lev, is everything okay?" Nikolai asked tensely, his face furrowing with concern as he leaned over and propped an elbow onto the arm of his chair. "You've been kind of strange lately, too. I've been meaning to try and sit you down to talk and see what's going on, but you're always running off before I get the chance."

Both my brothers looked at me with genuine concern, one of the more common looks, along with the 'what the fuck did you do this time' look. I may be the problem child, but I had my moments. They might not say it, but my brothers enjoyed the fact that I was a pain in the ass to them. I mean, how else was I supposed to show them that I cared for them? Still, no matter how tired they got of me a lot of the time, they cared for me deeply at the end of the day and watched out for me. They might not be as expressive or straightforward as now, but they had their ways.

They only ever intervened if things were *that* serious, like now.

"Lev." Stepan's stern voice softened more with concern with his expression. "What's going on? Does it have to do anything with the woman you had in the office last week?"

Well, that piqued Nikolai's interest with how his face lit up with curiosity as his head turned slightly to Stepan. "What woman?" His intrigued eyes peered over at me briefly.

Giving me a teasing, shit-eating grin, Stepan leaned back in his seat. "Oh, I don't know. I haven't asked him about her. Lev was all cute and cuddly with some cute chick last week when I entered his office to get something." His coyness made me want to punch him in the face.

Turning his head back to me, Nikolai studied me for a good moment before smiling and shaking his head. "I don't know if I should be worried or happy." Nikolai mused with a small laugh.

Slightly offended, I scoffed at my older brother. "Why would you be worried?" I was a grown-ass man who could very well make decisions that weren't utterly stupid.

Repressing a laugh, Nikolai looked at me with an 'Are you serious' look that had my eyes rolling in response. "Lev, all the women you've tangled with have either been gold-diggers, spoiled brats with no functioning brain cell, crazy flings, or flat-out psychos

." Nikolai deadpanned with a smug curl of his lips.

Opening my mouth, I was about to rebut him but quickly zipped my lips when Nicole's actions barreled through my mind like a derailed train on fire. "Oh, come on, don't act like your wives ain't crazy." Looking at Nikolai pointedly, I lightly jabbed a finger in his direction. "Angel is a sadistic psyyyy—"

The stern glare from Nikolai promptly shut my mouth. "In a good way." I nervously chuckled, diverting my gaze to Stepan, who raised an eyebrow at me. "You let Hanna chase you around with weapons and let her beat you up in the forest." Okay, it wasn't like *that,* but I needed to make a jab.

"All consensual fun," Stepan threw back with a smug grin. "Nothing wrong with a chase to get the adrenaline going."

Scoffing, I rolled my eyes and grumbled under my breath before stewing in an irritated silence. Taking a few deep breaths to calm myself, I let my question cook a bit in my mind. After an internal debate, I decided to bite the bullet. "How did your guys' wives claim you? Or, like, what mark did they leave on you to show the world you're taken?" Okay, maybe I should have sat on the question a little longer to make it sound less weird, but too late now.

A part of me wished I had a time machine to dial it back a few minutes when Nikolai and Stepan looked at me with bulging eyes. "Uhh, what?" Nikolai forced out, blinking his eyes a few times while rubbing his ear to clear it. "I'm going to need you to repeat that." His voice sounded wary and hopeful as if he hoped a different question would fly out of my mouth to prove that what he heard the first time was a fluke.

Nervously, I cleared my throat and sat up in my seat. "How did your girls mark you? Claim you." Okay, maybe I should have used my second chance more wisely because both my brothers looked at me with shocked faces. Judging by the look on their faces, they were probably debating whether or not to call Alexei in to do a psych eval on me. Yes, this has happened more times than I cared to admit.

"My wife gave me a ring?" Nikolai answered in a perturbed voice, holding up his hand to show the wedding band around his finger.

Stepan took a few more moments to join, sounding more unsure than Nikolai. "A collar? Ring?" The tan line caused by the leather cuff around his left wrist was visible after all this time. "I'm very confused. Is that what you were asking? Or what do you mean? Are you having a stroke?" Stepan's head tilted around, trying to get a closer look at me.

Annoyed, I scoffed and rolled my eyes. "No." I waved my hand in the air. "Like what did they put on your body, like what tattoo or scar or like permanent mark on your flesh." And cue the horrified and very concerned looks. If I was safe from a psych hold before, I probably wasn't after that.

"Lev," Nikolai groaned as he ran a hand down his face. "That should not have sounded as normal as it did, even for you." Sighing heavily, he leaned back fully in his seat, throwing back his glass of liquor. "Lev, do I even want to know the full story? Or am I going to need a full bottle of liquor before diving in?"

"You make it sound like I broke into Cortez's drug dens and stole their stash or went around terrorizing people for shits and giggles, which, no, I didn't do any of that," I quickly defended myself, glaring softly at Nikolai, who glowered at me from behind his empty glass.

The two of us stared each other down for a moment before I threw in the towel with a fed-up scoff. "I just... You know what, never mind." Throwing my hands into the air, I shot up from the couch and threw the bundled blanket onto it. "I'm going home."

At that, Stepan stood and got in my path, blocking me with his smaller frame. "Nah, ah," he objected, shoving at my chest. "You are going to sit your ass back down and give Kolya the migraine of his life," he demanded in a stern voice with a matching expression.

Gritting my teeth, I rubbed at my chest to ease the sudden, nagging ache. "I don't feel like it right now, and if you shove me again, I will knock your ass out." Brother or not, I wouldn't hesitate to push back if need be. Besides, it wouldn't be the first or last time we'd get into a tiff with each other.

"Lev, if you don't sit your ass down and start talking, then *I* will lay it out on the floor and start punching you until the words come out," Nikolai threatened me with a very heavy sigh and glare. "Don't make me get my wife."

Fuck no. I can't handle another psycho right now.

But speaking of my lovely she-devil of a sister-in-law...

"Oh my God, Nicki, I can't believe you did that, he's going to be so fucking pissed." Her faint laughter echoed from the kitchen, growing closer with her footsteps. "But come on, you gotta let me know who this man is. You can't keep edging me like this."

Nicki?

Shaking my head in denial, I forced all thoughts of her out of my mind. I fucking hated how hung up on her I was that hearing her name crashed her into the front of my head. I mean, Angel was probably talking to a different Nicki, for all it mattered. Nicki was a common nickname... Right? People used to tease Nikolai by calling him Niki until he smashed their faces and broke a few bones.

My nerves slowly settled as I rationalized everything.

If only it stayed that way.

If I wasn't stroking out before with my nonsensical question, then I would now at the sight of Nicole's smug face when she rounded the corner with Angel. "Oh, *đại ca*, you made it back." The damn minx had the gall to act sweet and innocent! Running up to me as if she hadn't just stranded me out in the middle of the road in the pouring rain!

Leaning up to her tippy toes, she grabbed the front of my shirt to pull me down a little. "Ange, meet my man." Nicole giggled, pressing a playful kiss against my cheek.

Angel choked on the water she had been sipping, going into a coughing fit until her face was red and to the point where I worried she might throw up because of how violently her body jerked.

Stunned, as if I'd been smacked in the face by a wooden plank, all I could do was watch Nikolai rush up to Angel and fret over her. Of course, Angel merely clung to him for support while waving his attempts off. "Oh my God, Lev, I am so sorry about your short life," Angel strained out between her struggles to control her fit.

"So much for not getting with a crazy chick," Stepan snickered, quickly stifling his laugh and covering it up with a cough.

Smiling innocently, Nicole looked up at me with devious eyes. "Told you I'd meet you at home."

"Blyat'."

Fuck me.

Chapter 18

Nicole

"YOU LEFT ME STRANDED in the middle of the road." Lev had to pause his complaining to sneeze. "In the pouring rain!"

Lev was quick to haul me over his shoulder like a sack of potatoes and took me to his place a little way from Nikolai's, after he recollected himself. So, we've been at his home (or was it technically ours now?) for a while now.

Suppressing my nervous chuckle, I awkwardly patted his shoulders a little before forcing him to lie down on his couch. "Now, now." Giving him a half-apologetic grin, I bundled his shivering body up tightly with the blanket. "I didn't leave you stranded... I left the bike for you," I retorted, letting my nervousness slip past my awkward lips with a curt chuckle.

Lev's body rumbled with his growl, and his beady blue eyes narrowed sharply at me. "It was locked for half an hour!" he half shouted before letting out another sneeze, followed by an annoyed grumble. "I swear, the moment I get better—"

I didn't give him a chance to finish his little threat. My index finger found the loop to his collar effortlessly under his turtleneck, curling around it and jerking his face to me as I leaned down close. "Now, now, I might give you some slack while you are sick—"

"Because of you!" Lev's voice cut out with a violent jerk of the collar.

Taking in a deep breath, I kept a rather sweet smile on my face as I kept talking, "As I was saying, I might give you some slack given your state, but that doesn't mean you can start mouthing off to me, got that?" My sweetened voice dipped lowly with danger toward the end as my face grew closer to his until there was only a mere inch between us. "Or you can continue to be a mouthy lil' shit and get punished for it later."

Out of the corner of my eyes, I caught the slightest glimpse of his neck muscles tightening. As his jaw clenched harder and harder, his eyes stormed over with conflict as he glared back at me. "You wouldn't. You're just an uppity little brat yourself who can talk a game, and that's it," he bit back with a challenging shine to his eyes.

Now, I expected to feel a little peeved at his doubtful backtalk, but I found myself laughing instead. I actually debated my sanity for a second there, not gonna lie. Getting a grip on myself, I let my laughter die out into an unpredictable grin that had Lev leaning back a little.

All bark and no bite, huh? We'll see about that.

Slipping more of my fingers under his collar, I hooked them around the thick leather and pulled him off the couch to the ground. "On your hands and knees," I commanded with an unhinged smirk to match my slightly crazed eyes.

When Lev showed no sign of following my order, probably because he was too busy ogling me with his wide eyes and gaped mouth, I gave his collar a firm tug. "Hands and knees, little lion. Don't make me repeat myself." To show him I meant business, I tightened my hold around the collar, making the leather creek under my grip.

His throat bobbed with a gulp before his eyes slowly looked away from me. "Y-yes, empress." His body shivered along with his words, and I couldn't help but smile from the surge of adrenaline bursting in my body.

Power burned proudly through my veins as I watched Lev shift around on the floor to his hands and knees. "Good boy." I barely recognized my own voice from how elated I sounded. "Now crawl." To encourage him, I lightly pulled him behind me down the hallway to his room.

Thankfully, Lev didn't fight me on that part. I wouldn't have been able to drag his heavy ass down the hallway if he decided to drop his weight. "Kneel and stay," I told him without a glance in his direction, leaving him at the door to go dig around in his drawers.

Of course, to no surprise, Lev had all I needed. It only took me a few seconds to pull out the rope, cuffs, and leather paddle. Tossing the items onto the bed, I took my sweet time strutting around the bed, slowly stripping to tease him as I stood at the foot of the bed. Casually, I finally turned my attention to Lev, who remained how I commanded.

Taking a moment, I drank in the image before me with a satisfied smile. Seeing Lev kneeling and watching me with such awe and desire in his eyes was so exhilarating. What made me puff my chest out with pride was seeing how Lev restrained himself to obey me. His hands remained on his thighs, but they constantly clenched and unclenched while his jaw ticked with every heavy rise and fall of his broad chest. The cherry on top of it all was the straining bulge in his sweatpants.

As much as I wanted to continue the fun, I could see the slight pallor on his tired complexion. "If you're too sick and tired, then we—"

Lev instantly shook his head in protest. "No, I'm fine to keep going, empress." The trust and happiness in his smile made it impossible to resist him.

"Safe-word?" I asked while picking up the leather handcuffs.

Sucking in a deep breath, his eyes lit up with excitement at the sight of the cuffs in my hands. "Bomb," he replied confidently with a widening smile.

"I won't cover your mouth or anything, but if you can't talk for some reason and need me to stop, then tap my shoulder three times, alright?" My wary eyes carefully studied his face and body for any signs of hesitation or reluctance.

Much to my relief, Lev displayed none of it. "Understood, empress." The way his shoulders fully relaxed melted my heart to lovey-dovey mush.

Cracking a proud and happy smile, I curled a finger at him to come hither. "Crawl to me, little lion," I commanded in a sweet and sultry voice. "But strip before you do." I wanted to see his body bend to my will; to watch every twitch of his muscles as he would move according to my commands.

Fuck, it was hard not to drool at the sight of his strong body becoming exposed to me. Every inch of this godly hunk belonged to me! Mine! He was all mine. All mine to touch, kiss, mark, and love. God, I wanted to jump him the moment he got on his hands and started crawling to me!

I've never felt such a rush like this, and I was sure that this would become a new addiction. Seriously, I was sure that I could possibly orgasm from ordering Lev around and watching him obey. Looking on in awe, I slipped my tongue out and licked my smiling lips. "That's it, that's my good boy, come to your empress," I praised him with a chest full of pride.

Letting out a content hum, I looked down at Lev as he stopped at my feet. "Look up at my cunt." The raw and lustful dominance in my voice took me back a little. "Look at how wet I am." I couldn't help but shiver with Lev when his eyes met my sex. "That's all you. You did that to me. Seeing you be such a good boy for me really gets me going." Reaching down, I gripped the back of his hair to force his gaze up at my thrilled face. "You like it when your empress gets wet for you for being good?"

My grip on his hair unintentionally tightened at the sight of his swollen cock twitching at my words, and another wave of heat consumed my body when I saw his thick tip weep with precum when he answered my question with a faint, "Yes, empress."

Releasing his hair, I apologetically stroked his head. "Here's what's gonna happen." Tracing his jaw, I gently cupped his face, smiling warmly when he leaned into my palm. "I'm going to put the cuffs on your wrists. Then, you are going to stand up and bend over the bed for a spanking." Lev's body tensed up with a sharp inhale before fully submitting to me again. "After that, you're going to get on the bed, and I'm going to cuff your wrists to the headboard before fucking you."

Lev's eyes darkened over with a deep want as his body subtly shivered under my touch. "Will you let me come in you?" His eyes softened pleadingly as he looked up at me with such hope.

Unfortunately for him, I was on too much of a trip to give it to him easily. My soft smile sharpened with an edge to it as my fingers gripped his chin. "Maybe, if you beg enough." Slowly, I ran my thumb teasingly across his bottom lip. "Ask me nicely and beg me."

Letting out a shaky breath, Lev leaned in close, caressing my thighs gingerly while peppering kisses to the inside of my thighs. "Please, can I come in you later when you fuck me? Please, will you let me fill your precious pussy with my cum? I need you to be full of me, please." His hot breath washed over my inner thighs and the edges of my aching sex, making me involuntarily shiver from the arousal that tightened my nipples into hard buds and caused my cunt to clench needily around nothing. "Please, empress, I need you to fuck me until I can't fill you no more until your womb is full of my seed."

Giggling, I leaned down and kissed his forehead. "You can breed me some other time when you are in tip-top shape, little lion." Tilting his face up, I take his shaky breath in a heavy kiss, groaning softly when I feel his tongue snake into my mouth.

Breaking the kiss with a satisfied sigh, I held Lev's face tenderly. "We also need to have *that* talk first before I let you fuck me, fill me, and knock me up," I remarked with a breathy chuckle. "For now, there are other—" To distract him, I pressed and rubbed the top of my foot against the underside of his pierced cock, making him gasp and grunt softly. "Matters for you to focus on."

Straightening myself, I dangled the cuffs in front of him. "Wrists," I demanded in a firm voice.

With an ounce of hesitation, he held his hands up to me with an eager smile on his face. "How many spanks are you going to give me?" His smile wavered slightly with wary as his head tilted and his eyes furrowed together.

Being the little shithead I was, I dragged out the suspense with a hum while I placed the cuffs on him. Seeing the way his chest rose and fell slowly with his tense breath was a little too amusing to cut short. I still couldn't get over the effect I had on Lev, how every little action or word could make him so happy or wary of me.

"Fourteen. Seven each side," I answered him after a very prolonged silence full of suffocating tension. "You can take it. I know you can." Playing with the loop of his collar, I lightly tugged at it a few times before firmly tugging it in the direction of the bed.

"Bend over, ass up," I commanded with a cheeky snicker. "Can't wait to mark that sexy ass of yours up." Well, it wouldn't be too bad today. I wasn't about to go hard with our first time.

Lev quickly rose to his feet and bent over the end of the bed, laying his upper body flat against the top of the bed with his bound hands stretched above his head. Then, slowly, he shifted his legs, relaxing them into a more comfortable position while taking some deep breaths.

Positioning myself right behind him, I reached out and grabbed his firm ass with a satisfied grin. Taking a moment, I groped him until the muscles of his back relaxed with his paced breathing and soft groans. Then, I picked up the flexible paddle, running it against the palm of my hand to get a good feel of the leather material along with how much give it had. After I got a good idea of the equipment in my hand, I placed the flat side of it against the curve of Lev's ass, shushing him softly when his body flinched in response. "I'm not spanking you yet, just letting you get a good feel of it." I wasn't *that* cruel, at least, not yet.

Inch by inch, I licked every inch of his luscious ass from bottom to top with the paddle until I had him shuddering under me. "Have you ever been spanked before?" I had to know to gauge the force behind my blows.

Craning his head back, he looked at me with half-hooded eyes. "No, but give me what you think I can handle. I trust you." His voice's lack of reluctance and hesitation instantly warmed my smile.

Patting his ass cheek reassuringly, I took a small step back to give myself some room to work. This all felt so surreal. I mean, my boyfriend was about to get spanked by me! The Lev Volkov, the Savage of the Volkov Bratva, was about to be spanked by *me*. Grinning madly, I pulled my arm back, keeping my eyes locked on his perky ass. "Count."

Smack!

Lev's body instantly jerked from the impact. "*Blyat'!*" He gasped while writhing against the bed.

I gave him a second to process everything before my anticipation built up. When the seconds ticked by and nothing else came out of his mouth, I pulled my arm back and delivered another hit to the other side—this one a little harder. "I said count," I reminded him sternly before pulling back and spanking his other side again.

Shoving his face into the bed, he let out a muffled cry with the next impact before coming up for a breath and counting. "Fuck! One! Two! Shit!"

Now, I had to give him credit for keeping his body fairly still. Not gonna lie, if it was me being spanked, I'd be trying to squirm away. I always had to be tied down or held down well if I ever took a spanking. So, the fact that Lev's stayed in one spot impressed me, especially with how hard I spanked him.

Smack!

"Ten! Fuck!" His body trembled with his heavy breaths, his toes digging into the hardwood floor to where they blanched.

Stepping up to him, I place my hands against his burning red cheeks. A low groan rumbled out of Lev's body when I softly rubbed and groped his ass. "You are doing so good, little lion." Leaning up on the bed, I ran my tongue along his muscular back to his ear, nipping it playfully with a giggle. "I'm so proud of you for being such a good boy for me. You're taking these spankings so well, and we're almost done. Just four more. You can do it for me."

Fisting his hair, I pulled his head back a little to claim his lips in a frenzied kiss. "Finish strong, and I'll let you cum in me all you want tomorrow." With one final kiss of encouragement, I pulled away and stood up straight behind him again.

The part of me that wanted to drag out the last four lost to my need to have Lev inside of me. In quick succession, the last impacts decorated his reddened cheeks with new marks, filling the room with the sweet sound of leather biting flesh and Lev's groans.

I didn't bother trying to catch the paddle when it slipped from my loosened grip. I was too busy climbing onto the bed and pulling Lev along until we were at the headboard.

Grabbing his face, I pressed a deep kiss against his lips, wasting no time shoving my tongue into his eager mouth and claiming every inch of it. Biting his bottom lip, I groaned hungrily as I pulled away. Hovering my face over his, I kept his face in my hands to look at his awe-struck expression and swollen lip for a few seconds before telling him, "On your back, arms up."

Chapter 19

FUCKING HELL, MY ASS burns! Fuck!

Seriously, I think I would rather take a damn bullet or a punch from Nikolai to the face rather than take another spanking.

I wanted to do nothing but lay on my front side and hope the stinging ache would go away sooner rather than later. Fuck, I knew things lingered and that spankings could be not fun sometimes, but fuck. Being on the receiving end of one definitely cracked my eyes open.

Although, as much as it sucked, a part of me quite enjoyed the pain. Yes, pain sucked, but the heat of pleasure that followed every throb heightened my body to new levels of pleasure. Fuck, I don't think my cock's ever been this painfully hard before. My hips were bucking against thin air in hopes of getting some kind of phantom relief to put me out of my lustful misery.

"Patience, Lev. You'll get fucked in a second." Nicole chuckled as she continued to fasten my wrists to the loops on the headboard.

I still had no idea how she would do that. My mind could only imagine her riding me, but something in her playfulness made me doubt its simplicity. At least I didn't have to wait long to find out because she didn't take long to restrain my wrists.

Settling between my legs, she leaned down and kissed me softly with such tenderness that shivers of warmth ran down my spine. "Relax, and let me take care of you," she whispered against my lips before kissing her way down my body.

Flashing me a wanton smirk, she pressed her tongue against the base of my cock, making me jump a little at the sudden heat and pressure against my aching member. Unable to help it, I threw my head back, letting out a strangled gasp of a moan when Nicole started to move up my shaft. Her lips curled around every piercing she passed, sucking and tugging at them until she got to my leaking tip. "Empress, please, I—*Der'mo*!" My body sunk into the bed as my hips bucked themselves at Nicole, needing to work more of my cock into her hot mouth and tight throat.

Nicole's hands pressed against either side of my hips, pinning them to the bed with a chuckle that had me shivering because I could feel the vibrations against my member. Gripping the rope that looped through the cuffs, I tugged at them in frustration when Nicole took me all into her mouth and throat but held my hips down. I wanted to thrust into her, fuck her pretty little mouth and tight throat—but I couldn't!

At least my torment didn't last long, thank fucking God. I only had to endure a few bobs of her head before she pulled off completely. I would've caved and begged her if she kept going for another second. Well, my desperate whimpers were probably close to full-on begging.

Her small hands pressed against the back of my strong thighs as she sat on her knees. Tiny pricks from her nails digging into me slowly turned painful the deeper they sunk into my flesh, but I didn't mind. My body shivered with delight in response to the pain. Now, what I didn't enjoy was the aching burn from her forcing my legs up and wide until I was spread with my knees to my chest.

Any discomfort I felt from being folded like a pretzel faded into the background the moment Nicole mounted me and slid herself onto my cock fully. The instant gratification made my eyes shut tight in bliss as my body shuddered delightfully with my audible gasp.

Nicole didn't give me more than a few seconds to adjust to her tight warmth before she started bucking her hips violently at me. Then, as if sending me into a whole new realm of pleasure wasn't enough, she threw me for a loop by spanking my aching bottom occasionally with her thrusting. "Look." Thrust. "At." Thrust. "Me." She demanded, rocking her hips harder with each word.

Forcing myself to come back down from the clouds, I focused my eyes on Nicole's smirking face. Shivers of excitement collided with my nerves at the sight of her darkened eyes full of lust and pride.

One look at her now, and there was no doubt in my mind that she was in charge.

For some reason, my body felt warm at the fact. All the tension in my body melted away to nothing the more I let myself go under Nicole's gaze that softened with each drag of a second. She still held the dominance in her strong eyes, but they gained an adoring fondness to them.

I didn't dare say it out of fear of fully manifesting it. I wasn't ready.

"I... Fuck!" Shuddering, I gripped the ropes again as I felt a wave of pleasure crash into me, pushing my need to empty myself into her hot cunt right to the edge. "Empress, please, I need to come," I whimpered needily, panting softly as I held myself back. "Can I come, please?"

Smiling down at me, Nicole shook her head with a chuckle. "Just a little more. I'm close," she told me between her moans.

Easier said than done with how good her hot walls felt squeezing me. "Nicole, I don't know if I can hold back for much longer. Your cunt keeps squeezing me." I strained out between my gasps and pants. "Empress, please."

"Just... One more... Fuck! Now!" Nicole's body tensed up with a deep moan, her hips jerking out of rhythm as her nails clawed at my legs.

The final vice-like squeeze from her shoved me over the edge into pure ecstasy. Groaning deeply, I bucked my hips up at her to bury myself as deep as possible. "Nicole!"

She moaned loudly after letting out a gasp. "Fuck! Lev!"

Fuck, I'm in Heaven.

I didn't care about how every fiber of my body ached with the after-shocks of my climax. Everything felt amazing, and I didn't want any of it to end. My balls ached with the need for another release, and I could feel my body responding to that primal want. I faintly registered the rocking motion of my hips through my hazy mind, and the feeling of friction from sliding in and out of Nicole pressed my protestant muscles onward.

"Oh fuck," Nicole groaned, pressing my legs down to the bed to keep my needy thrusting to a minimum. "Not tonight, little lion." She breathed out with an apologetic smile as her movements slowed to a stop.

Whimpering in protest, I continued to buck my hips at her. "No, please, empress, one more, please," I begged desperately through my struggles.

Just one more. I just need one more.

Nicole's eyes lightly scrunched with concern as she softly rocked her hips. "One more, but that's it. You're still sick and need rest," she told me in a soft and tender voice as she stroked my face with the tips of her fingers.

Pressing my legs apart more, she leaned down and kissed me softly with a big smile. "You are so amazing," she whispered sweetly against my lips before the movements of her hips became more exaggerated.

It wasn't like earlier. This time, her movements were deeper but slower. She wasn't fucking me this time. She was... Fucking hell.

"Don't fight it, Lev, just let yourself go. It's okay." Her sweet voice eased the rising tension to my internal conflict.

I couldn't bear to look at her, afraid that if I did, then my anxious eyes would find the underlying hurt breaking her pretty brown orbs. Even though she assured me otherwise, I caught the slight hurtful infliction in her voice—it was well veiled, though.

Shuddering, I let my head fall back against the pillow fully. I could face the music later. No point in letting my stupid stubbornness ruin this precious moment between us.

"*Zhizn moya*, let me touch you and hold you, please." The itching feeling in my hands turned into a full-blown ache that became rather hard to ignore after a while.

Smiling warmly at me, she carefully leaned down and distracted me with a sensual kiss, her tongue caressing mine as her hands slowly ran up my arms to my wrists. Some soft tugs followed by a few *clinks,* and my arms were free.

Immediately, I grabbed her face to deepen our kiss with a satisfied groan. Slowly, I trickled my hands down her body, feeling every inch of her tantalizing body to engrave her into my mind. My hands paused at her bubbly ass, squeezing and groping her round globes. The temptation to press her into me and speed things up twitched in my muscles, but I held the urge back.

"Fill me up again, Lev. I want your cum leaking down my thighs whenever I walk," she whispered against my lips before increasing her pace and force. "Let it all out in me." She spoke between her butterfly kisses on my face. "I'm still not on birth control."

And that did it. Hearing her tell me that, just, fuck.

Gripping her hips, I bucked into her once, twice, and the third was it. My overstimulated cock ached with my last release as my balls tightened rather painfully. Yeah, I was at my limit for tonight. Well, I hit my limit with the first release. This second one definitely laid my ass out.

"Nicole! *Blya, ya vlyublyayus' v tebya*," I gasped out between my tears.

I wasn't exactly sure why tears streamed down my face. Everything kind of broke with my climax.

The faint touch of Nicole's hands wiping my tears away kept me from totally losing it and making a fool of myself. "It's okay, *đại ca*." Her voice was so soft yet strong. "Let it all out. You're in a safe space, and I'm here." Her hands caressed my body in such a way that it was impossible not to lean into her. "You don't have to keep it all in with me. It's okay to be vulnerable with the right person and at the right times."

The right person...

It terrified me how I didn't question or doubt that one bit—Nicole being my *right* person.

Swiftly, in one smooth motion, Nicole set my legs to a comfortable position before laying down next to me, holding me tightly.

Together, we stayed in each other's arms for a long while. The air around me filled with Nicole's sweet nothings as her hands stroked the back of my head and neck soothingly. Besides her words, my soft sobs gripped the air. I stopped trying to control it after I found it futile; the tears and choked breaths came out whether I wanted or not.

"Will you be fine if I leave for a second to grab you some water and snacks?" She didn't sound eager to leave or anything. Honestly, she sounded reluctant to leave me.

Sucking in a deep breath, I nodded against her chest. "I think I'll be fine now. I... I don't know what came over me." I hated how vulnerable I sounded, but I couldn't steel my nerves back up right now. I felt exhausted for some reason, both physically and emotionally.

Nicole chuckled softly while giving me a look of understanding. "You had a drop, so it's normal. Besides, it's good to let it all out sometimes." Kissing my forehead, she smiles at me for a moment before slipping away from me.

As Nicole busied herself with gathering things, I slipped myself under the covers for some comfort. Thankfully, Nicole didn't take long to return with refreshments and some wet washcloths.

Smiling at me apologetically, she lowered the covers off my body to clean me. "It's okay, Lev. I'm not going to think or see you any differently. I know how tiring it can be to hold your head high and be the powerful leader everyone expects." Nicole was sympathetic and understanding, and the fact there was not an ounce of ridicule or judgment in her voice made me appreciate her more.

Forcing out a sad chuckle, Nicole gestured for me to sit up, waiting for me to do so before forcing me to drink some water. "I guess both of us are tired in a way." I couldn't really reply to her because she kept shoving handfuls of fruits and nuts into my mouth whenever I opened it. "We're both tired of being in charge all the time, me outside while you inside. It's going to be a good change for us both. You being in charge in the streets and me in the sheets." She gave out a soft laugh at the end before kissing my cheek.

A comforting moment of silence fell upon us as we sat there looking at each other as if we were the other's world. Well, that might be true for me the more I let myself get lost in her strong yet soft eyes and body.

Maybe my idea of straightening out our strange dynamic won't be too horrible. Not to say I had horrible ideas, but most of the time, they were on the fence at best.

Reaching out, she cupped my face and stroked my cheek with her thumb. "Rest." Her eyes gestured for me to lay down. "I gotta go talk with Angel for a bit, but I'll be here when you wake. I gotta go get some stuff to make us dinner, too."

"You and I have a lot to talk about later." My tired voice slowly faded as I felt the full effects of my crash.

I barely made it through three blinks before my heavy eyelids refused to open. It felt like someone superglued them down and slapped some duct tape over it for extra measure.

So much for closing my eyes for a few seconds.

Four fucking hours. I napped for four fucking hours! And that still wasn't enough.

When Nicole shook me awake, I wanted to knock back out. I probably would've if she hadn't been so insistent on getting my ass up so that I could eat.

Yeah, forget about the talk. I just wanted to eat and go back to bed at this rate. I could barely keep my eyes open while I waited for her at the dining table. Nothing against my lovely empress, but her voice grated my nerves the wrong way right now, too. My damn head felt so hollow that every little sound bounced around like a kid on crack in a bouncy house.

A hiss of pain slipped out between my gritted teeth from my body flinching at Nicole's concerned touch. "Lev?" Her frowning face moved within my sight as she sat beside me. "Did I push you too hard earlier? What's wrong? You're kind of scaring me." The tips of her fingers gingerly brushed my tousled hair out of my face.

Forcing a smile on my aching face, I nodded weakly. "Exhausted... It's not you. I was stubborn and pushed myself too much being sick." This cold was definitely going to get worse, and this wasn't me being a wimp with a man cold or whatever. Literally, I could feel the aches from my muscles seep down into my bones.

Sighing, Nicole's frown deepened as she leaned in and kissed my forehead. "I'm sorry. I shouldn't have engaged us in anything with you being sick." Her words rumbled against my hot body. "Eat up. I'll get you some meds and whatever concoction Angel and Alexei cooked up for you," she told me with a caring smile. "Then, we'll cuddle," she added with a bright grin.

Unable to muster the strength to respond verbally, I let out a small hum, smiling and nodding my head. Then, I turned my attention to the bowl of... Well, I don't know what it was actually. It kind of looked like porridge, but it was more mushy looking and white in color with bits of green onion, ginger, and chicken in it.

"Honey, it's not going to kill you. It's just some congee." Nicole's amused chuckle rang from the kitchen.

I wasn't inclined to believe that... Until I took a bite of it.

Now, I wasn't a picky eater by any means. Even if something was horrible, I usually grit my way through it unless it was *that* unpalpable, like now. The moment Nicole had her back turned to me, I spat out the mouthful I had back into the bowl with a silent gag.

"Hey, Nicki, I just don't have much of an appetite," I lied with a clenched heart.

The reasonable thing would be to tell her that the food tasted like utter sewage shit, but I couldn't bring myself to say anything bad about her food to her face. I didn't want to hurt her, which was stupid because I wasn't one to hold my opinions back.

"Try to eat some. You need some food in your body for energy," she spoke from the kitchen before the faint clinking of cups echoed through the air. "I hope you like it as it took me a while to make."

Fuck me.

Groaning internally, I hung my head in my hands, wishing the ground below me would open up and swallow me into a pit of suffering for being an ungrateful ass. Yes, it was a bowl of overly salted and sour mush, but she put her time and energy into making this for me.

Ugh! But I'll end up in the hospital with severe food poisoning if I eat more than three bites of this.

I mean, I could be a total asshole and tell her the truth... After I dig my own grave because six feet under was where I'd end up if I did tell her the truth.

On the other hand, if I lied and tried to eat this and somehow not die from it, then she might continue making it for me.

Either way, it was a lose-lose situation.

Fortunately, my muddled brain managed to cook up an idea that didn't seem half bad. "Actually, can you taste this for me real quick? It smells a little weird." She couldn't be mad at me if she tasted the bad food for herself.

A brief huff roughened the air up before the sounds of her exaggerated footsteps came my way. "Now I know you're full of bullshit because your nose is as stuffed as my cunt with your cum," she grumbled with a slight glare at me.

Mumbling disgruntledly, she snatched the bowl of food up, wafting it under her nose with a pensive expression. Her lips pressed into a thin line as her eyes darted to me suspiciously. "Did you spit in this?" she asked flatly with an unamused look.

Unable to help it, I let out a curt laugh. "Seriously? After you've sucked my face off and had my dick in your mouth, you're worried about a little spit?" I strained through a stifled laugh, snorting a little when my amusement slipped through.

Nicole gave me an offended scoff in response. Then, her foot shot out at me, kicking my calf. "Th-that and you spitting in food are two different things," she tried to argue with a waver to her voice. "It's just gross if you just spat in perfectly good food."

Crossing my arms, I leaned back in my chair. "Oh? Well, if it's perfectly good, then take a bite," I egged her on with a daring smirk.

Mocking me under her breath, she shot me a quick glare before shoveling a spoonful into her mouth.

One.

Two.

"Pleh!" Nicole's groaning mouth hung open with her tongue out. "What did you do to it?" she accused me emptily.

Scoffing, I laughed softly and rolled my eyes at her. "Nothing besides take a bite," I told her with a smug smirk.

Her fair face slowly blushed up with anger as she held a breath with puffed cheeks. "J-just go to the couch. I'm going to get some takeout," she said through gritted teeth, turning around and trudging away into the kitchen.

Barking out a victorious laugh, I half shouted, "Love you." It was meant in a playful manner, but maybe I should have used different words because the air around us stretched taut with tension.

"I know," Nicole teased back with a slightly forced chuckle. "Go get comfortable, turn something on the TV," she strained out with a smile on her face.

I felt like a complete asshole for hurting her, and I wish I could take it back. "*Zhizn moya*," I started with a regretful sigh.

"No," Nicole stopped me tersely with an outstretched hand. "Let's leave that bomb alone until you're ready to defuse it."

I hated the hurt in her smiling eyes, especially since I caused it. My mouth opened to protest, but my words refused to roll off my tongue. Closing my jaw, I turned around and went over to the couch in silence.

Great fucking job, you idiot.

Seething out a deep breath, I held back the urge to punch myself in the face. I really shouldn't have said *that* word. I mean, it wasn't as if I didn't mean it. Okay, never mind, that made me sound more like a jerk.

Sighing, I ran a hand through my hair, gripping at the honey-brown strands. I didn't know what to do. Apologizing and saying I didn't mean it *that* way would be a lie because I did love her. But fuck I hated that. Having feelings for someone, not the part about loving Nicole.

Ugh.

I was just a mess with my emotions. If it wasn't excitement or bloodlust, I didn't want to deal with it.

But that's not to say I didn't love Nicole!

I just...

Fuck me.

Chapter 20

~3 days later~

"Lev. Why do you have scissors to your neck?" Nikolai's heavy steps stopped with his tired groan.

"You know what? Don't stab yourself until I've had some coffee. I can't deal with your shenanigans this early in the morning without caffeine," he told me tensely with a hand held out in my direction. "Over thirty fucking years, and it never ends," he mumbled.

Scoffing offendedly, I loosely pointed the sheers in his direction. "Debating how much I value my life." I deadpanned, instantly regretting my choice of words because I didn't mean to sound like an ungrateful brat ready to end himself.

"Lev," Nikolai groaned into his hands as he ran it down his face. "We've talked about this. Not in the fucking house or my backyard. Listen, Stepan is just down the road." Okay, now he was fucking with me with how his voice picked up toward the end.

Rolling my eyes, I slammed the kitchen shears down onto the counter. "Kolya," I choked out, struggling for a moment to pace my breathing. "How do you do it? Love someone? How do you become fine with becoming so vulnerable?"

Dumbfounded, my older brother stood there, blinking at me. "Yeah, no, fuck this. I need my coffee first," Nikolai decided, before going about the kitchen, to put a pot of coffee on.

Sighing heavily, he leaned against the fridge and rubbed his temples as he waited for the pot to be done. "Lev, just spit it out because, honestly, you've been acting really strange the past few months." Nikolai's face softened with concern, genuine concern. "What is going on with you? Talk to me, please." It was rare for Nikolai to truly plead to anyone, let alone me.

Taking in a deep breath, I gripped the edge of the counter. "Nicole... I don't know what to do." I saw Nikolai's body twitch and his mouth open out of the corner of my eyes, but I held a hand out to stop him. "As in, I don't know how to process everything I feel for her."

Okay, maybe that didn't come out right either.

Frustrated, I ruffled my messy hair with both my hands. "I just..." Sighing exasperatedly, I pounded my fist against the marble countertop. "I know you and Angel didn't exactly start off normal and all, but how did you come to love her and just accept everything? Like I want to give Nicole my heart, but every time I think about doing it, I feel like an embarrassed clown. It makes me feel so broken and vulnerable." And now I probably sounded like a total wimpy loser.

"Ah, love." Nikolai gave a sympathetic chuckle before stepping up to me and patting my shoulder. "It's not easy."

Turning away for a moment, Nikolai rummaged through his kitchen. I paid him no mind because there was nothing to watch—I've seen him go through his own kitchen numerous times.

A sudden *clink*, along with the vibrations of thick glass next to my hand, made me give Nikolai my full attention again. "Kolya, even I'm not that stupid to drink at eight in the morning." I deadpanned, flickering my eyes at the bottle of vodka he set out.

Raising his eyebrow, Nikolai breathed out a chuckle. "Oh, you're going to need it. I'm just being nice and giving it to you beforehand," he joked with a dry chuckle. "You've got a long road ahead of you, little brother."

Going back to the coffee machine, he filled his mug. "Love is complicated, even when it is clear. It makes you turn into someone you are not, often for the better, though." Flashing me a sympathetic smile, he leaned back against the counter, sipping at his coffee. "It's going to be a hard one for you to swallow given how you are, but whatever is happening with Nicole, let it."

Reeling back a little, I crossed my arms and scoffed. "Who said it had to do anything with Nicole?" I got a little defensive because I hated how Nikolai pried at the right places.

Letting out a ridiculous scoff, Nikolai looked at me sardonically with a smug smirk and raised brow. "Lev, you've been acting strange ever since Nicole showed up in your life. It's not hard to put one and one together to make two." He mused with a chuckle.

Shaking his laugh off, he looked at me seriously. "Don't fight it, Lev. Yes, opening yourself to someone like that is scary, but trust me, it's worth it. If Nicole is the right one, then she will treasure the fact you made yourself vulnerable to her because you trust her," pausing, he took a few sips of his coffee with a satisfied sigh, "It's okay to let other people in Lev, especially if your gut and heart are pulling you in their direction. I know it's not easy for you to let people in. It's who you are, but don't let that stubborn shield of yours prevent you from having the best life."

Pulling his phone out, he smiles at the screen for a good moment before tucking it away. "I can't tell you how to love someone. That's something that comes naturally to you and your relationship with your partner. What I can tell you is that you really have a rough road, but there's a field of happiness at the end of it. Just... Have a lot of patience, don't punch first before you ask questions, or God forbid, shoot first before questions," Nikolai jabbed at me with a snicker on the last part.

"That, and a nice glass on the rocks helps," Nikolai added with a soft laugh. "Also, what were you doing with the sheers in my kitchen?" he inquired with a somewhat concerned raise of his eyes.

Smiling and chuckling awkwardly, I rubbed the back of my neck, tugging at the collar. "I was hiding from Nicole... While debating whether or not to cut her collar off." I also might have been hiding to avoid another potential case of death by poisonous food.

Yeah, Nicole was still in denial about her food being *that* bad despite being unable to stomach all the meals she had made for us. Every meal she tried to make us resulted in takeout. I really should ban her from the kitchen before the fumes kill us. Honestly, I adored Nicole from the bottom of my fucked-up heart, but that woman cannot cook and should not be allowed within a ten-foot radius of a kitchen.

The faint patter of footsteps had Nikolai and me looking over to the kitchen's entrance. "Oh, Lev, hey," Angel greeted me with a sleepy smile before going over to Nikolai and snuggling herself into him. Nicole's looking for you. I think she said something about sending you back home for breakfast?"

Instinctively, my stomach churned with a threat to throw up at the thought of putting anything Nicole made into my mouth. "Nope. Tell her I drowned in the pool or that Kolya finally had enough of me and punted me into a volcano." I threw my head back with a groan of complaint. "Listen, Nicole is lovely, but—"

"Yeah, she can't cook for shit." Angel laughed tiredly. "I'm surprised you're not in the hospital getting your stomach pumped or something." Angel's laughter was a little too amused for my liking.

"You just want to see me suffer, you sadist," I grumbled with a roll of my eyes. "God, you and all your friends are batshit crazy, I swear."

"Oh, as if you and the others are saints yourselves," she retorted with a scoff and chuckle.

"Compared to you? Yes," I playfully argued back.

To prove a point, I held my hand up and started counting off with my fingers, "You love to torture people, Hanna's another me, only more psychotic, and Nicole is a bomb obsessed techy who lost a few screws. Oh, and you agreed to marry Kolya knowing fully well who he is. Also, you get along with Alexei way too well, who, by the way, is a fucking psychopath." Holding up my other hand, I continued to list things off, "Hanna chases Stepan through the woods like a psycho-killer, and I'm pretty sure she and Stepan do a bunch of other shit that would be considered a little crazy."

Glancing over at the bottle of whiskey out of the corner of my eyes, I debated cracking it open for a few sips. I quickly shoved the thought aside, though, to continue. "Then we have Nicole, who loves bombs a little too much. I'm not even going to go into the virtual havoc she can cause nor the crazy shit she'll pull." Anyone ballsy enough to attack a gang member outright definitely had a few crazy bones in their body.

Snickering, Angel looked at me with a deviously cruel smirk. "Shit, like tattoo and collar you?"

Nikolai choked and spat out his coffee at his wife's words. "Excuse me, what?" He stared at me with wide eyes, hoping something got lost in translation.

Paying my brother no attention, I darted over to Angel, slapping my hand over her open mouth before she could spew more embarrassing shit. "Nothing, *bratok*, nothing." I tried to wave him off with a nervous chuckle and grin.

Prying my hand off, Angel digs her fist into my gut, shoving me away. "Oh, come on now, Lev, it's not as bad as high school prom night." I wanted to strangle her grinning face—not to kill or harm her, just playfully!

My head instantly snapped to Nikolai, and my face paled a little with horror as my eyes widened. "You told her?" There were some secrets between Nikolai and me that were sacred, prom night being one of them.

Angel spoke up for him before any words could fly out of Nikolai's stunned mouth. "Of course, he told me." With a devilish grin, Angel leaned up to my shocked face. "He's *my husband*, so he tells me everything." As if to further egg me on, she leaned even closer. "We tell each other *everything* and hide *nothing* from each other."

Directing everything to Nikolai, I stepped up to him, grabbed the front of his shirt, and jerked him a bit. "You said you wouldn't tell anyone about my dick getting stuck," I spoke in a rushed voice that was barely above a whisper.

"Oh, is that what happened? I thought it was about you being stupid." Angel's nonchalant sigh made me shake my brother again. "Or that time he had to pick you up."

"You told her *all* of that?" I freaked out slightly, feeling the world around me sink into my body, weighing me down with dread and embarrassment. "You promised me none of it would ever see the light of day...!" I hissed out in a raspy whisper.

Recovering from his stupor, Nikolai shoved me off. "You need to back off," he curtly told me with a jab to my chest with his finger.

Then, he turned his attention to Angel, who immediately wiped the grin off her face. "Wait, Kol—" Her words choked out with a gasp from Nikolai's sudden neck grab.

Pulling her right up to him, he leaned down until his face was mere inches from her. "You are going to march your bratty ass back to our room, bend it over our bed, and wait for me to come punish it. If you're going to be a brat this early in the fucking morning, then you damn well better be prepared to take it."

Now I couldn't help but be a smug asshole when I saw her get her dues. Lightening my expression, I gave her an 'Oh, you're in trouble' kind of look while flipping her off. As I watched the scene unfold before me, I leaned back against the counter with my arms crossed. Of course, once Nikolai was done with her, he turned his attention to me.

"And you." He jabbed a finger in my direction. "You need to stop jumping ahead of shit before you hear the whole situation." Straightening himself, he looked at me sternly. "I told her nothing about your high school prom night, where you had to call me after getting shit-faced drunk and got your stupid pierced dick stuck in a girl's braces." Then he had the gall to smirk and tilt his chin at me smugly. "Until now, because you were a dick to me."

Angel sputtered a laugh, holding onto her round stomach as she strained to stop. "For the record, Nikolai never told me anything." Breathing deeply, Angel held onto the counter for support. "I was just being a bitch and digging at you for the hell of it."

Motherfucker. I got played.

Growling out of frustration, I threw my hands up in the air and turned to leave. "You two are assholes," I half shouted as I began to walk away. "I'm not saving your asses in the field after this, " I half-joked, grumbling a bit under my breath.

Deciding to take my chances with Nicole rather than stick around with my brother and his wife and risk more embarrassment. At least I could still show my face with food poisoning. No way would Angel let the new ammunition about my high school horror go; it was only a matter of time now before she'd use it to blackmail me into something.

Going back to my place, I decided at the last minute not to enter, opting for my garden for some more moments of peace before I had to face the music of life. Don't get me wrong, I wasn't displeased with Nicole or anything like that. I really wasn't trying to avoid her for the sake of it; I honestly needed some fresh air and time to myself to go over the past few days.

Nothing exciting happened the past three or so days besides adjusting to Nicole being around. Things were fine, but we've been living in some strange honeymoon haze. I'd go to work during the day, occasionally chat with Nicole via text during my time away, grab little treats for her on the way home, come home to either takeout or dinner prepped for me to cook, and we'd cuddle and fuck before bed.

Life was good, ideal even, but there was always a tension between us about the shit we had to address. We haven't poked the situation with Nicole and her parents with a ten-foot pole, nor have we touched my bratva business. Truthfully, I didn't want to involve her with my family's mafia turmoil, but it would seem that she had her hand in the pot already via Angel.

After a little digging, I discovered that Nicole was the other techy genius behind Angel's success besides Bao, who apparently was her younger brother. Strangely, I didn't find anything about Bao and Nicole being siblings. All I dug up about Nicole's familial background was her mother, father, and two younger brothers. I met one of her brothers, the one who was currently CEO of N.Q. Tech. Yet, when I questioned her parents about her other brother, the middle child, I was met with extreme detest before it flipped to a strange denial.

Come to find out, Bao was cut out of the family for being gay, and apparently, his name wasn't Bao. He was born Jacob Chau, but after high school, Jacob dropped off the face of the earth from my search. From what

Bao and Angel told me, he came out to his parents at eighteen, and that was the last of Jacob Chau. His parents cut him off and out of their lives forever. Then, wanting a new identity for himself, he created new records for Bao Vu and has been living with Greg ever since his parents gave him the boot.

Even though their parents cut Bao out, Nicole still kept in contact and maintained the close relationship they'd always had growing up. Also, Nicole was one of the few who Bao came out to first and fully supported him through everything.

As crazy as Nicole was, after hearing about her softer side, I found a new fondness blooming for her. It would seem that her overly confident front was more or less a shield from what Angel and Bao have told me. Yes, she was a powerful and confident woman deep down, but she piled it on more than needed to make her mark in society.

No matter, she didn't need to do any of that with me. There won't be a second in our relationship where I wouldn't treat her like the queen she was. I'd stand before her out in the world, protect her from everything so she could live her best life. Then, at home, she could rule all she wanted over me.

"Little lion, there you are!" Her sweet voice brought an internal groan to my peaceful thoughts.

Lulling my head back, I watched Nicole come over to me with a bright smile beaming on her face. Just as she was about to sit down on the ground next to me, I threw my arms around her waist to pull her into my lap with a soft smile of my own. "I thought I made it clear that my lap is your seat from now on," I teased with a widening grin, earning a chuckle and a playful smack to the chest from her.

It only took a second for her face to twist into a stern and concerned expression. "What's wrong? And don't you say nothing or give me nothing either." Sighing heavily, Nicole straddled my lap to face me fully. "I know things have been really good between us the past few days, but we're both deluding ourselves into the whole white picket fence dream. There's a lot we have to talk about that we've been kind of actively ignoring."

Well, glad to see I wasn't the only one who thought so.

Smiling rather flatly, I reached out and tucked her hair away from her face. "I don't know where to start," I admitted with a sigh of defeat.

Pursing her lips in thought, Nicole laid her head against my shoulder. "Well, let's see, my parents stole my company from me, tried to ship overseas to marry me off for business connections, I ran away and basically went psycho, and now I got you," she lightly joked with a chuckle. "In all seriousness, though, we'll figure something out with my parents on a later day after I chat with Angel and Bao some more, once I get settled here."

Taking a deep breath, she snakes her arms around my midsection, squeezing me tightly. "Besides that, we need to talk about us." And here came the dreaded topic. "It's been quite a bit for both of us the past few days, and I know you've said you're fine and all every time I checked in on you after sex, I'm still just worried about you because I know this is all new for you." Leaning her head back, she looked up at me with scrunched eyebrows.

Assuring her with a confident smile, I leaned down and kissed her longingly. "Yes, I really am fine, and more. Yes, it's just taking me a little longer to process everything, but it's more of a me thing." Smiling tenderly at her, I stroked her cheek with the back of my finger. "I mean, I shoved my finger in your ass yesterday, and you took a few minutes to fully process it, so imagine it for me." I teased with a soft laugh.

Rolling her eyes, she flicked my nose. "Fair point, but it just worries me a little when you go a little quiet or disappear to go think without really letting me know." Her smile faltered into a lopsided frown. "I'm just afraid of you not coming back to me because I had pushed some limit I shouldn't have or done something wrong, or that I'd wake up to some note saying you can't do this anymore." She voiced her worries to me with a cracking voice.

The tension in my face softened as I cupped her face and shook my head in denial. "*Zhizn moya*, no, never. I would never be such a coward to slip from you like that without some word or explanation to your face," I assured her firmly.

The words gnawed at my tongue, but I couldn't get them out.

I love you too much to hurt you.

Chapter 21

Nicole

KISSING LEV DEEPLY, I let my hands caress the back of his head and neck before following the edge of his collar to the loop. "One step at a time, we'll make it," I assured him confidently. "As long as we communicate with each other, that's what matters."

I knew this was easier said than done. Communicating with a team or others without too much care for their feelings or knowing they don't have personal ties with me was different than communicating with my intimate partner. With Lev, I had to worry about hurting his feelings, wording things a certain way, watching my tone, and whatnot. I didn't want to be a dick to Lev, so I couldn't treat him like I would have my workers.

"I don't know what to do with my parents yet, as I've said. I mean, it would be easy to pull everything out from under them right now, but my gut is telling me it's a bad idea because no doubt they have some other plans in case shit goes belly up." Sighing, I gnawed at my bottom lip with irritation. "We just need to shut down all their escape routes before we strike."

My stomach churned with unease whenever I thought about what Lev told me about my parents doing some business off the books. I needed to figure that out before doing anything else. I already had a list of their business associates compiled from their electronic footprint, and I had other connections to reach out to get anything amiss if they didn't have some record of it online.

Which reminds me...

"You want to go out on a date tonight? Angel and I, along with the others, are gonna hit the autumn festival in Asian Village later tonight." It was meant to be a friends' trip for us to catch up and have fun, but Nikolai insisted on going with Angel, which then led to Stepan tagging along because of Hanna, so might as well add a third Volkov brother into the mess. "I'm also meeting up with some associates of mine to see if I can get more information about my parents."

"Like hell am I letting you go alone then," Lev immediately agreed with a stern look at me. "I would have agreed anyway because no way am I passing up a date with you, but knowing you're going to be conducting dangerous business? Like hell am I staying home after hearing that? What kind of boyfriend will I be if I let you go to a shady meeting alone?" His words rambled on and on about how I would even think about doing something so stupid alone and yada yada yada.

He didn't shut up until I grabbed his face and kissed him. "Got it, don't go anywhere without my *đại ca*," I teased with a giggle. "It's going to be nice knowing I don't have to be on guard all the time out on the streets now, so thank you." The mere thought of Lev being my personal bodyguard calmed my nerves. Even before we solidified our dynamic, when he was stalking me, I felt safe knowing he was there.

"How's bratva business?" I wasn't too involved much with his family business, not even with tech-related things. I used to help Angel a lot until I got too busy with my business, then after that was taken from me, I enjoyed my early retirement. For the most part, Bao handled things perfectly fine. Occasionally, I'd help if more manpower was needed or if the rare thing was out of Bao's scope—and that was really rare given how Bao knew all I did.

Lev took a deep breath before answering me, "Good, for the most part. Overall, everything has been pretty smooth, just some trouble stirring with those who were with the Qing Triad before getting a little too comfortable with us and trying to pull some shit."

Honestly, and I didn't want to say anything about it out loud, but I was thoroughly surprised at the lack of uprising from Lady Qing's loyalists. However, I wasn't at the same time, given the load of blackmail the bratva had on nearly all the members with their shutdown of Lady Qing. Now, digging out all the corpses from everyone's backyards was rather interesting, and I did take part in that because it was such a big project for Bao to handle alone.

Still, blackmail or not, I was surprised at the lack of resistance to the merge of the triad into the Volkov Bratva. I know a lot got screwed over with the merge. Well, screwed over in the sense that they couldn't run their business dirty anymore. The Volkovs ran things rather cleanly and had rules, while Lady Qing didn't. Honestly, the merge was akin to that of taming wild wolves with the acquisitions from the fallen triad.

So far, the brothers have done a rather good job keeping everyone in line, and if anyone dared to step out of it, then, well, there'd be a new person behind the line. That wasn't common, though, not after the house cleaning Nikolai and Angel did.

Unfortunately, some slimeballs, like my parents, remained. Of course, they had a close eye on them, but rats would be rats. There was no way for every second of their life to be tracked and reported.

Sometimes, I did feel a little bad for not helping more, knowing the situation of everything, but I just wasn't in it. I was tired and exhausted of everything and wanted a break from it all. Although, the break kind of stretched on and on until it hit this weird retirement funk I was in.

Not gonna lie, a big part of me deep down craved the action and chaos again. To hack into the enemy's system on a wire or send the enemy into a frenzy by whacking their system up was a rush I missed. Also, I missed blowing shit up. Angel was a little too passive to use the explosives I gave her, but I lacked such restraint. I mean, yeah, I was probably injuring or killing a few innocent lives too many whenever I threw a live one into the field, but why did that matter? They made their choice to work for the wrong side.

I had so many bombs sitting around in storage that I felt bad for. My poor babies would probably never see the light of day and experience the cathartic boom of glory unless I put myself back out there. Actually...

Slowly, my eyes trailed up Lev's body with a growing smirk. "Hey, if I gave you some bombs—"

Unfortunately, he didn't even let me finish before shooting me down. "My brothers would have my ass grilled and banned from the field if I ever caused that much damage, so no." At least I could appreciate his disappointment and his sense of responsibility.

Sighing with a pout, I pressed myself into Lev's body, remaining comfortably for a moment before playfully nipping at his neck with kisses. "Something is bothering you," I noted out loud with a concerned hum.

"It's... Complicated," Lev grumbled with a heavy sigh. "It's a me problem, mostly. The other thing that's bugging me is your parents and just everything with the old triad members and whatnot." Breathing deeply, Lev held me tightly against him and kissed my forehead. "But those things will have to take time, unfortunately."

Pressing my lips into a thin line, I held myself back from pushing Lev to open up. As curious as I was, I didn't want to push him away by accident. He'd tell me when he was ready, or at least I would give him more time to reach out to me before I pried at him.

So, relenting with a curt hum and nod of my head, I kissed the underside of his jaw. "Whenever you're ready, I'm here," I let him know with a warm smile. "Also, I'm here for everything, whether that be for you to vent about your day at the office or about the stupid man whose face you had to smash in." Reaching up, I played with the edges of his messy bangs. "I'm not some innocent housewife who's oblivious to everything, and you don't have to keep me in the dark for my sake either."

Unfortunately, I knew about all the ugly in the world and have dealt with them. As nice as it would be to live an ignorantly blissful life, I'd go mad with guilt. The only reason why I didn't pack my bags and move to some tropical getaway or the damn mountains was because I wanted to keep my nose in everyone's business. I wouldn't be able to live with myself knowing I could help Angel and the others with burning scumbags off the streets but didn't.

Me and my fucked-up morals.

"Oh, and we need to stay out a little late tonight. I have to meet with my supplier, too." Tonight was going to be a busy night for me, that's for sure.

However, speaking of supplies, that reminded me of something else. "We also need to go back to my cabin to pack my shit up and move it into your place. And I will probably need a shed or a work area." Okay, maybe not, probably because I will need an area. I couldn't stick everything into one of Lev's guest rooms and turn it into my office/workspace. I had too much shit and needed a lot of room.

Also, I was pretty sure Lev wouldn't want explosives inside his actual house. Personally, I kept work and home separate, except for right now, because I only have a cabin to work in. Still, I kept my worktable as far away into a corner as possible.

Shaking his head with a chuckle, Lev kissed my forehead before grasping my chin to tilt my gaze up at him. "Whatever my empress wants, she'll get. As long as you don't burn my garden down, I'm fine having a shed out in the back." His tone was light-hearted, but his intentions were serious. Without an ounce of hesitation, he asked in an eager voice, "How big of a work-shed do you want or need?"

"Uhh... Maybe like a thousand square feet?" I mean, ideally, the bigger the space, the better, but I was basically asking for a small ass house to myself the more I thought about the space I wanted.

Unsure, I scrunched my lips up while looking at Lev nervously. Then, much to my surprise, he didn't flip out on me. "Alright, consider it done, but it might take a while, a few weeks, give or take, but I'll get started on it in the next few days," he replied with a proud and determined grin. "Getting the materials will be easy. Just working out times to build it is going to be a little tricky, but I'll work it out."

Looking at him quizzically, I let my head naturally tilt to the side. "You make it sound like *you're* going to be building it." Unless I was sorely mistaken and misunderstood him greatly.

Giving me a confused look of his own, he studied me intensely with his mesmerizing blue orbs before his lips broke out in an amused smile. "Of course, I'm building it for you. You asked me for it, so I'm giving it to you. Like hell am

I going to let you work in some house that some other man built." He scoffed playfully with a dry chuckle. "I'm your man now, so that means I take care of you and everything pertaining to you."

Okay, that's rather sweet.

Unable to help it, I cracked a big, happy smile. "I can't believe I'm getting sappy with you," I voiced my thoughts out loud with a chuckle.

Snuggling into him, I enjoyed his presence for a long while, taking in the dream-like scenery of his garden basking in a lovely day. "Did you really make this garden yourself and kept it up to this day?" Honestly, it was a little strange for me to fully comprehend because a hulking bratva boss like Lev was the last person on this earth I expected to have such a green thumb and peaceful gardening side to him.

I couldn't help but giggle softly when Lev's face went bright red. "Y-yes, but don't tell anyone... Everyone thinks I hire people to plant and upkeep it all," he admitted with an almost cherry-red face. "It calms me and reminds me of my mother." His voice dipped with his sad smile as his eyes gained a nostalgic glaze to them.

Logic grabbed at my shoulders—and failed—to keep me from spewing my next question. "Where is your mother? If you don't mind me asking?" Maybe it was a little too soon in our relationship to ask about it? But curiosity killed the cat, as they all liked to say.

Thankfully, I had a lot of lives.

The air around us thickened with sadness as tension weighed his smiling face down. It made me feel bad for asking when Lev's eyes grew glassy and distant. But I knew nothing about his family besides his brothers and whatever records there were of his parents stored electronically.

"Gone, but in a much better place." His low voice cracked slightly at the end with his sigh. "Though, I suppose you want more than just the generic answer." He dryly chuckled.

Shifting around, he slouched a bit against the tree he'd been sitting against. "It was about five years ago," he started with a hard swallow. "It was... A heavy day... Nikolai had just come home from Russia with our sister's ashes, and the rest of us had gotten back from a long night of a violent turf war."

Averting his eyes to the ground, he stared at nothing as he mindlessly stroked my arms with his thumbs. "All hell broke loose after Nikolai told us all what happened over in Russia and what became of Natasha, and it just all kind of broke my mother."

I could feel his body tremble against me with his heavy breaths, and I gave him the space needed. Leaning against him, I calmingly stroked the length of his forearm, letting him know that I was there for him. "My mother snapped, attacked my father, and the two got into it for a while before my father left the house." Burying his face into my hair, he breathed deeply. "We all went to bed for the night after grieving together for a while, but we woke up in the middle of the night to my father and mother going at it again. By the time we got to them, my father had drawn his gun on my mother..." His shoulders shook with his hitched breaths. "We were too late to stop him from pulling the trigger."

The creaking of Lev's jaw and teeth grinding together echoed faintly in my ears. "He was pissed at her again for giving him useless children and whatnot because the bratva he married my sister off to get on his ass, before Nikolai tore their empire down to the ground and burned it all to ashes along with their bodies." Lev's voice perked with proudness but also with some jealousy. "Guess everything kind of spilled out with the alcohol in his system, and he really just exploded."

"Him pulling the trigger on our mother set something off in my brothers and me that night as well. We all jumped him and trapped him in the basement for a week, where we all took turns venting out all our years of pent-up resentment." The twisted smile that curled at his lips with each and every word sent a shiver of unease down my spine, especially when I caught the way his eyes sharpened dangerously with cruel pleasure. "Then, to watch the house burn down on top of him was fucking perfect." And now he looked and felt a little psychotic.

"Y-you had sister?" Maybe a change of topic would deter him from going batshit crazy on me.

The only person who was allowed to be a psycho in our relationship was me.

Inhaling deeply, Lev's crazed gleam faded from his eyes as he hummed and nodded in response to me. "Yeah, Natasha." His smile softened fondly as his fingers played with the tips of my hair. "She came after me but before the twins." Then, the warmth slowly faded to a stale sadness. "We all doted on her. Well," Lev scoffed, "everyone but my father, who only saw her as a means to an end."

Straightening himself out, Lev squeezed me tightly with a flat hum. "My father arranged her off into marriage to some rival bratva to form a truce and ally, but all they did was torture and kill her after my father shipped her over there." His voice sank into the depths of emptiness with his frown. "We tried to hide her, and we almost managed to sneak her out of the country... But he caught us by sheer luck at the last minute."

Frowning sympathetically, I cupped and stroked Lev's face. I hated how dejected he sounded. "Little lion, you guys did what you could, and sometimes, the universe is just a piece of shit to us despite our efforts." No doubt the near success got Lev to this day—the 'what if' of it all.

"After we got radio silence from the other side, Kolya took it upon himself to fly over to Russia to see what was going on and to bring Natasha back... But, he said he was far too late..." Dragging a hand through his hair with a deep sigh. "Kolya refused to tell us the full truth and still does to this day."

Now, it was my turn to frown deeply. Seeing the way his face tore with agony, sadness, and anger made my heart sink into my gut. "But you found out," I stated blatantly.

Almost robotically, he responded with a nod. "I contacted officials over there after drinking too much one night." Swallowing his feelings, he lulls his head backward to blink away the tears I saw forming. "And I've regretted it ever since."

Lev's body shivered with his hitched breath, and I could see him trying to hold himself together. I wasn't about to have any of that, though.

Prying his arms off and shoving them away, I slid out of his lap to the ground next to him. Reaching out, I coiled my arms around his shoulders and neck and tipped his big body over. "Lev." I sighed softly as I forced him to settle in my lap. "Let it out." I urged him with a comforting smile. "It's okay," I assured him with a kiss to his forehead. "I'm here for you."

Whoever said grown men shouldn't cry needed to go throw themselves off a cliff right into a shark's toothy mouth. Emotions were a vital part of being human, and that included expressing them. Lev could only put so many bullets into so many things or smash his fists into so many faces and bodies before another outlet would be needed. Besides, being a violent little shit won't do much to curb his guilt and underlying sadness.

Stubbornly, Lev resisted me with a blank stare, but something in him broke after a while. It started with a shiver, which turned into a shudder, then full-blown shaking as the tears came like a broken dam. Hugging my waist tightly, he buried his face into my lap and sobbed away.

Did seeing Lev cry make me happy? No, not in the slightest, but I knew how cathartic it could be.

Sitting there against the tree, I let my bratva boyfriend cry it out while soothingly petting his head. "I'm proud of you, Lev," I admitted with a prideful smile.

Chapter 22

Nicole

"TOP MIDDLE DRAWER OF the black dresser," Lev said lazily from the bed, not looking up from his phone.

Completely lost, I spun around with my hands on my hips. "Huh?"

Once again, without looking up from his screen, he replied rather flatly, "Your Ruggish Red lipstick is in the top middle drawer of the black dresser, specifically in the upper right-hand corner because it tends to roll around with how hard you open and slam the drawer."

Unable to come up with a proper response, all I could do was sputter and scoff as I trudged over to the black dresser and opened the middle drawer of the top row. Mocking him under my breath, I was about to spin around and snark at him that my lipstick wasn't there until I caught it in my field of vision at the last minute.

Zipping my lips shut, I pressed them into a tight line as I snatched the tube of lipstick up. Grumbling to myself internally, I applied the lipstick rather testily before slamming it down onto the counter. Crossing my arms, I spun around and glared softly at Lev with an angry pout.

Probably sensing my glaring eyes, Lev glanced up at me with a quirked brow. Silently, he stared at me quizzically before giving me his full attention as the corner of his lips smirked. "You always wear Magjik's Ruggish Red with your fancy clothes that are black or gray in color," he answered my silent question as if he had read my mind.

Okay, officially a little creeped out by Lev for the first time ever.

"What?" Lev shot back with a somewhat confused and offended look. "Why you looking at me funny for?" I didn't know whether he was serious or a really good actor with his dumbfounded expression.

"You're weird," was all I managed to stammer out bluntly before turning around on my heels to put my focus back on finishing my makeup.

Soft sounds of the sheets ruffling crumpled behind me. "What? What's weird about helping you find what you needed?" Lev's genuinely confused voice grew closer with his steps. "You were looking for your shit, and I helped out, so I don't understand what the weird look was for." Okay, now I felt like a piece of shit when I heard the hurt in Lev's voice.

Not wanting to see the possible pain on his face, I refused to turn around to meet him full-on, nor did I let my eyes wander to his reflection in the dresser mirror. "It's a little freaky how you read my mind," I muttered with a small shiver of discomfort.

I don't know why I felt so weirded out with Lev, who seamlessly knew my intentions without a hint from me. I mean, the damn dude literally stalked me for weeks, and this was what freaked me out about him!? Maybe I was a little crazy in the head, as he liked to claim.

"Read your mind?" Lev scoffed and snorted a snicker. "*Zhizn moya*, all I did was read your body language and study your beautiful face while putting it with what knowledge I knew," he answered merely as if it was no big issue. "You put on a fancy black and red uhh ow zai? Is that what they're called?"

Chuckling, I nodded in response to his—very surprising-ly—not-so-bad pronunciation of the traditional Vietnamese dress I wore, an *áo dài*. It was a very stiff pronunciation, but he got it maybe 80% right. "Very close for a first attempt," I praised him with a proud smile before quickly teaching him how to say the word correctly and urging him to continue with his train of thought from earlier.

Rubbing the back of his head, he flashes me a sheepish smile before picking back up, "Well, as I was saying... You put on your fancy outfit, and you usually get yourself all dolled up, like more than your casual makeup. Your eyes are all done, and so are your cheeks, so all you have left are your lips." Nonchalantly, he shrugged his shoulders with a slightly confused look. "So, it makes sense that you were looking for your lipstick, and rather you get all pissy and take longer, I figured I'd just help." His voice dipped at the end, making him sound crestfallen.

Yeah, way to make me feel like the jerk... Asshole.

Cracking a sad smile, I set the lipstick down and turned around, cupping Lev's face. "Thank you for helping me. I really appreciate it." Pity gripped my heart tightly until my chest ached from sadness at seeing Lev's eyes brighten up. "I'm not upset at you or anything. I was just kind of caught off guard with how observant you are." Not gonna lie, still freaked me out a little at how hard he tried.

Pulling him down, I pressed his head into the crook of my neck. Soothingly, I rubbed his neck and upper back. "It's okay, Lev, you don't have to put yourself out there like that for me." I stroked the back of his head and adorned his cheek and temple with kisses. "You'll never have to fight or earn my attention."

Lev said nothing in response as he buried his face deeper into me. "Probably wasn't easy being the middle child, huh? Nikolai naturally gets the attention being the oldest, Stepan is the second caretaker, your sister being the only girl, and the twins are the youngest." Middle child syndrome or whatever society liked to label it as. "You don't have to vie for my affection or attention. I can promise you that with all the certainty in the world," I assured him with a firm kiss on the side of his head. "All of me naturally belongs to you, just like how you are all mine."

Peeling his head back, he looked up at me with glassy, hopeful eyes. "Promise?" His low voice croaked with a smile.

Letting my emotions widen my smile naturally, I nodded with a hum before kissing him deeply. "You will always be the apple of my eye, little lion."

"Nicki, I'm pregnant, not invalid," Angel argued with a disgruntled glare.

Rolling my eyes at my good friend, I nudged her toward her husband. "And I told you before, this is my problem, not yours." Well, that was arguable, but I didn't want Angel to have a lot on her plate.

My parents, my problem... Unfortunately.

If I thought about it, I could easily feel the guilt of leaving my family's problems to Angel after I went deuces. I was no better than a coward pulling what I did—at least, that's what it felt like to me.

"Besides, it's just a meeting," I told her with a casual wave of my hand. "And," pausing to look up at Lev with a confident smile, I took his hand tightly, "I have my Lev." Knowing and having Lev next to me made me feel invincible and carefree. No more worrying about having my back exposed or looking every which way with anxious eyes and bated breaths.

Warmth coiled around my waist as Lev's large arms swallowed me into his hard body. "Don't worry, I won't let anything happen to my little empress." His chest vibrated against my back with his chuckle. "You guys enjoy your date." Lev's hand lifted from my body to give Angel and Nikolai small and curt flicks.

Clearing his throat, Nikolai lifted an eyebrow and tilted his head at us. "Lev." Nikolai's inquisitive voice was shot straight at Lev with a stern look.

Dragging out a sighing groan, Lev rested his chin on my head. "No unnecessary violence, no killing unless absolutely necessary, no lethal shots, yada yada." Lev deflated with a scoff. "You make it sound like I don't know what I'm doing at this point," he snarked at his brother rather playfully.

The two brothers quickly exchanged with each other in Russian before Nikolai took his leave with his arm protectively around Angel.

"I'm surprised he let her leave the house that pregnant," I commented aloud as I watched my friend walk away with her husband.

"You and me both, but I heard something about Angel threatening him with pacing around the house and stressing and possibly going into some pregnant crisis if she went another stretch of not having a date night with him," Lev mused with a low chuckle. "At least I know not to fall for any tricks from you once you're pregnant."

Now *that* made me whirl around and stare at him in disbelief. "Who said anything about me getting pregnant? Who says I want to have kids with you?"

Alright, I had to admit, that last part sounded silly because I obviously didn't mean any of it.

The blank expression on Lev's face barely lasted a second before an amused smirk sent chills down my spine. Pulling me flushed against his body, he leaned down until his lips brushed against the shell of my ear. "You say that, yet your body clings to me whenever I make any mention about stuffing you full with my seed until your belly is big with our baby," he whispered with a very deep chuckle, making me shudder from the tingles of excitement rushing my body. "Every time my cock is seated deep in you, you tighten and clench greedily around me as I fill you, and you squeeze out every last drop out."

Heat bombarded my face, particularly my cheeks, until I was sure I looked like a damn cherry. "You get so happy, so smiley, whenever I rub your stomach while we lay in bed and talk about our future." Kissing the side of my head, he remained there, letting me feel the widening of his lips. "The way your eyes sparkle and light up like the stars in the night whenever you look at baby names and ask me about them always makes my heart flutter with happiness for your joy."

Pressing his forehead against mine, he locked his hypnotizing blue eyes onto mine, staring deep into my soul. "What really gets me is when your whole face brightens up like the sun on a clear day whenever you sit there and stare at me with those lovey-dovey eyes of yours before you start talking about our future."

There were no words to describe the never-ending pools of adoration and euphoria in Lev's eyes that seemingly swallowed me with comforting arms. "I can't help it." My airy words fanned against our faces as I ghosted my lips against his. "Every time I look at you, it's like something flips a switch in my brain that constantly plays our happy endings." Kissing him softly and longingly with a big smile, I held his face against mine for a while. "It's getting to the point where I really can't imagine my life without you in it."

Well, if I were honest with myself, I wouldn't have been able to imagine my life without him for a long while now. Even if he started off as an annoying little puppy dog, he warmed his way into my heart. Honestly, he was like the stray that you couldn't help but fall in love with and take home. I mean, I kinda did just that... Kind of...

Technically, I barged into his life... After I tattooed him... And collared him... Yeah, I kinda gave him no choice with picking me out of all the women in the world, especially after I practically moved myself into his place. Yes, he offered his place to keep me safe, but I kind of planned to show up either way. His offer just expedited things a little, ignoring the part of me being hesitant because of my independence, of course.

"Good," Lev replied cockily with a big grin, laughing a little when I wailed at his chest with playful smacks.

Stepping away, I slipped next to him and looped my arm around his. "Way to ruin a moment," I remarked playfully. "Come on, let's grab a small bite real quick before the meeting." We had nearly an hour before the scheduled time, so might as well make some use of it. "So, lead the way because I can't pick." Seriously, if he expected me to pick *some* food items from *all* the delicious food that lined nearly half a block of this damn place, then he would be sorely mistaken.

Rolling his eyes, Lev chuckled down at me, kissed my forehead, and then dragged me down the aromatic and bustling street. Now, I let Lev direct us to the carts, but I ordered whenever we stopped at one. I was mindful to keep things light, though, not wanting to eat a full meal before a meeting, so I mainly ordered snacking food.

"I would ask if you could make these for us at home, but I rather like living. Or, at the very least, I like not puking my guts up." Lev stifled a laugh, clamping his jaw tightly and failing to keep a straight face.

Just because it was the truth didn't mean it didn't sting. Huffing, I dug my foot into the ground, snatching my arms back and crossing them while glaring at him. "You could learn to make it," I shot back with a sassy roll of my head.

"Set the stuff out then," Lev replied with a nonchalant shrug of his shoulders. "Just don't put the food on the stove."

Rolling my eyes, I mocked him under my breath before taking his arm hostage again in mine. "Let's grab something to drink, then head to the meeting spot." I needed something nice to wash down all the fried food we just ate.

Lev's wide strides slowed to stop, making us linger a few feet away from a bubble tea cart. "Do you think we can try that?" he asked in a low voice with a slight look of embarrassment.

Following his gaze, I wanted to know what he was referring to. "Bubble tea?" I kept my voice between us as I flickered my eyes between the food cart and Lev. "Babe, we can get whatever you want." I giggled warmly at him. "Nothing to be shy about either. Everyone loves bubble tea." If they didn't, then they were a psychopath—in my opinion (jokingly, of course).

Pursing his lips slightly, he frowned softly. "I've never had it... But Angel's always having Nikolai get some for her or getting some herself, and I'm just kind of curious." Rubbing the back of his neck, he let out a strained chuckling groan of sorts. "I've never worked up the nerve to go to a shop and get one for myself..." he admitted.

"What are you going to do when I get cravings when I'm pregnant then?" I teased with a cheeky chuckle. "What if I want something from a super girly café?"

Lev's eyes widened a little with his paling face. "W-well, that's for you and our baby, s-so I would do it no problem." Though shaky, there was an underlying confidence in his words that made it impossible for me to doubt him. Clearing his throat, he regained his composure. "If it's for you or our kids, I'd do it without question."

"What if our kids want to put frilly bows and paint your nails?" I tested him with a ridiculous, yet probable, situation.

Cracking a smile, he looked at me for a moment before shaking his head. "As long as they let me pick the color," he joked back with a hint of seriousness in his voice. "They can use me as their doll or dummy. I will let them yank me around all they want."

Oh, my poor heart. I could feel it melting at the conviction in his determined eyes. Seriously, how could this man get more perfect by the day?

Bouncing up onto my tippytoes, I pecked his cheek with a quick kiss before dragging him over to the drink stand. "Do you know what you want or like?" I asked, not taking my eyes off the menu.

"I'll let you surprise me," Lev replied with a trusting smile after peering his head into my vision.

Well, damn, alright then.

Debating for a moment, I weighed my options for a few seconds longer than anticipated before ordering for us both. It didn't take long for our drinks to be made and handed to us after Lev paid. "I got some taro and lychee. They're my usual favorites, so hopefully, you'll like one of them." If not, then, well, more for me.

The only two things in this world I'd ever be a slut for were Lev and food, especially anything sweet.

Lev slowly took the first cup—taro—and took a cautious sip, savoring it for a minute before switching with me to try the other. After the second taste, he held the cup up to eye level, studying it for a bit before trailing his eyes to the cup in my hand. His lips twisted in thought before speaking up, "I kind of like the lychee more. Can I keep it?" His hopeful eyes had a wary edge to them, almost as if he was anticipating a denial from me.

Not letting my pity surface to my lips, I forced all the warmth I had for him to mold into assurance. "Lev, you don't have to ask me for permission like that, ever. Also, I offered it to you, so, of course, you have first choice." Reaching up, I stroked his cheek with a deepening smile. "I'm never going to hurt you, either. I'm not such a bitch to dangle a prize in front of you, work you up, and snatch it at the last second."

Sliding my hand down his arm, I slipped it into his hand, intertwining my fingers tightly with his. The two of us slowly made our way over to the meeting area, taking our sweet time to enjoy the passing festivities.

The cheerful music and chatter slowly faded into the background the further we moved from it. Soon, it was barely a white noise to us by the time we made it to one of the warehouses at the nearby dock, where my two informants were already waiting for us.

They both greeted me with polite nods before gazing at Lev with widened eyes. "You are aware of who he is, right Nicki?" Matty questioned me with worry. "Listen, if you're in trouble..." His trembling hand rested on the gun in his holster.

Breaking out into a chuckle, I waved a dismissive hand at the two. "Lev is perfectly harmless." Okay, maybe that wasn't the right thing to say.

"Him?!" George pointed an accusing finger at Lev, who stood behind me like a protective statue with his arms crossed and an unreadable expression. "The Savage Volk, harmless?! You've got to be snorting some good ass shit to make a statement like that."

A short laugh echoed through the nearly empty warehouse. "Okay, I should rephrase that," I started with an amused smile. "He's harmless to *me*." I gestured at myself by splaying a hand against my chest. "I trust you two, but I can't be too careful given my situation. So, I hope you two can fully understand." The flat smile I flashed as a courtesy meant they had no choice but to either accept Lev's presence or face his—my—wrath.

"Fucking hell, Nicki." George sighed heavily with a shake of his head. "Just what shit did you get yourself into to be tangled with the Volkovs?" His concern for me was genuine, in a brotherly manner.

Tension tightened my shoulders in a curt shrug. "Whatever shit my parents put me into." Honestly, it all started because of them.

"Oh." Matty scoffed with a chuckle of disbelief. "Your parents are in something far worse than shit."

Hope widened my intrigued eyes as I took an eager step toward the two men. "What did you find out?" I couldn't help but rush them.

Running a hand across his jaw, Matty sighed. "They're planning to flee to Russia."

Russia?

I didn't need to voice it. The way my head turned and tilted with my narrowing eyes and scrunched-up face would have been enough of a question.

George's hands reached for his jacket, only to suddenly stop with a startle when Lev shuffled behind me. Lev's deep voice came out eerily steady and dangerous from behind me, "If you reach for a gun or any kind of weapon, I will stomp your chest in and bash your face to a pulp."

His threat made George go pale as a ghost as he kept his hands in the air. "I'd never harm Nicki, but understood," George stammered in response before his shaky hands made another go for the inside of his jacket.

Stiffly, he pulled out a folded manilla envelope and tossed it at my feet. "That was all we could manage," he apologized with a quick smile before averting his eyes to the ground. "They really didn't have much for us to pull electronically, and all the documents and any physical records were kept under tight lock and key in a safe at their estate."

Matty's throat bobbed nervously. "They've been meeting with a lot of people overseas, and they took a particular liking to some has-been bratva prince who managed to talk them into business with him with promises of giving them a part of Russia to run once he took over again." Reaching into his own jacket with much more confidence than George, Matty procured a manilla envelope of his own to throw at my feet.

Not taking my eyes off the two men, I reached down and picked up the two envelopes. "But what's any of that got to do with me? Why won't they let me be?" My role in their life and plans made no sense to me, maybe because there wasn't any sense to be made.

Honestly, they had everything I ever owned or created. I was literally nothing but a body to them now. So, why did they want me back so badly? To the point where they hired Lev to track and retrieve me.

"The Russian took quite a liking to you after seeing some of your photos, and it just so happens that he's in the market for a wife or two... Or three..." Matty's face twisted with disdain as his words trailed out. "Sorry," he apologized, shaking his head. "Got off track."

Straightening himself, he crossed his arms and leaned against a nearby crate. "From what I could figure out, your parents basically sold you to him to secure their business deal with them." Giving a nonsensical wave of his hand, he continued, "They promised him that you could do all the techy shit he wanted, hack the whole world basically, and a bunch of other shit."

As if that worked out great the first time.

Rolling my eyes, I opened the envelope from Matty first, pulling out a stack of photos. "And just exactly who did my parents betrothed me to?" I asked in a bored voice.

"Igor Petrov."

Chapter 23

Nicole

Slowly, I leaned over to Angel, who sat next to me on the couch. "Uhh, is this Igor guy really that much of a douchebag?" I whispered while keeping my eyes trained on Lev and his brothers as they prattled off in Russian.

Maintaining a calm demeanor, Angel nodded softly. "Besides the fact he tried to assault me in Nikolai's club, he's the oldest son of Ivan Petrov, one of the major conspirators who worked with Lady Qing to try and overthrow the Volkovs." Sipping at her water, she kept a steady eye on the group of Volkov men. "When we took down Lady Qing, Ivan and his sons disappeared with the wind, and we've been trying to locate them ever since because it's only a matter of time before they dig their roots somewhere and cause a huge problem for us."

Angel proceeded to explain the whole situation that the Volkovs had with the Petrovs, how the Petrovs tried to pull one over on the Volkovs and tried to get in their good graces when shit went belly-side up. Petrov's only daughter currently remained locked up in The Catacombs, but Ivan and his two sons, Igor and Nikita, were still running amok under everyone's noses.

Nikolai and his brothers didn't want Ivan to settle his business again and rise to power, given how twisted of a man he was under his old and charming smile. Also, they wanted to take care of him before he could strike them hard.

Word on the streets was that Ivan had a grudge against the Volkov Bratva for rejecting him and not sticking to the 'older' ways of the Bratva life. Something about how the whole situation was equivalent to the Volkovs spitting in his face from what some of their informants have told them.

Angel couldn't fully understand what the brothers were going on about because she couldn't keep up with their pace, but she got enough to surmise that they were frustrated about the new information.

"*Blyat*!" Lev exclaimed, throwing his hands in the air with an angry growl. Stepping right up to Nikolai, Lev jabbed his finger into his brother's chest with his firm words. "Kolya, I know you want to maintain this stupid, unstable peace we have, but it's obvious that some of our supposed allies are starting to doubt us and push their luck."

Lev's chest heaved deeply with every flare of his nostril as his heavy breaths came and went. "We need to act. We need to show everyone that we mean business and that how we are running things will be the new normal." His raised voice died down to a low but calculated one as he continued, "We have too many new acquisitions and 'allies' who don't respect us because they don't see reason to, and it's about damn time we demonstrate to them why *we* are the ones in charge and why *we* should be feared and respected."

Easing back, Lev slowly took a few steps backward. "I know you don't like to do things that way, *bratok*, but sometimes a stern reminder is needed." Hooking his hands onto his hips, he gave his brother a hard and stubborn look. "If we don't, people are going to end up teaming with the likes of Igor and shit. Then, things will really get messy." Breathing deeply, he kept firm. "You let a rat fester enough, and it'll come back with an army for an infestation of biblical proportions. It'll be way too fucking late for us to do anything at that point besides surrender everything and flee."

"I don't know about you, but we have put too much of our blood, sweat, tears, and souls into all of this to just give it up because we wanted to keep the peace. There will be no peace if we let trouble stir and storm, which is exactly what you are doing with wanting to play it safe." Lev's jaw ticked and tensed with a scowl. "You can try to be diplomatic about it all, take the long and tedious route. But I won't."

Okay, I did not like the sound of that one bit.

Shooting up from the couch, I closed the distance between Lev and me with a few big strides. My hand shot out, grabbing his forearm. "*Đại ca*, I think you need to take a step back and think about things after you've simmered," I suggested strongly in a very stern voice. "Starting a war over this stupid Igor person won't be a good idea for anyone." Given Lev's track record and from what I've heard from many others, nothing good would come from Lev going headfirst into things to prove a point. Yes, it would get the point across, but I fear it might do more harm than good in the end.

When his eyes landed on me, I could see his shoulders relax slightly. "I am not going to sit around and wait for them to harm you." His voice wavered with worry as he looked at me with sad eyes. "I won't wait around and risk losing you."

I did my best to reassure him with a smile, but I couldn't muster up the strength to give it to him fully. "I'll be fine. It's not like they can get me with you around or while I'm here." I wanted to sound confident, but the pressure gripping at my chest shook my words.

Which was strange because I was completely safe here at the estate. I was also safe outside of it because I had Lev literally at my back. There's no way anything bad could happen to me anywhere... Right?

Something in his eyes snipped at the safety blanket I'd wrapped myself in. It was as if he wanted to assure me otherwise, but deep down, he knew otherwise.

With a longing look of doubt, Lev sighed heavily as his head swung back and forth. "No, you're not ever truly safe." His eyes flickered over my shoulder to Angel. "They almost succeeded in kidnapping both Angel and Kolya while they were out together in public." Then, his eyes darted over to his brother, Stepan. "Hanna's family managed to kidnap her while she was with Stepan."

Okay, he had some fair points, and I couldn't argue with him there. If something managed to happen to those before us, then his doubt and wariness for my safety were more than valid. I mean, Angel and Nikolai were the head honchos, yet someone was gutsy enough to pull such a stunt. I couldn't say much about Stepan and Hanna, but I would've thought their reputation would be enough to keep people cautious and at bay.

Swallowing the lump in my throat, I pulled myself closer to Lev. "Then we'll figure out some other plan that doesn't result in you going out there and starting a violent blood bath." As much as I loved chaos, there had to be a good point and end to it.

"Is it wrong that I somewhat agree with Lev? Kind of?" Angel pipped up, making all of us look at her with wide eyes and aghast expressions. "Okay," Angel backed track, holding her hands out, "I agree to an extent, I should say. I mean, as much as I want to keep the peace, it's evident that some aren't too happy with the changes to the Volkov Bratva. Yes, they may still be in line with us, but I can still see the apprehension in their eyes." Taking a deep breath, she slowly let it out. "We do need to reassert our dominance with everyone, really give them a demonstration as to why they shouldn't even think about trying their hand with us."

Sighing heavily, Nikolai rubbed his temples. "*Lisichka*, if you want to torture someone, we have a whole dungeon full of people in the desert." Nikolai groaned, almost seemingly in pain. "We are not going to be shooting or beating people up, nor are we going to be trashing businesses just to make a fucking point when there are better ways to do so."

"I said I agreed with Lev, not his methods," Angel retorted with a roll of her eyes.

Honestly, the more I weighed things in my head, the more I leaned toward Lev and Angel. It'd take way too much time and effort to sit down with people and talk with them; actually, it'd be a big waste of time, in my opinion. "Why don't you just figure out who's iffy with you all or is thinking about other things, gather them, and just give them a real good scare or two... That might or might not send them into a heart attack." Maybe a few deaths gotta be enough of a shock to others. Besides, not like the people dying were innocent, so personally, I wouldn't lose any sleep over any of it.

"Actually..." One of the twins spoke up. Don't ask me which because I sure as hell didn't know how to tell them apart one bit.

To be fair, I haven't had much exposure to the twins. Sure, I've looked them up online, and if Alexei was in his scrubs or white coat, then I could tell him apart from his more charming half. Otherwise, it was a good fifty-fifty shot at who was who.

"Fucking hell, not you, too, Alexei," Nikolai grumbled under his breath while glowering at his younger brother.

Throwing his hands up in defeat, Alexei shrugged with a flat smile. "I don't see the problem with Nicole's little idea. It'll help us clean up some trash before it starts to rot, and it'll be a grand example for our doubters."

The soft sounds of feet dragging across the floor turned our attention to Stepan and Arseny as they slowly shifted more toward Lev's side. "You fucking traitors," Nikolai bit out harshly but almost playfully at the same time. "You know what?" His full attention was locked on Lev. "Since you came up with the brilliant idea, you handle its planning and execution."

"Fine." Lev took on the challenge with a puffed chest. "Just don't get pissy when my idea actually pans out well."

Chapter 24

"Zhizn moya..."

Before I could put my concern into words, Nicole shook her head at me with a heavy expression. "Not tonight, Lev, please." There was no energy to her voice, nor was there any to her shuffling feet as she dragged herself to the couch.

Being smart, for once in my life, I kept my mouth shut. She didn't need more shit placed on her right now after our impromptu meeting with my family. So, without a peep, I settled next to her on the couch and took her into my arms. "Do you want to be alone for a while?" I wasn't sure if my presence was helping or not.

To be honest, I wasn't sure of a lot of things when it came to Nicole and me. I wasn't doubting our relationship or anything like that; no, it was more that I wasn't sure what to do as a boyfriend. Even if I fooled around a lot in my younger days and somewhat recent years, I've never had a girlfriend before or engaged myself in any kind of committed relationship.

Long-term relationships have always terrified me. Yes, I was one of those cowards who was afraid of commitment—sue me. But, I also never felt the need to settle, until I came upon Nicole. Something about her drew me in and made me fall head over heels for her.

I thought Nikolai was bullshitting me when he told me a while back that he knew Angel was the one because he could see a life with her. Back then, I argued that a life with anyone could be painted onto a canvas if someone tried hard enough. Nikolai laughed at me and called me naïve, and I might have punched him in the gut for that. But I regret it now because clearly, he was right, like always.

One glance at Nicole was all I needed to have our whole life play out before me like a damn movie—I didn't even have to try and direct anything. I could see us finally having some peace and balance once her parents were taken care of. From seeing us sitting out in the garden watching our children play and grow to when we'd grow old and gray. Everything flowed smoothly like a lazy river.

Of course, thinking about it all made my muscles twitch with impatience. I wanted to go out and bulldoze everything over regarding her parents so she wouldn't have to worry about any of it. Unfortunately, that plan had to go into the trash because of Igor's involvement.

The damn rat.

Maybe it was too hopeful and stupid of me to think he'd run away and hide out the rest of his days in shame with his father after we busted Lady Qing and shut down her operations and some other major players.

Honestly, the whole thing was a huge headache and a half for all of us.

My train of thought came to a halt when I felt movement in my arms. "Yes, but I don't want you gone. I just need you to hold me for longer and be here for me in silence while I mull over everything." Her soft and tired voice made me frown with pity for her.

"Whatever my empress wants and needs." Placing a kiss on the top of her head, I laid down on the couch with her.

Thoughtful silence was probably needed for both of us because I needed to think of a plan to shove it into Nikolai's face. He may have given me the task of dealing with our skeptics and Igor, but I could see his wary eyes when he shoved it onto my plate out of anger.

I had nothing against my older brother, but sometimes, he took the peaceful route a little too far. I understood his reasons for running our family's bratva the way he does, given how our father used to run things with an iron fist, but sometimes, a firm reminder was needed all around.

At times, I wish Nikolai was more like his younger, unhinged self. I mean, he didn't get labeled the Devil Volk for being a pacifist. Everyone likes to think that I was the violent one, which wasn't a lie, but compared to Nikolai, I paled in comparison. Back in his prime, he really was a bloody demon in the streets and behind a desk. He still was a bloodthirsty asshole, but he kept a better lid on it now. But no matter how hard he tried to hide and deny that side of him, I could clearly see it whenever we went out on the field together.

No matter, Nikolai wasn't my problem—he was Angel's now.

Taking a deep breath, I let myself daze off while staring at the ceiling.

I wasn't too worried about the other people I had to terrify; it was Igor. I only had one shot at him, and I didn't want to fuck it up. If I did, then he'd get away from us for good this time. The solution seemed simple to me: figure out where he stowed himself away and attack him in his sleep. The only problem was that he was a slimy rat, and following him back to his hole proved harder than expected. Also, we had no idea about his forces or if he had any.

Going in blind was never a good idea, and as much as I craved some violence, I wasn't *that* much of an idiot. Additionally, I had to be cautious because of how closely involved Nicole was. The last thing I wanted was to have her caught in the crossfire or, worse, lose her altogether.

Looking down, I let my eyes wander about her features to distract myself. The thought of... No... I couldn't think about things like that. No point in planting seeds that I had no intention of growing.

Everything is going to be fine.

I repeated it in my mind in so many different ways until I lulled myself into a false sense of calm and security.

"Besides the meeting just now, did you enjoy tonight?" Nicole's voice broke the silence in the room. "Anything in particular you enjoyed or not?"

Forcing a smile onto my lips, I tightened my arms around her before replying. "A lot more food and festivities than I imagined, but it was nice and sweet. Seeing all the paper lanterns was nice, too." That was the part that surprised me the most, if I was being honest. Some of those were so intricate, like the dragons and phoenixes. Then, to hear they were all handmade really made them even more special to my eyes.

Chuckling, I lightly pinched her sides to tickle her. "I don't know how you ate all that food." Seriously, she ate as much as I did, and I ate *a lot*.

Her hands swatted at mine while her laughing body squirmed in my arms. "What can I say, high metabolism? I gotta get the energy to use my brain from somewhere," she stammered out between her laughter. "*Đại ca*, stop tickling me! It's not fair!"

Satisfied with getting my dose of laughter from her, I released. "Do you want to head to bed? Or are you going to tinker around a little with your stuff?" I nodded toward the spare room she had turned into her temporary office and workspace.

Nicole's body perked up from the couch, and her head darted between me and the room for a good minute. I don't know what ran through her mind, but whatever she decided on couldn't have been good with how she looked down at me with a rather devious smile and playful eyes. Leaning down, she slinked her way up my chest, hovering her snake-like face inches from mine. "You up for some fun tonight?"

My nervousness bubbled up and clogged my throat, forcing me to swallow hard. "I don't like how you asked that..." Fun for who? Her or me?

"Weeeell..." Her finger lightly danced around on my taut chest. "Depends on how you take it." Her lips curled to where she could pass for the Cheshire Cat.

I'm going to regret this, but fuck it.

Giving in with a sigh, I slipped away from her and stood, ready to walk to our bedroom, before my knees gave out from under me. The breath I'd been letting out knocked out of me with a grunt when I fell to the ground on my knees. Irritated and confused, I threw my head back at Nicole, who stood there smirking down at me. "Did I say you could walk?" The authority in her voice made me shiver with excitement and a need to bow my head to her.

Her pointed eyes remained on me as she strutted ahead. "Wait until I say, then I want you to crawl to the bedroom and wait by the foot of the bed." Her soft voice became firm and dominant when she gave me instructions.

Instinctively, I bowed my head slightly as I sat back on my legs. "Yes, empress."

All I could hear, besides her soft footfalls, were the sounds of drawers sliding and slamming. I couldn't tell if she had removed something from the drawers she opened. There was no telltale clink of chains, nor did I pick up the sound of fabric shuffling around.

What is she doing?

Anticipation crept up my body like cold, bony hands, making my skin crawl with goosebumps. Eager fear squeezed at my throat, causing my breaths to come out jagged and fast. An invisible fist slammed into my chest at the sound of Nicole's voice, making my heart explode and my ears ring.

Gulping, I lowered myself onto my hands and made the mile-long crawl from the living room to our bedroom. Okay, call me dramatic because it wasn't a mile, but it sure as hell felt like it. Seeing Nicole leaning against the doorframe with her arms crossed proudly made me feel smaller the more I crawled toward my destination.

"That's my good boy," she cooed her praise with an excited smile. "You remember your safe-word and gesture?" The excitement in her voice dialed down to press her seriousness across.

Letting out a trembling exhale, I stopped by her feet. "Yes, empress. Safe-word is bomb, and if I can't verbally communicate, then tap your shoulder three times."

Nodding her head and humming in approval, she pushed off the door-frame to walk back inside the room. I went to follow, but the sight of her luscious ass swaying back and forth with every accentuated step had me frozen and drooling. If it weren't for her prompting, I would have been more than happy to waste away in my spot as long as I could watch her strut around.

Fucking hell, we haven't even really started yet I could feel myself ache with a burning need in my pants. Every little movement I made to crawl toward her caused my rock-hard cock to rub against the thick center of my pants, sending pulses of pleasure through my body. With my desire for her ramping up until I was nearly mad with lust, I completely forgot about why I was here in the first place.

It would have stayed that way if it weren't for the slap in the face.

Stunned, all I could do was stare wide-eyed at the toy she dangled before me. "Did you just slap me with a dildo?" I scoffed offendedly.

Laughing softly, she waved the toy about carelessly. "Oh please, it was just a tap." The very cheeky grin made her words doubtful, but I let it slide. "The real smacking and slapping is next week." Sitting on the edge of the bed, she pulled her nightshirt off, revealing her nearly bare body to me. "We're going to see how good you can be for me tonight." The way her voice dipped deviously caused a shudder to rake down my body.

Her finger curled under my chin, lifting my face up to meet her smirking eyes. "Here's what's gonna happen," she started, giggling a little as she stroked my jawline with her thumb, "I'm going to tie you to the bed, then you're going to eat me out while I get your ass ready. Once I'm done, the toy is gonna go into your ass, and I'm gonna go finish up some work."

My legs clenched in anticipation, and I could feel myself tighten in fear at the thought of the toy going up my backdoor. The thing wasn't huge by any means, but it wasn't small, either. For someone who's never really taken anything but Nicole's fingers up there, the ribbed, phallic-shaped toy looked a little menacing. "Don't worry, I'll go slow and easy, and if you can't handle it or don't want to, then we can stop." Her voice softened tenderly as she assured me. "So, what do you say?"

I expected to feel some kind of hesitation or reluctance, yet there was none as I found myself leaning into her touch with a content smile. "I trust you to take care of me how you see fit."

A soft *thud* of the mattress cushioned my ears before the feeling of Nicole's hands on my face directed my full attention back to her as she kissed me deeply with a big smile. "On the bed," she whispered between heavy kisses.

Clumsily, I moved from the floor to the bed, keeping my lips engaged with hers as best as possible. I didn't want to break our connection, even if it would be brief. I was addicted to her and constantly needed to touch and taste her.

"Empress, please, get your cunt on my face, please," I begged needily with a groan as I pulled her down on top of me.

Chuckling chidingly, she wagged her finger at me while smirking cruelly. "Patience, little lion. You're still all dressed."

Her touches and movements were slow and deliberate as she stripped me at a torturously slow pace. No matter how much I begged and pleaded with her, she refused to go beyond the pace of a damn tortoise! Even when I was thrusting helplessly into the air for something—anything! Yes, call me impatient, but this was torture!

Crawling up my body, she straddled my face, hovering her hips inches from my watering mouth. "Hands on the bed," she commanded me with a stern look.

I opened my mouth to protest, but a twitch of an eyebrow was all she needed for me to promptly shut it and obey. Balling my hands into fists, I slammed them onto the bed next to me and gripped the sheets. I wanted to whine and complain, but that would get me nowhere besides possibly in trouble.

Shifting around, she positioned herself so we were in a sixty-nine position before pressing her delicious cunt against my face.

Fucking hell, whoever invented crotchless panties. I fucking love you.

Her juicy pussy lips were perfectly framed by the edged slit of her lace panties, and they helped spread her so well whenever she bent over or parted her legs.

The moment her sweet nectar touched my lips and her intoxicating scent overloaded my system, I was a goner. I dug my face into her vigorously, licking and lapping every inch of her exposed cunt. Her clit was perfectly positioned so that every slide of my tongue brushed right against it, and I was careful to stick my tongue out all the way at times to give her swollen bundle of nerves a nice, long lick.

I was so engrossed in the pleasure of feasting on her that I barely felt her lubed fingers prodding at my entrance. Well, it didn't help that I was being overloaded with pure delight. Her hot, tight mouth working my cock down to her throat was enough to dangle me over the edge. It'd be so easy to blow a load into her needy mouth right now, especially with how her skilled tongue worked my length in tantum with everything.

My resolve nearly snapped with my deep groan when Nicole pressed her fingers into me, right against my prostate. "Breathe, baby, breathe and calm yourself before you blow it." Her words vibrated against my cock as she adorned it with kisses. "You are doing so good for me."

Praise after praise, she cherished me with her sweet words as she fingered my ass to prepare me. I completely relaxed after the first few thrusts and rubs of my prostate, but I couldn't help but naturally clench at the feeling of something big and hard pressing against it. "Little lion, it's okay. Just the tip, and then we'll continue if you can take it." There was a bit of a challenge in her voice, almost as if she was taunting me.

Well, there was no harm in trying, and we were both in the mood. The only thing that would hurt is my ass, but that would go away quickly with time. So, with a deep breath, I spread my legs wider for her. Keeping my breaths controlled, I distracted myself with her cunt, hoping it would help keep me relaxed as she—

Gasping sharply, I threw my head back. "Oh fuck." My lips fell away from her sweet sex the more I dug my head into the pillow.

White-knuckling the sheets, I whimpered through my gasping breaths as my feelings stormed within me. I loved it, really, but the part of me that was conditioned to not enjoy it screamed at me to put a stop to it. But I didn't want to. It felt too good to stop. "Nicole, more, please," I groaned, thrusting my hips a bit at her.

I needed more to silence the objection blaring in my mind. None of this was wrong. There was no written or spoken law that said this wasn't right, just the stupid stigma and ridicule that came with time. But why should I care? Not like we were filming a porno and putting it online, nor were we shouting about our private life for the whole world to know.

There was nothing for me to worry about, so might as well indulge in the guilty pleasure.

"Shit," I hissed through gritted teeth when I felt more being pressed into me. It didn't hurt; I just didn't think it was *that* much that I had left to take. No matter; it was all in me now. Now, I could—

The gasping moan that choked out of me took me for a spin because I didn't want to believe I could make such a sound. "Nicole," I seethed at her with a quick glare before my writhing body pressed itself into the bed. "Why didn't you warn me...!" I gasped, struggling a little to adjust to the feeling of the vibrating toy thrusting against my G-spot.

And here I thought this would be easy. Fuck me for getting ahead of myself.

"Whoops, guess I forgot to mention the extra parts of it." Nicole feigned innocence as she crawled off the bed with a saccharine smile on her face. "Now, remember, no coming until I say so," she reminded me with a devious chuckle, making all hope of me getting off easy sink to the bottom of an endless pit. "And no leaving the bed."

Scrambling onto my hands and knees, I struggled to the end of the bed as I watched her sit in the lounger by the window. "Empress, please, you can't—fuck!" My fist slammed against the end-board of the bed as I groaned deeply.

The intensity and speed of the toy slowly ramped up the more I struggled to hold myself together. "Fuck you," I rasped out between gritted teeth, glaring at Nicole's smug face as she waved a small, black remote up in the air.

Yeah, holding myself back turned from hard to impossible with how Nicole yanked my chain around. If the toy was at a constant intensity, I could numb it out and endure it fine. But my damn minx kept randomly changing the setting on me, making it impossible for me to zone it out. All I could do was helplessly writhe around on the bed while I begged and pleaded with my empress for some relief, only to be denied each and every time.

I'd go insane if this stretched on any longer. Holding out for half an hour felt like hours to me, and Nicole happily typed away on her laptop without a care in the world.

Temptation ached at my hand to reach down and give my throbbing cock a few strokes to ease myself, but anytime I dared to make any indication of moving my hand near my crotch, Nicole would warn me with a side glare. Yeah, like hell would I risk some kind of punishment from her tonight after this. Also, the last thing I wanted was to go to bed with blue balls.

"How badly do you need to creampie me?" Nicole casually asked, not taking her eyes off the laptop screen.

Honestly, I felt like I'd die if I didn't get my cock inside of her tight, hot cunt right now. "I need it more than I need air right now, so please, let me fuck and fill you, empress, please." Screw oxygen; breeding Nicole's lovely body was more vital.

"*Pozhaluysta, lyubov' moya, mne nuzhno byt' vnutri tebya pryamo seychas, inache ya umru,*" I whimpered and groaned pleadingly while looking at Nicole deeply.

I don't know what happened, but Nicole's eyes gained a twinkle to them as her body straightened. She breathed out heavily with a seductive smile. "I don't know what you said, but holy hell did you sound hot." Hooking her finger at me to come hither, she set her laptop aside and climbed onto the couch.

Giggling, she leaned against the back of the lounger, gripping the edges as she got on her knees and stuck her ass out. "Keep talking Russian to me, and I'll let you fuck me until you can't come anymore." As if to tempt me, she gave a quick shake of her bubbly butt. "Would you like that, little lion?"

"Yes," I dragged out a low groan of victory as my cock twitched with the thought of relief. "*Pozhaluysta, ya budu tvoim khoroshim mal'chikom navsegda. Ya budu tvoyey khoroshey shlyushkoy.*"

Leaping off the bed, I closed the distance between us in three long strides. It took me less than a second to position myself behind her and enter her fully in a single thrust after wetting my cock with my spit. "*Blyat'!*" White hot pleasure blanked my mind as searing pleasure ravaged my orgasming body.

It felt as of my soul left my body with that first rush of my cum into her. I could feel my aching cock thrust in and out of her with abandon, but I don't recall *doing* it. My body moved on some primal instinct, it felt like, and every squeeze and sweet moan that fell from Nicole's mouth as I fucked her spurred me on harder.

Likewise, my tongue wove such filthy promises to her in Russian as I pounded her within inches of her life and probably mine as well. I wouldn't be surprised if she woke up with bruises on her hips and thighs from how hard I slammed my hips into her. Hell, I would be surprised if I didn't end up with bruises on my hips.

The lounger became a mess of our juices sooner rather than later, and Nicole's essence dripped down ours from how much I made her gush and squirt. Eventually, we moved back to the bed, just in time for my last round.

As much as I wanted to go all night with her, my overwhelmed body was beyond spent after busting two loads into her. That and the vibrating, thrusting toy in my ass didn't help me keep it together, especially not after Nicole turned it on max. Honestly, the fact I managed to hold out as long as I did without passing out from the absurd amount of pleasure that ravaged every single nerve ending in my body to the point of insanity was beyond my comprehension.

My last climax felt like a freight train to my whole body as I weakly gasped her name. "Nicole..." I didn't even have enough energy to moan out her name.

Utterly spent, I collapsed into a whimpering and sobbing mess next to her on the bed when my body just gave out. I fucking hated the drop and crash, especially this one, because I was edged for so long, and the sex was rather overstimulating.

A violent shudder shook my body when Nicole removed the toy, causing immense pressure to cut into my hot nerves.

Thankfully, Nicole was there for me. Like always, she took me into her loving arms, holding me and spoiling me with all the pets, kisses, and sweet nothings in the world. The vulnerable feeling I had at the start of all of this was a lot easier to deal with after I fully fell into Nicole's comfort and assurance. I had nothing to worry about with her around. She would take care of me and guide me back to baseline.

Exhausted, I found myself dozing off in her arms rather fast. I couldn't keep my eyes open when she left my side to go get supplies to clean me off. One heavy blink was all it took for me to slip into slumber's embrace when I watched Nicole's ass walk away from me.

"...YA tebya lyublyu..."

Chapter 25

~3 days later~

"Do you really have to go out tonight? It's supposed to rain pretty bad tonight, and I don't want you to get caught out there," Nicole worried from the doorway, half her body peeping around the frame into the artillery room.

Faking a smile, I turned around to fully look at her as I finished holstering my gun. "It's an important raid, and I plan on using tonight as an example to the others, too." Kill two birds with one stone. "The Hwangs and Hosths have been pushing it with us too much, and we let them get away with part of a shipment before." Grabbing my bag, I slung it over my shoulder. "We spoke with them, and of course, they gave us the whole crap about 'oh, we won't do it again' and shit, but obviously, that was a load of bull because I have to get my ass out there tonight."

Not that I minded. I'd been itching for some good action for a while now, so this would be very cathartic for me. I mean, shooting and punching at dummies in the backyard or sparring with my brothers and Hanna only took so much of the edge off.

I needed to kill.

And unfortunately, fratricide was very frowned upon. Not that I wanted to kill any of my brothers—well, not literally kill, anyway.

"I'll be back. I promise." I probably sounded a little too cocky about my survival rate out there, but I had to be.

Fake it until you make it.

I always did my best to stay alive out there. Even in my adrenaline-fueled haze, I had enough clarity to be wary and cautious. I kept myself alive thus far, and that was with no real motivation. Yeah, I tried harder to stay alive for my brothers' sake, but now, I had something more.

Slowly, my heavy steps approached Nicole until I could feel her body heat radiate onto me. "I promise, when you wake up tomorrow, it will be in my arms." I shouldn't make such promises, but if I put it out into the world, then that meant I had to keep it.

Frowning her eyes softly, Nicole huffed. "What if you got your arms cut off out there?"

A burst of laughter exploded from me at her ridiculous question. Okay, maybe I shouldn't be laughing because it was a possibility. Who knows, maybe I might encounter a machete-wielding maniac today who gets in the lucky swing. Chances of that happening were highly doubtful, but in this line of work, it wouldn't surprise me to come across something like that.

Hell, I couldn't say jack shit because my girlfriend was a bomb-loving techy who looked like she couldn't harm a fly. Seriously, one look at Nicole, paired with her history, no one would ever think that she was a bomb maker for the mafia.

To be fair, I grossly underestimated her myself. If I didn't, then I wouldn't have ended up with a broken nose or gotten drugged and tattooed by her... Nor would I fall victim to her antics. Yeah, she still liked to fuck with my shit, but only because I didn't know my limits.

It never thrilled me when she would shit my computer down in the middle of the night or limit the service to my phone, but it was for my own good. I never realized how much of a habitual problem I had working late into the night until Nicole started to nag me and control my life. But if it weren't for her, then I'd still be an angry, sleep-deprived asshole. Don't get me wrong, I was still an asshole, but the healthy schedule she had me on really helped regulate my energy levels to where I found myself being more tolerable and peaceful.

Clearing my head, I pulled her to me, hugging her longingly. "*Zhizn moya*, I will come back to you alive and with all my limbs intact and attached to my body," I half-joked with a flat chuckle. "If you don't want to be alone, then go be with Angel," I suggested, kissing her forehead.

"I'll keep myself busy with a project while I wait for you." I barely caught her mumbling words as she buried her face into my chest. Lifting her head, she looked up at me with her big eyes. "What are you planning on doing out there tonight?"

The corner of my lips stretched into an uncontrolled, bloodthirsty smile as I thought about my hectic plan. "Not much, just gonna make a bloody mess, maybe flay the bodies open and hang them up like Christmas lights, might leave some alive and send them back with missing parts." A hard drumming pounded in my ears from my heart beating in my chest, and I became more excited at the thought of the carnage that I was about to cause tonight. "And I might or might not personally pay the Hwangs and Hosths a visit after the fact."

With a cheeky grin, I slid my hands down and grabbed her ass, squeezing them tightly until she squeaked. Trapping her against my body with an arm, I grabbed the back of her head with the other. "You better be ready to spread those pretty legs of yours for me later, empress," I whispered hotly against her lips before swallowing her protest with an all-consuming kiss. "I'm gonna come straight home after my assignment, bend you over wherever you are, and take you until both of us can't come or move." The corners of her eyes sparkled under the dim lighting from her welling tears. "Make our bed and sheets all messy with blood and cum."

Grinning wildly against my lips, she giggled darkly. "You better come back tonight then, after threatening me with such a promising night like that." Biting her bottom lip, she looked up at me with darkened eyes. "Go out, have some fun shooting people, breaking bones, and being a menace. Then, come home and show me how a bratva boss fucks his whore."

The feral growl rumbled out of my chest in response to her words. *"Zhizn moya,* if you say things like that..."

Nicole might be the Dom between us, but there were some moments of switching in the bedroom. It wasn't often because we liked the dynamic we had set up, but sometimes she wanted to be the one dragged around. Not gonna lie, sometimes I felt the urge to dominate her as well. So, switching worked more than perfect for us to run our wants and needs out of our system.

"I need my bratva brute to remind me of my place," she teased, running the tip of her finger along my jaw. "To pin me down and breed me until your seed takes."

Damn this woman of mine.

She knew just the right things to say to get me going.

Grabbing her neck, I backed her up against the wall and attacked her with a frenzied kiss. "You better be wet and ready for me to go right in because the moment I step through that door, I won't have the patience for foreplay." Hell, I'd be lucky to get my clothes off in the moment.

Fight and fuck. Those would be the only two things on my mind once the adrenaline stormed my body later with the first taste of blood on the field.

Kissing her one last time, I pulled her away from the wall to give her ass a nice smack. "I suggest you test out those new toys of yours while I'm gone," I teased her with a hearty laugh before slipping away from her.

Soft pits and pats of Nicole's footsteps trailed behind me as I made my way out to the garage. *"Đại ca,"* she called out for me just as I tossed my bag into the passenger seat of my car. "Please, be careful out there." The worry in her voice ached my heart and made me feel a little bad about leaving her to risk my life out there on the streets. "I-if you die out there, I swear, I will put bombs in your coffin."

Amused, I let my body tremble with a soft laugh. "Gonna blow me sky high to Heaven?" I joked with a half-hearted smile. "I'll make it back to you, I swear," I promised her with a confident smile before climbing into the car.

It didn't take me long to reach the rendezvous point, where our men, Stepan, Hanna, Arseny, Greg, and Bao, were gathered. "Sorry for the hold-up.

Nicole was trying to convince me otherwise." If I wasn't so antsy for action, then maybe I might have pulled out of tonight to mess around with her.

As much as I loved sex with Nicole, passing up an assignment in my pent-up state was a huge no. It'd been at least two months since I'd gotten any good action with my men or brothers, so hell was I about to pass up tonight when they asked if I wanted to participate.

"Ew, can you not talk about my sister like that? It's just gross." Bao mocked his disgust with a soft frown as he recoiled a little. "Seriously, I can't believe you and Nicki are together." Bao looked at me with mock concern. "I don't know whether to help you get away from her or commit you to a psych house because you're insane enough to date my sister."

To be fair, I wondered about my own sanity—what was left of it—sometimes because it probably was a little insane for me to be with Nicole. I stalked her, only to be stalked back. She broke my nose, broke into my house, knocked me out, and tattooed me, then had the gall to strand me in the rain after jacking my car. Yeah, she was probably certifiably crazy, but so was I.

Chuckling sheepishly, I reached up and ran my fingers along the edge of my collar. "You should probably have me committed because after all that's happened, I fucking love her still and then some." And this would be the moment where I punch myself in the face for letting that last part slip.

Everyone's faces stretched tight with their wide eyes and shocked mouths. "Love?!" Bao looked like he was about to have an aneurysm as he frantically searched my face for some other answer. "Listen, if you need help, blink twice. I can get you a new identity and set up a new life for you in the blink of an eye. You just gotta say the word." I don't know if the worried look was for me or for his sister.

Honestly, it still boggled me how Bao and Nicki were siblings, given how laid-back and passive Bao was as a person, while Nicole was more headstrong and gung-ho about everything. Also, Nicole was a hell of a lot more violent and bloodthirsty than her younger brother. Actually, come to think of it, I don't think I've ever seen Bao intentionally harm anyone or even pick up a weapon. Oh, and Bao wasn't batshit crazy like Nicole.

My body jerked with a grunt when Hanna's squealing body tackled mine in a hug. "Aww, Lev, that's so sweet! I'm so happy for you and Nicki!" Hanna gushed with a happy grin. "Never thought I'd see the day you'd find someone crazy enough to tame your ass and love it." She laughed with a shit-eating grin on her face—a subtle jab.

Then, Hanna's face dropped and twisted in amusement. "Actually, I'm surprised you," Hanna jabbed her finger into my gut, "are crazy enough to be with her. I mean, I love Nicki, but girl is on another level of psycho compared to Angel and me." Turning her head to Bao, Hanna held her hands up in defense. "And I mean that in the most loving way ever. Nicki is great, but a little psycho, a good psycho."

I was pretty sure psycho could never be a good thing, but I kept that thought to myself as I looked over to my two brothers, who snickered amongst themselves. "Care to share you two?" I grumbled with a heavy sigh, knowing that whatever would come out of their mouths wouldn't bode well for me.

Smugly, Arseny crossed his arms and leaned against the armored truck. "Oh, Stepan here was just telling me how he wished he had earplugs in the office because of how much noise you made—"

"Blaph blah bla aaah!" Bao interjected with his nonsensical sounds while covering his ears. "New rule when working with B-Boy: no bedroom talk. I *do not* want or need to know who y'all screw on your time off, nor do I want any details about such activities." Spinning around on his heel, Bao glared at me accusingly. "Especially if it has to do anything about my sister."

We all laughed at Bao and dismissed him with playful comments in response. "Okay, all that aside, we need to get serious." Stepan pulled everyone back together with a few loud claps. "We don't have all night, and I'm sure all of us want some sleep tonight."

Recollecting myself, I straightened out and became serious. "Everything still like we planned initially? How's the enemy looking? Do we have a head count? Any changes to the layouts we've seen on surveillance?" My playful voice from before flattened to a stern one as I kicked my ass into business mode. "And everyone on our side is accounted for and ready?" One quick glance, and it looked like everyone was prepared and ready to roll out, but maybe last-minute prep was needed.

Letting out a deep breath, Bao tapped away at his tablet for a second before turning it around to show all of us a satellite view of the area we were set to attack. "The only change so far is the new cargo shipments that arrived hours ago. Other than that, it seems like the number of enemies is still roughly the same, about thirty of them, give or take a body or two." Bao slowly moved the screen around to show us the area along with the dropped pins of highly probable locations of guards.

"Alright, so we stick with the plan before. Two snipers up in the two towers and three ground teams," Stepan decided firmly, looking at everyone for any kind of objection.

When none came his way, Stepan continued, "I'll take one of the towers. Arseny and Greg will take the Alpha Team, Hanna will take the Beta Team, and Lev will take the Delta Team." Taking the tablet from Bao, Stepan circled certain areas before showing us the screen. "These are going to be our entry and exit points. Alpha Team will advance with everyone else but break off to storm and secure the back while Beta and Delta will deal with the front."

Studying the map for a minute, I reviewed Stepan's plan and played it out in my mind. Without a word, I took the tablet from Bao to play around with the satellite map. "*Bratok*, that won't work. There's a side entrance that needs to be covered, too," I pointed out, flashing the screen to Stepan. "It's not much of an escape, but they have some boats there they can run to."

"They won't have enough time to utilize that side escape," Stepan stated with a bit of doubt in his eyes.

"That might be true, but what if they do? Or what if somehow reinforcements come through that side?" I retorted with a skeptical look. "Team Beta can head straight for the front to secure and breech, but Team Delta is going to side before meeting back up with Beta inside," I told Stepan flatly.

I wasn't asking to alter the plan; I was altering it whether Stepan liked it or not. Something about that side exit and the docks tugged at my gut. Yes, it could be nothing like Stepan put it, but I didn't want to risk it. Besides, there would be no harm in taking the extra caution of securing that side door, in my opinion.

Stepan and I stared at each other in intense silence as we argued with each other through our hardened eyes. "Fine," he relented after a while with a soft scoff. His head did a quick sweep through our men. "Anyone else have anything to add or change?"

His question was met with quiet denial and shakes of some heads. No one really ever dared to go against Stepan's plans, but I didn't give a shit. If I was involved along with my men, then I wanted to do what I felt was right. Also, Stepan was my brother, so I really didn't give a single damn about it. If he had an issue with me, then we could work it out at home.

It wasn't as if I altered the plan to give my older brother a harder time. Contrary to what happened just now, I rarely made headstrong decisions like that without conversing with Stepan about it. If it weren't for my intuition, then things would've remained the same.

Something about that damn dock...

I couldn't get it off my mind as I made last-minute equipment checks. It felt like one of those creepy houses at the end of the street that gave off a bad energy. "Hey, is there something you're not telling us?" Greg inquired with a suspicious look, making me want to punch the cop in the face.

Irritated as to why I couldn't place a finger on the gut feeling, I huffed and shook my head. "No, it's just one of those gut feelings." I deadpanned, scowling softly at Greg when his expression didn't change.

If it wasn't Angel's brother or one of our trusted people, then his expression would have earned him a broken nose from my fist. To be fair, I did talk bad about Angel for a good while when she first came into the family, and Greg, being the protective older brother, didn't like that one bit. Angel held nothing against me, but I guess Greg did.

"Knock it off, you two. We're all buddies here." Arseny's awkward chuckle twisted the tense air between Greg and me. "Come on, whatever it is you two are fibbing about, let it go. Water under the bridge and shit." My younger brother's hands gripped each of our shoulders in a deadly manner.

Leaning in close to us with an empty smile, he threatened us, "I will make The Joker jealous of the smiles I will carve into your face if you two don't play nice tonight." The playful edge to his charming voice dropped almost completely, making the pitch of his voice lower to his natural one.

Shockingly, I wasn't the crazy one of the family. I might be the most physically violent and angry, but in terms of most deadly and dangerous, I definitely didn't come close to holding the title. Alexei and Arseny, the youngest of our family, were to be the most feared out of all of us, and everyone else would say the same if asked.

With Nikolai, Stepan, and I, the end was clear. With the twins? A person would be lucky to be killed within a week. The two were wickedly twisted—true sadists. Even if they were the least involved in the Bratva, they made their marks when they did partake in any activities.

Damn psychopaths.

Shoving at Arseny, I grumbled my compliance under my breath and rolled my eyes at him before going over to the armored truck assigned to my team. "Alright, boys, let's make this quick, violent, and bloody," I told them with a crazed grin before slamming the door shut and signaling for the driver to go.

The drive took about ten minutes, and it took us less than five to get into position. "Delta in position," I informed everyone over my earpiece.

"I need another minute, climbing the tower." Stepan's voice scratched through my earpiece.

"B-Boy needs a minute, too. I'm still setting the drones up," Bao piped up, making me roll my eyes.

"Bao, for the last fucking time, axe the nickname before I axe your tongue," Hanna snarked with a groan.

Moments later, everyone checked back in with their ready status. Once Stepan got confirmation from everyone a second time, he gave the order to go.

My team and I moved as planned. Starting at the southeast end, we swept our way up to the main building and broke off to the side door by the private docks where some boats idled. I stuck a hand out to feel the boats as we passed them.

Warm.

Something's off.

Every hair on my body stood on edge as I continued to advance with my team. Thankfully, there was nothing at the docks besides the boats. So, we moved our way to the side door. The sounds of gunshots and shouting filled my ears the closer we got to the building, and I practically felt like I was inside the room when I stood on the other side of the closed door.

Nodding at my men, I signaled them aside before kicking the door in to reveal the chaos of bullets, blood, and bodies on the inside.

Without hesitation, I raised my gun and methodically shot at every person I saw who wasn't on our side. Body after body, they dropped like flies. My body was on autopilot as the lust of battle surged through my veins and brought out a primal side of me.

Click. Click.

I didn't bother going for one of my spares the moment my main gun emptied out, nor did I bother clipping in a new magazine. Instead, I threw my piece to the side and went in with my hands, swinging wildly at any and every person within my reach.

Blood sprayed in every direction, hitting the objects around us, the floor, other people, and even my own body. None of it bothered me, though. Even when my vision clouded over with red from the blood spray across my face, I pressed on.

I didn't want to stop. There was this need, a hunger, for bloody deaths. My knuckles ached in protest with every punch, but the pain only spurred me on to the next victim.

It wasn't long until the pain of fatigue numbed out because of the buzzing excitement and adrenaline that consumed my body. Pretty sure the blood on my hands was a mixture of mine and the enemies. I knew for a fact that I cut myself on some teeth earlier from one of the first few guys I swung at.

This was getting dangerous, the haze of battle. I couldn't feel anything, which was good in the sense that my exhaustion meant nothing, but not feeling the pain of everything could prove to be reckless. I could have a stab wound or two and not know it until the physical damage became too much for my body to handle. Hell, there could be a bullet in me, causing me to bleed out, and I wouldn't know.

"Oof!" The wind got knocked out of me when a big brute tackled me to the ground.

Instinctively, I threw my arms up to block the hits flying my way. "Son of a bitch," I seethed through my grunts as I patiently waited for an opening to strike back.

Just as the man leaned back slightly with his withdrawing arm, I threw my upper body up and forward, wrapping my arms around his midsection and pulling him forward to kilter him off balance. Throwing him to the side, I flipped us over so I was on top. Headbutting him, I dazed him enough to get the upper hand in throwing my fists against his face. The hardness of his bones slowly gave with each blow until it felt like I was wailing on a sandbag that screamed back at me.

Even after his resistance stopped, I didn't. I had to be pulled off the man and held down. "Lev, quit it! Get ahold of yourself!" It was hard to tell who shouted at me because of the thrumming in my ears from my heart beating and environment being in a constant white noise.

"*Bratok*, stop. It's over." Okay, that had to be Arseny because Stepan wouldn't call me that. "We'll sedate you if we have to."

Like hell would I let that happen. I had a woman to fuck when I got home, and that couldn't happen if I was out cold.

I struggled to control my breathing as I forced myself back to reality. My whole body fought against the sudden shift, still wanting to grab people and break them. A burning sensation clawed at my chest the deeper my breaths became, and my lungs screamed in protest with each full breath of air I inhaled.

It took me a second to sort everything out in my mind once I came back down from my high. Slowly, I let my eyes take in every inch of carnage that filled the building. The more I took in, the wider my satisfied smile spread on my crazed face.

Mostly calm, I let my body slump against the bloodied ground. "I'm gonna need a whole ass bottle later." The crash later would be brutal.

On the bright side, it won't be as bad as my sub-drop, but it would be up there. Hell, I could already feel the fatigue and exhaustion seeping into my muscles and settling deep down in my bones. And I still had to get home.

Speaking of home...

"Get off of me, you oafs." I huffed with a slight struggle.

The moment I felt all the weight lift from my body, I shot up off the ground. "Let's get this shit show all set up for show and dip." I sighed tiredly when I got a better look at the mess we made.

Fuck this is gonna be a long night.

Of course, me and my big mouth. God really went 'ha, ya thought' with me tonight with the bomb he dropped on us—literally.

At first, I thought it was just my heart exploding inside my chest because of my excitement, and if it weren't for the flaming boat a few feet from me, I would've been inclined to whistle and walk away. Well, that and the panicked screams made it impossible to deny that shit was going down.

One after another, nearly all the ships blew up down the line, and out of the blazing wreckage were bodies flailing about in the water.

Then, to make things worse, the few boats that didn't go up in a ball of fire sped off like a bat out of Hell. "*Mat' yebanaya, ad!*" Just fucking great. "Get them out of the water!" I shouted at my men, rushing over to the dockside to start fishing people out of the water.

"Bao! Track those boats and see if you can get any of our men out on the waters on them!" I probably didn't need to shout at him through the communications system, but my voice came out how it did over the chaos.

"On it! Got some nearby. What orders do you want me to give them?" Bao nearly instantly replied.

One thing I really appreciated about Bao was his efficiency with every-thing, despite how laissez-faire he was as a person. Yet, when the time came, he always kicked his ass into the right gear. Well, guess that was one thing that ran through his family. Both he and Nicole had their work modes that were pretty intense if I had to say anything about it.

"Tell them to chase until they can't. Do anything and everything to shoot at least one of those boats down, and if they can snag anyone to be a prisoner, then better." I gave Bao the command to relay to the pursuers. "And tell them that if things get too dangerous, like crossing paths into another territory or Coast Guard, then retreat." As shitty as it was, I'd rather have live men than none or deal with a huge mess with the damn coastguard. The police were one thing, but the Coast Guard was a whole different ball game we weren't a part of.

"Want me to have one of them swing by and pick you and some of the others up?" I could barely make out Bao's voice through the crackling fire that made it sound like my head was in a damn microwave while a bag of popcorn was being made. The crashing water didn't help any either because it made it all the harder to discern the distressed shouts of the victims.

Gritting my teeth, I mentally debated my options, darting my head back and forth between the shrinking boats and the victims in front of me. "*Blyat*!" I hissed under my breath.

Sighing heavily, I replied to Bao, "No, it's too dangerous to swing a boat around this dock right now with the flaming wreckage and live bodies in the water." The last thing I wanted was for someone alive to be crushed or chopped up by the boat swinging into the place just to take me for a high-speed water chase. "Just keep monitoring them through your drones and what feeds you can, and keep me updated." I had to make do with living vicariously through Bao's nerdy little eyes, err words?

A loud bang rang out, and the whole place seemed to freeze for a moment as nearly everyone ducked out of fear of being hit. "Tell them to chase after the second one in line. I got a shot into it before it took off too far, and it's leaking," Stepan informed us, breaking the tense silence.

"You couldn't have given us a warning, *Styosha*? I swear, I'm going to shove that rifle up—"

"Ah blap blah blap! Nope! I do not want to hear you finish that!" Bao blurted, making a whole lot of us wince a little from the sheer volume.

"Hey, nothing wrong with enjoying some extra fun elsewhere," Arseny quipped with a laugh. "Come on, we still have people to get out of the water before they freeze to death or drown," he reminded us with a sigh before bending back over the dock.

"I hate fishing," I grumbled after a while to no one in particular, growing rather tired of hauling men, women, and children out of the freezing cold waters of the ocean.

Taking a breather, I peered down at the floating bodies that churned about with the water. An ache settled itself along my jaw as my whole body clenched up from the rising anger at seeing the needless destruction before me. So many lives lost, and for what?

As destructive as I was in the field, it was never mindless or bloody pointless. No matter how much shit I gave my brothers, it was to get on their nerves because how else was I supposed to show them affection or get their full attention and such? Either way, whenever I had my fill in the field, I was more than conscious about keeping casualties, especially ones of innocents or bystanders, to a minimum. Environmental destruction fell under the same rule. Nothing ever got blown up or torn down unless I was absolutely sure no one innocent would reap the consequences.

I might not have the best brains out of the bunch of us, but it worked where it mattered.

Shutting my eyes tightly, I took in a deep breath to calm myself before turning around to face the shivering victims we managed to save so far. "Stepan, Arseny, talk to those you can, to see if you can get anything useful," I said with a heavy sigh.

My body jarred a little from the sudden impact to my shoulder, and in my peachy mood, I snapped back at the person. Shooting my arm out, I smacked the whole thing against Stepan's chest, winding him and making him grunt. "Asshole." He strained out a cough and laugh before punching my shoulder again. "Just go home before you crash on the way back. We got the rest handled," he urged me with a sure smile and somewhat sympathetic eyes. "You need it, so go," he said in a firmer voice.

That tone of his meant there was no arguing. I would be going home, whether it be in my own car or in the back of one of the others.

Knowing better, I relented with a huff and glared at my older brother. "I hope Hanna shoves that—"

"Ey! What did I just say?" Bao piped up before I could finish, making me crack a smile.

"Well, keep me updated. I want to know about the whole shit show."

Chapter 26

GUILT EBBED AROUND IN my chest on most of the drive home because I felt bad about canceling on Nicole after working both of us up before I left, but I was exhausted.

Fortunately, I didn't have to pull out one of the lame apologies I cooked up. I don't know how or why, but when I was about a block away from home, a sudden surge of energy woke me.

It was like I'd snorted a line!

All I could think about then were the ways I'd take Nicole the moment I got my hands on her... and where I'd take her. Maybe I should drag her out back and fuck her in the garden under the moonlight; it was nice out tonight. The kitchen sounded like a nice idea, too. I mean, I was kinda hungry after my little frenzy; maybe I gotta hike her onto the island and feast on her until I was satisfied.

Fucking hell... So many places, so little time and loads. As pumped as I was, I doubt I'd be able to hit my usual three tonight. Actually, the more I thought about it, how the hell did I even make it to three loads nearly every time we screwed around? I mean, I was always exhausted and passed out nearly right away each and every time, but the fact I hadn't kneeled over and died yet was a shocker to me.

Whatever thoughts muddled my mind flushed down the drain the moment I pulled into my garage and killed the engine after throwing the car into park. The *only* thing on my mind now was Nicole.

Where the fuck is she?

My heart rammed against my chest in anticipation as my wild eyes frantically searched every inch of our house while my feet moved on their own.

Not the kitchen... Dining area no... Living no...

A light shining into the hallway from a room caught my eyes and caused my feet to shift to it. I broke into a brisk walk, nearly running into Nicole's makeshift office.

She barely got a chance to spin her chair halfway around before I roughly grabbed her by her arms and lifted her onto her desk after swiping everything off the surface with a wide sweep of my arm. "Le—mhmpfh!" Her muffled squeal blended in with the harsh rip of her clothes as I tore away at them while devouring her lips hungrily.

Her hands slapped against my chest in protest as I pressed into her, trapping her further against my body. Breaking the messy kiss, I grabbed her face roughly. "Safe-word," I demanded in a raspy voice that almost didn't sound like my own.

Nicole's whimper squeezed out between her squished cheeks, and her heavy breaths fanned my face. "Bomb, and three shoulder taps if nonverbal."

Whatever words came out of her mouth next was swallowed by my mouth as I claimed her lips again, this time shoving my tongue deep into her mouth until her body jerked against mine with her gagging. Her frantic hands switched between clawing, hitting, and grabbing me as I pressed more and more into her until she could no longer inch away from me with her squirming.

Growling against her lips, I grabbed her ass to press her lower body against mine. "You feel that, *zhizn moya*?" I growled out, grinding myself into her so she could feel how painfully hard I was. "Feel how hard I am for you?"

Glancing down, I couldn't help but let out a curt laugh when I saw the wet spot against my pants. "Fucking slut, already so wet, and I haven't done anything." Dragging my tongue across her lips, I slowly trailed it along her jaw to her neck.

Baring my teeth, I scraped it along her pulsating carotid as I continued to grind into her. I purposely rolled my hips slowly to get more friction against my aching member, but the tingling feeling zipping along the underside of my length made my pace pick up to press more into the feeling. It was only a few thrusts before I got too annoyed and pulled away with a frustrated hiss.

Grabbing her thighs, I pulled her to the edge of the desk until her ass hung off it. Spreading her legs wide into the air, I looked down at her nether regions. "What the..." My confused expression quickly shifted to an amused smirk. "Naughty girl." I chided playfully as I eyed the vibrating jewel plugging her ass.

Licking my lips, I stepped right up against her. With one hand firmly holding a leg of hers, I used the other to haphazardly undo my pants and pull my throbbing cock out. Quickly, I spit on her pussy, making her whimper and twitch.

Grinning down at her, I sloppily swiped the tip of my dick against her wet petals, spreading her slickness and my spit around to lube myself up. "Have you been thinking about this cock all night, my little whore? About how much I'm going to stretch this tight cunt of yours and how full I'm going to stuff it?" Leaning down, I breathed hotly against her ear before biting it. "About how you'll feel every inch of me thrust in and out of you?"

And just because I was an asshole, I slowly slipped my tip inside of her, but I stopped right after the first piercing slipped past her entrance. "Did you think about being taken from behind?" I chuckled deeply as I eased another inch into her moaning body. "So you can feel every bump and rub of my piercing right against your g-spot."

Unable to hold myself back any longer, I let go of my member to grab her other leg again. Spreading her legs as wide as possible, I pressed them down until she was almost bent in half. Then, with one hard thrust, I sunk myself balls deep in her with a feral groan. *"Svyatoye der'mo."* I choked out a ragged breath while digging my fingers into the back of her plush thighs.

Shit.

The butt-plug in her made her already tight cunt impossibly tight to where it kind of hurt a little to be in her fully. Well, at least the passive vibrations from the toy made things a little more pleasurable and bearable as I adjusted fully.

God, if it sucked a little for me, then... "Empress, how are you feeling?" It was a little hard to discern whether the discomfort twisting at her face was a good one or not.

Her head nodded in response as her pursed lips let out a trembling breath. "Yeah, I'm okay." Wincing, she dug her nails into the flesh of my bottom. "Just feels so full," she shuddered.

Wanting to give her some mercy, I gave her some long and slow thrusts while she adjusted—it was also for me to adjust, too. But I stilled in her after a while when I noticed her relaxing expression.

"Lev, please," she begged through a sobbing moan, her hands pawing at my ass to try and push me more against her.

Scolding her with a tut of my tongue, I pulled back to just the tip and slammed back into her, violently jerking her. "Needy little whore, aren't you?" I teased with a dark chuckle, giving her lazy thrusts to tease her. "Please, what?" Reaching a hand down, I took one of her hard nipples between my thumb and forefinger, pinching it harshly enough to make her scream a little.

Whimpering pathetically, she looks at me with needy, wanton eyes while death gripping my hips and ass. "Please, fuck me like your whore." Her hips rocked against me with her pleading words. "Please, I need your cock to break me again."

Her insistent grinding made it hard for me to think straight. So, I pressed down hard against her, trapping her completely against the desk. Taking a moment, I let my burning eyes admire her beautiful body for the millionth time. I'd never get enough of the subtle curves of her waist or the flare of her hips that made her shapely legs look long and perfect. Her small breasts looked so perfect right now, all pressed together with how I had her body folded, making them pop slightly.

She was fucking divine.

A low hum rumbled from my chest as I ran a hand down and up her body, stopping at her neck to wrap my thick hand around the slender column. Pulling her up as much as possible, I leaned down the rest of the way until I was a hair away from her parted lips and half-hooded eyes. "Here's what's gonna happen," I started, staring deeply into her awe-struck eyes. "I'm going to ruin and break you, then I'll cherish you."

Kissing the corner of her lips, I dipped the tip of my tongue into her mouth teasingly. "I am going to fuck you like I don't love you," I whispered deeply against her lips with an intense gaze.

Nicole's eyes widened brightly in a smile at my words. "Y-you love me?" Her hopeful voice trembled against my lips.

Naturally, my lips warmed up in a genuine smile. "Of course, but those three words won't do my feelings for you any justice." I pressed my lips against her in a deep and passionate kiss, letting all my adoration and devotion pour into it. "So, I will show you how much I love you."

The blissful smile on my face quickly sharpened into a malicious one as my grip on her neck tightened until I heard her gasping breaths hitch sharply. "After I return the favor for all the things you've done to me." Taking her bottom lip between my teeth, I bit and pulled hard. "I am going to fucking break you until all you can do is beg for my cock to be in you twenty-four fucking seven."

"Oh God." Nicole shuddered under me, biting her bottom lip with her muffled moan.

Barking out a ridiculing laugh, I pulled my hips back and slammed into her a few times to work her up. "If that's how you see me, then you better start worshiping my cock like your life depends on it."

Carefully, I adjusted my hold on her neck to not crush her as I slammed into her harshly, making the desk bang against the wall with every thrust. I'd probably damage the wall or even put a hole through it after I was done with Nicole, but fuck it. There was no way I'd ease off, not with how Nicole's eyes rolled to the back of her head as her happy mouth hung open to sing her beautiful moans. The only thing I was mindful of was Nicole's head.

Yeah, I wanted to fuck her until there was not a thought in her head, but I rather not give her a concussion in the process. I was careful to keep her head from hitting the wall with my hard thrusts so far, but one slip and my brothers would have another embarrassing story to put into their blackmail treasure box.

Sucking in a sharp breath, I let go of her neck and moved that same hand to the back of her head. "Shit, you're squeezing me so much," I remarked with a breathless chuckle.

Nicole could barely get out a full sentence through her dazed moans. "Coming... Too good... Fuck!" Her body tensed and trembled with her soft sob as she orgasmed again.

Gritting my teeth, I sucked in another chilling breath as I felt the familiar ache in my balls. Every orgasm from her made it harder and harder to hold myself back from exploding in her with how perfectly her soft walls clenched around my thick cock.

Even if this first load didn't mean the end tonight, I wanted this rough fucking to last a little longer. I wanted to push beyond that edge for as long as possible. Also, I had just a little more pent-up energy to expend.

Hearing her scream my name in such lustful anguish brought a twisted smile to my face as I watched her come undone. "Lev, I can't! Too much!" she sobbed loudly.

Fortunately for her, that big orgasm of hers drew my own out with a deep groan. "Fuck, that's it, Nicole, be my good girl and squeeze out every last drop," I encouraged her with a soft smile and some butterfly kisses to her face as I slowly pumped in and out to work out the ache in my balls.

Burying my face into her neck, I inhaled her scent to calm myself as I lowered her legs and wrapped them around my waist. "Breathe, baby, breathe," I shushed and soothed her, stroking her messy locks. "Thank you," I whispered sweetly into her ear. "You were so amazing and perfect."

Slowly and carefully, I stood up straight and picked Nicole up, being mindful to keep us connected as I moved us to the bedroom. "I'm going to be so sore tomorrow, but I don't care." She chuckled weakly against my neck between her little nips.

Chuckling along with her, I carefully laid down in the bed with her. "When are you not sore after a night of sex?" I remarked with an arrogant smirk, earning a smack to the chest.

Wincing softly, she shifted her hips to straddle me more comfortably. "Just because I let you be in charge tonight doesn't mean you can be an asshole, you jerk."

Her chest heaved against mine, and her heavy breaths chilled my sweaty chest with each exhale. "We are so going to have to shower after this somehow..." She chuckled dryly. "You're still covered in blood and sweat from your assignment, and now it's all on me."

Maybe that was why I found her a little more alluring. I didn't take much notice of the fact that I had dirtied her with my tainted body. Well, the riveting thought sped away as it came when my anger started to boil a little in my blood.

I could feel my eyes narrow as my nostrils flared with each seething breath. The fact that she was covered in some other man's blood was unacceptable. Granted, it was my fault, but still, I didn't like anything of another man touching her or staining her body.

So, with an audible huff, I hauled us off the bed and took us to the shower in a brooding silence. I wanted to get the blood off her this instant. No, scratch that. I *needed* to remove it from her and then mark her as mine again.

Without a word or sound, I turned the water on, letting all the shower heads drench us with hot water. I didn't bother grabbing the sponge or washcloth to clean her. My hands were more than enough to rub away all the blood smeared on her face and body. Some bits took a little more effort to remove, but I didn't stop touching every inch of her until she was pristine again.

Once she was clean, I grabbed her face and kissed her deeply. She kissed back for a moment, but her hands wailed against my chest in protest after a few seconds. "Lev, what the hell? What's going on with you? What's with the grumpy silence? Did I say or do something to set you off? And why the hell did you just drag me into the shower like this when we were comfortable in bed?"

Question after question flew out of her mouth, each one growing in pitch with her irritation as she stood there with her arms crossed.

Clicking my tongue, I turned my back to her for a minute to recollect myself. I don't know why I found it difficult to verbalize my frustration to her right now. I mean, it shouldn't be this hard to tell her how I hated the sight of another man's blood on her. Yet, here I was, pouting in the shower like some petulant child.

Nicole's sigh was almost lost to the shower, but I caught it. "Little lion." Her soft voice echoed throughout the shower.

The warmth of her body was stark in contrast to the hot water, surprisingly. Silky softness snaked around my waist, holding me against my lover's tantalizing body. Oddly enough, a chill ran through my body at the contact with Nicole before I felt myself naturally relax into her.

Her soft voice rang out throughout the shower again, coaxing me. "Talk to me. I won't get upset or mad or anything. I just want to know what made you flip a switch." The pads of her fingers danced along my abdomen and pelvis, following the contours of my muscles.

Closing my eyes, I let my head fall back to let the water pelt my face for a while. Then, my head fell forward, and I sucked in a deep breath. "I..." I thought I was ready, but my words caught themselves in my throat. Shutting my mouth, I moved my tongue around to loosen it up. "I got upset at the sight of another person's blood on you," I strained out in a single breath. "I don't want any part of another man to touch you or be on your body for any period of time," I admitted in a small voice as I stroked the back of her hands with my thumbs.

Nicole's arms loosened, and a soft push pressed into my hip, prompting my body to turn around. I braced myself to face a disappointed or irritated girlfriend, but much to my surprise, I was met with a proud smile. Her body pressed itself fully against mine again, and a kiss was placed on my chest, right over the tattoo she gave me. "Good job. I'm proud of you for telling me," she praised me with a soft grin. "And thanks for not overreacting because I sure as hell would have thrown a huge ass fit if the situation was reversed," she mused with a chuckle.

Cracking a smile and chuckle, I hugged her back for a long minute before letting go to finish our shower. I still needed to make love to her and cover her body with kisses to taint her my essence again.

Actually... Maybe I should cover her in my cum instead.

The dirty thought sent a shiver of excitement down my spine as I let my eyes linger on Nicole while she dried her hair without a care in the world. I was already done and remained leaning against the bathroom doorframe with all the patience in the world for my lover to finish.

Fortunately, Nicole wasn't one to have some hour-long bedtime skincare routine or some ridiculous ritual. I wasted no time scooping her into my arms when she turned her head and flashed me a cheeky smile.

Giggling, Nicole tightly wrapped her arms around my neck. "I'm surprised you didn't fuck me in the shower," she commented with some confusion laced in her voice.

Snorting out a short laugh, I shook my head softly as I carried her to bed. "I'm not making love to you for the first time in the shower," I remarked, grinning at the sight of her cheeks blushing up. "Plus, you've made it clear that you don't like shower sex." Apparently, shower sex wasn't all it was cracked up to be for Nicole, and after we tried it a few times, she struck it from our list of places to fuck.

Once we reached our bed, I threw her on it rather unceremoniously, causing her to giggle and glare at me playfully. "Jerk," she shot at me with a roll of her eyes.

Chuckling, I pounced on her, caging her between my arms and legs. "If I'm not a jerk, then something is seriously wrong with me," I retorted with a small laugh.

As I lowered my head, I took her face in my hands to hold her still. "So fucking perfect." Kiss. "Divine." Kiss. "Lovely." Kiss. "Beautiful." Kiss. "And you're all mine." My voice dipped lower and lower with each word until I practically growled.

Carefully, I gingerly trailed my hands down her body, cupping her breasts and fondling them. Reluctantly, I left her lips to kiss down her face and neck.

Hearing her soft sighs and moans of pleasure jolted my heart to pump harder until it was banging in my ears.

I left no inch of her neck untouched. It was a constant barrage of kisses, nips, and licks, along with the occasional love bite that would last for days. Once I was satisfied with leaving my mark on the side of her neck, a nicely drawn out 'L' with hickeys, I moved down to her lovely breasts. Of course, I didn't leave them unscathed. Her chest and breasts were adorned with scattered marks varying in size and shape.

As I busied myself with painting her body with my marks, I carefully pinched and pulled at her sensitive nipples until I had her grinding against my thigh shamelessly. "Don't come," I whispered against her nipple before taking it into my hungry mouth.

Sucking and licking, I spent a good moment teasing her nipple before pulling off with a soft pop. "Work yourself up, but don't come. I want you to hold it all back for when I'm in you. I don't want you clenching around nothing when my cock is here to receive it," I told her with a teasing smile before going over to her other nipple to give it some attention.

Much to my surprise, she listened. I half expected her to shoot me a 'fuck you' glare before taking her orgasms for herself. So, when I felt her juices coat my thigh but never felt the rush of her gushing or squirting, I was thoroughly impressed. "Lev, please, no more teasing," she begged between her gasping moans after she tangled her fingers into my hair. "I need you in me." Her legs shifted to coil around my waist, and she pressed me against her by putting her feet against my ass. "Right. Now," she demanded, grinding her slickened cunt along the underside of my cock, making me groan.

Smiling happily, Nicole gripped my shoulders as she slowly rolled her hips against me. "Fuck I love your cock so much." She sighed out a moan. "Your piercings always feel so amazing, and the way you know how to work your cock to get every spot of mine... Just..." Biting her bottom lip, she let out a deep moan as she pressed herself harder against me.

Then, her smile widened into a small laugh. "You know," she started, locking her eyes with mine, "You never told me the story about your piercings."

The mention of my hardware made me groan internally as my eyes rolled. "And I never will for as long as I live," I grumbled, turning my face away to hide the embarrassed flush of my cheeks.

There were only two people in the whole world who knew about how I ended up with a full Jacob's Ladder on my dick, me and Nikolai; the ladder only knew because I had no other option, but I made him swear to secrecy.

Nicole's amused and cheerful laugh filled the air. "Oh, little lion, who said I'd give you a choice?" The dark edge of determination in her voice sent shivers down my spine.

But it went as fast as it came. Her sharp smile softened back up as she stroked my face tenderly. "Well, we can bring that back later." Her hips lightly bucked at me, pulling my mind back to the activity at hand.

Sliding my hands around her body, I slipped one arm around her waist, lifting her hips a little as I did so. My other went around her upper back, and I cradled the back of her head with the same hand. Holding her body fully against mine, I let my lips ghost against hers as I moved my hips around until my tip pressed into her. Keeping myself barely in, I held myself back from fully entering her.

This would be a first for us. We've fucked every which way til Sunday and beyond, but never once have we taken it slow and sensual.

Never have we made love to each other.

Until now.

"I love you," I confessed with a shaky breath and groan when I slowly filled her to the brim. "So much," I breathed against her lips, shivering a little as the sound of her blissful moan sang beautifully in my ears. "I love you so fucking much, Nicole." My voice cracked from the overwhelming crash of emotions assaulting my body.

Resting my forehead against hers, I kissed her lips with a soft whimpering sob. "I'm so sorry for not admitting it before, for being such a coward about it." The number of times I withdrew from her when I saw the closeness in her eyes or heard the dreaded four-letter word fall from her mouth was a few times too many.

Nicole's body arched more into me as her mouth hung open with a silent moan. Her soft walls gripped my cock in a vice grip as her orgasm shook her delicate body. It took her a few seconds to come down from the high of her orgasm enough to smile brightly at me with teary eyes. "Lev." Her own tender voice cracked a little as her hand stroked my cheek. "It's okay. I know you love me, that you always have." Bigger, her smile grew until she was full-on beaming at me with so much giddiness that I thought she'd explode into a ball of sunshine. "I always saw it in your eyes whenever you looked at me before you would start to fight yourself on it. I never pushed you to admit any of it because I wanted you to come to things on your own terms."

Her lips met mine in a soul-stealing kiss; to say that it was breathtaking would've done it an injustice. Those soft brownish amber eyes of hers melted my heart the longer she gazed into my icy blues. "I'm so happy you came to it sooner rather than later." She mused with a giggle before kissing me again. "I'm so proud of you, little lion." Her praise caused a zap of pleasure to shoot down my spine straight to my cock, causing me to twitch inside of her. "I know it couldn't have been easy for you one bit, so I really am so proud of you."

Gulping, I forced out a chuckle and bucked my hips a little, making Nicole's breath hitch. "Trying to butter and sweeten me up, *zhizn moya*?" I teased, grinding my hips more to rub my piercings against her sensitive walls. "You're going to give me an ego if you keep praising me like that," I joked with a hearty laugh that mixed with hers when she joined.

"Oh, shut up and show me how much you love me," Nicole murmured against my lips. "Show me how a bratva boss properly loves his woman."

"With pleasure." I grinned smugly before drowning my groan out with her lips.

Tightening my arms around her waist, I angled her hips slightly to easier thrust at her sweet spot with each movement. My hips moved at a rather slow pace, dragging out the pleasure for both of us with sensual strokes rather than ravaging her with hard and fast thrusts that would break her body. "Fuck you feel so amazing, baby," I groaned breathlessly against her lips.

Breathing heavily, Nicole smiled against my lips, darting her tongue out to run it along the seam of my mouth. "I really love how big you are and how you fill me just perfectly every time." She giggled before busying herself with kissing my face. "Fill me with your cum, Lev. Stuff me and get me pregnant."

It was hard to maintain my slow pace after hearing that. Holding her firm, I started to move her body along with my thrusts, bringing her down to meet each and every buck of my hips. My strokes were still full and sensual, being careful to pull out nearly all the way before going to the hilt on the way in.

Paired with her sweet moans and pleas to knock her up, the feeling of her walls squeezing me to coax my release out made it impossible for me to hold it back after a while.

An ache gripped at my clenched jaw as I gritted my teeth and groaned loudly. "That's it, baby, squeeze me just like that." I gasped with a jagged breath. "Oh fuck, Nicole, fuck, that's—shit! Mhmm, take it all, take all my cum into your greedy little womb." My hips lightly bucked and jerked in short bursts to try and work out as much of my seed as possible.

Looking down at her, I could perfectly imagine the feeling of her round belly pressing against me when I'd take her in such a state.

Fucking hell... She's gonna look so adorable all round and pregnant.

The image of her smiling warmly at me while rubbing her swollen stomach sent a shiver through me and caused my throbbing cock to squeeze out one last spurt.

"I love you so much, Lev." Her voice sounded so ethereal in my post-climax haze.

Smiling like a dope, I kissed her languidly. "I love you too, Nicole."

Slumping down beside her on the bed, I pulled her close and held her tightly. "I'm not pulling out," I murmured against her hair as I felt myself drifting in and out of sleep.

"You can't stay like this all night. You're gonna cramp up or something," she worried with a weak chuckle.

"Don't care. Worth it." My words slurred out groggily as I lost my fight with the impending darkness.

"Good night, *zhizn moya*."

"Good night, *đại ca*."

Chapter 27

Nicole

~1 week later~

Going back to what used to be my company felt strange, more so than I expected. What used to feel like home felt so foreign and cold with the strange looks everyone flashed me when I walked in.

"M-miss Le." The receptionist's face paled upon recognizing me. It was as if she'd seen a ghost. Clearing her throat, she averted her eyes to something on her desk. "This is unexpected. Um... Do you have an appointment?"

I don't know why, but the frankness of her attitude, along with how she actively avoided eye contact with me, pissed me off. Approaching the fancy desk, I slammed my hands on top of it. "Do I have an appointment? At my own company that I started from the ground up?" Narrowing my eyes into dangerous slits, I scowled at her. "Don't think that you are going to escape from this unscathed." The threat was meant to be empty, but from how she flinched and shrunk away from me, I couldn't help but wonder if she had some part in my usurp.

"Tell my sperm donor and child bearer that I will be in my office," I commanded the receptionist in a low and stern voice. "And tell them, don't be late."

Not bothering to wait for a response, I pushed off the desk and made my way to the private elevator at the back of the lobby, carrying my head high and chest proud the whole way.

Stopping at the keypad, I pulled out my phone to load the digital keycard to swipe. Obviously, it wasn't my original one when I worked here, but it was child's play to create a new one after hacking my own company. Actually, with how bad my company's tanked, even a tech-illiterate person like my little lion could hack the damn place.

Just as I expected, the doors opened after the swipe, and I stepped in along with Lev and some of his men. No, I wasn't raiding my parents or shooting the place up. This really was meant to be a peaceful meeting—just talk. All of us were dressed professionally, as in business professional, not tactical gear.

No one dared to stand in my way as I strutted down the hallway to the grand room that used to be my office. Well, everyone probably avoided me because of the six rough-looking men who trailed behind me. Lev insisted on bringing some backup just in case things went haywire, and I wasn't in the mood to argue with him about it when there was really no harm in having extra manpower. Granted, I hoped this meeting wouldn't end up in a shoot-out. I wasn't so much worried about Lev or our men getting into it; it was my parents and their idiots who I worried about.

Barging into my office, I paused at the entryway when I saw my brother sitting behind the grand desk. Before the shock got him scrambling to put himself together, it was obvious what I had interrupted.

Fucking gross.

"Get out," I bit out with a disgusted scowl.

Can't believe this is the idiot they gave my shit to.

With one hand holding his pants up, he fumbled around on the desk for the emergency button. "G-guards!" he shouted, his hand throwing papers and folders randomly aside in search of the button.

"It's under the desk in the first drawer, you fucking idiot." I deadpanned, watching as he followed my direction.

It was a little amusing to watch his face light up with hope before realization smashed it. "Guards!" His desperate shout echoed throughout the room and down the hallway.

"Are not coming," I merely told him as I walked over to the desk calmly. "Maybe if you'd pay them decently and treat them well, then maybe, just maybe, they wouldn't have been so easily bribed," I told him matter of factly, with a smug smile that lasted a second before my face turned deadly again. "Now, you have ten seconds to get your pathetic ass out of here before my men throw you out." It was his final warning, and the grave infliction in my voice would have made it evident.

Guess my brother decided to be utterly stupid today. He got his scraggly ass all up in my face while the poor girl who had been servicing him scrambled out of the room. "No, you listen here." I didn't budge or flinch as he spat in my face. "You do not belong here, so you leave before someone throws you and your loser thug heads out."

Now, I did move when he decided to lay his hands on me and shove at my shoulders. I quickly caught myself before I could trip on my own feet, and I struck back. I felt no guilt in backhanding my younger brother. Unlike me, he fell to my feet with one strike. "Lev, I'm fine. Put the gun away." I could see Lev's outstretched hand pointing a gun in my brother's direction in my peripheral.

Looking down at my brother with a dead expression, I nodded toward the door. "Leave and be lucky I'm not picking my bone with you today, or possibly ever because you're not worth a second of my time."

Sure, my younger brother was a brat, and I didn't like him, but I didn't really have anything against him. Unfortunately for him, he was a product of our parents. He couldn't help how they raised him, and I definitely had no say in them raising their damn golden child. And maybe I held out a little hope for him in the end because I think deep down, he had the potential to be a good man; he just needed to get his ass kicked and set straight and removed from my parents.

That hope was short-lived, though. Getting back up to his feet, he got in my face again. "You are such a bitch. You know that? Always walking around like you own everything, that you are the shit." His seething face was inches from mine, letting me smell the alcohol and weed on him very clearly. "You're just a selfish cunt who wants everything for herself. I mean, you can easily create another company or give me some money to help me start my own, but no! You refused to help your own brother start off a good life!"

Confused, I lightly furrowed my eyebrows together and opened my mouth to speak, only to have my brother silence me with a finger to my face. "No! Don't you dare try to gaslight me and shit." He scoffed spitefully. "And, of course, when things don't go your way, you through a bitch fit and ruin things for all of us." Turning on his heel, he walked away a few steps before whirling back around to continue his nonsense.

"Would it have been so bad to marry Phi? He would have given you the damn lavish life ya wanted, given you more companies to be a tyrant over, but no, you wanted to be a stupid 'I don't need no man' feminist and didn't even show up to your own wedding." Throwing another accusing finger at me. "You have any idea how much shit we got from them? How much money we lost? How much shame was brought upon us?"

Yeah, color me confused because I truly had no clue, not even a shred, about what he went on about. "Are you high? Drunk?" Was that the reason for his outburst?

Before I could question my brother, a new voice took the spotlight from us. "Liam! That's enough!" Lazily, I turned my head over to the doorway, where my red-faced father stood with my mother right behind him. "Leave! Now!"

Liam instantly apologized, bowed his head, and left with his tail tucked between his legs.

Fucking coward.

Taking a deep breath to recenter myself, I pulled the jacket off the back of the desk chair and set it on the seat. After seeing what gets done in this chair, no way would I sit on it without some kind of barrier. Hell, I wanted to burn my eyes after seeing the initial scene, and I was sure that these clothes would end up in a bleach bath or in a fire pit once I got home.

Suffocating silence filled the room, following the doors slamming shut. For a long while, I sat there, glaring at my parents with spiteful, dead eyes. "I would say I love what you've done to the place, but lying is unbefitting of a humble woman," I snarked at them with a fake smile. "But, who am I kidding." Dropping the act, I let the loathing edge inside me sharpen my voice. "I'm not a humble woman."

Scowling deeply, I propped an elbow onto the desk and leaned my head onto my hand, and my other hand drummed at the desk's surface. "Since everyone's so convinced that I'm such a bitch, then I might as well start acting like one." I scoffed, shaking my head disapprovingly at my parents, who stood there in a brooding silence. "Igor Petrov," I demanded with a hardened expression. "And don't you dare feed me some bullshit of 'oh, I don't know what you're talking about' and shit because I know you've been meeting him in secret, and I have proof of it. So, start entertaining me before I let Angel handle you two."

Slow steps interrupted the silence in the room as Lev moved next to me. "Talk," Lev demanded menacingly from beside me. "Now!"

My parents flinched at Lev's raised voice. My mother started stammering for a split second before my father silenced her with a hand in her direction. "How dare you," my father started, taking a step in my direction, only to stop when the men who surrounded him drew their guns at him. "You have no right to trespass and demand things of us."

"Igor. Petrov. Now," I repeated, not wanting to engage in useless conversation with them. "Why are you meeting with him? What is he doing here in Nespin? What does he want?"

"That is none of your business." My father stood firm, not running his mouth. "You're wasting your time, so unless you're going to tell me that you're coming back and going to be the obedient daughter you're supposed to be, leave."

Well, this was going how I somewhat expected.

Forcing out a short, ridiculing laugh, I shook my head. "You fucked over my life one too many times." Leaning back in the chair, I defied them with an arrogant look. "You already have everything I owned in name, so why even need me back?" I questioned in a bored voice. "And this is your last chance to talk. If you don't, then I suggest you start getting used to the idea of living in a three-by-eight-foot room."

When I was met with another stretch of silence, I sighed heavily. "Fine. Have it your way." Lifting a finger, I signaled the men to act. "Cuff 'em, and we'll take them to The Catacombs."

Needless to say, my parents weren't too thrilled being walked out like perpetrators. No matter how much they protested, though, they wouldn't give me what I wanted, even when I gave them one last chance before they were thrown into the car.

"Wait," I half shouted at my men, making them stop right before they put my mother into the car. "Put her in mine and Lev's," I commanded, nodding toward our vehicle.

"Martha! Don't—"

My father's shouting became incoherent after I slammed the car door on him. "Oh, shut it!" I hissed under my breath.

The fake smile I flashed my mother would've put a snake to shame. "Let's go for a drive, mother."

If anyone between my parents were to break, it would be my mother. The only problem was my father, who controlled her. Not to say she was a good person without him around because she wasn't, but she was easier to manipulate without my father to block any attempts.

As expected, my mother trembled like a leaf in the wind the moment we started driving in a dead silence. "You know," I spoke up after we left the city limits. "I wonder how long it'll be before Liam's body turns up in the morgue. I mean, without mom around to feed him and tend to him, how is he going to survive? All that booze and drugs will get to him faster without anyone around to help curb his habits." My eyes glanced up at my mother's reflection in the rearview mirror. "I say the company bombs and tanks within three days max, and it'll just all blow up real quick after that."

No one at the damn company was loyal to my parents, at least not without the right incentive, which they wouldn't receive with my parents locked away in our desert prison. "Actually, it might be less than that." I sighed in disinterest. "It'll only take me an hour or two tops to completely drain every account you have in existence while I have some men tear your homes apart from the foundation up."

I wasn't serious about everything I spoke into existence. It was all to scare my mother into spilling about Igor and whatever else they had up their sleeves. "No money, no home, no company, just what will your poor Liam do besides drown his sorrows until his heart stops? And what will you have to come back to if you ever live through this?"

"Nicole, please, have a heart and reason. Your father and I just want what is best for you. We always have. We were taking away the stress of the company from you and setting you up with a good life with a rich man who would have spoiled you with all you could ever think of." If it weren't for the sheer desperation and lack of emotions in her voice, I might be inclined to somewhat believe her.

Too bad I knew better now.

"And I don't want to hurt you. You're my mother." Turning around in my seat, I looked at her with a frown and sad eyes. "This is why I wanted to have you with me in the car. I know I can talk to you." I continued to play the caring daughter despite the fact it made my stomach churn my lunch back up my throat. "Listen, whatever this Igor person is offering you, it's nothing compared to what the Volkovs—"

Out of nowhere, my mother shot up, leaning toward me. In a low voice, she spoke in Vietnamese, "The Volkovs can go eat shit!" Whoa, did not expect the sudden outburst from her. "Everything was going perfectly fine until they took over, and we had to obey their stupid rules. You have any idea how restricted we became? Our profits were cut in half overnight, and we've been on a downward trend ever since your stupid friend merged and gave leadership to her husband."

From the corner of my eye, I could see Lev flash me a look of concern. "Little lion, it's okay," I assured him with a wave of my hand. "Just drive, okay?"

Then, I turned my full attention back to my mother with a fake smile plastered on my face. Switching to Vietnamese, I conversed with my mother. "And Igor is much better? You know he has next to nothing, right? The takedown ruined his whole family. Even if you help him, that won't be enough.

He has no funds, no men, no army, nothing. If you go to Russia with him to try and retake what his family lost over there, then I hope you're prepared to have an icy grave because the Volkovs control quite a bit of Russia and outpower Igor by far." Honestly, what the hell were my parents even thinking? It really made no sense to me, business-wise or not.

"The Volkovs are about to fall because of their stupid rules. No one likes them. They are all teaming with Igor," my mother told me in a slightly hushed voice. "It's only a matter of time."

Well, ploy or not, she had my interest piqued. "Oh? Who then? It doesn't matter if they're little people." Time to see what information I could pry from her.

My mother quickly prattled off a list of names, nearly all of whom have been dealt with accordingly rather recently. However, it would seem as if my mother had no idea about the recent shift in leadership and loyalty. "Oh? Wow, I didn't think there were that many." But her ignorance would bode well for me. "So, Igor, he's got a shot then? Like a good shot."

Realization beamed on my mother's face as she fell for my act. "Yes, exactly. Everything will return to how it was before with Lady Qing." Then, her face grew brighter with a hopeful grin. "And you know what? He's taken rather a liking to you and wants you as his wife. Isn't that amazing? You'll have all the power in the world with him as your husband, and our family's alliance with him will be complete."

And there it was, just as my informant told me. "Really? Why me?" Might as well dig for the whole treasure if I was getting dirty already.

"He really loves how you look, and he needs a woman by his side to look better for all the followers. It's actually one of the conditions he gave your father and me that for this working business between us to fully work, you had to be the one to solidify it through marriage." I didn't like how comfortable my mother was getting, as if she'd just won the lottery. "So, come on, stop this nonsense with those useless Volkovs and come back to your father and me. We can be a family again, and everything will be wonderful again."

A part of me hated how genuinely hopeful she seemed. This whole thing was nothing more than a grand delusion, in my opinion. Sadly, it seemed like she'd fallen for it all—fallen to the bottom of the pit with no chance of help. Granted, there was no help for her before, but it was pitiful how she'd deluded herself.

If I had more of a heart to give her, then maybe I could care enough to try and save her, but she was way beyond saving. She was too set in her old ways. I would always come third to her, Liam and my father being first and second. Whatever money I'd throw at her would go straight to one of the two men in her life, and even if I got her help somehow, she'd pull Liam along.

Unfortunately, it was the stupid dance of old customs and culture with my parents, and it was one I refused to partake in. For crying out loud, we were in the twenty-first century and in America. Women had rights, we had autonomy, and we definitely didn't have to bow to some stupid patriarchy.

Tearing my attention away from my mother, I leaned over the center console and hugged Lev's arm. "Hey, are you going to be fair to our children?"

Lev's arm shook gently with his confused chuckle. "What do you mean, *zhizn moya*? Of course, I'm going to treat them fair? I mean, if one of them needs more discipline or something, then obviously I gotta treat them a little different." His gaze fell down at me briefly before snapping back to the road.

Okay, I probably should have worded that a little differently. "I meant like our girls and boys like you won't favor our boys over our girls, right? Or treat them better and shit." I couldn't help the slight disdain from slipping into my words.

"Of course not," he quickly replied in a firm voice. "I don't give a shit about gender." He scoffed softly and muttered something in Russian before flashing me a playful grin, "Though, if I'm being honest, I might spoil our girls more than our boys." His soft laughter filled the car, along with the sound of my hand hitting his shoulder. "I'm going to treat and raise all of them the same, and according to who they are as a person. All our girls will know how to kick ass like our boys. And all our boys will know how to cook and clean just as well as any girl."

"Girls and boys? Plural?" I questioned him with a playful wariness. "How many kids do you want?"

Lev shrugged his shoulders with a hum and chuckle. "Like enough to fill a van? So five? Six?"

Staring at his cheeky face for a second, I waited for him to change his mind to a lower number. When it was obvious that wasn't happening, I smacked his arm again while rolling my eyes. "Let's start at one or two, mister, then go from there." I decided for us with a soft chuckle and warm smile.

The thought of having to wrangle more than two kids seemed exhausting to me. If I was being honest, thinking about raising one child was enough to get my hair to fall out. I mean, what if I fucked up at being a mother somehow? What if I was an oddball where my mothering instincts don't kick in? Would I even be a good mother? Why didn't I think about any of this before agreeing to roll the dice with Lev and kids?

A soft pinch to my thigh derailed me from my train of worries. "Hey, look at me." Lev's prompting got my body moving accordingly. "Our children are going to be perfectly fine. We have all the money in the world to provide amazing lives for them, and we're going to be amazing parents." I don't know how he could sound so assured about something so unstable and unpredictable, but I'd take the comfort. "Or, at the very least, we know what *not* to do as parents." He barked out a curt laugh and grinned goofily at me.

I mean, he had a good point there. Even if we might not know the rights when it comes to parenting, at least we know the wrongs to avoid at all costs.

Kissing Lev's arm, I squeezed it in a brief hug before turning back to face my mother. "It's a shame. Lev's an amazing boyfriend, and he would have been an even better son-in-law." Sighing disappointedly, I shook my head at her. "Too bad you'll never know from The Catacombs."

Chapter 28

"ARE YOU SURE? I mean, I said you can pick anywhere," I questioned Nicole's choice of venue with a raised brow.

Bouncing a little in her seat, Nicole hit the 'go' button on the navigation screen. "Hey, small family-owned places are the bomb. I'd pick them over a freaking five-star Michelin restaurant any day," Nicole retorted with an excited grin.

Rolling my eyes, I snorted softly as I reached over to pause the navigation, earning an angry pout from my hangry girlfriend. "Hey! You said I could pick," she snapped, balling her fists up in her lap and glowering at me.

If looks could kill, then I'd be burning in Hell already. "Empress, I just got done beating your dad bloody, and I'm covered in his blood and spit. Even if we're not going to some high-end place, I want to get decent at the very least." If it was a small splatter here and there then I wouldn't have minded, but I had it all over my arms and face. Also, dried blood was a bitch to scrub off.

Huffing in defeat, Nicole slumped in her seat with her arms crossed. "Fine, I guess you can go clean up," she grumbled, rolling her eyes.

"Baby, there's some snacks in the glove compartment and in the bag in the back." The drive home from our desert compound would be a long while, and the last thing I needed was for Nicole to rip my head off halfway through the trip.

Without a peep, Nicole trifled through the glove compartment and the snack bag after snatching it up. Thankfully, her munching kept her occupied for a good portion of the drive.

After a while, I broke our peaceful silence. "So, what are we going to do with your parents now? Just keep them locked away in The Catacombs until they die? What about Igor? I mean, they were our only lead to him so far." Unfortunately, these things couldn't wait.

Sighing, Nicole ran a hand through her hair, pushing it out of her face. "We'll see if they talk once Angel or one of the twins have a go at them, then we'll figure things out further." She didn't sound too confident, which made the corner of my lips frown. "We're going to need to have another go at the people who are supposedly in cahoots with Igor, and if we're lucky, one of them will squeal sooner rather than later."

The leather seat creaked with her movement as she leaned her head against the window. "I'll have to dig around with Bao to take a look at everyone's accounts. There's bound to be one idiot who did something electronically that will give us the thread that will lead us back to Igor." Her words grew in frustration as she spoke with heavy sighs.

Reaching over, I settled my hand on her thigh, offering her a soothing rub and pat. "Don't dwell too much on it, empress. We'll handle it one day at a time." We couldn't rush it if we wanted.

Yes, the possibility of Igor fleeing and resurfacing was a huge problem, but tracking people down and capturing them took time, same with going through their electronic footprint. As good as Nicole and Bao were, their fingers could only code and scroll at a certain speed, and their programs could only process so fast.

Keeping a hand on her thigh, I continued to drive for a little bit in silence to simmer the tension out. "What were you and your mom talking about earlier? I kept hearing 'Volkovs' every now and then." We hadn't had a chance to talk about the brief conversation in the previous car ride, and my curiosity was starting to burn holes into my brain at this point.

Lifting her head off the window, she gave a soft, questioning hum and blinked at me a few times before I saw the light bulb go off in her head. "Oh, that?" Sitting up straight, she continued to hum for a second before leaning over to me and hugging my arm. "She was going on about how there's a lot of people unhappy about the Volkov Bratva, the ones who were with Lady Qing before. Then, she tried to convince me to leave you to go marry Igor because, apparently, that was a condition of his for my parents to go fully into business with him."

Hearing the little bit about her mother telling her to leave me for Igor made my grip on the steering wheel tightened to where it squeaked under me. "Like hell are you ever leaving me for anyone." Over my dead body because I'd fight whoever tries to take her away from me or whoever she tries to leave me for.

Laughing softly, Nicole kissed my shoulder. "I'm pretty sure that's my line. After all, I was the one who tattooed and collared you," she retorted, reaching up and tugging at the ring of my collar.

"Still can't believe you were thinking about cutting it off." Her voice flattened with her words, and a sharp pinch to my arm followed them. "Not that you would have been able to, but still, the fact you held those sheers to it."

Angel snitched me out to Nicole the other day about the one morning I hid out at Nikolai's place. Come to find out, if I did try to snip my collar off that morning, then I would've failed because there was metal in the damn thing.

"I said I was sorry, and it's not like I did it." I tried to defend myself, but the deadpanned expression she shot me meant I'd get nowhere. "I was confused and terrified, I told you." Still didn't make me feel less guilty about it all. Even though she waved it off back then as she did now, the hurt in her eyes was as clear as day to me.

Yeah, I was more than prepared to spend every day apologizing for almost making a huge mistake. Well, at this point, that would be the case. My sore ass served as a good reminder.

Speaking of my ass, the thought of punishment later tonight had me squirming in my seat with a slight grimace. Needless to say, Nicole definitely wasn't letting me forget her gracious gift to me, nor was she letting me forget who was in charge between us and who owned who.

Memories of the other night flooded my mind, making shivers trickle down my spine in response to the sudden heat blooming in my body. I knew what happened behind closed doors would always remain so, but it was still a little embarrassing to think about. No one would ever take me seriously if they ever found out about how I'd let Nicole—

Everything came to a screeching halt from the sudden jolt of pleasure shocking my unexpecting body. Sucking in a sharp breath, I glanced at Nicole briefly. "N-Nicole, I'm driving," I strained out through gritted teeth before letting out a trembling exhale.

"And?" she remarked smugly, and no doubt with a devious smirk etched on her face. "You don't need your dick to drive." Nicole snarked, snickering darkly as she leaned over more to my side until her upper body was all up in my lap.

Dragging out a playful sigh, she slowly worked my pants open, pulling my throbbing cock out. "Now, just what is my little lion thinking about to get this worked up? Hm?" Her soft hand squeezed my aching shaft tightly, slowly stroking and being careful to press against my piercings.

Frustrated, I let out a brief shout and pounded a fist against the steering wheel. "God damn it, you're going to make me crash." I gasped sharply and shuddered at the hot feeling of her mouth swallowing my cock. "Nicole!"

God fucking damn it! This woman!

Slamming my head back against the headrest, I let out an anguished cry as I breathed deeply.

The fuck do I do?!

My fingers went numb from how hard I gripped the steering wheel while my knuckles turned deathly pale.

Should I pull over? Keep going? Pull her off? Fucking hell!

"Focus on the road, little lion." Her voice insisted through my indecisive haze. "Just worry about getting us home safely." Her soft tongue ran along the underside of my length, starting from the base all the way to the crown of my tip, where she teasingly swirled her tongue around. "And I'll worry about taking care of you." She chuckled deviously before taking a good few inches into her needy mouth, causing me to shudder violently.

I don't know how I didn't fucking crash with how well she took me for the remainder of the ride. I nearly pulled over a few times when she somehow worked my pierced cock down her throat, especially when I heard her struggling with it. Her sweet gasps and gags as she choked on my member were like music to my ears. It was so lovely that I couldn't help myself from reaching down and grabbing her head to keep her there a few times, which earned me some smacks to my arm and chest, but the consequences were worth it.

Thankfully, I managed to blow my load before I threw in the towel and pulled over—I did come very close, though. Right as I was slowing the car down to pull over, I felt the familiar squeeze and rush. So, I continued down the road while Nicole sucked out every last drop from me.

When she went to pull off, I stopped her by holding down the back of her head, forcing her to remain pressed against my pelvis. I couldn't tell what her expression was because of our positioning, but her confused hum and muffled protests made it clear that my antics didn't amuse her.

Relaxing in my seat, I patted her growling head. "Since you can't seem to get enough of my cock, then you might as well stay on it." I laughed teasingly, earning a smack to the thigh from Nicole. "Love you too, *zhizn moya*." My laugh grew louder with amusement the more Nicole reacted.

Luckily for her, we were close to home, so she didn't have to stay like that for long. I don't think she would've complained much, though, because her protesting died down rather quickly. Though, no doubt I'd be paying for this later tonight or within the next few days. But, again, it was worth it.

Once we got home, I took a quick rinse to freshen up and threw on a pair of dark jeans, a fitted tee, and some black combat boots, looking rather casual compared to Nicole's business-casual outfit, which consisted of a powder pink skirt with black edges, a black blouse with a blazer thrown over, and a pair of black ankle boots.

Nicole wanted to change when we entered the house, but I convinced her against it with a teasing idea. Dinner and a fuck in the streets. A little roleplaying never harmed anyone, so it didn't take much to convince her to play out a date where she'd end up bent over in an alleyway and ravaged by me. The sweet and powerful businesswoman who's looking for love, only to come across a ruthless bratva boss who claims her in a not-so-romantic place after wining and dining her.

Of course, she only agreed if I agreed to one of her ideas, which was to reenact our little moment when she tattooed me. It seemed harmless enough of a trade to me, but in hindsight, I probably should have prodded her for details before agreeing blindly. Oh well, not like she'd kill me or something after all this time. The worst I could think of coming from the scene would be me ending up with her name tattooed on me this time.

After we settled into the car and hit the road, I double-checked with her on our destination. "Are you still sure about your choice?" Well, she had until we were sitting down in the place to change her mind, but I didn't want to end up parking and walking only to bust a U-turn and do the whole dance again. Not that I would nag her about it or make my displeasure known because it would lead us to a pointless argument.

"Yes, I want dim sum, and that's one of the best dim sum places," Nicole answered confidently, beaming at the road with an excited grin. "Seriously, it's the best in terms of quality and quantity for the price, and the atmosphere is so nice." Leaning over to my side of the car, she trapped my arm in hers. "None of the other places stack up to it, and a lot of them left me sorely disappointed. I mean, nearly thirty bucks for four small ass pieces of seafood shumai, and it tasted bleh. Honestly, if I'm paying thirty bucks for any kind of food, it better be a loaded ass plate and taste good, or it better give my mouth an orgasm with one lick."

Don't say it, don't say it, don't—

And my intrusive thoughts won. "You know, for a person who cooks like shit, you sure love food." I better start writing my eulogy because I doubt I'd be leaving this car alive.

Offended, Nicole scoffed loudly and punched my stomach, knocking the wind out of me. "I will put you in the corner, mister," she threatened me playfully. "And my cooking abilities have nothing to do with me liking food. Those two things are completely unrelated," she retorted sassily.

"You can't make good food, yet you enjoy it. I feel like enjoying food and being able to make good food for yourself goes hand in hand." That's how it worked, did it not?

"Honestly, have you been surviving on takeout your whole life?" Now that I thought about it, I only ever saw her eat out or order in when I stalked her. Her trash was constantly filled with local takeout boxes and bags, along with instant meals, chip bags, and all that jazz. Even now, unless I cooked, our meal was some kind of takeout or instant meal that only an absolute idiot could fuck up. Not that I was complaining; she could actually do quite a bit with some packets of ramen and some extra things.

Her nervous chuckle plucked at the air, making me roll my eyes and groan internally. "I mean, my family has a chef... And I lived with my parents up until they tried to ship me off to Vietnam..." she said sheepishly. "So, I never really had to cook for myself at any point in my life, and if the chef had the day off or something, then I had the money to eat out or order in," she added nonchalantly. "And when I had to live on my own... I just... I mean, the instant meals are easy, and making stuff from scratch is so much work and time-consuming and just ugh."

Rolling my eyes, I reached my hand up and pinched her face. "You are so lucky I'm a decent cook. I might not be a wonder chef like Stepan, but I make it work." It was rather adorable that my older brother thought his love for the kitchen was a well-kept secret. Actually, it probably could've stayed a secret if he was more careful about it. All of us have caught him in the kitchen numerous times over the years, and he may deny it all he wanted, but we weren't *that* stupid.

"Well, I'll leave the kitchen chores to you." Nicole chuckled softly and kissed the back of my hand after grabbing it.

"And the laundry, dishes, cleaning, and gardening," I added with a grumble, wondering just how the fuck I ended up with all the housework.

Yeah, I was definitely not the man of the house. Don't know how that fucking happened, but no point in arguing over it with Nicole. Besides, it wasn't even that bad to do all the house chores. It wasn't as if Nicole and I were slobs, and Nicole picked up here and there, which made things a little easier for me. Also, not like I had something else to do when I got home from work or during my free time when Nicole would be occupied in her office.

As tiring and boring as it got sometimes, I really had no issues with it. So, I really don't understand why so many men out there make such a big fuss about it. The other part that boggled me was the whole house chores being a woman's job debacle. Why sit around being a fucking lazy ass turd while your woman is stressing about? Why not help because you fucking can? Chores had no gender labels on them, and anyone who liked to argue otherwise was stupid in my books.

"I really love you so much, you know that?" Nicole buried her face into my arm with a giddy giggle.

Rolling my eyes, I let my hand fall to her thighs. "Oh, I don't know. I mean, you haven't put permanent cuffs on my wrists and ankles yet, nor have you tattooed your name on me yet," I snarked back with a snicker.

I could feel Nicole's body slither up my arm. Then, her breath hit the shell of my ear. My body shivered involuntarily at the sound of her wickedly playful whisper, "Oh, don't worry, your limbs are free for now because they're not done being made yet, and I ain't gonna tattoo my name on you because that's just a little too tacky for me." The heat of her body pulled away from my head as she returned to her seat. "So, my signature is gonna have to suffice," she told me matter-of-factly.

Slowly, my face scrunched in thought as her words sank in fully. I opened my mouth to ask if she was serious or not about the cuffs, but I quickly zipped it. Knowing her psycho tendencies, she'd just toy with me more rather than give me a straight answer. If anything, I might have dug my own grave with my jest before. So, might as well keep quiet and hope to God she won't act on it.

I mean, cuffs in the bedroom, fine, whatever; permanent cuffs, though, were a whole different story. The collar already pushed it for me. I don't know how Stepan does it with his wrist cuff, but personally, I didn't like the thought of such items on me 24/7.

Being a spoiled pet? Yes.

Being a slave? No.

Shoving the thoughts aside with a sigh, I lightly squeezed her plush thigh. "Why me?" I stammered rather hesitantly. "Of all the guys out there, why me?"

There was nothing special about me. Okay, let me rephrase that: there was nothing special about that was good. I was nothing but a huge pile of red flags. Granted, Nicole wasn't exactly normal, but still. I didn't see what about me was 'lovable' or relationship material.

"Pull over," Nicole demanded after a few seconds of silence.

Without questioning her, I obeyed. Veering off the road, the car rocked a little when I drove onto the uneven dirt and gravel that crunched under the car's weight. It didn't take long for me to have a hard time discerning whether the cracking noise was the ground outside or my buzzing nerves crowding my eardrums the more I slowed the car down. For a moment, I could've sworn my anxiety killed my heart when I killed the car's engine.

Fear kept my slumped body rigid in place as a chilly silence filled the car. I don't know why or how the question left my mouth. Sure, it had been something on my mind for a while, but it was a stupid question. So, I always held myself back from asking Nicole her reasons for picking my broken ass over someone decent. That, and I was afraid of the possible answers. What if she didn't have any good reasons, and my question was the start of our end when she'd realize what a bozo I was?

Even the sound of her body shuffling around couldn't get me to turn my head the slightest in her direction. The only reason why I even looked at her was because I had no choice when she plopped herself onto my lap and grabbed my face. "The simple answer is everything," she started, with a half-smirk that slowly grew into a smile. "But you're not simple, so that answer won't do."

Her head darted forward, and a kiss pressed itself against my tense forehead. "You're stubborn about me. And yes, I know, I was your assignment, but even after you found out the truth and decided to drop it, you still cared enough about me to have my back." Keeping her head against mine, she lightly stroked the side of my face with her finger. "I admire your persistence and devotion and how you genuinely want what's best for me and protect me because you care for me. You never ask for anything in return from me." She had to pause for a second to chuckle. "Well, besides my happiness."

Looping her arms around my neck, she tangled her fingers into the back of my hair, curling and tugging at my locks. "I also love how observant and thoughtful you are when it comes to important things. Like yeah, it's a little creepy how much you know me more than myself sometimes, but it's sweet in its own way." A brief chuckle came out with her heavy breath. "You may be a violent brute, but you're a big softy underneath with a good heart."

Okay, I couldn't help but flash her a questionable look at that last part, making her laugh softly. "Okay, a good heart to me, which might be considered twisted or dark to some." She corrected herself. "But back to what I was saying... You're thoughtful, and everything you do, for the most part, has your good intentions behind it."

Cupping my face with both her hands, she looked deeply into my eyes with such tender affection. "Most importantly, you accepted me for who I am. You didn't rip my head off when I broke your nose with that wooden plank, nor did you try to get revenge for me tattooing my signature on you." Her eyes softened further with gratitude as she continued to speak, "Never once have you tried to change me ever since you met me. You've never asked me to be less crazy or to ease back on my hobbies with the bombs and tech. You never nagged or guilted me into doing more feminine things like tending to the house or being more ladylike and shit."

It started as a gleam before her eyes turned glassy with tears. "You actually love me for me, and you only ever want to bring out more of it rather than try to drown or snuff it out."

Tightly, I engulfed her with my arms and pressed our lips together in a frenzied kiss filled with lust, passion, and gratitude.

Nicole was just like me.

We were both confident and independent individuals who wanted nothing more than to have that special person who would have our backs. The missing piece of our souls who would complement and complete us rather than change us. The other half who would accept us for who we are and love us wholly.

Two twisted souls finally united.

And we won't let anyone stand in our way.

Chapter 29

Nicole

"I'M SURPRISED I ATE more than you," I commented as we left the restaurant with our satisfied stomachs.

Chuckling softly, Lev slipped an arm across my lower back, splaying his hand and fingers against my waist and hip before shoving me across his body. Giggling, I gave out a protestant 'hey' from the sudden shift in position. "Gotta make sure my girl is safe," he replied with a grin, holding me close with his other arm around my waist.

With a playful smile, I dug my heel into the ground and stepped in front of him with my arms crossed. "Your girl?" I shot back with a cocky smirk. "We only went on one date, and you're already calling me your girl?" Leaning toward him, I wagged a finger in his face. "Nah ah, I don't think so, bucko. It's going to take more than one simple dinner to sweep me off my feet."

Game on.

Lev's eyes clouded over with confusion for a second before they sharpened with a dangerously playful gleam. "Oh? I don't think you've fully grasped the situation yet, darling." Closing the small distance between us, he pulled my body right against his. "You were mine the moment I laid eyes on you and decided so. This date was a mere formality to make your new life a little easier to ease into."

Defiance sharpened my eyes and lips as I pressed my hands against his chest to shove myself away, only not to budge a single inch. "I don't belong to anyone, let alone to someone like you." I shot at him with more bite than I intended.

Clicking his tongue, Lev raised a brow at me as he backed me into the alleyway nearby. "Someone like me?" His voice dipped dangerously low, sending shivers down my body. "Now, what could that mean, hm? Do tell." It sounded more like a demand than a question.

Gulping, I jumped a bit when my back hit the wall. Another jolt of exciting fear chilled my body from Lev slamming his hands on either side of my body and trapping me. "J-just, you're a little rough around the edges... That's all." I chuckled nervously as my eyes darted around for an escape. "I just don't think we're compatible. I mean, we're from two different worlds, we wouldn't—"

My jaw remained unhinged from Lev's hard grip. "What? Think you're too good for a gangster like me? Does little Miss High and Mighty not want her hands dirty with my crimes?" I barely recognized his raspy voice as his face got all up in mine. "Well, too fucking bad, little empress, because I'm dragging you into my fucked up world whether you like it or not." I couldn't help but suck in a sharp breath from his voice rumbling next to my ear.

A strangled whimper forced itself out of my body when Lev hiked me up the wall and forced my legs apart. Instinctively, I wrapped my legs around him out of fear of falling on my ass if I didn't anchor myself to him. Of course, in doing this, I could clearly feel the excitement tenting in his pants. "Lev, please, we're in the middle—"

Another strangled sound choked out of me from the sudden thrust from Lev. "I own these streets, so I will do whatever the hell I want in them." His lips crushed mine in a starving kiss that sucked my soul out of my body. "Including you."

The front of my shirt bunched up in his large hand, and I braced myself for the rush of cold air that would hit my bare skin at any second.

But it never came.

Instead of chilly air biting my skin, the warm splatter of blood slapped my unexpecting face. "Lev!" The sounds of the bullets whizzing by us disappeared into the background as all I could worry about was Lev.

Could it have been me that was hit? Maybe, but I didn't feel any pain. So, it couldn't have been me, right?

With me tucked against his body, he ducked behind a dumpster. "I'm okay." Lev hissed with a deep scowl as he shielded my body with his. "Fucking nerve of these idiots..." He grumbled under his breath.

Kissing my forehead, he pushed me against the wall. "Stay," he commanded, pointing a stern finger at me along with a hardened glare.

"Oh, I was thinking of going out there to be turned into Swiss cheese." I snarked back very sarcastically.

Bringing my purse into my lap, I opened it and pulled out a pipe bomb. "I got a bomb. Do you want it?" I offered, probably sounding too casual about it. "If you want one with shrapnel, I got some of those as well."

For a brief moment, Lev stood there staring at me all flabbergasted. His eyes constantly cycled between me, my open purse, and the bomb in my hand as the gears in his head turned. Shaking his head, he ran a hand down his face and held his open jaw for a second before closing it. "Just... Stay," he stammered, turning around after drawing his gun.

Right as he was about to peek around the dumpster, he turned his head back at me. "And do not throw a bomb." He deadpanned with a glare before resuming his course.

Lev waited until the gunfire ceased before throwing himself around the corner and shooting. He only got a few shots off before ducking back next to me because of the return fire. "Give us the girl, and we'll let you live!" a voice demanded.

Scoffing in disdain, I rolled my eyes and tossed the bomb up and down in my hand. "Ya sure I can't bomb them?" I was more than willing to bet my parents sent them after me, so might as well take care of the trash now before it became a rotten issue.

Rolling his eyes, Lev snatched the bomb from me, "Give me that!" And stuffed it in his pocket with a scolding glare. "You can't just chuck a bomb at every problem that crosses your path." He chided before turning his attention away from me to address the enemy.

His chest expanded with his deep breath. "You can go back to whoever sent you after us and tell them to either fuck off or to stop being a coward and come get Nicole themselves!" His projected voice carried clearly throughout the alleyway. "You also have five seconds to leave before I put a bullet through your heads!" he warned them while readying his gun for another round.

Laughter from the crowd of men echoed from their end. "There's only one of you and seven of us! You stand no chance! Your Volkov name don't mean shit in this situation!" One of them bellowed loudly.

A wicked grin of excitement stretched at Lev's lips. "Fine! Have it your way!" Rounding the corner, Lev let off exactly seven shots.

Silence followed the dying echoes of the gunshots, and the only disruption to the chilling peace was the sound of bodies hitting the hard ground.

Looking over, I gawked at Lev, who stood there perfectly poised and composed. His chest rose and fell in a perfect, steady rhythm with his controlled breaths. Besides the injuries he had sustained before, he didn't have a hair out of place.

God, he looked so perfect in his element like this.

Seriously, it should be illegal for him to look so damn immaculate and natural handling a gun and shooting down seven men within a blink of an eye.

As fucked up as it sounded, I wanted to see him do it again.

"Empress, if you don't stop looking at me with those 'fuck me' eyes, then we're going to have problems," Lev growled, snapping me out of my stupor.

As much as I wanted to pull him down by the collar of his shirt and have him take me right then and there in the alleyway. The moment of clarity drew enough sense out of me to take note of his injuries.

Whatever arousal woke my body went back to sleep as I rushed up to him, grabbing and touching every inch of his body to get a better understanding of his injuries. Lev wasn't having any of it, though. He was quick to let his annoyance known with groans and sighs as he tried to knock my hands away. "*Zhizn moya*, I'm fine," he told me with a heavy sigh after bunching my hands in his. "Really." His irritated face softened with reassurance. "They're just surface wounds, grazes."

Sighing, I relented, pulling my hands back and dropping them to my side. "We should head back so Alexei or Angel can have a look at you." Sex was the last and furthest thing on my mind.

All I wanted was to get back home and get Lev checked out. I wouldn't rest easy until I saw all of his wounds with my own eyes. He didn't look like he was bleeding out anywhere, nor did I see any holes in his body, but still.

Grabbing his wrist, I dragged him out of the alleyway toward the car with hurried steps.

What should have been an easy trip turned dicey when we encountered a small group of men who blocked our way. Lev and I immediately stopped in our tracks, and before I could make a move to threaten the men, Lev shoved me behind him. "If you know what's best for you, then you'll move," Lev barked out in a low and threatening voice. "Your buddies already pissed me off tonight, and I won't mind more live targets for practice tonight."

"You're delusional." One of the men scoffed with a mocking laugh. "There are five of us, and you're just one injured person."

Not liking the dreaded feeling in the pit of my stomach, I quickly reached into my purse, using Lev's bulky body to hide my movements. Tossing a bomb with Lev and me being this close was a little risky, but it was better than nothing. I mean, surely Lev would sustain a direct shot or two if he pulled his gun right now. If it was just him or if I was hidden somewhere relatively safe, then his chances of getting away unscathed would be high. Sadly, he had me to take into account right now.

Lighting the fuse, I watched the ring of light eat away at the wire with a bated breath. It felt like seconds for the fuse to be lit to where I wanted it, even if it was less than a second in reality. When the time came, I almost hesitated because I was afraid of throwing the bomb too soon, but logically, I knew otherwise. I couldn't hesitate. If I did, then the risk of being caught in the blast with Lev would increase rather drastically. Worse, the bomb could go off way before reaching the enemy and harm just us.

A tense and confused silence filled the air the moment I stepped out from behind Lev and threw the bomb. I thought surely they'd scramble out of the way before the bomb landed by their feet, but that was too much credit. The stark realization didn't twist at their face until the bomb landed and bounced once, twice...

"Shit!"

My whole body quaked with the small aftershock of the bomb that caused my own heart to explode with happiness. The sight of everyone scattered on the ground, all dazed and groaning in pain, brought a twisted grin to my gleeful body. "Ooooh that worked out so well, definitely need to make note on that one to make more of," I commented out loud, mainly to myself.

I didn't even take note of Lev's concerned look until he spoke up, "Holy shit, you're a fucking psycho." I couldn't tell if that was meant in a good way or a bad way with how unchanging his face was. Although, when was a statement like that ever good?

Well, I didn't have to wonder for long because a crazed smile flashed across Lev's face right before he grabbed my face and kissed me. "I fucking love it." Then, he kissed me again. "But we are so going to talk about the fact you're walking around with bombs in your bag." He chuckled nervously after breaking the kiss. "Come on, let's—"

Without a thought, I shoved Lev out of the way, grabbing his holstered gun in the same action. Now, this whole thing went a lot smoother in my mind...

Bang!

Lev's cry of pain and anger shook the ground. "*Blyat*! Nicole!" Glaring at me scoldingly, he snatched the gun away from me, flicking the safety on and holstering it. "Okay, new rule: you are not allowed to touch any kind of firearm," Lev gritted out, very unamused and ungrateful for how I just saved his ass just now.

"He was going to shoot you," I argued with a soft huff, letting Lev drag me to the car in a rush.

Grumbling, Lev threw me into the passenger seat and crossed the car to the driver's side. "You could have just shouted at me. I would've reacted in time," he said while buckling me in. "Hang on." Was the only warning I got before my body slammed back against my seat with how he floored it.

Rolling my eyes, I glared at Lev out of the corner of my eyes. "You had your back turned..." I continued to argue with him.

I should probably drop the subject, but I was rather proud of what I did.

Raising his voice slightly, he scoffed, "You fucking shot me!" At least he wasn't totally upset with how he mocked me almost playfully.

Slamming a door on my rising guilt, I swallowed the lump in my throat. "Not on purpose!" I defended myself in a shaky voice.

Sighing heavily, Lev ran a hand down his face and slumped in his seat. "Nicole, you don't ever shoot a gun unless you have a clear shot and are a hundred percent confident." And here comes the lecture. "Listen, I know your intentions were well, and I appreciate it, I do, really. But for the love of all that is holy and unholy, please don't ever do anything like that ever again until I've taught you how to properly handle a firearm and you've grown comfortable with doing so."

Okay, maybe it wasn't as bad as I psyched it up to be. Don't get me wrong, I wasn't thrilled about the lack of initial gratitude, even if my actions were rather mindless and risky. In hindsight, I probably shouldn't have done what I did. If anything, the safest thing to do during that time would've been to shove Lev aside completely and let him handle the situation after he recovered enough.

Stewing in silence, I sat with my legs curled up on the seat. Awkwardly, I forced my concern out. "I didn't actually put a bullet in you... Did I?" I probably should've asked him earlier, but I was too irritated to think straight.

Breathing deeply, Lev reached over and placed his hand over mine, squeezing it softly. "Just a bad graze, so I'll live." There was some chagrin to his reassurance, not that I blamed him.

If the situation was reversed, then Lev's head would've been rolling down a hill by now. So, honestly, I'd count myself lucky with how tame he was in response to me.

Swallowing my pride, I sank in my seat a little as I gripped his hand. "I'm sorry." I had to force it out of myself, but it was genuine.

A long sigh dragged out of Lev before I found my hand being moved. Then, the familiar ticklish feeling of his beard scratching the back of my hand preceded the warmth of his lips. "As long as you can promise me no more gun-toting Nicole, then I'll forgive you," he joked flatly with a very dry chuckle.

Humming softly, I nodded my head and leaned against his arm. "I'm tired..." Whatever adrenaline buzzed at my nerves took my energy away when it died down.

"Rest, don't fight the crash," Lev encouraged me with some more kisses to the back of my hand. "I'll be here to watch over you."

I tried to fight it, but a wave of dizziness forced my eyes to shut when I shook my head.

Needless to say, my eyes refused to open back up.

Chapter 30

~3 days later~

"Still can't believe this is where you've been the whole time..."

All this time, Nicole was literally right under my nose. My family's fucking vacation cabin. I literally could have just happened upon her at any time if I'd decided to take a decompressing trip!

Yes, my pride was a little hurt, I'd admit that. I mean, for being so observant to a fault, and a damn good tracker, I literally missed her when she was right in front of me. It never even occurred to me to check any locations the bratva owned! I don't know why. But also, why on earth would Nicole be hiding in *my* family's property in the first place?

"*Đại ca*, are you still beating yourself up about all of that?" Nicole chuckled with pity as she looked at me apologetically. "It's nothing to get hung up on. I mean, the point of me being in hiding was to remain hidden. Besides, I had Angel's help, who had a lot of resources at her disposal because she married Nikolai." At least I could appreciate the effort she made to downplay my fault in this. "Also, it was just sheer luck you never found me here. I mean, like you said, if you had decided to take a vacation and picked this cabin, then that would have been either a very awkward meeting or the end of my days of freedom."

Sighing, I set the moving box I'd been carrying down by the front door before turning my head to give her a deadpan expression. "*Zhizn moya*, I appreciate you trying to make me feel better, but all the reasons don't excuse my sloppiness and carelessness in overlooking this place." Well, at least I knew better from now on. Private bratva property or not, it needed to be checked.

Pushing the topic aside, I stood by the boxes with my arms crossed. "You have a slight hoarding problem, you know that?" I commented while running my eyes over the various boxes.

For the past two days we've been stormed in at the cabin, and we've done nothing but pack all her things up while we were stuck. All ten boxes stacked by the door were barely half her shit! All of them didn't contain any personal items and effects—they were all her office and materials.

Not gonna lie, it was a little worrisome to know nearly all those boxes contained bomb-making material. If it were a small crew or some bomb-obsessed psycho, then I wouldn't be too worried, but all this for one tiny woman was a little terrifying. Granted, my Nicole was a bomb-loving psycho... A good bomb-loving psycho, though!

Yes, I called her a psycho quite a bit sometimes, but it was mainly in jest or in an affectionate way. I mean, she was my psycho, and that was all that mattered. The little nickname was rarely used, though, and only ever behind closed doors or moments of extreme excitement that was fitting. Like when she blew those men up the other day—that was just amazing.

Honestly, just when I thought I couldn't fall in love with her more, she blew me away. And if I wasn't careful, she'd probably *literally* blow me away... Or to bits and pieces.

A brief scoff came from Nicole before the sounds of her footsteps came to a stop behind me. "I do not have a collecting problem," she argued with narrowed eyes. "I need everything."

Rolling my eyes, I reached into a partially open box we hadn't taped up yet. From it, I pulled out a small bag of mismatched wires that varied in length and size. "Empress, you do not need a wire that's barely a centimeter long. I mean, what the hell are you even going to use it for?" Shaking the bag in her face, I spoke again. "This is a bag of trash wire. You literally can't use a majority of this shit unless you're gonna painstakingly connect all these wires somehow. Even if you did, whatever bomb you're gonna use them in won't be reliable."

Without anything to say in return, Nicole just clicked her tongue at me and glared with her arms crossed. Staying like so for a good while, she angrily tapped her foot against the wooden floor. Then, she nervously licked her lips and jutted her chin out at me. "W-well, I could say the same for you and your weapons. I mean, who the hell needs that many handguns?" She tried to rebut me weakly.

Unable to help it, I laughed a little at her cute attempt. "Guns and knives do not count or factor into this little tiff of ours." I flashed her a smug smirk while loosely crossing my arms. "And I dispose of my weapons once they are no longer of use."

There was no winning for her.

Letting out a frustrated growl, she grabbed the front of my shirt and pulled me down to her displeased face. "Listen here, you little lion, that is my shit, and I like my shit. So, I am keeping my shit. If you try to make an issue out of some habit I don't have, then don't come crawling to me if you wake up in a bed full of volatile explosives," she threatened in a low and dangerous voice.

If she was joking somewhat, then I would've laughed her off, but the determined blaze in her eyes burned her serious intent into my very soul the more she bore those stark orbs of hers into mine. I mean, she wouldn't do all of that... Right? Or at least, not to the scale that she implied... I hope.

Grinning nervously, I grabbed her hips and rubbed them lovingly with my thumbs. "Empress, you know, what's some bag of wires gonna do, hm? I mean, no harm, no foul." I tried to sweeten my way out with her, but the unamused look on her face meant I probably wasn't getting anywhere.

Pulling out my best pout, I leaned in and nuzzled her neck. "Come on, I'm sorry, I'll drop it." I wanted to cringe at how weird I sounded cooing. "Don't be mad at me, please."

Scoffing and chuckling, Nicole shoved me away playfully. "Don't do it again, and I won't," she told me with a roll of her eyes. "And please, don't ever talk like that ever again. Seriously, you sound so weird and cringey."

Well, good thing I wasn't the only one repulsed by it.

Smiling, I snatched her by her waist and brought her into a long and sensual kiss. "Can't wait to get back home with you," I groaned against her lips.

Giggling deeply, she looked up at me with curious eyes. "Oh? Why? What's so different there and here?" she questioned while pulling me toward the couch. "Or are you hinting at something?" Her voice dipped suggestively as she pulled me down on the couch. "Hm?"

Instead of answering her with words, I let my actions speak for me. My lips devoured hers in heated passion. My hands greedily grabbed at every part of her body that was a work of art on its own. God, she was so fucking perfect, something I'd never get over. It was as if she was carved out of marble from the high Heavens for me.

Only me.

"Fuck me, empress, please," I begged wantonly, nipping at her bottom lip and kissing every inch of her face. "Please, I need you."

Pushing me up, she gestured for me to switch positions with her. With a happy grin, I grabbed her hips and flipped us so that she was on top. I was more than prepared for her to strip me and burn every part of me with her luscious lips and skilled hands, so I flashed her a confused look when she got off me with a smirk.

"Be a good boy and strip," she commanded me with a powerful smile. "And stay," she said, pointing a stern finger at me before disappearing down the hallway and into the bedroom.

A part of me wanted to call out to her for answers, but the side of me that knew her held me back. She wouldn't tell me, even if I begged.

So, with a calming breath, I took off every piece of clothing from my body until I laid there bare on the couch, shivering in anticipation. I had no idea what she could be grabbing from her room; I hadn't gone through her stuff here yet, and she was a little secretive with packing her personal items. Actually, she didn't let me linger around her when she was packing up her personal space. So, whatever was in those drawers and the closet was beyond my knowledge.

"Close your eyes, little lion!" Her voice echoed down the hallway.

Oh God, what is she planning?

Letting out a shaky breath, I let my eyes shut. I tried to maintain a calm demeanor with controlled breaths, but every little tick and creak around me made my muscles tense and twitch with anticipation. I nearly bolted when I felt a warm presence crowd my space, even if I knew it was Nicole because of her soothing scent of gunpowder.

"Lev, breathe. It's okay." Nicole's giggle above me made my whole body shudder with nervousness. "I'm just going to blindfold you real quick, and then I'm going to get you ready to be fucked," she told me in a calm and collected voice. "And I'm going to try something a little different, but don't worry, it's nothing crazy." If it weren't for the stability and reassuring tone, then I would've called bullshit on her.

"Alright, empress." This was a little crazy. To go through something for the first time blindfolded was a little nerve-wracking. "I trust you." But I wasn't known for being sane. Besides, I knew Nicole wouldn't wrong me, as crazy as she was.

Instinctively, my face twitched when I felt something soft and smooth brush over my eyes. "Shh, it's okay, just a blindfold." Her calming voice eased my rising tension a little before a quick spike gripped my body at the feeling of her securing the fabric around my head.

Shivers ran down my body at the feeling of her nails raking down my sensitive body, along with her hot breath against my neck. "I fucking love how good you are for me." My body jolted with a sharp gasp from the sudden grab at my aching cock. "Already so hard for me."

Her soft lips brushed over my hard nipple, and her tongue teasing it got a small whimper to fall from my lips as I arched my body into her. "Can I touch you, please?" I barely managed to restrain my hands by gripping the couch. The need to feel her soft skin under my fingers burned at my fingertips.

Sparks of arousal shot throughout my body in response to her fingers running down my arms to my wrists. "Yes, you may." I breathed out a sigh of relief when she gave me permission, and I wasted no time feeling around blindly until my hands found their home on her delicate curves.

"Thank you, empress," I replied shakily, too focused on appreciating her divine body with my rough fingers.

As she moved down my body, I did my best to hold on, but I could only reach so far without seeing.

Soft warmth engulfing my cock suddenly jarred a sharp, gasping moan from me as my hips instinctively bucked at her hot mouth. Then, it barely felt like a second of bliss had gone by before a familiar pressure pushed against my asshole. Nicole didn't take it slow like usual this time. Her mouth and tongue gave my pierced member the perfect amount of attention and love while her fingers thrust in and out of my ass at a rather fast and hard pace. She barely gave me time to adjust to the first finger before adding a second and third shortly after.

Being ravaged with such lustful rapture drove my mind high into the sky. "Shit, empress, I—"

And just like that, everything came to a terse stop, making me let out a whimpering sob; I didn't know my body could make such a desperate sound until now. "No, please, I was so close." My hips bucked relentlessly at the air, hoping to catch some part of Nicole or press against something to give me some relief.

"Empress, plea—ah!" My words became strangled with my gasping moan when I felt a sudden tightness choke my aching cock.

Even though she's put me in the Amazon position so many times now, my body still fought it initially out of habit.

As she rocked her hips and fucked me, I felt something else along with her thrusts. A light tap, right against my ass. It was something semi-hard, but it didn't feel like a whip or a flogger.

Before I could ask her what it was, the feeling of her fingers spreading lube and toying with my backdoor distracted my mind. "You ready to really get fucked, little lion?" I could hear the devious edge to her voice.

The hell did she me–

The pitched, strangled, whimpering moan that escaped my mouth was definitely a sound I did not think my body could make.

I couldn't get a single word out between my jagged breaths as I struggled to adjust to the sudden penetration that stretched me wide like never before, and the depth in which the object slid into me was what caught me off guard.

This wasn't a small toy or a plug; it was way too big and long.

Fuck, did she...?

"Shh." Her soft kisses fell upon my gasping face as her hands stroked my body lovingly. "Breathe. You're taking it so well." Surprisingly, my body responded to her soothing words. "Deep breaths, babe, nice deep breaths for me."

They weren't smooth, but I managed to strain out some deep breaths for her. "More of a warning next time would be nice," I lightly snapped—playfully, of course—at her after I got a better grip on myself.

A cheery but devious giggle shook from Nicole's body. "You would have clenched if I told you I'd shove a dildo up your ass," she retorted. "You feeling okay, though?"

Oh, now she asks.

My eyes rolled along with my sarcastic thoughts, and I let out a small scoff as I relaxed on the couch. "Just give me a few more seconds to adjust," I replied in a small voice, feeling a little embarrassed about the situation a little.

Learning to accept our dynamic was one thing, but getting fucked by my girlfriend was another. This probably wasn't the time to be reflecting on it all, but having a dildo shoved into my ass was a new limit we were testing. It wasn't breaking me or anything; I just wasn't expecting it!

"Let me know when I can move," she told me between her peppering kisses along my body. "You look so wonderful right now, though, so fucking hot." Her hot words fanned against my chest with her soft chuckle. "Feels so good to be connected to you like this. Your cock in my cunt while I reward you for being a good boy by fucking your ass." Her excitement slipped through with some small thrusts—she probably couldn't help herself.

I couldn't see what she meant, but the image painted in my mind by her words got me shuddering and bucking my hips at her. "Fuck, you're so crazy for even thinking and planning something like this." Breathing deeply, I shifted my hips a bit to make it easier for her to be situated over me. "Don't go too fast. I'm still adjusting."

Her laugh echoed through the air, causing goosebumps to wash down my shivering body. "Honey, I just rammed a dildo up your ass. That's about the extent of my evilness today to you," she assured me with a rather hearty giggle before I felt her body slowly ease off until she was almost off my cock.

Gritting my teeth, I squeezed her hips to still her. The feeling of her tight walls working the length of my cock paired with the feeling of the dildo stimulating my sensitive ass was more overwhelming than I anticipated. "Slow, please," I reminded her in a pleading voice.

Keeping my hands on her in case I needed her to stop, I softly nudged her to continue. Then, I felt her lower herself back down on me with a low moan that blended in with mine. "Shit... I don't know how long I can hold back if this is how good it feels." And here I thought that vibrators were my worst enemies.

"You and me both." Nicole's breathy moan barely made it through the pounding in my ears. "I've never been so stuffed before," she strained out between her heavy breaths.

My hands never left her hips as her pace picked up slowly. Hanging onto her was more for comfort and ease of mind the more lost I became to the endless waves of pleasure crashing against my body.

"Shit!" I strained a groan through gritted teeth at the feeling of her cunt squeezing the life out of my cock. "Fuck, *zhizn moya*, if you—shit!" It wasn't even a second before I felt her squeeze me again with her next orgasm when she bottomed out on me.

"Sorry, too good, can't help it," she moaned happily as her hips jerked out of rhythm.

"Empress, if you don't stop coming, you're going to make me lose it." I could only take so much more before I completely lost it.

It was already taking so much out of me not to bust my load and paint her insides with my cum. God, she'd probably get out everything so easily with how filled she was with the added dildo.

Unfortunately, Nicole had other ideas.

The only warning I got to brace myself was the feeling of Nicole pressing my legs toward my chest more before the hard thrusts literally slammed into me, knocking my breath away for a split second. I didn't even get a chance to warn her about my release—it just came.

Immense pleasure consumed me like a raging inferno when my climax hit. Whatever shred of sanity and clarity I had burned away as I let myself be used by Nicole. It was so much. I could feel myself become overly stimulated to where my emotions went haywire. My body and mind didn't know how to begin processing all the stimulation that wrecked me all at once.

A painful ache tightened at my sobbing body following a second release that slammed into me out of nowhere like some derailed train. "Nicole! I can't!" I barely recognized my own voice because of how vulnerable and broken I sounded. "It's too much... I can't—"

Nicole shut me up with a deep and adoring kiss as her hips slowed to a stop. "Shh, breathe. It's okay. You are okay." Her soft voice was so loud to my sensitive ears.

Pulling out and off of me completely, she laid down on the couch next to me and held me tenderly. Nuzzling my head into her face, she stroked the back of my head with her dexterous fingers. "You did so well, so fucking good." Her lips soothed my forehead with kisses as she continued to speak, "I am so proud of you for being able to take all of that. You have no idea. Then, to fill me twice, I can't thank you enough, my good little lion."

I was a silent and tearful mess for a long while before I could recollect myself enough to fully process the life-changing sex we had. Somewhat shell-shocked still, I tried to voice my thoughts in hopes of easing the tension that threatened to snap in me, "That was..." I was at a loss for words.

Flashing an understanding smile, Nicole brushed her thumb against the seam of my lips. "Intense? Overwhelming? Shocking? A lot?" She offered some options with softening eyes. "It's okay. It was a lot, so just take your time to process it." Kissing my nose, her face brightens with a widening smile. "Don't force yourself to dance if you're not ready. I will be here, waiting and ready."

An appreciative spark warmed my body as I looked at my empress in awe. Just how on earth did I end up with an amazing woman like her? How patient Nicole was with me and our whole relationship would never cease to amaze me. Honestly, she was a saint in her own twisted way.

"Thank you." It was all I could manage out as I held her back and eased myself into her presence.

Playing with my hair, she hummed softly in response. "You don't have to thank me for anything, my little lion. I'm only giving you all the attention and love you've always deserved."

Cracking a quick smile, I leaned up and kissed her chastely. "I love you, Nicole, so much." I knew those three words would never be enough to fully express the never-ending devotion and intimacy I felt for her from the depths of my soul.

Pressing her own smile against my lips, she whispered, "I love you too, Lev, so much that my heart explodes with happiness with just the thought of you." Kissing me deeply, she let her hands cup my face.

Breaking the kiss, Nicole sucked in a deep breath as she kept her forehead against mine. Slowly, her eyes twinkled with curiosity as they trailed off to the side a little bit.

An involuntary shudder shook my body when Nicole pressed her fingertip against the top of my facial scar and traced it down my face. "How did you get this scar exactly?" she asked tentatively, her wary eyes searching mine for a response.

Placing my hand over hers, I held it against my face for a moment before my mouth moved. "The short answer, my father." I dryly chuckled at the sight of her flat glare. "But you want the full story, I know."

Before more words could come out, Nicole's finger shushed me. "Let me get you cleaned up and fed a little before you start," she told me with a soft kiss, slipping away from me for a moment before returning with an armful of water bottles, snacks, and washcloths.

Sitting next to me, she sits me up a little and makes me hydrate myself before leaning me back against the couch. "Go ahead and tell me while I get you cleaned up," she urged me with a warm smile before the slight chill of the washcloth touched my body.

Taking a deep breath, I reached out and played with a strand of her hair to help keep me distracted enough so that I wouldn't slip into some angry haze. "It was about ten years ago when I was around twenty-five or so," I started, pausing for a second as I felt a slow burn nag my chest. "I was at home with my mother that day because I was too injured from an assignment the night before to go to work."

Everything around me slowly faded back to the day the further I dove into the story. "My mother babied me the whole day, fretting over me and making me eat and drink her concoctions that she always swore by. Overall, it was a normal day for us." An unconscious smile pulled at my muscles. "We even got to tend to the garden and pick some apples that day to make apple tarts later that night for dessert."

A stinging pressure spread across my face when I let myself get lost in the memory. Nostalgia twisted at my heart, and the darkness of truth snuck in. "I was helping her set the table when my father came through the front door reeking of sex and booze, and I'm pretty sure he was high, too, because of how crazed his eyes were." Tightly shutting my eyes, I tilted my head up at the ceiling, hoping to keep my tears from spilling. "The state he came in was no surprise to any of us, but the aggressiveness in which he went after my mother was unexpected."

Letting go of Nicole's hair, I covered my scar with my hand, pressing hard against it in response to the phantom pain flaring. "There was no warning. He walked up at her while yapping at her, bitching about everything in the world and about us, then he laid his hands on her." Shaking my head, I had to pause for a moment to take some calming breaths. "Usually, we'd be able to see it coming, but there weren't any signs of escalation like all the other times. One second, he was running his mouth, spitting everywhere like a disgusting bastard, and the next, he was throwing my mother across the table."

Though years ago, the sound of the plates and cups shattering by our heads and feet rang so clearly that I could've mistaken it happening right now. The whish and whizz of the wind would hit my face before the sharp shards flew and scratched at my flesh. Feeling the soft brush of air from the air conditioning in the room made me flinch because my mind was pulled back to the day, and I honestly thought it was another plate flying by me.

If it weren't for the sight of Nicole, then I might have let myself be immersed in the flashback. Seeing her strong and beautiful face was the breath of fresh air I needed to drag myself back to the present. "My father eventually approached us and threw me aside to strike my mother with a broken bottle, but I shielded her with my own body in the nick of time."

My fingers dragged themselves along my scar, causing a shiver to roll down my body. "The bottle caught me, leaving a deep wound that probably won't ever disappear." My vision in my left eye was never the same after that night, either. I wasn't completely blind or anything, but the difference between my left and right eye was pretty stark.

A sad but grateful smile curved at Nicole's lips as she stroked my face, giving my scar a little more attention than usual. "Thank you for telling me, Lev." She sounded proud, making me puff my chest out a little at the satisfied feeling welling up inside of it.

Taking her hand, I kissed it with a smile. "Thank you for being patient with me, for not pushing me until I was ready, and for staying with me despite how difficult I am as a person." I mean, I wasn't the worst person to be with compared to a lot, but I knew I was a huge pain in the ass still.

Giggling, Nicole leaned up and kissed me longingly. "It should be me thanking you for not running away from my crazy ass and learning to love all my strangeness." She rebutted, laughing softly as she pinched my cheek. "Seriously, I thought for sure you would have run off after I chloroformed your ass and marked you," she reminded me with a hearty laugh that lasted a short second before her face turned saccharine. "Not that I would have let you because, ya know, you are mine and all."

"There's my little psycho empress," I mused with a chuckle.

Chapter 31

Okay, sounds in the middle of the night shouldn't be too odd out here in the wilderness, especially in the middle of the night. But sometimes...

Creeeeeeak...

I did not like the way my heart clenched with fear at the sound of wood giving under some weight. Sitting up in the bed, I reached over to the slumbering giant beside me and shook him. "Lev!" I shouted at him in a hushed whisper.

Creeeak... Creak... Creee...

The sinking feeling in my gut was validated when Lev instantly shot up in bed and grabbed his gun at light speed. Jumping out of bed, he moved to the door, pressing his back flat against the wall next to it. "Nicole, go hide," he commanded me in a sturdy voice, nodding toward the closet. "There's a saferoom in the closet. Code is six, six, eight, five, seven, zero."

Scrunching my face up into a scowl, I glared at him defiantly as I got out of bed and reached under the mattress, pulling out some small bombs. "I can help." Well, I might do a lot more damage than anything, but it was better than him handling whatever was out there on his own.

Too bad Lev wasn't gonna have any of it. "No. Either you behave and hide, or I will knock your ass out and shove it in that closet." He set my two options out in the open with an unmoving expression. "I am not having you risk your life when you don't have to."

My scowl deepened with displeasure as I gripped the handful of bombs tightly. "No, we are in this together. That means I fight with you, not go run and hide while you take care of our issues." Not the wisest time to start an argument, but like hell was I gonna let him boss me around like that.

I barely caught the sight of his chest rising with his deep breath in the dimly lit room. "Nicole. I swear to God, I will fucking knock your ass out in the next ten seconds if I don't see you moving." And he was probably smart for not engaging my stubborn ass.

Creak. Creak. Creak. Creak. Creak.

"Nicole!" Lev barked at me in a hushed voice, his glaring eyes burning holes toward the closet.

Biting my tongue, I huffed and retreated to the closet without any fight. Lev needed to have his full focus on whatever was beyond that door, and the more I thought about it, the more logic sunk into me.

Whatever made the noise that crept closer and closer to us would be right on the other side of the bedroom door in a matter of seconds. So, we were basically cornered. Throwing a bomb in an open street or an alleyway was one thing, but throwing a bomb in this situation was a bad story waiting to be written to life. The chances of Lev and I being caught in the blast were pretty high. I wasn't willing to risk it like I did the other day with the goons my parents sent after us.

Making my way to the back of the closet, I quickly located the keypad after feeling around for a quick second. Punching the numbers in the dark was a bitch, though. I was about to slam my fist against the wall when the thing beeped at me in error for the fourth time I fucked up the code. Thankfully, the fifth time was the charm.

Standing at the threshold of the saferoom, I turned my head back to look at the parted closet door, debating for a split second if I should try to help Lev. Inching in the direction of the closet's door, my feet threatened to carry my body back out until I forced myself into the metal room and slammed the door shut behind me.

The room wasn't huge, but it was roomy enough. Inside the metal room were boxes of canned food, M.R.E.s, boxes of bullets, guns, knives, radios, batteries, an old-ish computer system, and a wall of screens with active video around the cabin.

My frantic eyes carefully scanned the screens, stopping at the one that showed the hallway. "Oh no."

I could feel a chill settle in my paling face when I saw the number of armed men lining the hallway and crowding around our bedroom door. It was hard to make out the exact number of men with the poor lighting and grainy feed, but I counted at least ten.

I have to help Lev.

The shittiest girlfriend in the world title would be waiting for me if I didn't try to help Lev out of this jam after seeing what he was up against. But what could I do? All my drones and other materials were packed away and sitting pretty in boxes by the front door, and the only bombs I had on me were too dangerous to set off inside the cabin.

Shit, shit, shit. Come on, Nicole, think, think!

Pacing around, I tapped my fingernail against my teeth. Then, I made the mistake of peeking at the screen again, making my panic rise a little when I saw how much more crowded the hallway became.

I needed to calm down. I wouldn't be any help if my thoughts raced out of my control.

Fucking hell, there are so many men. There's no way Lev stands a chance against all of them, not with—ah hah!

It was right in front of me, and I was too stupid not to take any kind of notice. I wanted to slap myself in the face for being so blind in my frantic state.

Rushing over to the table and wall of weapons, I grabbed the assault rifle and disengaged the magazine, grumbling to myself when I saw it to be empty. "Why the hell wouldn't you have a ready weapon," I complained to no one in particular as I quickly loaded it.

Pulling a handgun off the rack, I quickly checked and loaded that as well before grabbing a knife and exiting the safe room. Of course, Lev wasn't too happy to see me again, which I didn't blame him for.

Before he could scold me, I held a finger at him to wait. "I'm not staying, promise. I just wanted to give you some stuff to even the odds." I set all the items on the ground and slid them over to him. "There's at least fifteen out there on the other side, all armed like some Call of Duty game. I don't know how much help the extra weaponry will be to you, but it's better than the single handgun you have."

Taking out a lighter and some of my bombs, I slid those over to him as well. "Don't use them unless you have to or if we're outside."

Then, with one last look and a wary smile, I blew him a kiss. "Be careful. I love you."

At least he managed to smile at me reassuringly, so I was thankful for that. "I love you, *zhizn moya*." Picking up the items, he quickly stashed them away on his body and held the rifle. "Now, go. I'll see you in a bit."

Believing him, I went back into hiding and watched the gunfight go down behind the screens until the cameras got taken out by bullets. All I could do after that was sit there and wait with bated breath for Lev to open the door so that I could run into his bloody arms like some fairytale.

I wish I had some way of knowing what went on beyond the heavy metal door. The walls were so thick, and probably soundproofed, that I couldn't hear anything happening on the other side.

It was torture to sit there in a dimly lit metal box that was too silent for its own good. The silence was deafening after what felt like forever—it was only ten minutes (I checked my damn phone). It was so quiet that my worries about how Lev was out there sounded like they were outside my head.

Another stretch of silence trudged on before a clicking sound made my head snap to the door.

The breath I'd sucked in dizzied me when I let it out with my wide grin. Excitement filled my racing heart when the door slid open, and I was about to run up to Lev until...

"No..."

For once, I was at a loss for words because I was too consumed by shock.

This wasn't how it was supposed to turn out.

Lev and I should've been embracing each other and celebrating his bloody victory, not forced away into separate cages after an apparent defeat.

We were supposed to be either on the road home or safe at home, not here at some unknown place located somewhere only the high Heavens knew.

All of this was bullshit!

The fight wasn't fair!

Lev should have won! He would have!

He nearly killed everyone in that damn hallway, and we would have gotten away if it weren't for the flashbang that was thrown his way. He could have gotten away if he'd jumped out the window, but he didn't want to risk leaving me.

That was what he told me when we were stuck in the back of the van together for the ride here.

...It's my fucking fault he got taken down...

"Grah!" My fists slammed against the metal bars of my prison cell with my angry outburst, rattling the rusty things.

Letting out a livid sob, I slumped against the bars and looked at Lev with apologetic eyes. My poor Lev was all beaten and bloody, and he was tied to a chair a few feet from my cage. "I'm so sorry." My cracked whisper barely cut through the air to his dazed self.

Wincing, Lev did his best to smile at me. "*Zhizn moya*, no. You have nothing to be sorry for. I made the stupid decision to stay. I should have been smarter. I could have jumped out of the window and jumped back into the room after the flashbang went off." He sounded regretful about his split-second decision that put us in this situation.

"Lev, what are we going to do?" I didn't see how we would get out of this.

I was locked up, and Lev was halfway to Death's door from the looks of it. They stripped both of us of our weapons and anything that could be used as a weapon, so we had nothing on but pants and a shirt.

His strong smile wavered for a second before he firmed it back up. "I don't know, but I'll figure something out, promise." If he was worried or anything, then he sure did a good job hiding it. "I'll get you out of this if it's the last thing I do."

It's not that I didn't appreciate his determination, but given the situation, I didn't want those words. Shaking my head with a frown, I refused to accept his promise. "Don't say that." I couldn't keep my voice strong or loud; I felt too beaten to hold my head up.

"The last thing you are allowed to do is grow old with me after we've raised our little gaggle of children together into wonderfully crazy adults," I told him with a forced chuckle in an attempt to lighten up the mood between us. "We'll get out of this. Together." Somehow.

For a moment, the two of us had some peace.

Too bad it didn't last long.

Our sweet moment ended with the door slamming open, followed by a cruel laugh. "If I had a heart, then I would feel a little bad for cutting your last moments together short, but I've got too much of a bone to pick with both of you to give a shit." Some man's spiteful voice filled the air, turning it rather volatile.

The yellowed fluorescent lights above us flickered on, causing my eyes to ache slightly from the sudden shift. It was only then that I saw the prick who's been a nuisance to the Volkovs and me by proxy. The sight of him brought an immediate frown to my face, causing him to tut at me.

"Now, now, that's not a very becoming face of you to make toward your husband." He chided me with a silent anger in his voice. "I suggest you change it before I do it for you," he stated harshly, glowering at me warningly.

A sudden shout of rage shook the room, along with the rattling of a chair. "She is not your wife!" Lev spat at Igor with the deadliest glare I've ever seen from someone in my life. "And I swear, if you dare lay a finger on her, I will rip you apart, limb by limb, then have rats eat you alive!" The raw wrath in Lev's booming threat shook me to the very core.

If the situation was in our favor or any different, then I would've laughed a little at how Igor's face paled with his widening eyes. Honestly, he looked ready to shit or piss himself with the way his body trembled with terror as he avoided Lev's gaze.

Fucking coward.

Clenching his eyes shut, Igor lashed a shaky hand out at Lev, landing a weak punch to Lev's face. The impact barely twitched Lev's head, and it even got Lev to bark out a m0cking laugh. "Come on, I can't even do shit to you all tied up like this, and you still fear me." Okay, Lev sounded a little too arrogant for his own good right then. "You better count your fucking seconds because you're not going to have days to live. You're dead the moment my brothers storm this place."

If they can find us.

I'd sent an SOS to Angel and the others while I was in the safe room, but there was nothing for them to track us to our current location. So, Lev gambled quite a bit with his threat.

Igor's hands balled up into tight fists as he glared down at Lev. "The only thing they'll find here is your dead body once I'm done with you." He bit back with some conviction. "And the last thing you'll be doing is begging me not to take your life before I do."

Throwing his head back, Lev let out a crazed laugh that had all the men in the room looking at him with wary eyes. "You know, if my sister-in-law didn't kick your ass half-drunk, then I'd be more inclined to take your pathetic threats seriously." Lev's laughter cut off with a winded grunt when Igor planted his fist into Lev's stomach.

Worried, I grabbed at the bars and shook them, frowning at the sight of Lev coughing. "Lev!" I cried out instinctively.

His reassuring gaze and bloody grin flashed at me. "I'm fine," he strained out.

Chewing my bottom lip, I looked over at Igor. "Let him go. It's me that you want, so let him go." I tried to keep my voice from wavering, but the idea of trying to bargain with this disgusting rat made me want to hurl.

"No," he flatly denied me, not even bothering to turn his attention to me as he was too focused on burning holes into Lev with his eyes. "The Volkovs made a mockery of my family, tore it apart, and burned it to the ground. So, I'm not going to take mercy on any of them."

What happened over the next few minutes made my heart crack. "Igor! Stop! Please!" My incessant begging fell on deaf ears.

No matter how much I pleaded with Igor, he wouldn't stop driving his fists and feet into Lev, who had toppled over with the chair. Even if Lev wasn't wincing in pain or reacting appropriately, I knew the blows had to hurt to an extent. Also, surely, he'd suffer the aftermath of it all, and I was worried that he might have an internal bleed with how many hits he took to his unguarded abdomen.

An outcry strained out of Igor when he realized his physical abuse of Lev did nothing but cause Lev to laugh like a complete maniac and spit balls of blood at him.

Yeah, good luck getting him to break.

Although, I may have spoken too soon.

I don't know what shit went on in Igor's head, but his head suddenly darted to me. Next thing I knew, his body appeared next to the cage and the door was thrown open after he unlocked it. My instinctive move to scramble away from him didn't amuse him one bit because once he locked his fat hand around my arm and hauled me out, he slapped me right across the face.

Now, that got a reaction from Lev. "*Ty, chert voz'mi, ublyudok!*" I don't know what he said, but he was very angry.

Being rather pissed about being physically assaulted, I whipped my scowling face at Igor and lashed back with my own hand, clawing him across the face and digging my fingers into his eyes. While my hand attacked his face, I leaned my body in and bit his hairy forearm that was exposed from his pushed-up sleeves, gagging a little when I felt the hairs in my mouth.

Fuck it, if I threw up, then it sure as hell would be all over him.

No matter how hard he tried to shake me off, he couldn't with how deep I latched onto him. It was only when he slammed me against the cage did I let go because it felt like he broke my fucking spine.

I was then thrown to the ground next to Lev, who was still shouting angrily at Igor in Russian.

Unfortunately, Igor didn't even give me a second of reprieve. His grubby hand fisted the back of my hair, forcing my head back to an unnatural angle that caused pain to stab at my neck. "You fucking bitch, you are going to regret that." He seethed at me, earning a bloody ball of spit to his face from me, which in turn got me a slap from him that split my lip open.

Shoving my face into the rough, concrete ground, he pressed my face into it until I felt the prickly ground scrape my face raw. "You know, I was going to wait until after we left the States to start breaking you, but I guess there would be no harm in starting early."

The feeling of his hand snaking under my shirt and grabbing me instantly kicked my body into survival mode. My legs kicked wildly like a herd animal fending off a predator while my arms clawed and pushed at Igor's heavy body to try and keep him as far from me as possible.

Screams of protest scratched my throat raw until it felt like my vocal cords would snap if I made even the faintest of sounds.

Then, my poor eardrums deafened after a while of hearing myself along with Lev's protestant shouts.

But, no matter how hard I fought... I couldn't stop every person's worst nightmare from coming true.

Chapter 32

I'M GONNA KILL HIM. I'm gonna fucking kill him!

It fucking killed me to see Nicole like this—broken. My heart broke into so many pieces being forced to watch... Watching her walls be torn down and smashed to nothing, for her to be reduced to...

Forcing the ordeal into a burning pit, I focused my attention back on my empress. "It's okay, I got you, it's okay." But was it? Would it ever be okay? Would we ever be okay after this? Was recovery possible?

"I'm sorry." All of this was my fault. None of this would have happened if I had been more wise back at the cabin. I should have tried harder to save Nicole, too. Yet, I did nothing; I was fucking useless while the damn bastard... "I'm so sorry."

After Igor was done, he threw Nicole back into the cage and left with his men. I managed to struggle myself over to Nicole, and she undid the rope that bound me. It hurt like hell to kick in the cage door enough to budge it open, but I gritted through the pain. Besides, I had no right to complain or give up. Nicole needed me, and she literally went through Hell. So I could endure some nonsense pain.

I don't know how long we stayed in each other's arms; not like it mattered to me. As long as I had her in my arms, that was all that mattered. Also, giving her comfort and being there for her was all I could do for her.

No matter how much I wanted to, I couldn't take her pain away. There was no way for me to erase what happened to her from her mind. Nor could I ever take the trauma away from her body.

A muffled noise from Nicole made me look down at her as I pulled her head back. "You'll still love me, right? You won't leave me, will you? I didn't want him or liked what he did. I only thought about you, I swear." Her frantic words spilled out of her nonstop with her tears that burned my skin like acid when they fell on me.

Immediately, I shot her down and shushed her gently as I held her face in my trembling hands. "Nicole, no, never. I would and will never think or see you any differently because of something like that, ever. I swear on my life and my mother." It hurt me so much to see her in shambles like this.

Giving her a stern look, I kissed her deeply. "And don't you ever question me and or anyone like that after the fact. And if anyone ever leaves you or changes the way they look at you because of something like that, then you punch them in the face and throw them into a landfill." I tried to lighten the mood a little by forcing out a bit of a serious joke at the end, along with a smile.

Hesitantly, Nicole cracked an awkward smile and chuckled very dryly. "I'd rather blow a bomb in their face, but I guess your way works, too." Her words were a little choppy and forced, but at least she was trying.

Although, as soon as it left, it came back. Her eyes darted away from mine to the ground, and her face fell completely. The air around us turned somber again as she slumped against me almost lifelessly. "How can you even see me the same after that?" Her worries reared its ugly face again.

Kissing her temple, I rubbed her arms soothingly. "My love, no, I don't see you the same, and I never will." Curling a finger under her chin, I lifted her face. "You aren't the same, not after that, but not for the reasons you are probably thinking about." Brushing a thumb across her lips, I smiled at her proudly. "I will always see you as better than me, the stronger person."

As I continued to hold her, I slowly brushed my fingers over the marks that marred her once-pristine body. Bruises in various stages of forming littered her extremities and face from where she was grabbed and held. Scrapes and cuts from the ground reddened her joints and face, making her look really battered and battle-worn. To be fair, she fought like a hellion until the very end, so I would've been surprised if she didn't up with battle scars.

God, I hated how she had to fight alone. I was fucking useless, tied to a chair. All I could do was scream and shout helplessly while she suffered.

Taking a deep breath, I kissed her cheek. "You literally got dragged to Hell and left there, but you pulled yourself out without giving yourself any time to grieve. You fought the damn devil tooth and nail throughout it all, despite knowing the end result, and never once did you give up." Nuzzling her face, I gave it tender kisses. "I will always see you as the better between us from now on, and I will always see you on the higher pedestal. I wish I could say I'd do the same in your situation, but I know for a damn fact that I wouldn't."

As much as I wanted to say otherwise, I would've been in a worse state than Nicole if someone forced themselves on me in front of my significant other. I'd be broken, inconsolable, and mentally unaware.

"You are so strong, *zhizn moya*, and I couldn't be more proud to call you mine," I said against her lips, kissing her deeply. "You are a fucking survivor who crawled out of the depths of hell with a crown of victory."

Hugging her tightly, I swore to her, "We'll get out of this together, and we'll burn the bastard alive."

The only problem now was how all of that would happen.

"Are you sure your body can handle that? You're still pretty banged up." Nicole eyed my various injuries with concerned eyes.

Taking in a controlled breath, I nodded my head in confirmation. "This is the only chance we got. The moment they move us to the new location, we'll be at a huge disadvantage," I whispered in a hushed voice as the two of us sat in the back of the car.

Sighing, Nicole leaned into me. "I just... It's a cramped car. Are you sure we can pull it off?" Her nervous eyes looked out the window, watching everyone scramble about to finish loading various vehicles for the move.

Before I could reply, the door by Nicole flew open, making me scowl. "So pathetic," Igor scoffed, reaching in and grabbing Nicole by her arm.

For a moment, the two of us glared at each other in a silent exchange of anger. "You know, I was going to take *my wife* back, but considering how your time with her is going to be limited, I'll take some mercy on you and let you enjoy what little time you have with her." If only he left it at that.

Damn bastard had the nerve to grab Nicole's face and plant a nasty one on her. Nicole's muffled scream shook at her thrashing body before a sharp slap rang through the air from Igor backhanding her. "Fucking bitch, you're lucky I don't gag you," he spat at Nicole with a deadly glare while holding his bleeding lip.

I couldn't help the proud and elated grin showing on my face as I watched Nicole spit his blood back in his face and tell him to fuck off in Vietnamese. "Enjoy your last moment with your rabid dog, *wife*." Igor seethed at Nicole before slamming the door in her face.

Spitting onto the floor, she wiped away the remainder of Igor from her mouth. "Fucking bastard, I swear, I'm going to gut him and stuff him full of bombs and make a bear chase him," she said with a determined glare out the window. "If he thinks I'm going to marry him, then he's got another thing coming for him. I'll fucking kill him in his sleep or slit my own throat if everything else fails."

Putting my bound arms around her, I held her close. "If only we can revive him to torture him over and over." I sighed disappointedly.

Honestly, there was so much I wanted to do to Igor, all ending in death. Too bad he only had one life and a set of body parts. "As long as you let me get my hands on him, I'd love to rip his puny dick off and make him choke on it while he runs for his pathetic life." I would much prefer to tear him limb from limb, like I said before, but Nicole had the final say after everything.

"I don't know how we're gonna pull off your plan with our hands cuffed." Nicole huffed, wiggling and gesturing at her bound wrists and mine.

Chuckling, I rolled my eyes and took her wrists into my hands. "Cuffs like these are easy to break." After a quick look to make sure no one was paying attention, I gave her a very fast crash course on breaking handcuffs. "But don't start until I tell you to. We don't know how many men are going to be in the vehicle quite yet. I just formulated the plan based on the hunch that there will be a driver and passenger, but if they decide to stick someone back here with us, then I'm gonna need a minute to adjust."

Thankfully, they didn't try to stick a guard into the back with us, so we had to deal with only the driver and passenger. The only shitty part of it all was that our car was more toward the front of the line, so we really had to punch it the moment the plan went into full swing.

I waited until we had driven out of the more remote parts of the woods before nudging Nicole and glancing down at her cuffs. Using my body to hide her attempts. It was probably risky to bank on their stupidity, but their lack of observational skills worked well in our favor. Honestly, all it would take for this whole plan to go bust was for one of them to look back and notice us acting strange. Luckily for us, they were too busy chatting about what they were going to do after payday.

Unlike Nicole, it didn't take me long to snap the links on my cuffs. Not that I was knocking at her skills or anything; I'd been trained to escape cuffs ever since I was a child back in Russia.

Carefully, I looked at Nicole and flashed my eyes at the driver before rubbing my left side to indicate the position of his weapon. Then, I waited for Nicole to nod in response before counting down from three on my fingers.

Nicole's nimble body shot out from the back, slipping up to the front through the space at the center. Ignoring the shouting passenger, she crawled into the driver's lap and fought with him for control over the steering wheel and pedals.

Meanwhile, I reached up and grabbed the passenger, taking his gun from him after he pulled it out and put a bullet through his head, splattering his brains all over the windows on the right side. Then, I turned the gun onto the driver, sending him to the afterlife with a shot to the temple.

Fucking hell.

I thought with a groan as I squeezed myself up to the front and pushed the passenger side door open, causing Nicole to swerve a little from the sudden rush of wind that threw the car off balance. "Shit! Damn it, Lev!" She hissed while jerking the wheel.

"Jerk it to the right," I told her with a grunt as I shoved at the dead body to get him out the door.

The car violently veered to the right, throwing the man fully out with the momentum. With the seat freed, I slipped into it and wrestled the door shut to stabilize the cabin again. "Holy shit! Drive! Drive! Drive!" I rushed Nicole when the sounds of bullets hitting the car echoed in my ear.

"Oh, no, I was thinking of cruising at five miles per hour and enjoying the scenery," Nicole snarked in a giddy and very sarcastic voice, her empty smile flashing at me for a second before her face dropped to a glaring scowl. "The fuck does it look like I'm doing!?"

Hanging onto the grab handle and the center console, I kept myself as steady as possible as Nicole drove like a madwoman down the road, sideswiping and straight-up bashing into any vehicle in our way.

A pained grunt strained out of me from a sudden hit that tilted the car and smashed my side in a little. "Shit!" I grunted again when the car next to us bashed us again.

"Motherfucker..." I seethed under my breath as I kicked the broken door off the car.

It probably wasn't a good idea to waste bullets like this, but like hell would I sit here and let this asshat bash my side in fully. Pressing my legs against the frame to steady myself, I aimed and shot at the driver of the other vehicle repeatedly until the bulletproof glass gave, and a shot went through to his body. The car's tires squealed as the vehicle spun out of control and into another behind us.

"Lev, don't waste your fucking bullets," Nicole told me before letting out a short scream when her side got hit by a vehicle.

"Fuck!" I hissed under my breath, quickly catching and bracing myself using the frame when my body was nearly thrown out from the hit.

Crawling into the back seat, I pulled the handle and kicked the back driver-side door open into the car hanging around Nicole's side. Grabbing onto the rail, I used the door to repeatedly bash the enemy's car until it spun out of the way.

Unfortunately, my makeshift door bat only survived that one car. Some speeding truck tore the thing off its hinges by driving straight into it. Luckily for me, the truck had its windows down because the passenger was trying to take a shot at me. At least I didn't have to waste any bullet to take him and the truck's driver out for the count.

"Lev!" Nicole's shrilling scream made my head snap back up front, where a man had hopped into the car through the doorless passenger side and struggled with Nicole.

The car jerked randomly with the steering wheel being in a game of tug-of-war with Nicole and the man, making it hard for me to keep my balance a little. It was almost impossible to properly aim at the man with how much we were all being thrown around in the car. One jerk and the bullet could end up through Nicole instead.

For a split second, the car steadied, and I immediately lunged for the man, grabbing him by the neck and blowing a hole into his head after digging the gun into the side of his head. Then, out his body went, becoming roadkill after the car next to us ran his body over.

Leaning around to the front, I kissed Nicole's cheek with a victorious smile. "We're almost to the main road." It was right there, just another mile, and we'd be safer with the crowded streets.

Sadly, a clean getaway wasn't in the cards for me.

"Fuck!"

Thwump!

"LEV!"

Chapter 33

Nicole

"LET ME IN!!!" I pushed my raw throat to the brink of snapping my vocal cords when I suspected to be within earshot of the guards who stood at the front of the Volkov Estate.

Half my body hung out of the beaten Jeep Wrangler, one hand gripping the wheel while the other waved madly to get attention drawn to me. "OPEN THE GATES!!!"

My battered body popped back into the car when a bullet whizzed past me and grazed my outstretched arm.

Hyperventilating breaths matched my racing heart as I kept my foot flat to the floor, still pushing the vehicle to go at max speed despite the mansion coming into view. I was afraid to ease off the gas pedal, afraid that the car would slow down just enough for my chasers to catch me at the last minute before I could get to safety. I'd probably wreck a few things and tear up the landscape beyond the gates, but I wouldn't stop until I was inside the mansion's doors.

As I got closer, to the point of nearly crossing the threshold of the opened gates, I could see armored SUVs and fully armed men spill out into the road, forming a blockade with a spot just wide enough for me to slip through.

I couldn't pay attention to anything else around me as I zipped past them at an ungodly speed. God, I thought I would pass out from the lack of oxygen in my body. It wasn't until I cleared the armored blockade and crashed into the fountain at the front of the mansion that I sucked in a proper breath that burned my lungs as if I'd inhaled acid.

"Oh my God! Nicki!" Angel's shocked voice was right there, and I could see her rushing to me with Nikolai right behind her. Yet, she felt so far.

Splash!

The chilly water did nothing to shock me out of my stupor when I stumbled out of the doorless Jeep and landed in it. The only thing it did was put me into shock. I was drowning in inches of water, but my arms and legs had no strength to move my body out of danger or lift me above the water. I had to be dragged out by a set of arms.

Fresh air mixed with my drowning lungs, sending me into a violent coughing fit as Nikolai and Stepan dragged my soaked body inside the house.

Everyone rushed me in the blink of an eye, toweling me down, wrapping me in blankets, settling me on the couch, and Angel even managed to get a damn I.V. in me so Alexei could run fluids and nutrients into me.

I wanted to tell them all so badly, and I knew time was of the essence. But my mouth refused to open, and when I somehow forced it open, words and sound refused to leave. I needed to tell them about Lev before it was too late, but my body repelled every effort. Even when my frustration spilled over into tears, no sound came out with my angry sobs.

Lev needed me, yet I was fucking useless!

"Hey, shh, hey, it's okay." Hanna's softened voice soothed me as she held me tightly. "You're safe. You're alive and safe. You're okay now."

But that's what was wrong! I was okay while Lev could be dead!

I couldn't stop crying for the life of me.

It was like my body had a mind of its own. I was no longer in control. At the very least, my rational side wasn't in control. If I had to wager on it, I was willing to bet that all the events of the past days, all the trauma and repressed rage and sadness, finally reached a breaking point.

The volcano of emotions finally blew.

"We're gonna have to sedate her," one of the twins, probably Alexei, said, making my panic rise.

I didn't need to be sedated! I couldn't! If I was out of it, I wouldn't be able to tell them about Lev!

Immediately, I struggled against Hanna, who was actually trying to help me by shielding me from Alexei. The young doctor was by far amused, and he fought his way through Hanna to stick a needle into my neck.

Whatever drug he hit me with kicked in immediately. No matter how much I fought it, my muscles refused to tense and move, and my head fell over onto Hanna's shoulder as she grabbed ahold of me again. My heavy eyes drifted over to Angel, pleading silently with her for some help, but Nikolai and Stepan held her back by actively blocking her path.

Fucking Volkovs...

If the reason for my head was a hangover from one hell of a night, then I wouldn't be so pissed.

If my man's life wasn't on the line, then I wouldn't be so fucking pissed.

If Alexei would give me some kind of fucking reaction to my rage, even the slightest twinkle of fear would do, then I'd be somewhat satisfied with threatening to blow his ass sky high to where he would meet God.

But no!

The damn psychopath wasn't fazed one bit!

Heavy, seething breaths heated the air in the living room up as I sat there glaring at each and every Volkov man. "I'm going to fucking kill all of you if Lev doesn't," I grumbled with a very pissed-off scowl.

"Well, you weren't going to be of any help being in shock like that, and you weren't showing any signs of improving," Alexei remarked casually in his usual collected tone. "So, I made a judgment call."

"Well, I didn't consent to having my ass sedated," I snapped back with a snarl.

Smug little turd had the audacity to crack a smirk and shrug his shoulders. "You weren't of sound mind, therefore cannot make any informed consent."

Unable to think of a good comeback, I settled for flipping him off and telling him, "Go put your dick in a shredder."

Taking a few deep breaths, I calmed myself down enough to get some mental clarity. "What's our plan for getting Lev back?" I asked with a somewhat sour face, still pissed at his brothers.

"I wish I could give you more information about Igor and his plans, but he didn't give us anything to go on." But did that really matter? Igor would cease to exist the moment we strike him down. Of course, we had to get to that point.

"And how do you know he won't kill Lev?" I knew keeping calm under pressure was probably some supreme bad guy 101 kind of thing, but everyone was too calm about Lev's disappearance.

"Igor contacted us the other day, the morning after you and Lev were kidnapped, and made a ransom demand for Lev. He wanted his sister, Natalia, back along with the section of the city that his father owned before we ran him out," Nikolai answered me with a long exhale. "Obviously, we're not going to give him what he wants, but if he kills Lev, then he has nothing."

Sighing heavily, Stepan leaned forward in his spot on the couch and ran his hands down his face. "But the issue with us gambling like so is the fact Igor is potentially a man with nothing to lose. So, we're really hoping he wants his sister and turf badly enough to spare Lev long enough for us to find out where Lev's located and rescue him."

Huffing, I snatched the laptop from Bao the moment he came within arm's reach, startling him. "Whoa! Freaking chill sis. He's not gonna get any deader if he's dead already," my younger brother quipped at me, earning a nasty glare in return because this was not the time for that kind of joking.

Rolling my eyes, I booted the laptop up and immersed myself with pulling up the tracking program and pinning down Lev's location. I wasn't a religious person, but I sure as hell prayed to everything out there in the universe for Lev to still have his collar on.

By some miracle, he did.

I zoomed in with a bated breath when I saw the blinking rot dot on the satellite map. I hoped it wouldn't be an empty road or some random spot in the forest. I nearly screamed with joy when the grainy image cleared up to show a shittiest building next to some abandoned dock.

Jumping up from the couch, I showed everyone the screen while bouncing on the balls of my feet with glee. "Come on, let's go get him!" I urged everyone with an eager grin, practically throwing the laptop onto the coffee table and turning to shoot out the door.

Unfortunately, I only made it a step before a body blocked my path. "You're not going anywhere in your current state." Stepan's stern words made me glower at him in defiance.

Stepping right up into his face, I held a finger up to him. "For one, I'm not even going into the midst of battle." Lifting a second finger, I continued, "Secondly, if you think you're going to keep me home while my man is out there needing to be rescued, then you're fucking delusional." Holding up a third finger, I narrowed my eyes more at him. "Thirdly, I am going."

Thankfully, my girls had my back—literally.

"Angel, if you don't get your ass over here right now—"

A pointed look from Angel was all Nikolai needed to shut up. "You can't say shit. If it was me out there, you'd be dragging yourself to me even if all your limbs were gone." Crossing her arms, she stepped up next to me and glared at her husband challengingly. "Likewise, if it was you out there, I would stop at nothing until I dragged your ass back home myself. Which, by the way, has happened."

Then, before Stepan could get a word out of his open mouth, Hanna dug into him. "Nah ah! Nothing out of you Styosha, not unless you want to be sleeping outside," she threatened her own husband confidently. "And it's not like you can argue either because you put your stupid ass up there on a damn roof to save me when you should have been resting in a hospital bed."

"And you two." Angel's head locked onto the twins, who looked rather conflicted. "If you dare say *anything*, and I mean *anything*, I will make you regret it. No woman, no opinion."

With all the hardheaded men shut down, Angel picked up the laptop and studied the map closely for a silent stretch. Once the lightbulb in her pregnant brain went off, she returned the device to me and looked at her husband. "You have fifteen minutes to get your ass out that door with our men and the others, *Nicole included*, before I gear my pregnant ass up and march out there myself to run the damn mission."

That surely got Nikolai's feet moving at top speed, much to his brother's surprise. His body practically flew around the place, making various trips to some room down the hallway and dropping off various pieces of equipment on the coffee table with each round. After the third round, he skidded to a halt at the hallway's entrance to bark something in Russian at his brothers with an angry and somewhat panicked face.

They all looked at their brother with wary eyes, not budging from their spots until he shouted at them again, this time with more urgency. I don't know what Nikolai told his brothers, but it got them scrambling to gear up in a flurry—even Alexei got his ass geared.

Leaning over to Angel, I asked in a hushed voice, "Uhh, what did he yell at them?" If anyone—besides his brothers—was to know what Nikolai said, Angel would be our best bet because she'd been pretty active with learning Russian out of all of us.

Scratching her temple, Angel mumbled the words repeatedly for a moment before her lips twisted with unsureness. "Uhh, something about how he'd out them with something, but don't quote me on that."

All of us, minus Angel, were out of the house and on the road in less than fifteen minutes. Everyone was in their own vehicles to the destination, and we were all connected on a group call to work out the impromptu plan as much as possible before shit went down.

"Three groups, Alpha, Beta, and Delta. I'll head Alpha. Stepan and Hanna will take the lead for Beta while the twins lead Delta. There aren't any good spots for sniper nests, so we're all going in on foot." Nikolai paused for a second before continuing after clearing his throat, "We'll forgo a sweep as long as Bao and Nicole can cover that end for us with their drones. Alpha team will come in through the front, Beta will handle the side, and Delta will be the back."

"What about the waterfront?" Alexei questioned, sending an eerie silence through the call. "We're going to need—"

A heavy breath crunched through the speakers before Nikolai's low voice rumbled through. "We are not going in for a full takedown. Our priority is to get Lev and do what damage we can during the process, but we are not focusing on Igor. If he escapes, then so be it. We can always find some way to track Igor down again and kill him, but we only have one Lev."

"Bao and I will handle surveillance. You guys just worry about going in there and giving them hell and saving Lev," I told them flatly while messing with my tablet.

Feeling a wave of unease trickle down my arm, I glanced over in the direction I felt the chill. "What?" I snapped softly at Bao after muting the call.

Bao's eyes nervously glanced at me as he continued to drive, and his tongue kept darting out and licking his lips as he hesitated. It wasn't until I glared full-on and snapped at him again that he got his words out. "You're going to do something stupid." He let out a defeated sigh as if he accepted the fact before it came to fruition.

"Depends on how you define stupid," I muttered, rolling my eyes.

Waving a dismissive hand at my brother, I told him, "Just focus on driving. Don't worry about any of it."

As if I would let the others have all the fun. Also, my impatience may or may not be playing a huge part in my rash plan.

"Uhh, does it have to do anything with what you had me gather..." Bao questioned warily with a glance at the back of the van.

Once again, not wanting to deal with possible pushbacks from anyone, my brother included, I waved him off. "I said, don't worry about it," I bit out sternly, throwing him a warning glare.

Sighing heavily, Bao dropped it and unmuted the call so we could participate again. There wasn't much from me and Bao, mainly because we didn't have much to comment on. Well, I wasn't participating because I was too busy running my programs to make sure things would run smoothly later.

The last thing I wanted was for something to blow up in my face or Lev's—literally.

Just as I thought, we didn't immediately jump into action when we reached our destination. Everyone was too busy trying to finalize the last-minute plan to march their ass into the place. Also, they were waiting around for Bao and me to finish our sweep, which took longer than I anticipated as well.

"Nicki... What are you doing?" Bao hissed over my shoulder. "We're done with our part, so why the fuck around you still cruising around?" He reached around me to shut the screen off, but I slapped his hand away.

Then, his mouth opened again, but no words came out when his eyes landed on the other computer screen. "What is that? What are you trying to hack?" He moved his hand for the mouse, but I stopped him with a grab to the wrist. "I'm not going to shut it down," he remarked with genuine eyes. "I just want to see what you got going on because it looks weird."

Letting go of his hand, I turned my attention back to my drones. "It better be a good weird and not a bad weird," I muttered. "Do not touch the codes..." My voice trailed out with reluctance.

I didn't want to tell Bao that the program I had running was a proto-type of sorts, so the lines of codes were kind of... Experimental, so to speak. I mean, this wasn't the first time they've been used or tested—technically. I've only ever tested things through virtual simulations and on a very small handful of unlucky people with a success rate that was rather low. It was probably risky of me to use it today without having all the kinks out, but what better way to figure out if my last round of patches worked or not than to test it out firsthand?

Oh yeah, I was more than prepared for this shit to blow up in my face. But fuck it.

"Do I even want to know?" Bao sighed heavily as he plopped down next to me.

"Probably not," I answered him truthfully with an innocently wicked grin. "But you should help me either way because you're the best brother ever."

"I'm your only brother where it matters." Bao deadpanned before pulling the keyboard closer to him. "I'm gonna ignore what diabolical plan you're executing over there to fix your whack-ass program." He jabbed at me playfully with a chuckle.

"There is nothing wrong with my program," I retorted, scoffing in slight offense.

"Your shit is gonna make phones blow up." Bao deadpanned with a slightly raised voice.

Rolling my eyes, I shot him a flat stare. "That's the point."

"W-well then, your shit ain't efficient in that manner either," he stammered with a shaky confidence. "Your code that causes the relay and overload is slow."

"Then fix it, mister smarty pants," I snarked with a playful smile.

Bao stuck his tongue out at me for a split second before focusing on the screen.

Entrusting Bao with the bomb phone program, I let him be so I could go back to navigating and positioning my drones.

I really shouldn't be doing this. It was one thing to bomb an area I knew or had a good view of, but to go off of only thermal imaging? Yeah, I was essentially blind. All I could do was make very educated guesses about the figures I saw on the screen. It was probably safe for me to assume that the mobile figures weren't Lev because why on earth would Lev be given free roam around the place?

After scanning the place carefully a few times, I somewhat confidently determined the figure off in the southwest corner to be Lev. The figure hadn't moved to a different location the whole time, nor had it been mobile. Also, it looked to be sitting. Well, it could be someone hiding out to take a break or something, but given the actions of the other figures, I doubted it.

Another moment passed before I got everything in position. "Bao, set them off," I sternly ordered him, glancing briefly at him out of the corner of my eyes as my finger hovered over the ENTER button of my keyboard.

A look of reluctance and defiance crossed my brother's eyes for a hair for a second before he gave in with a sigh and shake of his head. "I am so going to get shit about this later from the others," he uttered before finishing a line of code and hitting enter.

Seconds later, nearly all the figures on the screen made the same movement of pulling something from their body and holding it before them, which was a cue for me to set off the next chain of events.

"Bombs away bitches."

Chapter 34

A PAINFUL COUGH FORCED itself out of my scratchy throat from the hard punch to the gut from Igor.

His hand buried itself into the top of my hair, yanking my head back. "I should just feed you to the sharks," he seethed inches from my face. "Better yet, I should send you back to your family in pieces."

Pooling up the blood in my mouth, I spat it at him with a challenging smirk. "Do it, and you'll get your sister back in pieces the same way." Letting my smugness come out, I slackened my body. "If they don't decide to let Angel torture her. And you better hope Angel doesn't get her hands on Natalia."

Dealing with Angel in the torture chamber was worse than a death sentence, in my opinion. "She'll probably start off by sticking needles under Natalia's nails before ripping them off with pliers and then slowly chopping her fingers off by the joint until there's nothing but nubs left." I shouldn't open my mouth and make my dire situation worse, but if I was gonna die here, then I might as well have some fun. "Imagine how many days worth of mail that'll be to you." I cackled madly before a punch to the face shut me up.

Throwing my bound body off the chair, Igor kicked my midsection until I hacked up blood all over the dirty floor. I was hauled back up into the chair before my heavy head was wrenched back at a painful angle. "I am going to fuck your stupid whore over your grave every damn day after I make her my wife."

A wave of fury heated my body for a split second before an amused laugh barked out of me. "If your words held any promise, then I might take you seriously and snap at you." Deep down, I was furious, but I knew for a damn fact he would never get his hands on Nicole if I were to die.

The deep-seated rage quickly surfaced despite my efforts to keep a lid on it. My heart pounded in my chest while my bound hands clenched into tight fists behind my back. Every seething breath burned as it entered and exited my body through my flared nostrils until it felt like I constantly breathed fire and smoke. "I am going to make you pay for what you did to her once I am free, and if I die, then I will come back and drag you down to Hell and torment you for all of eternity." It wasn't a threat—it was a promise.

Sneering, Igor threw my head and punched me across the face before stepping back. "You're fucking delusional if you think you're going to make it out of this alive."

Mocking him with a sneer of my own, I set my eyes on him in a death glare. "And you're delusional for thinking you'll have any success when you have nothing."

Igor's prideful laugh filled the room, throwing me for a loop. "I have everything I need to overthrow you Volkovs." Slowly, he paced back and forth in front of me. "I've taken more than half of your allies, who have helped me gather a vast amount of wealth to sustain."

A crazed grin inched itself onto his face as he continued to spew shit from the garbage can he called a mouth, "You Volkovs got too cocky and comfortable with the merge that you failed to realize how many were actually against you. I mean, for crying out loud, I got your whore's parents on my side, and it's thanks to them that I am going to be successful in taking you and your stupid brothers down."

Maybe he was a tad out of touch with reality, or stupid... or ignorant... Or all the above. From the sounds of it, he might actually be unaware of the fact that what he prattled about was gone.

My brothers and I had little to no trouble with tracking down and taking care of the traitors on our payroll. We thought taking care of the trash would be difficult, but we didn't struggle one bit because Nicole and Bao took little to no time tracking everyone down. It didn't take much for us to compile a complete list of people either; a lot of the people we captured initially were more than eager to spill with some false promises.

Needless to say, we removed all the rotting bits. Granted, there would always be the risk of someone turning on us in the future, but that was a problem for later when or if it arose. For now, we regained control and respect.

Of course, Igor didn't need to know about any of that. If he didn't notice before, then that was on him for being an ignorant little shit. Besides, if I burst his bubble right now, then he might actually kill me when his perfect little plan imploded on him.

I have no idea what Igor went on about as he continued to run his mouth; I stopped listening long ago. His voice was also very annoying, and I couldn't help but feel sorry for anyone who had to put up with him for more than five minutes.

I didn't bother zoning back in until he stopped midsentence. I had to know what made him shut up. Much to my disappointment, it was his phone. I was about to zone back out until I noticed how his face twisted with confusion momentarily before it stretched out in surprise. A string of curses flew out of his mouth when he let his smoking phone fall from his hand and clatter against the ground.

What the hell is going on?

Then, it hit.

"BLYAT'!"

Deafening booms popped my eardrums and caused a constant ringing to echo in my head. The place was instantly filled with dust and debris as the building slowly came apart from the seemingly endless explosions.

Was this an earthquake? The whole place shook and trembled like it was caught in one, and maybe the explosion was from some generator going off because of the earthquake.

The inclination of this being an earthquake crumbled away when the ceiling gave in, and flashes of light tore through the place. I felt myself getting winded by the force of the explosions that ended up knocking me over with the chair.

Despite my broken and aching body protesting, I forced myself to worm away behind a slab of metal that had fallen against the wall and made a nice little tent—one I barely managed to fit my fat ass into.

Tucking myself up as much as possible, I silently laid there praying to whoever was in the sky that I'd survive this. This attack couldn't have been from my brothers; they weren't this destructive, nor would they risk my life like this. Nicole did cross my mind for a split second, but the explosives came too close to me, and I doubt she was *that* insane for gambling with my livelihood like so.

My chest ached from how I struggled and strained to contain my coughs as I breathed in the dusty air around me. If I had an option, then I wouldn't breathe at all because everything fucking hurt like hell. Also, I was pretty sure a few of my ribs were busted up—bad. If I was lucky, then maybe I'd make it out of this without a punctured lung.

Big if.

My internal bleeding would probably get to me before my brothers would.

Letting out a deep breath, I let myself slump fully against the wall. I was so exhausted. The only thing that fueled me this far was my rage against Igor, hope to see my brothers again, a want to see my first nephews, and my hope and dreams to see Nicole again. To be able to hold my empress in my arms, kiss her heavenly lips, feel her soft body, and have a whole life full of wonder and joy with her.

I wish I could say it'd be fine because I would finally be able to see my mother, but there was no way I'd end up in Heaven with the life I have lived.

God, how did I fuck up so badly this time?

If I had paid more attention when we were escaping, I wouldn't be in this mess. I should've noticed the enemy, and I would've if I hadn't let my guard down. The enemy wouldn't have been able to sneak up on me and get enough of a hold on me to yank me out of the car if I had been more attentive.

Squeezing my stinging eyes shut, I let the stray tears escape down my face. No one was around to see me cry, so screw it. Besides, maybe it was the dust and not my emotions. Also, if this was it, then who the hell cares?

I'm so sorry for being a little shithead, Kolya. Sorry, I couldn't have done more, Stepan. Arseny, fuck you, for one, but I hope Mia knocks some sense into you and you two find your peace. Alexei, you fucking psychopath, I don't know what to say to you besides I hope you find your heart again.

I shouldn't be so pessimistic, but it really did feel like this was it for me. So, might as well say what I needed and not leave with any regrets or unspoken things.

Exhaling slowly, I struggled to lift my heavy eyelids every time I blinked. A nap really sounded good right about now, though.

...Just a few seconds won't hurt...

I love you, Nicole... Maybe I'll dream of you.

I couldn't fight the darkness anymore. My eyes refused to open with my last blink, and the bog of slumber swallowed my mind.

Endless peace beckoned me away from the fading world around me, but a faint voice made me turn my head.

"... Want... Body... For..." The distant and muffled voice sounded familiar, but who was it? "... Lev...!"

Nikolai... He didn't sound angry at me, so I wasn't in trouble... Right?

A sharp screech made me scrunch my face up as it felt like a knife into my ear. "Here!" Not Nikolai... Stepan?

There was a lot of shuffling in my direction before I felt an immense amount of pain shoot through my body, making me wince. Unfortunately, that wasn't enough to get my eyes to open. Well, at least I could peep them, even if it was just a crack, and for less than a second.

"Shit!" A sharp sting landed on my cheek, followed by one of the twin's hissing. "Damn it, Lev, don't go to sleep." My brain rattled in my head from someone shaking it. "Wake up, stay with us," my younger brother pleaded—I still didn't know which one.

Nikolai threatened me with a pleading playfulness, "Lev, I swear, if you don't stay with us, and we end up dragging your dead body out of this damn place, I will tell them *everything* that's supposed to be a secret between us." The hope in his voice, hope for me to snap back at him, cracked at his voice. It was almost as if he was begging me to open my eyes and glare at him.

I mean, I would if I could, but it felt like someone stitched my eyes shut after supergluing them.

"Lev, come on, don't do this to us." It was Stepan this time. "Don't you dare fucking die on us." I could hear his emotions cracking through as well. "This isn't some damn blaze of glory, so you can't fucking die on us."

"Can't believe I'm saying this, but please don't die." It was one of the twins again. "You know I can't go to an actual therapist. Otherwise, I'm going to end up in maximum lockdown at a mental prison." Arseny; it was Arseny because he was the only one who ever referred to me as his therapist. Also, he was the only one of the twins to actually converse a lot with me.

"Alexei, anything?" Nikolai inquired.

I assumed the sigh I heard was from Alexei. "Can't say for sure until we get him back home and I properly examine him." Always the oh-so-careful doctor—this asshole. "But I still feel a pulse. It's really thready, but it's there."

It wasn't long until my lungs screamed with happiness as a natural warmth blanketed my body.

Fresh fucking air, thank God.

Forcing my chest to expand—bad fucking idea—I took in as much oxygen as possible. My whole body convulsed with my violent coughs as I hacked, what felt like, my life out; I couldn't stop no matter how hard I tried to tighten my torn muscles to suppress my coughing.

At least the stark pain shot my eyes wide open.

Spitting out the pooled blood in my mouth, I weakly looked at my brothers with the best smile I could muster up in my state. "... I fu..ckin g...love...you...all..." I could die on the way home for all I knew, so it was better to get it out now, just in case.

"Hey, hey, hey." Alexei's hands grabbed my falling face, holding it up. "Do not close your eyes! I don't care what you do or say but do not fall asleep. You understand me?"

I wanted to roll my eyes at him for ordering me around, but I was afraid that if I did, then I'd pull my eyelids down. "Fu...ck...y...ou..." I garbled out, causing some more blood that had pooled again in my mouth to spill over.

The four of them practically ran to the nearest vehicle and threw me into the back with the twins. "Kolya, you better drive like your wife's in fucking labor," Stepan joked in a serious voice as he slid into the passenger seat.

"No, I was planning on going twenty under the speed limit," Nikolai snarked at Stepan with a sneer. "Just shut up and hold on tight."

"Oh, this is going to be a ride from Hell," Arseny commented as he held my body down with Alexei.

"Or a ride to Hell," Alexei muttered.

Oh boy, this might be my last car ride if things went as I thought.

Fuck me.

***

My fucking head.

God, someone shut that beeping up.

Groaning, I strained out a few coughs as I tried to turn my broken body, only to be stopped by a set of hands. "Whoa, whoa, whoa, no, do not do that." God, never thought I'd be so happy to hear Angel scold me. "You need to stay on your back. Otherwise, you're going to pop your stitches and compromise your breathing."

Taking a slow and painful breath, I forced out a weak chuckle. "Well sh...it... That..." Fucking hell, I couldn't even finish a short quip back at Angel.

A soft whirring sound buzzed in my ear, and my upper body was lifted up into a half-sitting position. Thank fucking God because that made breathing so much easier and better.

Lulling my head to the side, I looked at Angel with grateful eyes. "Thank you." I barely managed to get the two words out above a whisper.

Smiling happily at me, Angel leaned in and hugged me very carefully. "I'm so glad you're alive." Her voice shook with relief as she clung to me for a bit.

Her happy smile straightened out sternly after she pulled away. "Try not to move too much yet. I still have to secure your dressings and give you an abdominal binder and a rib belt." And there was nurse Angel—great. "If you bust a stitch and we have to put you together again, I will feed you Nicole's chicken noodle soup."

Grimacing a smile, I strained out a chuckle. "I think I'd rather spend an hour in the torture chamber with you than have a lick of my Nicole's food." At least I wouldn't end up with food poisoning with Angel.

"Hey! That's just rude!" And there she was. "Move!" Nicole practically ran up to Angel and playfully nudged her away to throw herself all over me.

"Hey," Angel scolded Nicole, smacking her on the back. "Careful, he's injured! You're going to make him worse!"

"Nikolai, your wife is putting too much stress on the babies by yelling at me!" Nicole shouted toward the door before looking at Angel and flipping her off.

Everyone filtered into the cramped room within seconds of Nicole shouting. I swear, it was as if they were all waiting by the door or something. "Get off of Lev, Nicole." Alexei chided with a sigh as he elbowed himself through everyone to my bedside. "Angel is right. His condition isn't fully stable yet, so you could do some damage to him." He proceeded to carefully pry Nicole away from me.

Letting my head fall back against my pillow, I slowly turned it around to look at everyone in the room with appreciative eyes. "You all have no idea how fucking happy I am to see you all." I wasn't an emotional person by any means, but fuck, I couldn't hold my tears back.

"Think you gave him too much pain meds, Alexei." Stepan cracked a soft laugh with his joke.

Everyone held it in much better than me, but I could see it in their eyes. They were all relieved and elated that I was up and talking. Although, I could see some puffiness around their eyes that weren't bags.

Sucking in a sharp breath, I twitched my hand in Alexei's direction when he pressed against my stomach. "Son of a... A warning would have been appreciated...!" I hissed through gritted teeth. "Fuck..."

Squeezing my eyes shut, I breathed deeply. "What even happened anyway? And what's the damage to my body?" I could still feel and move everything, so that had to be a good sign... Right?

Taking a deep breath, Alexei stuffed his hands into his jacket, then listed off everything wrong with me, like some grocery list. "Slight concussion, busted eardrums, right dislocated shoulder, bilateral fractures to your ulna and radius, a few broken ribs, some bruised ribs, left lung puncture, mild internal bleed, right fractured tibia, and the rest of your body is scattered with various scrapes, cuts, and lacerations." It creeped me out a little at how nonchalant he sounded, but I knew he cared because of the little warmth and worry in his eyes when he looked at me.

Blowing out a heavy breath, I tried to lighten the dense air with a chuckle. "Well, that would explain why I feel like I've been mauled by a hippo." At least my awkward joke got a few chuckles.

With my condition out of the way, all that was left was, "So, what happened then?"

Immediately, everyone's head turned to Nicole accusingly, who returned all the gazes with an offended scoff. "You were all taking too long, and they could have killed Lev by the time you got to him," she defended herself with her chin held high.

Groaning from the growing headache, I brought a hand up to rub my aching temples. "*Zhizn moya*, what did you do?" I already sounded fed up and ready for the chaos that would come from her mouth.

Don't get me wrong; I wasn't upset or angry. I just knew it wouldn't be anything good given everyone's deathly glares, and given how she was as a person.

Giving me a lopsided smile, she chuckled very nervously. "I uhh might have gotten a little impatient with waiting for your rescue mission to get under way... Sooooo I uhh..." Her eyes slowly trailed around the room as she rocked back and forth on the balls of her feet. "I might have gone a little crazy with the explosives..."

"A little?" Arseny questioned while looking at her with calculating eyes as if he was trying to figure out whether or not she was sane. "You blew up a whole fucking building until it was dust after turning everyone's phones into bombs."

"Well, it took care of everyone faster than you guys would have," Nicole retorted smugly.

"You could have hit Lev, or he could have been caught in a blast," Stepan interjected with his own worries.

Deadpanning at Stepan, Nicole loosely crossed her arms and rolled her eyes at him. "Seriously? You think I'm that careless?" she asked with mock offense. "I might have only had thermal to go off of, but I guessed right and avoided the right person."

If I had a drink in my mouth, then it would have ended up all over everyone in the room. "You what?" Maybe I misheard?

"Well, who else would look like they're bound and in one spot?" Nicole tried to defend herself with a nonchalant shrug of her shoulders. "And, I mean, I was careful not to drop any bombs close enough to actually do real damage... Maybe just a popped eardrum or smack to the gut..."

I had to take a minute to accept the fact that Nicole really gambled with my life. There was no doubt that she was mindful of where she dropped the bombs, but there was no way she could have known the exact results of the damage. Stunned, I stammered out, "You dropped bombs close to me without being a hundred percent sure that I would survive?" My question came out closer to a statement rather than a question.

"Woman, you are fucking psycho." I had to take a moment to really look at her and recollect myself.

Waving her closer, I waited until she was within reach before grabbing her and pulling her into my lap with a pained groan. "And I fucking love it." Grabbing her face, I pushed through the pain of my screaming body and planted a hard one on her lips. "But please don't do something like that again."

An awkward chill weighed the air around the bed down, making me look around at everyone who eyed me like I was some alien.

"What? Don't act like you haven't kissed your woman in front of me."

Chapter 35

~1 month later~

"*Zhizn moya*, that's enough."

Lev's large hand engulfed my wrist, putting an immediate stop to my mindless scrubbing.

Snapping out of my daze, I blinked a few times before looking at Lev with furrowed eyes. "*Đại ca*... What are you...? You're getting yourself all wet."

Lev was still fully geared in tactical clothing as he stood there under the showerheads, getting completely drenched. But he didn't seem to care about it with how he kept his concerned eyes trained on me and remained unmoving despite my shoves.

Sighing heavily, he took the coarse sponge from me and dropped it onto the tiled floor beneath us. "Empress, you're going to hit bone next if you don't stop," he joked flatly with a troubled smile.

Without a word, he took me into his arms and held me tightly. An arm anchored itself around my whole backside while his other hand stroked at my wet strands.

Something about his simple but tender action blew my dam wide open. All the anger, regret, resentment, sadness, self-loathing, just everything spilled over. Acid-like tears streamed down my face uncontrollably, mixing with the shower water that cascaded over me. The tears wouldn't stop, and soon, my body shook like a leaf with my loud sobs.

Lev's soothing shushes barely cut through the sounds of the rushing water as he rocked me softly. "*Vso v poryadke, zhizn moya. Vypusti vso naruzhu. U menya yest' ty, i ya nikuda ne uydu.*" His rumbling voice shook my nerves back into place. "I got you. I always will, just like how I will always love you, no matter what." His lips comforted every inch of my face with kisses. "Like I told you before, I don't see you the same." Pulling back, he held my face with both hands and kept our eyes locked. "I see you as better, stronger."

Leaning down, he kissed me deeply with a content groan. "I love you so much more, and I am very proud to call you mine," he whispered after sucking in a deep breath. "I will never see you any less because of what happened. I will never see you as ruined, stained, or tainted. So, stop cleaning yourself raw." He meant every single word, and he was also concerned about my well-being. "I see the way you avoid your reflection. How you're taking long-ass showers and how red, raw, and tender your body is after you come out of these showers."

His furrowed eyes softened with concern and sadness with each word, looking like they would melt out of his eyes at any moment. "And I just... It pisses me off how I can't help you." His voice cracked as the tears slipped from his eyes. "I'm fucking useless to you, and I hate it. And I know it's nothing that either of us can fully control, but it still sucks."

For a long and silent moment, we stood there in each other's embrace. Our bodies trembled and shook as our cracked walls eroded with our sobs. We were both broken over what happened, but I don't think either of us ever properly processed and grieved over it.

Forcing out a chuckle, I looked up at Lev with a smile of disbelief. "Maybe everyone has a point with us needing to see a therapist." It was obvious that neither of us were coping properly. "And I don't even know where to start the healing process."

No matter how many self-help articles and books I trifled through, none of the information seemed to help. If anything, reading everything made me more overwhelmed and withdrawn. Yet, the thought of reaching out for professional help felt like I was throwing in the towel; it meant I was really fucked up beyond normal help.

Lev's body shook against mine with his chuckle. "I'll start looking for someone who we can pay off not to turn us into the authorities." He was serious, even if he tried to make light of everything with his uplifted tone. "I'm willing to do anything at this point because I really don't know where or how to start helping you or myself." Forcing out a short chuckle of defeat, he shook his head slowly. "I thought I could just power through it like everything else, but I can't."

The two of us became silent again as we looked at each other with understanding eyes that slowly morphed into appreciation and adoration. Soon, our frowning lips curled into smiles that broke out into full grins until our mouths were open with our laughter that echoed throughout the bathroom. "God, we are so fucked up, but I'm so happy that I have you by my side at the end of the day and that you are going through every step with me." My hands stroked down his face to his neck, and my arms coiled themselves around him until there was no space left for even air to pass between us.

"Thank you, Lev, thank you so much," I whispered against his lips before completely closing the space between us with a heart-shattering kiss.

My feet stumbled backward until my back hit the shower wall with a grunt. "You don't ever have to thank me for doing what I am supposed to do." He breathed heavily against my lips. "I swore to always be there for you, no matter what, to always love and cherish you until we are six feet under. Through sun and hail, through the good and the shitty days, everything. I will always be by your side or watching your back as we move forward together."

A cheery laughter rang from me as I slapped his shoulder playfully. "I swear to God, you better not get down on one knee and propose to me in the shower."

Rolling his eyes, Lev tickled my sides with a playfully offended look. "*Zhizn moya*, what kind of man do you take me for?" he retorted with a playful quirk of his eyebrow. "The only thing showers are good for is cleaning off blood and fucking you."

I could feel my own eyeballs roll slightly at the feeling of his hand slipping between my legs and stroking the length of my cunt. "Then why aren't you making good use of it then?" I challenged him with a smirk, spreading my legs a little for him to have better access.

Two of his fingers slowly slipped into me, curling up against my G-spot and making my back arch with a moan. "Because I have a better use of our energy later." Now, this perked my interest, and I urged him to continue with a raise of my brow and tilt of my head. "If you're fine with it, I was thinking we finally pay Igor his long overdue visit and show him how it's properly done. Show him who you really belong to, who your body responds to, who your heart belongs to." His voice shook with uncertainty as his nervous eyes searched mine for an answer.

A stark chill gripped my body, making me grimace. "I don't know..." I answered truthfully. "Give me some time to think about it... Like it's a bold idea, but... I don't know..." I wasn't completely against the idea, shockingly, but the part of me that never wanted him to see any part of me ever again and give him even the slightest satisfaction rejected Lev's idea.

Humming, Lev nodded his head before distracting me from my thoughts with his fingers. "Let's put that aside for now, then." His lips quickly occupied mine with some butterfly kisses as his fingers picked up in pace. "Let me take care of you, empress. Let me worship every inch of your perfectly flawed body and replace all the bad with better memories."

My shoulders relaxed with a deep breath as I let myself melt into Lev's touch. "You're always doing that. Thank you for it." My words came out breathy and hot like the steam fogging up the place as I closed my eyes and let my head fall back against the shower wall. "Love me, Lev, please."

"Always and forever," he promised before the sounds of his zipper coming undone echoed in my ears.

Chapter 36

Nicole

"ARE YOU SURE YOU are ready?" Lev's concern brought a sure smile to my face as I turned my head to look at him. "It's not like he's going anywhere any time soon... or ever."

Looking down at our intertwined fingers, I squeezed his hand reassuringly. "I'm ready to start his end." My smile grew confident with each step we took toward the private chamber that imprisoned Igor.

"I need this," I told Lev with a serious expression.

It's been a month since Lev and I started therapy, both individual and couples. Emotionally and mentally, I was still a mess, but I would get through it. The road to full recovery wouldn't be easy, but at least I started and made good progress so far since I started therapy.

Come to find out, I went through three of the five stages of trauma pretty fine on my own and with Lev's help. My problem was the fourth stage: depression. Apparently, that was where I got stuck. Well, I was still in the stage of depression, but at least I had options given to me in terms of treatment.

Even if I was a little reluctant at first with the therapist, she eventually warmed her way into me. I needed to get rid of the weight on my shoulders however I could, and it took me a little while to figure out what she meant in regard to me. So, after I got my head back on my body, I figured it was time to kill the monster who haunted my mind and body.

The only thing that could help me move on was Igor's torment and death. He took a part of my life away from me, so it was time I returned the favor. Of course, the only struggle I had was deciding on how I would make him suffer.

As much as I wanted to see him dead at my feet, I didn't want to kill him because a quick death was too much of a mercy. So, unfortunately, I would go down the route of slow and painful.

Pulling myself from my head, I wrapped my other arm around his, hugging it tightly. "Alexei, is there what I asked for?" I asked just as the door came into view.

Lev kept a straight face, but his eyes clouded over with some curiosity. "Yeah, though you still haven't told me what you need all that stuff for? Or what your plan is exactly..."

Of course, I wasn't the only one who would find closure today. I might have been the one Igor brutally raped, but Lev was forced to watch helplessly and be taunted throughout the whole thing.

Like me, Lev hasn't been the same since. Besides being physically banged up from the whole kidnapping and rescue, he's been much more paranoid and overly protective. If I thought his over-observant habit was annoying before, then it was outright irksome now. He would walk over every inch of the house and our property whenever time permitted, and if anything was a hair out of place, he'd flip. Every sound made him jump for a gun, even if it was some stupid bug hitting the window.

Then, whenever it came to me, he clung to me like a baby monkey would their mother. As much as I love Lev and his attention, it was way too much. Contrary to that, our sex life has been out of control because we fell into some cycle of constantly needing each other. I needed him to touch me and make me forget about Igor, and Lev needed to prove to me that he still loved me despite everything—it wasn't healthy.

We've been more regulated since therapy, though. We weren't back to baseline by any means, but we were getting there.

Our steps slowed to a stop when we got to the heavy metal door that looked grim and menacing in the dim lighting of the corridor. It was a little scary if I really thought about it. Beyond this thick slab of metal was a demon of a monster.

Placing his hand on the door's handle, Lev gripped it until his knuckles turned white. His head looked down at me for a few seconds to let his eyes search my face for any signs of reconsideration. "Remember, at any time, and I mean *any* time, you feel uncomfortable or change your mind about facing Igor, you let me know." The seriousness of his tone meant his words were more of a command than a reminder.

Nodding firmly, I took in a slow and controlled breath. "Yes, *đại ca*." I knew I needed to push myself, but I also knew that I couldn't go too far into the deep end yet.

Taking a deep breath of his own, Lev squared his shoulders, puffed his chest out, and threw the door open with so much force that it nearly flew off its hinges as it slammed against the wall with a loud *boom* that shook the whole room like a damn earthquake.

Igor's tense face twisted into a smug and cruel smirk upon laying his eyes on us. "Come to bring my wife back to me?" His taunt was void of spunk, just like how his eyes were hollow with defeat.

For a stupid man, he was smart enough to know the direness of his situation. He was a dead man, and he knew it. It was only a matter of time now.

Purposely ignoring him, I tutted my chin and turned away to look at Alexei. "Alexei, priapism, what is it again?" I intentionally exaggerated my question and spoke loudly enough to ensure Igor would hear me.

"The short version: an erection that lasts more than four hours, usually painful," Alexei replied casually as he remained sitting in his chair by the table of weapons and other various torture equipment. "Would you like to know more?" Now, he was just playing along with me.

Out of the corner of my eye, I could see Lev sneakily cross his legs in a protective manner. If I wasn't trying to maintain a somewhat serious demeanor, then I would've chuckled. With my attention fully on Alexei still, I replied,

"Well, I suppose it'd be good to know why an erection that long wouldn't be good." I dragged out a sarcastic sigh as I eyed Igor curiously.

"Well, with that much blood flow to your penis, your body's gonna get less perfusion, but, of course, that's not the main concern with priapism." Smirking cruelly, Alexei held up a bottle of pills, shaking it. "Not only is it really painful, but after a while, with all the blood being pooled there and not going back up, permanent damage can start happening. If left untreated, then a person's penis would slowly die, rot off their body, and the infection doesn't stay localized." Shaking his head, he looked over at Igor with a twisted gleam. "The infection goes to your blood, and sepsis sets in."

It took a few seconds for the realization to pale Igor's face. "Wait, you can't be serious. That's just a stupid and insane idea, banking on me being able to keep it up that long," he stammered nervously, tugging at the restraints that kept him bound to the metal chair.

I had only intended to let out a chuckle, but it came out as an evil laugh that would put an evil queen to shame. "Oh, honey, you make it sound like you're going to have a choice." Reaching out, I caught the bottle of pills after Alexei tossed it to me.

Holding up to Igor's face, I shook the bottle with the label facing him as I held it inches from him. "Recognize these little blue pills? I mean, you should since you probably use them a lot." I sneered mockingly at him. "You know, I thought about stuffing you full of bombs and letting you live in paranoia of not knowing when I'd set them off on a whim, but this just felt a little more fitting after a lot of thought."

"If you think I'm going to drink that, then you're fucking delusion, you crazy bitch," Igor spat back at me with a seething scowl as he continued to struggle.

Tilting my head at him with a smirk, I chuckled. "Again, you make it sound like you're going to have a choice in the matter."

Throwing the bottle back to Alexei, I went over to the table and leaned back against it with my arms crossed. "Do it," I commanded the younger Volkov darkly.

Getting up, he snapped on a pair of gloves and grabbed some tubing off the table. "Oh, with pleasure." His controlled voice broke with a crazed uplift.

Rounding Igor like a predator would its injured prey, Alexei motioned for Lev to come over with a nod of his head. "Hold his head back so I can shove this tube down his nose and throat."

Sneering, Lev smirked darkly as he approached the struggling Igor. "No promises about not breaking his neck in the process." He barked out a short laugh before grabbing Igor's head and forcing it back over the back of the chair.

The next few seconds were filled with Igor's screams of protest and suffering as Alexei shoved the tube down into his body with an unhinged smile that made me question Alexei a little.

I mean, he was the reserved one out of the five of them. Although, it did throw me off a little with how calm and collected he always was. Yeah, Lev and Stepan have told me numerous times that the twins were psychopaths, and with Arseny, I could see, but it was always a little harder to believe with Alexei. Well, at least until now.

I doubt he needed to take a whole ten minutes to put the tube into Igor. Alexei kept pulling back and going forward, only to pull back again because 'it went down the wrong tube' or 'it went out the mouth' or some line of excuses to keep flossing Igor's body with the feeding tube. All the while having a sadistic sparkle in his smiling eyes.

Yeah, note to self: don't fuck with the twins.

Once the tube was in place, Alexei secured it before crushing up the Viagra and pushing it through the tube into Igor's system.

"Well, that'll take about an hour to kick in, and of course, the guards here will monitor him and keep administering the medication as needed to keep him in that state," Alexei said collectedly while dusting his hands. "I have to get ready for a shift."

And just like that, the good doctor left as if he didn't just get his rocks off torturing a man just now.

"And you call me the psycho?" I scoffed and deadpanned Lev with a raised brow.

Walking up to me, he leaned down and caged me in with his arms. "Hey, I mean it in a loving way," Lev defended himself with a chuckle.

Gripping the edge of the table, he leaned in and kissed me softly. "Now, what would you like to do, empress?" he whispered against my lips.

I leered at Igor after peering my head around Lev. For a pensive moment, I let my spiteful eyes look at his disgusting body for a very quick moment before deciding, "Rip his nails off, toes and fingers, then break every bone in his feet and hands." The lack of care in my very cruel tone surprised me as much as it did Lev, who looked at me with stunned eyes for a split second.

Then, my twisted man cracked an excited grin before his hand grabbed a hammer off the table. "Consider it done, my love." Right before his body turned away from the table, his other hand snagged a pair of pliers.

Once Lev approached Igor, it took less than ten seconds for his screams of bloody murder to bounce off the metal walls and resound in my ears like the perfect carol. Agonized screams, pleas for the torture to end, nasty comments, and slurs said in between. None of it bothered me because, after all, they were the ramblings of a dead man.

"Did the meds work?" I asked Lev, refusing to trail my eyes down to see for myself.

Movement was caught by my eyes, and I could see Lev moving the hammer down to Igor's pelvic area. Then, Lev's mocking chuckle rang through the air. "If I can even find it."

A splatter of bloody spit landed right at Lev's feet before Igor remarked something to Lev in Russian, only to be met by a burst of loud laughter from Lev.

Spinning around, Lev came back over to me with a lustful frenzy in his eyes. The moment he was inches from me, his hands grabbed my face to bring me into a heated kiss. "Get on the table and spread your legs, empress," he groaned against my lips, grabbing the back of my thighs to help hike me up.

"What are you doing?" My airy voice trailed the more I melted in Lev's loving hands as they wandered my body.

Holding my face tenderly, he looked down at me with pleading eyes full of warmth and want. "Do you trust me?" he asked with a confident smile.

There was a twinkle of darkness in his eyes that sent a small tingle of nervous excitement down my spine. I probably shouldn't, but I nodded my head in response and leaned into his touch. "Yes, always." Unless this was the moment that would break it.

Snaking his hand under my skirt, he brushed his thumb against my clothed sex, rubbing my clit until it throbbed with pleasure. "He won't see you, I promise," he whispered reassuringly against my lips before kissing me deeply.

Carefully, he positioned himself between my legs to use his big body to cover me before undoing his pants and slipping himself under my loose skirt. Spitting in his hand, he slicked himself up before pushing my panties aside and positioning himself at my entrance. "Hold onto me, and don't hold back, *zhizn moya.*"

I didn't get a preparatory swipe or teasing thrusts; he shoved himself all the way to the base with a single, hard jerk of his hips. Instinctively, my body arched against his as a loud scream of pleasure escaped from my open mouth. Shudders trembled my whimpering body as I tried to release Lev's shoulders from my clawing grip.

"Lev, claim me, please," I begged through a shaky exhale. "Show me how much you love me and want me."

Chapter 37

I WAS WARY OF our trip to The Catacombs when Nicole demanded to go out of the blue. Yes, demanded, not asked, demanded. I tried to talk her out of it, afraid that she was being a little too rash or impulsive or that she was losing it just a tad. Even if she had been making great strides over the past month since she started therapy, I still worried about her quite a bit.

But when she was rather adamant about going to see Igor to settle the score, I was somewhat inclined to let her have it her way. Well, I still fought her about it a little bit because I didn't want her to get triggered. Even if she never really showed any signs of it before, trauma was something I didn't like to play around with. Besides, the last thing I wanted to do was end up in a situation like Nikolai's when he decided to present Angel's ex to her and almost sent her into a crisis.

Thankfully, Nicole kept her head on straight the whole time, which made my admiration for her rise to a new level. If it were me, or if I hadn't promised Nicole that Igor was hers, then I would have ripped into him the moment I stepped into the room. Don't get me wrong, I was furious under my calm demeanor, but this closure was Nicole's to take. Besides, it wasn't as if she didn't let me participate.

When she told me to pluck Igor's nails off and break his bones, I was more than happy to oblige. The bastard deserved far worse, in my opinion, but I guess having his dick rot off and then dying from a bloodstream infection was worth it in the end.

Thinking about that happening made me shudder and clench protectively. I don't know how or where she came up with the idea, but as long as it wasn't me on the receiving end, then I didn't care. If Igor wasn't such a bad person, then I might have felt a little bad for him about his impending death.

No matter, he dug his grave himself. I was merely helping him along to it.

Much to my surprise, he was no fun to torture. Unfortunately, he didn't fight back as much as I had anticipated. Yeah, he spat out nasty words and begged a little, but he didn't struggle or plead genuinely—it wasn't from his soul. He did do a good job of pissing me off, though.

Sure, therapy has been as beneficial for me as it has been for Nicole, but I knew for a fact that my anger toward the whole situation wasn't something I'd fully accepted yet. It was less often now, but I still beat myself down for being a helpless sack of shit during that time. Yes, I know the situation was out of my control; I didn't ask to be tied up or wanted to be bound to the chair, and my strength and skills could only do so much in the situation. Still, it was a constant knife to the heart that would occasionally twist.

It also felt like no matter how much I adored Nicole and tried to prove myself to her, it was never enough. Okay, I know I didn't have to do that, but I felt compelled to. Which apparently wasn't a healthy thing. I was trying to overcompensate for my failure to protect her, even though it was out of my hands.

The whole thing was more confusing than it sounded, and I hated how I couldn't fully accept everything. Everything the therapist pointed out made absolute sense, but I couldn't accept it for some stupid reason. Well, the damn shrink got deep with me, explaining how it was my inability to accept failure.

Like, she may be right, but I didn't want to admit it.

Yes, maybe I was reluctant to accept my failure because I didn't want to admit to myself that I failed Nicole. It was my job to protect her, save her from shitty situations, yet that horrible ordeal happened right in front of me.

And I did nothing.

And yes, I know, it wasn't my fault.

Nicole has told me so many times, but I was a stubborn asshole.

I didn't plan on having sex with Nicole in front of Igor like this, but I really wanted to shove it in his face. He may have taken her, but she didn't enjoy one millisecond of it. So, I wanted him to see what he failed to achieve from his deplorable act.

A tight squeeze from Nicole's cunt drew me out of my head to her smirking face. "Better not be thinking about another woman in that noggin of yours," she teased with a snicker that cut short when I gave her a firm thrust.

Wrapping my arms tightly around her, I kissed her temple. "Oh, please. You and your crazy side are more than enough for me," I joked back with a grin. "Now brace yourself."

The items on the table's surface jostled and clattered around with my thrusts that pushed Nicole's body more and more into the table. Soon, the whole table itself inched along the floor with my hard thrusts. But neither of us cared much about the shifting; we were too caught up in each other.

"Lev, right there," Nicole moaned happily into my ear. "Your piercings are rubbing me just right, and it feels so fucking amazing."

"You're so tight, and you keep squeezing me so well," I groaned lowly into her neck as I buried my face into it. "I'm so sorry," I whispered in a cracked voice. "I'm so sorry for not being the man I promised to be, but I swear, I will always do my best to be the man you deserve from here on out." I could feel her top becoming a little damp from my tears, but I couldn't stop them from coming out.

"Oh, Lev," she cooed lovingly and stroked the back of my hair. "You are more than enough, and I couldn't have asked for anyone more perfect. You have been there for me when anyone else would have dipped. You still hold and love me every day despite all that has happened, and you don't ever blame any of it on me. That is more than what I could ever ask for." Her soft lips pressed against the side of my head, and her giggles soothed my tension. "You have nothing to apologize for, and even if you did, I have already forgiven you. So, it's okay to let go, Lev."

A soft tug at the back of my collar made me pull away a little and look at her. "We will both let go." Her eyes were full of promise and life.

She was finally ready, and if she was ready, then so would I.

"I love you, Nicole." Something within me snapped the moment I gave her a genuine smile full of nothing but hope and happiness.

That knife in my chest dug itself deep one last time, causing a wave of doubt to cascade over me, but I turned my head to it.

I am not a failure.

Nicole didn't see me as one. She doesn't hold anything against me. The only thing that held me back was my own stupid ass.

"I love you too, Lev," she moaned breathlessly against my lips before capturing them to muffle her scream of pleasure.

Letting my own groan be taken by her, I let my thrusts become sloppy with the height of my release until I stilled myself within her tight walls. "That's it, empress, squeeze me just like that," I encouraged her with a soft roll of my hips. "Get all of me into you."

Once her heavy, jagged breathing evened out, I slowly pulled out of her and fixed her clothes before turning my body a bit to smugly smirk at a rather red-faced Igor. "What? Smaller than you thought?" I mocked him with a laugh as I tucked my still-hard cock back into my pants.

Looking at the messy table, I danced my fingers over the various objects for a minute before picking up a wooden mallet. "Wonder how many bones I can break today before you pass out on me," I wondered out loud as I approached a sweating Igor.

"Maybe we'll take mercy on you and actually let you die." I dragged out my words as I lightly tapped the weapon along random parts of his body as if I were trying to decide what to break first. "We could always let the sepsis run for a bit but load you up with antibiotics at the last minute and save you, only to do it all over again." I sounded rather nonchalant as I spoke, "Or we can heal you, then stuff you with bombs as Nicole initially wanted."

Pulling my hand back, I brought the mallet down onto his already crushed hand, making him scream bloody murder. "Or just load you up with a paralytic and let rats eat you alive." I tossed out another idea before whacking him across the face with the wooden weapon, knocking out a few teeth.

Standing before him, I leaned down and glared at him menacingly. "There are so many options. It's just a matter of how creative we get and how long we want to drag this out." Discarding the mallet, I balled my hand up into a fist and punched him square in the face, breaking his nose.

After winding him with a blow to the gut, I grabbed his head and forced it back. "Welcome to the wolves' den."

Epilogue: Nicole

~2 years later~

"NICOLE!"

Lev's fury shook the walls of our home, along with my laughter in response to him.

"You psycho! Get your ass out here and uncuff me! How dare you chloroform my ass like that and tie me up!? Naked too!? Is that really necessary!?" Even though he was in the living area, it sounded like he was right next to me with how his voice carried. "Nicole!"

Taking my sweet time, I let Lev stew there for a moment before sauntering out of my office and down the hallway. My feet stopped at the entrance, and I leaned against the wooden frame seductively to show off my lingerie-clad body, making the red in Lev's angry eyes disappear. His narrowed eyes widened with wonder and excitement as his mouth hung open. He didn't even try to hide his blatant staring as he looked me up and down without blinking.

"Holy shit..." His Adam's apple bobbed deeply with his gulp. "This is not fair." His groan of complaint echoed into the air when he threw his head back.

Giggling seductively, I slowly strutted up to him, purposedly giving my hips an extra sway for effect. When I stood before him, I nudged his legs open to get on my knees between them. "Just sit back, relax, and enjoy the first part of my anniversary gift to you," I told him with a cheeky grin.

"Fuck, Nicole you do—agh! Shit!" His gasps and strained groans were like music to my ears as I worked his thick cock with my mouth and hands.

"W-wait, anniversary?" Looking up, I could see the gears turning in his head with how confused his eyes looked. "We're not getting married until next month, the fuck you mean anniversary?"

The cuteness of his confusion caused me to lose control and gag on his cock as I had him down my throat. Pulling myself off completely, I waited until my coughing calmed down before snickering at him. A soft sigh squeezed out of my chest as I leaned in and rested my head against his thigh. My hand lazily stroked his throbbing cock to keep him stimulated as I replied, "The anniversary of when I claimed you." Walking my fingers up his body, I let the rest of my body follow until I hovered over him. "Of when I tattooed you." Softly, I traced the tattoo of my signature on his chest with a proud grin.

Lev's shoulders slumped with relief before his chest shook with a chuckle. "You've never celebrated that before." He eyed me suspiciously for a second before looking around the room as if he expected something to blow up or for someone to pop out.

"What are you—" I immediately shut him up with my lips, not wanting to engage in a game of twenty questions with him and ruin the mood.

Breaking the kiss, I tucked my bottom lip between my teeth and smirked at him as I raked my nails down his chest. It aroused me to no end seeing how Lev's eyes darkened so much with lust at the simple action.

Teasing his body with kisses, I took my sweet time to mark up and taste every inch of his muscled body before straddling him. Pressing his cock flat against his abdomen, I nestled him between my cunt and grind myself along his length. "If you want to get fucked, then you better start begging." There was a devious bite to my giggle as I used him to get myself off.

Bucking his hips at me, he looked at me with needy, pleading eyes. "Empress, please fuck my cock with your tight cunt. Please, I need you so badly." The way his voice became whispery and how he whimpered so sweetly made it hard to deny him.

For once, I decided to take it easy on him. So, I reached a hand down to grasp his cock and position him properly at my entrance. I took him nice and slow, wanting to feel every bump and rub of his piercings as he entered my tight walls. I also wanted this moment to last a bit.

Fully seated on his cock, I stayed like that for a moment to fully savor him before I started bouncing. Holding onto his shoulders, I moved at a rather teasing pace. I intentionally exaggerated my rocking hips to get as much friction as possible to stimulate him and keep him on edge.

Sliding a hand across to his neck, I looped the leather leash around my hand, and with a firm jerk, I pulled him towards me. "Who do you belong to? Who do you kneel to at the end of the day? Who owns this cock of yours?" I asked with a power-hungry grin.

Lev shuddered and bowed his head slightly. "You, my empress. I belong to you and only you." His jaw clenched shut with a whimper when I slammed myself down on him hard. "I crawl and kneel to you and only you." His answer came out a little strained and breathy. "My cock belongs to you. It's your cock."

"Good boy," I praised him with a big and proud smile.

But that was the end of my sweetness.

Grabbing his face, I pressed my thumb against his bottom lip, dragging it down a bit. Then, I leaned in and kissed him passionately with a deep groan. "That's right, you belong to me, and only me," I growled possessively against his lips before kissing him aggressively.

Breaking the kiss with a heavy breath, I pulled at the leash and grabbed his collar. "Don't you ever forget whose collar adorns your neck." My deepened voice rumbled in my chest as I spoke.

Lev's body fell back against the chair when I released the collar and slackened the leash. His glistening chest heaved with each breath he took, making me smile at how my mark on him danced with life.

Dragging my nails along his body teasingly, I traced the tattoo proudly once I came to it. "And don't you ever forget whose mark is on your body," I told him in a slightly dazed voice as I was too busy admiring the work on his body.

Snapping out of it, I leaned up and hovered over him with a dark, possessive grin. "I fucking own you, and don't you ever forget that."

His neck craned toward me, his eyes begging me for a kiss. "Yes, empress, I won't ever forget," he whimpered, his lips pursing slightly in a silent plea.

Running a hand down his arm, I quickly unlatched the cuff from one of his wrists. And the moment his hand was free, it shot up and wrapped itself around my neck, choking me softly. With some force, he pulled me down to get that kiss he desperately wanted.

"Nicole, please, let me come," he begged sweetly against my lips, bucking his hips to urge me.

Not wanting to drag this on any longer, I picked up the pace and force of my movements until I had both of us moaning uncontrollably with pleasure. Not once did my movements falter until my orgasm hit me full force.

Sitting fully on his cock, I slumped against him as my tight walls clenched and twitched around his throbbing cock as he filled me with his cum.

Once the aftershocks of my orgasm died down enough for me to get ahold of myself, I released his other wrist. I kept myself pressed against him, though. We might be done with round one, but I also had something else for him besides sex.

Weakly, I fished around under the seat of the chair until I felt the item I had taped there before I even knocked Lev out. I feared the thing might snap with how tightly I clutched it in anticipation as I sat up and looked at Lev with a tearful smile. "Close your eyes, *đại ca*," I commanded in a soft voice.

Lev looked at me warily, but he obeyed. "I swear, if you're going to whack me in the face with a plank of wood..." he grumbled with a playful chortle.

Memories of that day flashed through my mind at his mention of it, making me laugh a little. "No, no, nothing like that, I promise." I might be a little mean to Lev, but bodily harm like that was a little too far.

Nervously, I held the item in my hands and looked it over one last time to ensure everything was still perfect before holding it toward him. "Alright, open your eyes." A shaky exhale squeezed out of my tight chest as I watched his eyes flutter open.

His face fell at the sight of the object. Disbelief bulged at his eyes, making me worry that they might pop out of his head. My concern and anxiety skyrocketed when he sat there stunned.

"Le—ah!" I cut out with a squeal that turned into full-blown laughter because Lev shot up to his feet with me in his arms.

Spinning around, Lev shouted excitedly into the air and laughed with me as he practically danced around with me.

"Lev, you're gonna make me throw up," I remarked, slapping at his shoulder.

Quickly, he apologized and set me down on my feet. Then, he grabbed my face and kissed me deeply with a happy chuckle. "*Zhizn moya*, are you really? Please tell me it is real." His tearful eyes begged me with so much hope.

Immediately, I smiled brightly at him while nodding my head, "Yes, I really am pregnant." Tears streamed down our cheeks with my confirmation, and we held each other for a long while on the couch.

After two long years, it was finally happening. We were finally going to have our family—our child.

Not gonna lie, it has been disheartening for me when month after month would pass with negative results. There was nothing wrong with us health-wise, and technically, I wasn't infertile because my eggs were healthy. Biologically, there was no explanation as to why we didn't conceive within that first year of trying.

When the second year of our relationship rolled around without any positive results, we began to talk about other means, such as IVF or adoption. We had both decided to put it off until after the wedding, not wanting to add more stress than necessary to our lives.

So, imagine my surprise when I decided to pee on a stick a few days ago on a whim and had it come back positive. Of course, being the paranoid little shit I was, I took five more in total in the days to come to make sure the first wasn't some fluke. I also had our doctors collect my blood as well to verify my hormone levels. The only definitive answer was an ultrasound, which was scheduled for today.

Looking up at the clock on the wall, I beamed with excitement when I noticed the time. With a giddy giggle, I tapped Lev's chest repeatedly, urging him to get up. "Come on, let's go see our baby."

I could see the questions and confusion written all over his grinning face, but I guess he was too ecstatic to burst the bubble right now. He waited for me to get up completely before he sat up and wrapped his arms around my waist, pulling me in for a tight hug. With my stomach leveled with his face, he buried it softly into me, being extra gentle. "I really can't believe it." His muffled words tickled me a little, causing me to giggle.

His head rolled back to look up at me with his infectious grin and lovely blues that were full of nothing but pure gratitude and adoration. "Thank you, and I know those two words will never be enough to express my eternal gratitude, but I will spend forever showing it to you every second of every day for the rest of our lives."

Pressing his face back into my belly, he spoiled it with loving and tender kisses.

Unable to help it, I buried both my hands into his hair and pet his head. "You are going to be an amazing father, Lev."

Chuckling softly, his tender eyes looked back up at me. "And I never would have gotten such a chance if it weren't for you, Nicole, so thank you for imploding yourself into my life. Thank you for giving me a chance to love you and for letting me knock you up."

The stifled laugh turned into a full one when I failed to contain my amusement from his words. "Oh, little lion," I sighed playfully and lightly slapped his pouty cheek. "It's cute how you think you had an option in it all," I half-joked, throwing my head back slightly in a rather boisterous laugh.

My cheery laugh warmed up the whole air around us until the walls lit up with their own delight from the overwhelming amusement that radiated from me. "Oh, Lev," I sighed through my dying laughter.

Taking a moment, I looked at him adoringly, smiling at his cute face. "The moment I decided to turn the tables on you was when your choice in loving me went up in flames." Pressing a deep and possessive kiss against his lips, I groaned deeply with him as I claimed him roughly. "Don't forget, little lion, I always get what I want no matter what."

A spark of fight lit up his eyes right before they rolled away from me with his widening smirk. I watched as his mouth opened and remained so for a moment before he changed his mind with a chuckle and shake of his head. "I love you, Nicole."

If it weren't for the way his eyes completely melted with ardor, then I would've poked and prodded at him until he confessed to his fleeting thoughts. Well, that and the fact we had an appointment to see our baby took precedent over toying with Lev.

Rolling my own pair of eyes, I let him win with a relenting sigh as I took his wrists into my hands to inspect them. They were a little chaffed and red, but they weren't bleeding or showing signs of possible bruising. Peering up at him with a soft and tender smile, I brought his hands up to my face, kissing every inch of them before comforting his wrists with my lips. "We'll leave after I get some ointment on you, and I'll feed you in the car," I told him with a flash of a big smile right before peeping up to my tippy toes and kissing him chastely.

After tending to his reddened areas with some ointment to ease any discomfort he'd possibly feel—and to help him heal properly—I forced him to hydrate himself before letting him into the car to drive us to the doctor's office. And, yes, he drove like a fucking maniac because he was too excited to see our baby. I barely managed to feed him properly because of how much he caused the car to jerk with his acceleration. Honestly, how not a crumb or drop of sauce fell onto the pristine floor or leather seat was beyond my comprehension.

"Hey, little lion, can we drop by the office building on the way? I just want to pop by and check things out." Well, I probably could've told him to swing by the place, but I felt generous and wanted to actually ask.

Blowing up my own company all those years ago wasn't for show or anything. Okay, maybe a big reason was to stick a huge ass middle finger to my parents basically, but that was besides the other plans and reasons I had. Aside from wanting to wipe the slate clean, I knew Angel's little safe haven business needed to expand. So, since I had plans to be involved greatly in the whole business, I figured a central place of operations for us and our workers would be grand. Also, the property was big enough to build a secondary building that we turned into a housing place for the victims under our care and protection.

"Yeah, it's on the way, so I don't see why not," Lev replied with an indifferent shrug.

Humming softly, I pulled one of his hands away from the steering wheel to rest it on my lap. Mindlessly, I played with his fingers while looking out the window, pulling myself into my head.

Sometimes, it was hard to believe that two years had gone by and that we'd be married soon. Hell, it was crazy to think about all that's happened in those years. All my friends and Lev's brothers were all settled nicely and starting families of their own; the psycho twins included—shockingly.

Lev and his brothers had their businesses, both legal and not, that flourished with each passing day. Angel and the lot of us girlies had our own thing going on with the safe haven business that Angel started up after her marriage to Nikolai. For the most part, half of us had a day job to report to, but then there was the other half where the safe haven business was our job.

Take me, for example; I didn't have a day job. Sure, I could've started up another tech business, but I didn't feel like it. If I started another one up, then my heart wouldn't be in it. Thankfully, Angel was more than happy to shove the safe haven business into my hands, given my business experience. Angel was still the head of it all, but I was co-CEO, basically. I handled the business front, all the tech work, and some of the equipment management for the safe haven business. And by equipment management, I meant I made the bombs, killer drones, little nifty techy devices, and things of that nature.

It only felt like yesterday that Angel threw the idea at me, and I accepted. One blink of my eyes later, and apparently, two years had gone by. With the Volkov Bratva expanding to nearly all of California over the years, we've had to expand the safety net for victims with the brothers. We were gonna have to look at getting more trustworthy managers and such under our belt soon to keep our plates from getting too full, but I'd bring the issue up to Angel after she popped out her latest children.

"You alright, *zhizn moya*?" Lev's deep voice distracted me from my thoughts, and if that wasn't enough, he fully snagged my attention when he grabbed my hand and kissed the back of it. "You have your thinking face on, and I don't want you muddling up your mind too much and stressing. It's not good for the baby."

The sweet and warm smile graced my lips at the sound of his worried words. "And you're worried that you're going to be a bad father," I teased, snickering a little. "You're already worrying about our little one, and they're not even out in the world yet."

"W-well, worrying about you and our child is different than actually raising them," he retorted with reddening cheeks.

Smiling at him reassuringly, I leaned over and hugged his arm. "Don't worry, I'm not stressing. I'm just thinking about how the past two years have been and how there are still big things to come." Okay, that might've sounded better in my head, but it really wasn't anything tasking on me. "I'm just so happy and glad that I have you by my side." Honestly, I didn't know what I'd do without Lev sometimes.

Breathing deeply, I patted his arm softly. "Just drive. I wanna just sit in silence with you and enjoy your presence." More often than not, him being around was more than enough for me.

Peaceful silence befell us for a long stretch until Lev spoke up. "Do you want to stop by the flower shop?" The car slowed to an idle roll as a quaint little shop appeared ahead of us.

Looking beyond a nearby café, I stared at the floral shop with pressed lips and a pensive scrunch of my face. "Maybe after the doctor's appointment." I was in a good mood, and I didn't want to add any tension to sour it right now possibly.

"Are you going to tell them?" Lev questioned with a quirked brow, sounding a little apprehensive underneath all the curiosity.

Sighing heavily, I shrugged my shoulders in response. "We'll see. Let's just keep going for now."

I didn't want to deal with my mother and brother right now. Well, more so I didn't want to interact with my brother.

After I effectively put my company into the ground all those years ago and dragged my parents to The Catacombs, things with my mother and brother have been rather strange. My father was dead, bits and parts of him at the bottom of the ocean or swimming around in a shark's stomach until it'd eventually be excreted and sink down. My mother got the help she needed at The Catacombs. Extensive therapy later, and she was a different woman.

Too bad the same couldn't be said for my brother. While my mother was on the straight and narrow... Yeah... I just wished the same could be said about my brother. He was still a fucking asshole and a half, though he had his good moments. He needed help badly, but he always refused it. Of course, my poor mother didn't want to let him go because he was somewhat all she had left.

Bao was still reluctant to reach out to our mother, for which I didn't fault him, given the treatment. I wasn't particularly close or fond of her; we've established a stable-ish relationship with each other and have learned to live as friends or something along those lines. We definitely weren't cozy and best friends or some mother-daughter duo. We kept in touch with each other, and I visited her from time to time just to make sure she was okay.

I couldn't help but follow the shop with my eyes as we drove past it, only tearing my gaze away when it went out of view. "It probably sounds stupid of me, but I somewhat wished things would've turned out differently." Call me silly for wishing and wanting that perfect family, but that was the only thing missing from my life.

"The world would be too happy of a place if everyone had the perfect family," Lev joked, chuckling dryly. "Well, whatever went wrong with your parents is what we won't do with our kid."

I waited until Lev parked the car in front of the business building before grabbing his face and pulling him down into a deep kiss. "I love you, Lev." Warmth filled my heart, and I smiled as I looked up at him deeply. "Thank you for putting up with my craziness and trusting me."

Of course, he had to ruin the moment with his snarky words. "Well, I've been known to make bad decisions that work out." His mirthful laugh made my eyes roll in response. "I love you so much, and I can't wait until I have someone to share my suffering with." That last part was meant in jest.

Slipping a hand down my body, he rested it against my stomach, rubbing at it with the most loving look and eager eyes.

Epilogue: Lev

~20 years later~

"Lev, can you find Nolan for me? I need to finish setting food out."

Nicole didn't even turn her head to look at me the instant I entered through the door, making me roll my eyes out of irritation.

After hanging my keys onto the wall, I went over to my busy bee of a wife and grabbed her by the hips, stopping her and spinning her around into a stunning kiss. "Hello, *zhizn moya*, I'm so happy to see you after a long day of chasing idiots around, and of course, I'm okay even though I'm half mummified in bandages," I snarked playfully, drawing her full attention to my battered body.

Her mouth dropped open with a scolding scoff, and she smacked my chest. "Lev, what happened? Why didn't you tell me anything? Should you even be up and walking?" Whatever she was doing was completely forgotten as she dragged my ass to the living room. "Why didn't I get a call? Who did this to you?" she fretted, grabbing at my shirt to lift it and see the damage.

Chuckling, I grabbed her hands and pulled her down onto the couch with me. "Empress, I'm fine. I just took a tumble down a hill." A rocky hill, but she didn't need to know that. "Just got a little banged up on the way down, that's all. I'm perfectly fine, though. Alexei and another one of our doctors checked

320

me out and cleared me, so really, you don't have to worry," I assured her with a warm smile.

Taking in a deep breath, I held her tightly against me to fully relax. "Why is Nolan hiding? Did he get into your stuff again and blow something up? Or did he hack the Pentagon and get caught?" I half-joked with a dry chuckle.

Rolling her eyes, Nicole nuzzled her face into my chest. "Still can't believe he forgot to cover his tracks properly. I mean, who forgets to set up three proxy chains at least?" Her complaints slowly trailed out. Okay, maybe they didn't trail out; it was more like I zoned her out.

Hearing her huff made me tune back in. "God, could you imagine if we had more than one kid?" Nicole mused with a dying chuckle. "I mean, sometimes I kinda wished we did, but I'm glad we got some sense kicked into our asses and decided one was enough."

Letting out a deep breath, I couldn't help but agree with a nod and chuckle. "What were we thinking when we wanted a whole van full?" I mused with a soft laugh.

After watching Nikolai and Angel's twins, Nicole and I quickly changed our minds about the number of kids we wanted. The twins weren't even that hard of kids, yet we found ourselves wanting to tear our hair out whenever we babysat for my older brother. So, yeah, one was more than enough.

Besides, Nolan was a handful from the moment he became mobile and sentient enough. The little troublemaker took after both Nicole and me, which made him amazing but also a big handful. He was too smart for his own good, thanks to Nicole, and like his mother, he loved to tinker around with explosives and tech. From me, he got his hard head and relentless spirit. Thankfully, he wasn't an aggressive or violent little shithead like me.

We were more than happy with Nolan, and we wouldn't want him to be any different. No matter how much trouble his curious mind got him into, we were always there to help him out and love him at the end of the day. Even if we bailed him out of trouble, we didn't spoil him. We always made sure he learned his lesson at the end of it all. Besides, it wasn't as if he was a budding career criminal. The trouble he often got into was little things like hacking people's phones to change their ringtones to embarrassing things or other electronic objects for harmless pranks. He has set off quite a few bombs, though... But those were mostly in a controlled environment...

I wasn't too concerned in that area of his life anymore because it seemed to be a phase that he got over. Occasionally he got into Nicole's stash still, but it was for stupid shit like wanting to make something awesome for a girl he wanted to impress or to make smoke bombs for escapes.

And yes, our little genius somehow managed to hack the FBI just to prove a point to his cousins after they kept taunting him. Yeah, everyone got in trouble that day.

Imagine my surprise to open the door to the fucking FBI!

That really was a shit show and a half, and I was glad we made it out unscathed. It was one thing to get caught with local law enforcement, but going higher than the state was a whole new level of risky.

Looking down at Nicole, I appreciated her for a long moment as I stroked her hair. "We've done good, though. We made it through, and we did amazing."

Sometimes, I was afraid to wake up. I feared that this wonderful life I'd lived was all some kind of dream, that one day I would open my eyes to an empty bed with no Nicole in sight and an empty house with no family photos or happy memories.

Not a day went by when I wasn't eternally grateful for Nicole and the life she'd blessed me with.

"Thank you, *zhizn moya*," I whispered against her head before kissing it. "I love you so much."

Giving her a tight squeeze, I breathed in a lungful of her scent with a happy smile. "Go finish up what you need. I'll deal with Nolan," I told her, kissing her one last time and slipping away to search for my son.

On a hunch, I went into my office and rounded my desk. Lo and behold, there was my son, all scrunched up under my desk with his laptop propped up on his curled legs.

Honestly, I don't know how the hell he even still managed to fit his 6'0 body under there. Sighing, I pulled my office chair out and stood there with my arms crossed with an unamused smirk, "Nolan, you're going to get your fat ass stuck one day, I swear." He wasn't bulky like me, but he still had some meat on his body. "Come on, it's almost dinner, so get your ass up." I signaled for him to get up with a wave of my hand.

His head of dark brown hair popped out, and his amber-brown eyes shined up at me sharply. "No, because I actually want to live long enough to make it to my graduation," he snarked with a roll of his eyes. "I ain't eating anything mom makes."

Nicole was still banned from cooking anything besides packaged food after all these years, but that didn't stop her from trying to learn. Unfortunately, anything she tried to make from scratch always ended up inedible somehow.

So... Yeah... It sounded like it would be one of those nights.

Sighing, I ran a hand across my graying beard and gave my son a calculating look. "I'll buy you that new laptop you want," I shamelessly bribed my son.

Instantly, he shot out fully from under the desk and got up in my face. He crossed his arms and glared at me defiantly. "Hell no, I took the bite last time, and ain't nothing is worth doing it twice in a row." Nolan vigorously shook his head as he dug his heels into the floor.

Leaning in slightly, he mocked me a bit with a pressed smile. "I'd rather be target practice for Uncle Stepan because at least my survival rate is higher than mom's food." Before a single sound could come out of my open mouth, Nolan held a finger up to stop me. "And, if somehow I get shot, at least I know I'd die rather quickly."

Huffing, Nolan sat down in my office chair and spun around in it. "Honestly, why can't you just tell mom her food is crappy? And tell her not to cook anymore?"

Grabbing the back of the chair, I quickly tilted it over to pour him out of it. "You act like I haven't been doing that for the past twenty-something years," I retorted, rolling my eyes at him before grabbing him by the back of his shirt and dragging him to the dining room.

"I'm going to hack everything you own," Nolan threatened me with an unpromising glare as I dragged both of us to our dooms.

"Yeah, you do that and face your mother's wrath," I barked back with a curt laugh. "I will be the least of your worries."

Throwing out an exasperated groan, Nolan rolled his eyes so far back that I was surprised they came back. "Ugh! You two are such buzz kills."

Hauling my son into his seat, I looked at Nicole, who looked at the two of us with raised brows. "I'm blaming you for this typical teenager attitude," I commented, jabbing my thumb at our son. "I was not this angsty at his age." I was a whole lot worse.

"You had no time to be moody because you were too busy getting your ass beat by Uncle Kolya for catching the latest STD or for getting caught and thrown in jail," Nolan retorted with a smug snicker, earning a stifled laugh from his mother, who covered it up with a cough when I glared her way.

Scowling at my son, I grabbed a plate of food and shoved it into his face. "Oh, shut up and get your monthly dose of food poisoning," I grumbled, earning an offended scoff from Nicole.

"Don't you glare at me, *zhizn moya*, you already know how it always ends when you make food." Well, Nicole had no one but herself to blame. I mean, I could only sugar coat it for so long before I had to be blatant with her. "At least Nolan gets his cooking abilities from me," I joked with a snicker.

Biting out a growl, Nicole waved her spoon at me threateningly. "Oh, shut up before I—"

Nolan's hands instantly slapped over his ears. "Ah ah ah! Nope! No no no no noooooo! Noooope! I do *not* want to hear you finish that!"

Unable to help it, Nicole and I laughed at Nolan's reaction because Nicole was always careful about keeping things tame with Nolan around.

Reaching out, I wrapped an arm around Nicole to pull her to my side. Gazing down at her lovingly, I chastely kiss her forehead. "God, I love you all so much." I could feel the happy tears burning in my eyes, but I held them back as I threw my other arm around Nolan's shoulders to hug him.

"Dad, will you really not be upset with me not being in the family business?" Nolan's small voice made me frown a little because of how ashamed he sounded.

Gripping his shoulder, I assured him with a proud smile. "Nolan, you could go be a damn stripper for all I care, as long as you're happy." Okay, maybe I should have thought that one out better in my mind. "As your mother and I have told you many times, it's your life. We will always support you, whichever way you go."

"As long as you are happy with what you choose, then that's all that matters to us," Nicole reaffirmed my words with a warm, motherly smile. "We didn't have you to take our place in the bratva. We had you because we wanted to spread our craziness to the next generation." Nicole's seriousness went out the window with her laughter after she said the last part.

Grinning cheekily, I threw my son a devious look. "Well, I mean, we had you because we—"

Nolan's protest came immediately as he covered his ears again. "God, you two are so gross!"

And once again, Nicole and I couldn't help but laugh in response.

"We really did do good, little lion," Nicole whispered to me after her fit of laughter died down. "Thank you." Leaning up to her tippy toes, she kissed my cheek. "I love you, Lev."

Returning her adoring look with one of my own, I smiled at her for a while before kissing her forehead. "I will never be able to thank or love you enough in this lifetime, *zhizn moya*, but I will try my best until my very last breath."

Glossary

- **Anh:** A Vietnamese term of endearment for a male.

- **áo dài:** A traditional Vietnamese dress.

- **Blyat':** Fuck

- **Blya, ya vlyublyayus' v tebya:** Fuck, I'm falling in love with you.

- **Bratok:** Brother

- **Bud' zdorov:** Be healthy.

- **Đại ca/đại ca:** A Vietnamese term of endearment for a male that means boss in this use and is typically geared more towards those in gangs.

- **Der'mo:** Shit

- **Mat' yebanaya, ad:** Mother fucking hell.

- **Pozhaluysta, lyubov' moya, mne nuzhno byt' vnutri tebya pryamo seychas, inache ya umru:** Please my love, I need to be inside you right now or I'll die.

- **Pozhaluysta, ya budu tvoim khoroshim mal'chikom navsegda. YA budu tvoyey khoroshey shlyushkoy:** Please, I'll be your good boy forever. I'll be your good slut.

- **Rasplata eto suka:** Payback is a bitch.

- **Shakhta:** Mine.

- **Svyatoye der'mo:** Holy shit.

- **Ty chertovski bozhestvenna:** You are fucking divine.

- **Ty, chert voz'mi, ublyudok:** You fuckign bastard.

- **Ty, malen'kaya shalun'ya, ya sobirayus':** You little minx, I'm going to...

- **Vso v poryadke, zhizn moya. Vypusti vso naruzhu. U menya yest' ty, i ya nikuda ne uydu:** It's all right, my life. Let it all out. I have you, and I'm not going anywhere.

- **YA tebya lyublyu:** I love you.

- **Zhizn moya:** My life.

Thank You

If you enjoyed the story then please take a second to drop a review/rating! They mean a lot to Indie authors like me, and they are the best way to support us!

Thank you so much for reading The Bratva's Bounty, the third installment in my interconnected standalone Volkov Bratva Series. I hope you enjoyed Lev and Nicole's story and that you stay tuned for the first of the twins. Arseny's charm hides a bloody smile, and his empire is made up of more than money and women, something Mia finds out once she is caught in his shop with no escape. While you are waiting on his book, feel free to check out the other Volkov brothers, Nikolai and Stepan, in their perspective books! Or, if you want a break from the mafia, then I have some lovely novellas with shadow demons that are good cleansers, or if you still want something dark but lighthearted, then check out my Serial Lover series.

If you wanna keep up with me, get sneak peeks at upcoming works and all the little goodies, then follow me on social media or join my Discord!

Discord: https://discord.gg/keu5YTsvyS

tiktok.com/@rose.chase.author

instagram.com/rose.chase.author/

facebook.com/rose.chase.author

amazon.com/author/rose.chase

About the Author

ROSE CHASE, A DEDICATED nurse and loving mother to two boys, discovered her passion for storytelling in middle school on online forums and Wattpad. Despite her busy life, she delves into the captivating realm of contemporary romance, with a particular fascination for dark romance and morally gray characters. Through her skillful storytelling, Rose navigates the intricate dance between love, desire, and the shadows of human nature. When not saving lives or caring for her family, she immerses herself in the world of fiction, inviting readers to explore the depths of love and passion while confronting the complexities of the human heart.

tiktok.com/@rose.chase.author

instagram.com/rose.chase.author/

facebook.com/rose.chase.author

amazon.com/author/rose.chase